Praise for the novels of Heather Gudenkauf

"Masterful... Intelligent... Thought-provoking."
—Sandra Brown

"An action-packed thriller."
—Mary Kubica

"Crackles with tension... Taut suspense."
—*Kirkus Reviews*

"Thrilling... Will appeal to fans of Lisa Scottoline and Jodi Picoult."
—*Publishers Weekly*

"Deeply moving and exquisitely lyrical."
—Tess Gerritsen

"Fans of Jodi Picoult will devour this."
—*Red* magazine

"An emotional roller coaster of suspense that will keep you guessing."
—Jennifer McMahon

"Relentlessly suspenseful."
—Diane Chamberlain

"Remarkable."
—*Fresh Fiction*

Also by Heather Gudenkauf

The Weight of Silence
These Things Hidden
One Breath Away
Little Mercies
Missing Pieces
Not a Sound

BEFORE SHE WAS FOUND

HEATHER GUDENKAUF

PARK
ROW
BOOKS

PARK
ROW
BOOKS

ISBN-13: 978-0-7783-0773-0
ISBN-13: 978-0-7783-0862-1 (Library Exclusive Edition)

Before She Was Found

ParkRowBooks.com
BookClubbish.com

Printed in U.S.A.

For my parents, Milton and Patricia Schmida.
Thank you for teaching me the meaning of home.

BEFORE SHE WAS FOUND

Jordyn:
Going 2 Coras at 6

Violet:
Me too. Are you going to bring it?

Jordyn:
Yeah

Violet:
R we really doing this????

Jordyn:
Yes! Unless UR 2 scared

Violet:
What if we get caught?

Jordyn:
Just keep your mouth
shut and we won't

The air is cold, but she barely notices. It's the dark that fills her chest with terror, makes her limbs heavy with dread. But she feels something else, too. Something that she can't quite name. It reminds her of how she feels the night before her birthday or on Christmas Eve but not exactly the same. Thinking about her birthday and Christmas makes her feel good, warm. This feels more like slowly climbing the ladder to the high dive at the swimming pool or like when the roller coaster at Adventureland reaches its highest peak just before it plunges straight down and she just knows she is going to die.

The train yard, filled with the carcasses of gutted-out buildings, is illuminated by only a wispy, wayward eyelash of a pale moon. She stretches out her neck, tilting her ear toward the tracks, hoping to get a sense as to where the others have gone but all she can hear is the wind whispering through the tall grass.

Too much time has passed. They may already be looking for them. It's now or never, she thinks nervously. She can do this; if she doesn't he'll never show up. That was the deal. Together in the bedroom, door locked, they planned everything so carefully right down to the day and hour.

In her right hand dangles the hawk-billed knife they secretly took from a kitchen drawer. Her other arm hangs loosely at her side. At first they considered bringing a crowbar but decided that it was too big, too heavy to lift. This fits her fingers better, feels comfortable, reassuring in her palm. She will use it if she has to.

Over the past month or so he's written messages, love letters, really. Sweet, sentimental words that if she could, she would tuck inside her secret shoebox filled with lucky coins and heart-shaped rocks found over the years. But he warned her, said they could get in trouble, so instead she memorizes each sentence and murmurs them at night before she falls asleep and it's almost as if he's right there with her.

She picks up her pace and moves toward the tracks, dulled and worn down by time and elements. The rail ties are barely visible through the weeds, half-buried sun-bleached bones. She's breathing hard and suddenly realizes tears are rolling down her cheeks. On the opposite side of the tracks where the last year's winter wheat stands, unsown and bent like a wizened old man, is a field that in a few months will be filled with alfalfa. There she sees something. He is hidden in the shadows but she knows it's him. He's come. He beckons her with a raised hand and her heart leaps.

Out of the corner of her eye she sees a familiar shape sitting on the train tracks, knees tucked beneath her chin. The girl turns her head as she approaches, stretches out her legs, holds her injured arm close to her side. They don't speak. She trusts her. Of course she does.

The figure in the dry grass tilts his chin as if to say, *Go ahead. Do it. I dare you.* Her legs are not her own as she approaches, the knife bouncing lightly against her thigh. She stops in front of the girl who stands and smiles crookedly up at her through tears, her small teeth flashing white. Beneath her feet the ground vibrates, warning her of the coming train. She has to hurry; once the engine comes into view it will be too late. He'll leave.

In the distance a dog barks. The rumble of the train grows louder.

She strikes quickly, without thinking. The cold metal rips through fabric and skin easily. She thought it would be harder, take more effort. The girl looks at her in confusion, presses her fingers to her abdomen and pulls them away. The girl looks surprised to find them wet with blood.

The tracks shiver and shake with the approaching engine. The girl tries to squirm away but she yanks her backward and the slick knife slides through her fingers and to the ground; she slams the girl's head onto the track, the rusty bolts tearing at the girl's cheek, the delicate skin below her eye. Again and again she thrusts the girl's head down until her muscles burn and the girl goes limp. She considers leaving her on the tracks but in a burst of adrenaline she pushes the girl off the rails.

As she breathes deeply, her eyes search for him but he's gone. He's slipped back into the tall grass. He can't leave her behind. He promised. A wail from deep inside tries to find its way out but she finds she can't make a sound.

The freight train bears down on her with a long mournful cry and she considers staying still, allowing the engine to pull her beneath its iron wheels, but somehow her legs carry her over the tracks. She sees herself pushing through the plumes of winter wheat, painting them red as she brushes by, and finally catches sight of him. He pauses and turns to face her. He looks pleased.

Sept. 5, 2017

Today was my first official day of sixth grade and it actually went really well! Middle school is a lot bigger than my elementary school because three dinky towns have to share the building. For once I'm going to school with kids I haven't been with since preschool.

The good news is I don't have any classes with Melody Jenkins, who was awful to me during fifth grade. She's the one who sent the top four lists all around school. I was at the top of each one. Dumbest, ugliest, weirdest, most likely to be a virgin. That last one is just stupid. I tried to not let it bother me but it did. And I only have lunch and one class with Jordyn Petit. Jordyn isn't as bad as Melody but last year she did tell everyone that I liked Dakota Richter. NOT true!

The best news is that I have lunch and social studies with Gabe Shannon, who I've liked forever and I think he might actually like me, too. This summer I helped my mom in the elementary school office where she's the secretary and Gabe helped his mom set up her kindergarten classroom for the new school year. We hung out a bunch this summer and really got to know each other.

Anyway, I've got social studies with Mr. Dover, who is cute and is supposed to be a really fun teacher, and I'm even thinking about going out for volleyball. My mom says that it's really important to be "a joiner" in middle school in order to discover what I like to do and to meet some new people.

My sister, Kendall, says that this is Mom's way of saying, *Don't be a loser, Cora. If you don't make some friends now, you never will.* I think that Kendall is probably right. She's super popular and pretty and outgoing. I mean, I'm not a monster, but I'm definitely not as good-looking as Kendall. I'm pretty much her complete opposite.

The good thing is in middle school everyone who goes out for a sport is on the team. They don't cut anyone, which is a huge relief because I know I'm going to be terrible at volleyball. My only other option is joining the cross-country team and I can't think of anything worse than running on purpose. So volleyball, it is. The first practice is tomorrow. Wish me luck—I'm going to need it!

I've been called a lot of things in my thirty-six years: trash, slut, home wrecker. And much worse. All true, I guess, if I'm being completely honest with myself. But one thing I won't let people get away with saying about me is that I'm a bad mother. Those are fighting words. Just about everything I've ever done has been for my two children. I may be stupid when it comes to men but I'm a good mother.

Seven months ago I quit my job as an administrative assistant at an office supply company, loaded our belongings and squeezed a reluctant Violet, a pissed-off Max and Boomer, our basset hound, into our car that was more rust than steel and began the twenty-five-hour drive northeast from Algodon, New Mexico, to Green Bay. The plan was to begin a new life with my boyfriend, Jerry, who moved there to take a job with Proctor & Gamble a few months earlier.

I had some hard selling to do but by the time we reached Kansas City I almost had them convinced that even though we would be giving up Picacho Peak we would get Lambeau Field and the Green Bay Packers. And though we were trading in the Rio Grande there would be Lake Michigan where we could go fishing and water skiing. And though we would miss driving through the Mesilla Valley and seeing the fields of cotton, white, fluffy and soothing against the dusty, dry ground, once in Wisconsin we would have piles of crisp clean snow to build snowmen and have snowball fights.

Max wasn't buying it but Violet was easier to convince. Always in her own little world, Violet would retreat into her notebook of drawings and stories and a few hours later she'd look up, blinking rapidly as if trying to bring her surroundings back into focus. Max, on the other hand, wanted nothing to do with the move. He was completely content in New Mexico and didn't even try to hide his hate for Jerry. It's to Max's credit that he didn't say *I told you so* when the car broke down in the middle of Iowa and Jerry suddenly had a change of heart and got back together with his ex-wife.

Long story short, we stayed in Pitch, a dying railroad town with a population of about two thousand. We were rescued by a nice lady by the name of Tess Petit, who has a granddaughter the same age as Violet.

I know I should answer the phone but for the first time in almost a year a man is beneath me and inside me. Our fingers intertwine and we move as one person. The phone rings and rings and I briefly think of my kids. Violet is spending the night at Cora's house and Max, I hope, is fast asleep downstairs. Usually Boomer alerts me to the comings and goings of my kids but I have been a bit distracted for the past hour or so. Sam reaches out and cups my face in his palm, his fingers pressing into my cheek, keeping my eyes on his, and I push any thought of my children aside.

Finally, my heart stops galloping and Sam presses his face to my neck, his beard velvety against my skin, and I remember the ringing phone. It's late. Or early, depending on how you look at it—1:00 a.m. Way too late for any good news.

"Don't worry, they'll call back if it's important," Sam murmurs in my ear, reading my mind. We doze. Then that voice, that good mother voice that I so pride myself on having says, *Get dressed, you don't want Max or Violet to see you like this.* But instead I move closer to Sam all the while thinking it's been so long since someone has held me like this.

It isn't Max or Violet or the telephone that wakes us up, it's the sirens. At first a single alarm whoops off in the distance and then is joined by several more. I scramble from the bed, pulling the sheets around me, and run to the window and crane my neck to the left and the right, hoping to catch sight of the emergency lights. No such luck. No streetlights line our road and the houses across the street are still dark.

"Max," I breathe, somehow sure that the sirens are for him. That he has been in a car accident or is out doing something stupid—hanging out on the train tracks, drinking with friends. "Max!" I shout as I quickly throw on the clothes I wore earlier. "Max!"

I move through Violet's side of the bedroom that we separate with one of those room partitions. On my side of the partition I have pictures of Max and Violet and an old one of my parents. On Violet's side are a few hand-drawn pictures of unicorns and fairies and landscape sketches of the railroad tracks west of town.

I rush down the steps and to the family room. Max's bedroom door is open and I slap at the light switch on the wall. His bed is unmade, but that doesn't mean anything; he rarely makes it, anyway. I turn and push through a second door, the bathroom—empty—and a third door that leads to our narrow galley kitchen, also empty except for a few dirty plates and silverware in the sink. Max has been here between the time I snuck Sam up into my bedroom and now.

"Try and call him," Sam says, coming up behind me and laying a hand on my shoulder. His fingers feel like lead weights and I shrug them away. I suddenly want him out of my house. Gone.

The sound of sirens fades and I allow myself a moment of hope. Pitch is tiny. Too little to have emergency services like a hospital or ambulance or a fire station. For these we rely on Oskaloosa to the south of us or the city of Grayling, about a half an hour northeast of Pitch. We do have a police department that consists of a chief, one full-time and two part-time officers.

I run back upstairs and fumble around for my cell phone and finally find it on the floor next to the bed. I call Max's phone and it rings and rings until it goes to voice mail. Behind me I'm aware of Sam pulling on his shoes.

"No answer," I say. I'm trying not to panic. This isn't the first time Max hasn't come home by his midnight curfew. I was hoping that this rural Iowa town might be good for him after Algodon where he had fallen in with a rough group—drinking, smoking and God knows what else. But I guess even Pitch has its share of wild teenagers. So now I get to worry about him being out at all hours of the night, raising hell in a cornfield or on the railroad tracks instead of in the mountains. Same problems—new setting.

"He's probably just at a friend's house," Sam says, pulling a sweatshirt over his head. I nod, wanting it to be true. "Do you have a picture of him? I can drive around, see if I can find him."

"No, no, that's okay," I tell him. "I know the places he goes." This is not entirely true. I know that Max hangs around with a boy named Clint, who either wears the same camo pants every day or owns a pair for each day of the week. Clint, when he comes over to the house, won't look at me and answers questions in the fewest amount of words possible. He has close-set, ferrety eyes and always has a pissed-off look on his face. I don't know much about his family except that he lives in a trailer east of town with his mom and two brothers.

"Do you want me to stay here, then? Wait and see if he comes back?"

There's no way that I'm going to leave this man alone in my home. "I think it's best if you just go," I tell him. "I'll go and look for him myself. Thanks, though."

"Let me drive you around, then," Sam says, looking at me as if he really wants to help. "You can keep trying to reach him while I drive."

He has a point. Though Pitch is just a speck on the map, I'm not so familiar with all the back roads.

My thoughts turn to a girl that Max doesn't know I'm aware of. "There's a girl," I say. "I think she lives out near the fairgrounds." I think her name is Nikki. She's pretty in a too-much makeup, overplucked-eyebrow sort of way. She comes into the convenience store where I work several times a week—Pitch Fuel and Feed. Seriously, that's its name. She nearly always buys the same things: a can of Red Bull, cinnamon-flavored gum and a pack of powdered-sugar donuts. Sometimes she comes in by herself and sometimes she comes in with a girl of about five who has Down syndrome. I assume she's Nikki's sister.

Nikki always waits patiently while the younger girl wanders the aisles with a dollar bill clutched in her hand. She doesn't roll her eyes or heave big sighs when her sister chooses a pack of gummy worms, puts it back and then reaches for a bag of potato chips. The sister does this three or four times with different snacks and eventually always settles on the gummy worms. Nikki just waits, absentmindedly spinning the metal rack that holds everything from key chains to sunglasses. When her sister finally makes her decision, they lay their purchases on the counter and I ring them up.

I want so badly for Max to talk to me about Nikki but whenever I ask him about his friends he just says that everyone in Pitch is stupid. I try not to push it, afraid that if I do he will stop talking to me altogether.

Sam pulls open the front door for me and waits by my side as I debate whether or not to lock it. Max has a key but Violet didn't bring hers to the overnight. "It will be fine," Sam says. "You'll probably only be gone for thirty minutes, tops. Your daughter's got a phone, right?"

"Yeah, but I better leave a note," I tell him and then dash back inside and scrawl a few words on the back of an envelope. *Violet, went looking for Max. Lock the door behind you if you get home before we do. Mom.*

Outside I find Sam sitting in his car, the engine idling. My car—not the one that we arrived with in Pitch, but one with fewer miles and fewer dents—is parked in the driveway just in front of Sam's SUV. The night air is chilly and I wish I would have thought to grab a sweatshirt. I climb in next to Sam, who, seeing me shiver, cranks the heater to the highest setting.

"Where to?" he asks. Though I'm grateful for the ride, for his willingness to come along with me on this trek, a persistent voice in my head is telling me to get out of his car and into my own.

"Let's check his friend Clint's house first," I say. "He lives out on Highway 162 about four miles." Sam backs out of the gravel driveway before stopping in the middle of the street.

"Or," Sam says, sliding his eyes toward me, "we can follow the sirens. Might put your mind at ease."

His suggestion makes sense. We can drive all around the county and not come across Max, but if we go toward where we think the emergency vehicles went, then I'd know for sure that Max is safe. Or not.

"West, I think," I say and Sam throws the car into gear and tears off toward the railroad tracks that split Pitch in half. No one can say that one side of Pitch is any better than the other. The north side has the Lutheran church, the library and the Fuel and Feed while the south side has the Catholic church, the middle school and the old opera house. Both ends of town have their share of foreclosed homes.

Sam turns onto Main Street and I tap my foot nervously as we pass the hardware store and an antique shop with a vintage soda machine sitting out front. He reaches for my hand and I pull it away to cover up a fake cough.

I should never have invited him over. Though tonight was our first official date, Sam and I have spent time together. He comes into the Fuel and Feed twice a week—the first on his way to see his parents and the second on his way back home. He buys a cup of coffee or a pack of sunflower seeds and we talk.

He learned that after coming to town, instead of fixing my car and heading on to Green Bay, I got a job at the convenience store, rented a two-bedroom house with peeling paint, no air-conditioning and a temperamental furnace and enrolled my kids in school. I learned that he grew up in Pitch, now lives forty miles away in North Liberty and works as a researcher in the College of Dentistry at the University of Grayling.

Tonight, with Max out with friends and Violet spending the night at Cora's, Sam and I drove to Washington to eat at an Italian place he knew about, and after one too many glasses of wine, we ended up in bed together. Big mistake. But big fun.

We glide pass the post office and two empty storefronts with soaped-out windows and past Petit's Bar and Grill. The closer we get to the railroad tracks, the faster my foot taps against the rubber floor mat. I want to tell Sam to turn around, to go back to the house. Max has been out all night before, shown up in the wee hours, bleary-eyed and rumpled and probably hungover, but he always comes home.

I'm afraid of what I might find once we reach the police cars or ambulances. I strain to see if I can hear the sirens, even roll down the window, but all I can hear is the rumble of the car's engine and the creak of branches rubbing against each other as we drive down Main.

Sam slows to a crawl as he crosses the railroad tracks but still the car bounces and pitches as it rolls over the uneven iron rails. I expect Sam to make a left on Depot, a street that runs parallel to the tracks, but he keeps going. Once over the tracks we pass the bank and the tiny grocery store, and then three blocks filled with single-family homes.

I glance down Juneberry, the street where Violet is spending the night at her best friend's house. Cora Landry invited Violet over so they could spend their free day off school together tomorrow. I breathe a sigh of relief. No ambulances down that way.

Pitch ends suddenly as if the town's forefathers somehow knew that it would never really grow into the buzzing railroad town originally planned. Main Street turns into a country highway, treeless and lined with deep ditches and acres of farmland now hidden by the black night. The road dips and winds and gradually rises and I turn in my seat to look out the rear window. From here I can see Pitch below us.

"There," I say, grabbing at Sam's arm. On the western edge of Pitch right along the railroad tracks and the old millwork district I see the rhythmic swirling of red lights. Sam knew exactly what he was doing coming up here.

Without slowing down, he makes a U-turn and I clutch at the dash to keep myself from sliding across the seat. There is no train in sight. Surely if there was an accident with one of the freight trains that runs through Pitch four times a day, it would have stopped. Unless, of course, the engineer didn't know that he hit someone. Sam pulls off to the side of the road and punches the hazards with one finger.

"Try and call Max again," he says and I lift the phone to my ear and this time it goes right to voice mail. "Do you want to go down there?" he asks.

Apprehension, thick as mud, fills my chest. I've always known I would never have much money, never have a big house to live in, never have some great job, probably never get married again. And because I've expected so little I don't think I'm asking too much that my kids stay safe. God and I have always had a complicated relationship, but I never held anything against Him. But if something bad happened to Max or Violet all bets are off. I don't want to find out what's going on down there. I will my phone to vibrate, but it stays still.

"Go," I finally say. I'm guessing that we won't get very close to the scene, anyway, but I have to do whatever I can to find out what's going on. Sam pulls back onto the highway and he speeds toward the train yard. He doesn't have to worry about getting pulled over. It looks like every police officer and sheriff's deputy in Johnson County is parked down there.

In less than three minutes Sam manages to park just a block away from where all the emergency vehicles have converged. Two sheriff's cars and the police chief's SUV barricade the only entrance into the train yard where the depot is boarded up and empty boxcars, abandoned years ago, sit. An ambulance is parked a bit off to the side facing the road ready to leave in a hurry. A deputy strides toward us as we approach. He's young. Tall and broad across the shoulders. His eyes dart left and right as if on the lookout for something or someone. He looks scared. Ill.

"You can't be here, folks," he says, trying to usher us back toward the car.

"We heard the sirens, saw the lights," Sam explains. "What happened? Is everyone okay?"

"Sorry, you can't be here," the officer says again. Behind him someone turns on their headlights and the darkened train yard suddenly comes into view to reveal a flurry of activity. A woman wearing running tights and tennis shoes is talking to another officer. With hands tucked inside the sleeves of her sweatshirt she gestures toward the tracks and then rubs at her eyes, leaving behind a streak of red across her face.

"Is that blood?" I ask louder than I intend. Hearing me, the woman looks down at her hands and cries out.

"Ma'am," the young officer says more sternly, "you need to leave this area." This is when I see the EMTs come toward us carrying a stretcher to the ambulance. A small body is strapped securely to the stretcher. My breath lodges in my throat. She is shaped like my Violet. Thin with long dark hair that could belong to Violet, too, but the child's face is nearly unrecognizable. Bloody, swollen, grotesque.

I try to push pass the officer but he steps in front of me and I bounce against his solid form and stumble backward. Sam is quicker than I am and skirts past the cop to get a better look.

"It's okay, I don't think it's Violet," he calls back to me.

"Are you sure?" I say, wanting so badly to believe him, but Sam hasn't met my kids yet—how would he know?

"What color is Violet's hair?" he asks.

"Black." My heart pounds wildly.

"Then it's not her. This girl has lighter hair." I want to cry in relief.

From my spot on the hard-packed dirt I can now see it isn't Violet. The girl's ears do not belong to my daughter. The hair I thought at first glance was Violet's isn't naturally dark but slick and blackened with blood. This child looks a bit thinner than Violet. Still…there is something familiar about her, but it can't be. It doesn't make sense.

Sam comes back to my side and helps me to my feet. My stomach churns. What has happened to this little girl? What could cause this kind of damage? Not a car accident; there are no other vehicles besides the ambulance and the police cars. A fall from a bike? She's deathly still and I wonder if she's breathing. She looks like she could have been mauled by a dog or some other large animal. A flap of skin hangs loosely from her cheek and blood bubbles from her lips.

The EMTs lift her into the ambulance and are quickly on their way and the scream of the siren once again shatters the late-night quiet. I watch as it speeds away, the tires kicking up clouds of dust, and wonder how they are going to find out who the injured girl is. I'm just getting ready to ask the cop this question when I realize that everyone else is looking back toward the railroad tracks.

Another small silhouette appears. This time on foot, emerging from the tall winter wheat that fills the field on just the other side of the tracks.

Again my heart nearly stops.

It's Violet.

She is moving toward us as if in slow motion. Eyes unfocused, unseeing. The front of her white T-shirt blooms red. Her hands look like they've been steeped in blood. Something tumbles from her fingers and lands on the dirt at her feet.

"Oh, my God," I breathe. "She's bleeding! Call another ambulance!"

It feels like forever until I finally reach her. I sweep her up in my arms and run my eyes over her, searching for the source of all the blood. "Help her!" I cry, laying her gently on the ground. "Please," I plead. "What happened?" I ask Violet. "Who did this?"

Suddenly I know exactly who the other girl is. Violet's best friend, Cora Landry. I feel arms pulling me backward and hear Sam telling me to let them do their work. Violet's lips move but I can't quite make out what she says.

Every doctor has a case that haunts them. A patient that runs through your thoughts while you sip your morning coffee, that tags along during rounds and therapy sessions. The case that sits shoulder to shoulder with you during the quiet moments and slides between the sheets with you at night and whispers in your ear, *You could have done more. You could have done better.*

For me, that case is the girl in the train yard. She's how I measure time. Before and after.

Disorder—easy enough to define, right? *A state of confusion. A disturbance that affects the function of the mind or body.* Obsessive compulsive disorder, anxiety, ADHD, eating disorder, autism spectrum disorder, schizophrenia, mood disorder, posttraumatic stress disorder. And hundreds more.

Every day, through a combination of talk, behavioral and pharmaceutical therapies, my primary goal was to provide an organized clinical experience to my patients in the evaluation, diagnosis and treatment of children, adolescents and their families.

In the twenty-odd years I had walked the halls of Grayling Children's Hospital, first as a medical student and then as a psychiatrist, I'd seen it all. I've seen children who compulsively eat dirt or paint chips or sharp tacks, and emaciated sixteen-year-olds who refuse to eat anything at all. I've counseled children who have been neglected, beaten and sexually abused.

If it sounds like I say this with pride, I must admit that I do. Psychiatrists are scientists, after all. We are fascinated by the brain and all its intricacies. It's not uncommon for us—in closed circles, of course—to refer to a patient by their diagnosis. *I've got my mood dysregulation at nine and my trichotillomania at ten.*

We talk this way, as if the disorders are our own. It's challenging, at times, to remain detached, to always approach each case with a clinical, dispassionate eye. We work with children, after all. It's easy to become enamored with the idea of playing God. Desperate parents at a loss in how to help their child who is in pain. Mental anguish is just as excruciating as physical pain, if not more.

The girl in the train yard. According to the referring doctor it was a simple case. I imagined meeting with the child once or twice. I would listen to her story. Certainly scary and traumatic, but not the worst I've encountered. I would nod my head in all the right spots and ask questions about what happened in the train yard. But not too pointed that she would shut down and not feel comfortable talking to me.

I would instruct the parents on what to look for in their daughter in the coming weeks: intrusive thoughts, avoidance, negative moods, anxiety. I would tell them to seek follow-up professional care for her if any of these symptoms persisted.

I wasn't worried. I was intrigued. As I learned more I became more invested, more absorbed. *Three twelve-year-old girls walk into a train yard and two come out unscathed.* What doctor wouldn't be fascinated?

I often wonder what would have happened if Dr. Soto had called another psychiatrist. Perhaps the end results would have been different. But I picked up the phone and I made the long walk down to the emergency room.

Sept. 9, 2017

Well, volleyball lasted all of four days. I knew I would suck but I figured some of the other girls would be just as bad as me and we'd just end up on the B team. No such luck. There is no B team and I actually am the worst player.

Of course Jordyn is also on the team and really good. I swear she kept serving the ball right at me and I couldn't bump a single one. This happened like eight times in a row. At first the girls on my team were really encouraging and said, "It's okay, Cora, you can do it!" and "Shake it off!" But after a while it was pretty clear I couldn't do it, so they stopped saying anything.

I tried, I really did. I even dove for one of Jordyn's serves and ended up twisting my ankle. It didn't really hurt but I started crying. Why do I do that? The coach told me to go get a drink of water and sit out until my ankle started feeling better. I sat on the sidelines the rest of practice. Afterward, when we were changing our shoes, everyone told Jordyn how good she was. No one said anything to me, not even to ask me how my ankle was.

I told my mom and dad that I got hurt and didn't think I'd be able to play anymore. Of course my dad was like, "You can't quit! Landrys aren't quitters. You'll be fine!" and I had to go to practice the next day. And the next. And the next.

Then it was like I had a target on me. Jordyn wasn't the only one serving the ball right at my head. EVERYONE started trying to serve or spike the ball at me. Even the ones who are nearly as bad as I am. It was so obvious. Even Gemma, who is normally nice, got this mean look on her face just before she served. I swear she glared right at me and aimed. At that point I didn't even try. I just stood there and the ball hit me on the shoulder. Everyone laughed. Except the coach and I bet that's because she's paid not to laugh at the kids.

When I got in the car after practice my mom asked me how it went. I told her that I wasn't going back. "You can't quit," she said and I started crying and I couldn't stop. When we got home my mom tried to get me to tell her what was wrong but I couldn't. It was so embarrassing. I finally told her that I hurt my ankle again and I might have sprained it or maybe even broke it.

She got me an ice pack and told me that she'd make an appointment with the doctor. Obviously, the doctor didn't find anything wrong with my ankle but he did say that I should take a few weeks off from playing.

At school today Jordyn asked me why I hadn't been at practice and I told her that the doctor said I couldn't play anymore and she said that was too bad. She said it in a way that I thought she really meant it. She was so nice that for a second I actually considered going back to practice and trying again.

Gabe and I haven't had much of a chance to talk since school started. He sits with his friends at lunch and we don't sit by each other in social studies but he says hi to me in the hallway and my stomach does a flip every single time.

Guess what! A new girl showed up at school today. I can't remember the last time someone actually moved to Pitch. Usually people move away from here. Or die of old age. My best friend since kindergarten moved to Illinois last year when her dad got a new job. Ellie's mom said that Pitch was a dying town and I guess she's right. Once the packing plant closed down lots of families left but no one who I liked as much as Ellie.

Ellie and I wrote letters and emailed back and forth for a while but then I guess she's made new friends that keep her pretty busy. I haven't heard from her since summer. I miss her so much that my stomach hurts. It's so hard to go from having someone you can talk to about anything to having absolutely no one to hang out with.

After Ellie left, the world suddenly became very quiet. I can go days without anyone my age speaking to me. I told my mom that it would be much easier to keep in touch with Ellie if I had my own cell phone so we could at least text back and forth. Of course my mom said no. My parents think that I'm too young for one. *Check back in when you're fifteen,* my dad said. I told him that by then everyone will have forgotten that I exist, so never mind.

The new girl's name is Violet and she has pretty black hair and is from New Mexico. Jordyn said that her grandma saved Violet and her mom and brother when their engine exploded outside of town. She said they were standing in the dark on the side of the road when her grandma pulled up next to them in her truck. They all piled into the front cab and Mrs. Petit drove them into town and dropped them off at the Do Pull Inn.

I don't know if I believe Jordyn. She doesn't always tell the truth. I guess Violet and her family are going to stay because Violet says that her mom got a job at the gas station and they rented a house on Hickory Street.

I felt kind of sad after she told me that. Violet seems nice but my mom will never let me go over to her house. Hickory Street is where my sister, Kendall, and her best friend, Emery, say the meth heads live. I asked Emery how she could possibly know that and she told me to get a good look at their teeth. Without trying to be too obvious, I tried to see Violet's teeth and they seemed just fine to me. Emery told me to check again in a few months. It takes time for enamel to turn to mush.

Not to brag, but we live in a pretty nice house. It's made of brick that my mom says is salmon-colored. I think it looks more pinkish but whatever. I have my own bedroom and we have a rec room in the basement where we keep the foosball table, the karaoke machine and the Xbox. We have a huge trampoline in the backyard with a net around it so no one falls off and breaks their neck.

Last year, after we got the trampoline, lots of my classmates came over to try it out but that stopped once school started again and it got colder. Kendall says it's because I'm weird and if I tried harder I'd have friends.

In social studies class we sit in pods and Mr. Dover pulled an empty desk from the corner and added it to my group so Violet would have somewhere to sit. She didn't say much, just sort of watched everyone.

At one point, when Mr. Dover said that we were going to take the ITP tomorrow and it was a very important test that the Department of Education makes every student take to see if we could make it to college, I thought Violet was going to start crying. Violet told me that she hasn't been to school much in the last couple of months because of the move and all.

I whispered to her not to worry, that it wasn't that big of a deal. That all teachers seemed to talk about anymore was "college and career readiness." I made air quotes with my fingers and Violet smiled. I was hoping that Violet would sit next to me during lunch but Jordyn got to her first. Oh, well, maybe tomorrow.

I ended up sitting next to Joy Willard, which is okay. One thing I like about my school is that they don't let people get away with saving seats or telling people that you can't sit next to them. If Mrs. Morris, the lady who supervises the lunchroom, sees you don't have anyone to sit next to she'll send you to a specific spot. I swear she's got this superpower that kicks in the minute you carry your tray from the food line. She sees you desperately looking around the cafeteria for a place to sit and then she swoops in and points. "No argu-

ing, Landry," she'll say. "Sit there and start eating. This isn't Perkins, you know."
Even the jerks don't talk back.

Then at lunch I felt something hit me in the back. I turned to see what
it was and I saw a tater tot on the floor behind where I was sitting. I
turned back around and it happened four more times. Plop, plop, plop, plop. The
last tater tot landed in my hair and stuck there. I pulled it out and turned
around to see who was throwing them. Jordyn and some other girls were sitting at the table behind me and were trying not to laugh. I know it was her.
Violet was just staring down at her lunch tray like she didn't see what happened. At least she wasn't laughing.

When I got home and took off my shirt there were four dark spots on the
back. Like four greasy bullet holes. I don't know why Jordyn's being so mean
to me. I've never done anything to her. Ever.

At least I have just about every class with Violet. Everything but math and
home base, which is what they used to call homeroom in elementary school. My
mom is the school secretary at the elementary school I went to last year. It's
kind of weird not being in the same building together anymore, but I'm glad.
I would never tell my mom that, though. She keeps saying things like, "Don't
you miss seeing me every day, Cora?"

I really don't miss it. I never realized how awkward it was having my mom
around all the time. She knew every move I made. Let me tell you, the school
secretary knows everything and I mean everything.

Last year I found out that my second grade teacher was having an af-
fair with the gym teacher. Of course, my mom didn't come right out and tell
me this; I overheard her telling my dad. I also learned that Mr. Simon, the
custodian, had brain cancer and that Darren Moer, a kid in my class, had
lice again for the third time. Needless to say, having a mom as the school
secretary had its perks, but it feels kind of freeing knowing that she's a few
miles away and can't peek in the classroom at any point during the day just
to see how I'm doing.

After the last bell rang I started turning my combination lock—56 left,
13 right, 2 left—when Tabitha came up behind me and reached over and
spun the lock in the wrong direction, screwing everything up. I started over
and then Charlotte did the same thing. My mom was waiting outside for me
and I knew she would be mad at me for taking so long. I tried to open my
locker for the third time and Jordyn came up and messed me up all over again.

I leaned my head against the locker door and tried not to cry, then I heard Gabe say, "Real mature, Jordyn." And like it always does when I see Gabe, my stomach flipped. Gabe was sticking up for me!

"We're just joking around," Jordyn said. "You're not mad, are you, Cora?" Jordyn asked in this fakey voice. I shook my head even though I felt like slapping her. "See?" Jordyn said, looking at Gabe all innocent.

"Here, let me help," Gabe said. "What's your combo?" The last thing I needed was having Jordyn know my locker combination so I waited until Jordyn left before I told him the numbers. Gabe opened my locker and said, "Just ignore her. Jordyn can be such a bitch sometimes. See you tomorrow."

My face was burning up I was blushing so hard. Jordyn and some of the other girls might not like me but Gabe does. I grabbed my book bag, shut my locker, and that's when I saw Mr. Dover watching me from his classroom doorway. My stomach flipped over again, but not in a good way.

They load us into the back seat of a police car telling me that in the time it takes for another ambulance to arrive we can get to the hospital. I hold Violet close to me, doing my best to keep her as still as possible as we wind through the countryside. The nearest emergency room is twenty-five miles away in Grayling and the officer is determined to get us there in record time and I'm worried that the bumpy ride will injure her further.

I've given up trying to find the source of the blood that blooms across her chest but am fairly confident that she isn't bleeding anymore. Instead I focus on keeping her eyes open and on me. Violet's skin is a scary shade of white and she seems to be floating in and out of consciousness. She isn't going to pass out—it's not that—but every few moments a light seems to go out behind her eyes and she disappears into some unknown, private place.

"Violet, honey," I say, shaking her lightly. "It's going to be okay, I promise. Can you tell me where it hurts?" No response. "Stay awake. Keep looking at me." Her dark lashes flutter, casting fanlike shadows across her cheeks. I smooth her hair away from her forehead and tell the officer to drive faster. My mind is swirling with questions. Who could have done this? What kind of sick monster would attack two innocent girls? The injuries on Cora are horrific. Has she made it to the emergency room already? Is she still alive? I think of her parents and wonder if they have been called. Another girl, Jordyn Petit, was supposed to be at the overnight, too. Where was she? Was she attacked, as well?

The air is filled with the earthy, rich scent of newly tilled fields. The once hard-packed ground now loosened and velvety to the touch. So different than the red soil back home. We are approaching the city of Grayling and the officer merges onto Highway 218 and vehicles move swiftly to the right so we can pass. Signs for the University of Grayling Hospitals and Clinics let us know that we are getting close. Traffic thickens the closer we get to the hospital and despite the sirens it feels like an eternity for vehicles to get out of our way.

Finally, we pass by a handful of restaurants, the university softball fields and a number of university buildings. We arrive at the newly constructed children's hospital, a beautiful structure built of steel and glass that rises high above the others. The officer bypasses the main doors and drives directly to the emergency entrance. "They are expecting us," he says, pulling to an abrupt stop.

Three hospital workers converge upon us and Violet is carefully but firmly taken from my grasp and laid out on a stretcher. The officer reaches for my arm and Violet is whisked inside without me. "My name is Keith Grady and I'll be right in. Keep trying to see if she can tell you anything, anything at all about what happened."

I nod and rush through the doors, looking left and right for any sign as to where they have taken my daughter. She's gone. "Are you the mother?" A heavyset woman rises from behind a counter.

"Yes," I say. "Where is she?" My voice shakes and I press my hand against my throat as if to steady my words. "Can I be with her?"

"The doctor is looking at her right now. Let me get some information from you and then we'll take you back to her." I answer her questions as quickly as possible and then take a seat to fill out the reams of paperwork. When I get to the section that asks for a list of family members I think of Max.

I forgot about him. I pull my phone from my pocket. He still doesn't answer and I shoot off another text to him telling him to call me immediately. "I'm going to kill him," I mutter and am immediately sorry. How can I say something like that after what happened to Violet and Cora?

"Ms. Crow," the receptionist says, approaching me. "I can take you to see your daughter now."

She leads me down a hallway to a boxy room where Violet lies atop an examination table, face turned away from the door. Her bloody clothing has been removed, snipped from her body and tossed to the floor. All she is wearing is her underwear and a training bra that she doesn't really need. Both are streaked with red. Her hands look as if they've been dipped in red paint, a stark contrast to her pale forearms. I scour her skin in search of any wounds but find none. I look to the doctor, a tall man who gives me a reassuring nod. "Looks like only a few bumps and bruises but we'll check her over carefully." He turns to one of the nurses. "Let's get a heated blanket on her and then we can get her cleaned up."

"But all the blood…" I begin.

"It's not your daughter's," he says and I nearly collapse with relief. "I'm Dr. Soto. You can come on over next to her," the doctor invites and I go to Violet's side.

I bend over her and lay the palm of my hand against her cheek. Her skin is cold to the touch. "Violet, honey," I whisper, "what happened?" She blinks up at me and I see no recognition in her eyes. She opens her mouth but no words come out, only a weak croak. I think of head injuries, drugs and monstrous acts that might leave a child speechless. Panicked, I look to Dr. Soto, who has stripped the bloody gloves from his hands and drops them into a hazardous waste container.

"She's in shock," he explains as if reading my mind. "We'll get her warmed up, give her fluids and watch her vitals. Barring any complications, she most likely will be able to go home today."

"I want to stay with her," I say, bracing myself for a fight. There's no way I'm going to leave her side.

"Of course," Dr. Soto says and drags a chair from the corner of the room and situates it right next to the examination table. "Judy here will take care of you. I'll be back in just a bit." Dr. Soto briefly puts a reassuring hand on my shoulder and exits the room. I sit down next to Violet, who still doesn't seem to register my presence. Judy, a woman around my age with deep commas etched into the corners of her mouth, speaks to Violet in a low, soothing voice.

"A little pinch here, Violet," she says and I wince when she inserts a needle in the crook of Violet's arm. She doesn't even flinch. Judy draws several vials of blood and then sets up an IV drip of clear liquid. Then she reaches down with gloved hands and picks up Violet's shorn clothing. I expect her to toss them into the wastebasket but instead she places them inside a plastic bag, seals it and affixes a label to the front. She reaches for a cell phone sitting on the metal tray and drops it into another bag and seals it shut.

"Now I'm going to get you cleaned up, Violet. Does that sound like a good plan to you?" the nurse asks. Violet gives no indication that she hears the question.

"Why won't she answer?" I ask, tears stinging my eyes. "What's wrong with her?"

"Like Dr. Soto said, she may be in shock. It happens sometimes when there's a traumatic event. You'll come around, won't you, Violet?" The nurse smiles down at her. "We'll have you sitting up and talking in no time. But for now we'll keep you warm and get all cleaned up." The nurse holds up a small blue hospital gown. "First thing we'll do is get you into this lovely outfit." Judy deftly dresses her, nimbly shifting Violet's weight so she can button the gown into place. Violet is nearly swallowed up in the fabric.

"Do you know if Cora is okay?" I ask Judy, who situates a metal cart with an arrangement of paper envelopes, jars in a variety of sizes, a large tweezer, a camera and several other items I can't identify next to Violet's bed.

"Cora?" Judy asks. I glance over at Violet to see if hearing her friend's name brings any reaction. It doesn't. "I don't know who that is."

"She's the other girl who was brought here. She came in an ambulance," I explain. "She looked like she was hurt pretty badly."

"I wouldn't know anything about that. Let's just focus on Violet right now," Judy says, holding up a small spatula-shaped tool. "See this, Violet? I'm going to use this to clean your fingernails, okay? It won't hurt a bit." I watch while Judy uses the spatula to scrape dried blood from beneath Violet's fingernails and deposit it within one of the paper envelopes.

This is when I understand that this nurse isn't just treating my daughter for shock or dehydration, she's collecting evidence. This is why they bagged up Violet's bloody clothing and cell phone. That's what the camera is for and the thought of others seeing photos of my daughter, half-dressed and covered in her best friend's blood, is too much.

My stomach lurches and I leap from the chair, unable to speak. I stagger out to the hallway in search of a bathroom. Probably from the look on my face, a woman pushing a cart of cleaning supplies points me in the right direction. I make it to the toilet just in time before I start heaving. The sour tastè of the chicken marsala and wine Sam and I ate fills my throat.

Who could have done this? She's nearly catatonic and they are poking and prodding her to gather evidence. I think again of Cora, somewhere in this hospital being treated for terrible injuries. I need to know what is going on and at the same time want to know nothing. I only want to take Violet home with me and try not to think about any of this.

I sit on the floor for a minute catching my breath before pushing myself up from my knees and flushing the toilet. I try to rinse the bitter taste from my mouth with water from the tap. I run my fingers through my hair and take several deep breaths before stepping back into the hallway. I'm still not ready to go back into Violet's room. God, I'm such a coward.

Dr. Soto is standing outside Violet's room talking with the officer who drove us to the hospital. Dr. Soto glances my way, his face grim. My first thought is that Violet must have taken a turn for the worse and I press my fingers against the wall to steady myself. The officer turns and I register the worry in his eyes, the tightness around his mouth. I will my legs to move me forward but I don't want to hear what they are going to tell me. I have only been away for a few minutes. What possibly could have gone wrong?

Dr. Soto and the officer move toward me and for an instant I want to run. If they can't catch me they won't be able to give me the news. My thoughts travel to the darkest corners: collapsed lungs, a brain bleed, a ruptured spleen, internal injuries that might have gone undetected. I can't catch my breath and as they draw closer I press myself more closely to the wall, trying to make myself smaller, trying to disappear.

"Ms. Crow," the officer begins.

My eyes are on Dr. Soto, who must recognize my terror and lays a reassuring hand on my shoulder. "Violet's fine," he says.

I want to cry. I want to lash out at them for scaring me so badly. "What is it?" I ask, unable to keep the anger from my voice but instantly I'm sorry for it. "Is it Cora, then? Is she okay?"

Officer Grady ignores my question. "I really need to ask Violet a few questions," he says. "We need to get as much information about what happened as possible."

"I told him that he needed to talk with you first before speaking with her," Dr. Soto says before excusing himself.

"I don't know," I hesitate. "She's in shock. I don't think she's in any condition to talk to anyone. She tried to say something at the train yard but I couldn't hear what it was. Maybe one of the other cops heard what she said." Officer Grady shifts from foot to foot, runs a thumb across his lips but doesn't say anything. "What?" I ask. "Do you know something? Did she say who did this?"

"I just really need to question your daughter. The more time that passes, the harder it will be to work out what happened. Do I have your permission to talk to Violet?"

"No," I say. "No one is talking to Violet. Not until you tell me what you know. Who is he?" Again, the worst pinballs through my head. A sex trafficking ring, a deranged drifter, a serial killer. "If you won't tell me, I want to talk to someone who will."

"One of the other officers did hear Violet say some names," Officer Grady tells me, though I know he doesn't want to.

"Names?" My stomach clenches again. "There was more than one person?" It's bad enough to think that one horrible person attacked Violet and Cora, but the thought that there were two monsters is too much.

"Yeah, Violet said two names. Joseph Wither and something that sounded like George or Jordan."

"Jesus." I lean against the wall for support. "Jordyn Petit. She's a friend of Violet's. She must have been there, too. Did you find her? Is she okay?"

"I don't know anything about another girl but we have a guy back in Pitch checking into it."

"It's Jordyn Petit. I know it is. You have to send someone to find out if she's okay."

"Don't worry, we're on it," he says and I want to scream. How can he tell me not to worry? I'm about ready to ask him this when it hits me that he mentioned another name. "Wait," I say. "You said another name—Joseph…"

"Wither," Officer Grady finishes for me.

I've heard the name before. Something to do with a school project, I think. I've been working so many hours lately. I really haven't been paying attention as much as I should have. "Who is he?" I ask. "Did he do this? Is someone out looking for him?"

Officer Grady sighs and he looks oddly at ease. "There is no Joseph Wither," he says. This isn't the response I was expecting.

"What do you mean?" I ask in confusion. "He didn't do this?"

Officer Grady shakes his head. "No, he didn't. He's not real. Not anymore, anyway. Joseph Wither, if he is still alive, would be a very old man today. Can you think of anyone who might want to hurt the girls?" he asks.

Officer Grady can see that my mind is still stuck on this Joseph Wither person and he holds up his hand to stop me from questioning him any further. "Trust me, Joseph Wither doesn't exist. For every minute that passes we lose precious time finding Jordyn and who did this." Impatience is creeping into his voice so I let Joseph Wither go for the moment.

"They are twelve," I say. "I can't think of anyone who would want to hurt them. No one. Do you think someone was trying to kidnap them?" I ask, my stomach churning as sex offenders and human traffickers and other dark thoughts lodge themselves in my brain.

"I promise you, we've got someone checking out that possibility. What about the girls?" Grady asks. "How did they get along with each other?"

It takes me a second for his question to register. He can't possibly think that Jordyn did this to Cora. I open my mouth to tell him he's crazy, wasting his time, but then shut it again. I've only met Jordyn a few times, and while she is always polite to me, I get the sense that she is the queen bee of the group. Violet and Cora watch her carefully, gauging Jordyn's reaction to what they say, what they do, how they dress. But violent? No way.

"Ms. Crow?" Officer Grady raises his eyebrows, waiting for my response.

"No," I say firmly. "Jordyn gets along just fine with Violet and Cora. I can't imagine her hurting anyone."

"What about Violet?" he asks pointedly. "Has she had any physical confrontations with anyone? With classmates? Friends?"

"What? No!" I say. "Violet's never been in a fight with anyone. You don't think Violet had anything to do with this, do you?" I ask.

"I have to ask," Officer Grady says. "Can you think of anyone who would target the girls?" he asks, moving on, but the idea has been brought up; it's crossed his mind. Officer Grady thinks that Violet and Jordyn may be behind the attack.

A shrill ringing yanks Thomas from his sleep. With his sons grown and his day-to-day role as owner of Petit's Bar and Grill greatly diminished, Thomas thought perhaps he would finally be able to start sleeping past 6:00 a.m. In the early days his schedule had been brutal. For years, he tiptoed into bed well after 1:00 a.m., careful not to wake his wife and kids. The couple would get up just a few hours later to head next door to Petit's to prepare for the lunch crowd.

He is in the house alone. A predicament that is both unfamiliar and unsettling. Tess, his wife of forty-five years, is convalescing in a skilled-care facility in Grayling after a nasty fall and his granddaughter, Jordyn, is spending the night at the Landry girl's house. The ringing continues and Thomas realizes that this won't be his day to lounge beneath the covers. With effort he sits up, shoves the down comforter aside and eases his legs over the edge of the bed until his toes find the cold wood floor. He shivers through the thin fabric of his boxer shorts and T-shirt.

Each step sends bolts of pain through the soles of his feet and coursing through the ropy purple veins that line his legs, the result of years of standing behind the bar. As the day goes on, the aches will become less pronounced but until then he will limp along, clutching at heavy pieces of furniture to keep upright.

"Dammit to hell," he mutters, nearly tripping over Jordyn's soccer ball, and the house phone stops ringing.

Thomas wishes briefly that he had kept the smartphone his youngest son, Donny, sent him last Christmas. "This one works just fine," he said, holding up a flip phone that Jordyn called archaic. A word she said she learned in English class. *It means old, Grandpa, just like you*, she teased. "What do I need a fancy phone for?" Thomas asked incredulously.

"Emergencies," Tess said.

"Shopping," Donny offered.

"Snapchat," Jordyn giggled.

Thomas gave them a look that let them know the topic wasn't up for discussion and the phone disappeared back into its box and then reappeared a few months later on Jordyn's twelfth birthday. Now he is considering buying two smartphones. One for Tess and one for himself.

With the house quiet once again, Thomas debates whether to go back to bed or keep pushing forward to the kitchen. Again, the phone begins its maddening trill, making Thomas's decision for him. He picks up his pace, trying to ignore the needle-sharp prickles of pain that he thought he would have become accustomed to by now. No such luck.

"Hello," Thomas says into the receiver, not bothering to disguise his irritation.

"Mr. Petit?" an official, unfamiliar voice asks.

"Is my wife okay?" Thomas asks. A shiver of fear runs down his spine. He knows how quickly hip injuries can lead to something even worse like pneumonia and blood clots and infections of the bone.

"Mr. Petit, this is Officer Blake Brenner from the Johnson County Sheriff's Office. Does a child by the name of Jordyn live in your household?"

"What happened now?" Thomas asks. He loves Jordyn beyond words but drama seems to cling to his granddaughter like cockleburs. Last month, the local police brought Jordyn home after she was caught climbing the Pitch water tower east of town.

"Relax, Grandpa," Jordyn had told him. "It's no big deal."

"Sir, does Jordyn Petit reside in your home?" the officer asks firmly, his voiced edged with tension.

Thomas leans against the corner of the kitchen counter. "Yes, she's my granddaughter. Is she okay? She's supposed to be spending the night at a friend's house."

"Is her mother or father available?" the officer asks.

"No. My wife and I are her legal guardians. Jordyn's parents aren't able to care for her." It pains Thomas to admit that his eldest son and Jordyn's mother were deadbeats. Unfit to care for Jordyn. "Did something happen?" Thomas asks, finally registering the concern in the officer's voice.

"That's what we're trying to find out. So, you're telling me that Jordyn is not at home right now?"

"No, she's at a friend's house. Cora Landry's," Thomas says but uncertainty pricks at the corner of his thoughts.

"Jordyn isn't at the Landrys' home at this time. That I can confirm," the deputy says.

"I'll go check her bedroom," Thomas says. "Maybe she came home and I didn't hear her. Can you hold on a second?"

Thomas lays the receiver on the counter and moves as quickly as he can to the bottom of the stairs. "Jordyn, are you up there?" he hollers. There's no response. With a sigh he begins the ascent, one knee catching and crackling with each step, the other refusing to bend. By the time he reaches the landing, he's out of breath, damp with sweat and thoroughly irritated.

"Jordyn!" he booms, pushing through the bedroom door, finding it empty. Grabbing tightly to the banister, Thomas makes his way back down the steps and picks up the phone, hoping that the officer hasn't hung up, impatient for his return.

"She's not here," Thomas says, anxiety squeezing at his chest. "Tell me what's going on."

"We'll send an officer over to your house, Mr. Petit. She'll fill you in on what we know."

The line goes dead and Thomas slowly lowers the receiver from his ear. He and Tess have raised Jordyn since she was four, after their oldest son, Randy, came back home and dropped her off. "I can't deal with her," Randy said, "and I can't find her mom." Then he left. They hear from him only a few times a year by way of a phone call, a postcard or birthday card.

Thomas wanted to tell Randy to stop calling altogether. That the sound of his voice and his letters made Jordyn sad and out of sorts. But Tess told him that barring Randy from Jordyn's life would be a mistake that Jordyn would hold against them one day. So he held his tongue.

Jordyn is the daughter he and Tess never got the chance to raise. Betsy, their third-born, didn't live to see her first full year and Tess never quite recovered from the loss. She loved her boys but they weren't Betsy, and Jordyn reminded them of their daughter.

If Jordyn wasn't at the Landry house, then where was she? The bar and grill, Thomas thinks. Maybe Jordyn went next door. She spent a lot of time in the office and the restaurant part of the business. Thomas limps to his bedroom and pulls on a pair of jeans from the bureau and a shirt from the closet.

Despite the recent trouble with the local police, the over-the-top drama, the slammed doors, the icy silences that come with a preteen girl, Jordyn has been more joy than trouble over the years. Tess taught her how to make gingerbread and *ptichie moloko*—birds' milk cake—and how to knit. She braided her hair and told her about growing up on a farm, the daughter of immigrants from Russia, and stories of Baba Yaga and Kikimora, the House Hag.

For his part, Thomas taught Jordyn about how to run a business. Put her to work sweeping and taking inventory, taught her, much to Tess's chagrin, how to mix drinks. All alcohol-free, of course.

Thomas pushes through the front door, the newly risen sun momentarily blinding him, the air mild against his face. Holding tightly to the wrought-iron railing, he picks his way down the four concrete steps that lead to the sidewalk. Directly next door is Petit's. The twin buildings are two stories tall and made of red brick and weeping mortar.

When the boys were small they lived above the bar in the

cramped second floor but eventually bought the building next door after Tess complained that the noisy patrons kept the boys up late into the night and filled their ears with crass language and their heads with unsavory ideas.

By the time Thomas climbs up the steps to the bar he is breathing heavily and sweating. Peeking through the window he sees Kevin, the young man who has taken over the day-to-day duties of running the bar, wiping down the scarred mahogany counter. He tries the door handle but it doesn't open. Kevin keeps the door locked before opening time to ensure that no one wanders in with hopes of getting an early-morning cocktail.

He raps on the door but Kevin doesn't even look up. Thomas can hear the faint trill of the phone and bangs harder, the glass shivering with each strike. He must be listening to music, he thinks. That's why Kevin doesn't hear the bar phone ring, why he can't hear him knocking. He waves his hands in front of the window and Kevin finally glances up. Kevin takes his time unlocking the door and when he does Thomas reaches up and rips the earbuds from his ears.

Kevin looks down at him, startled. "Jesus, you scared me. What's wrong?" he asks.

"Jordyn," Thomas says, his voice cracking. "Is Jordyn here?"

"She's in the back," Kevin says, hitching a thumb toward the kitchen. "Why?"

"Jordyn," Thomas calls, brushing past Kevin. "Get out here."

"Jeez, what?" Jordyn rounds the corner in exasperation and halts at the sight of her grandfather's angry face. She's dressed in a pair of flannel pajama bottoms, flip-flops and a T-shirt as if she's just rolled out of bed. "What did I do now?"

"Why don't you tell me," Thomas says, hands on hips.

Jordyn looks him directly in the eye and lifts and drops her shoulders and as if daring him to contradict her says, "I have no idea."

Thomas wants to shake the defiance from her face. He wishes

that Tess were here. She'd know what to do and say. She would go to their granddaughter, pull her into a hug and Jordyn would apologize for making them worry. But Tess isn't here and Kevin has returned to scrubbing the bar, earbuds placed firmly back in place. It's just the two of them.

"The police are looking for you," Thomas says. "What are you doing here? Why aren't you at Cora's house?"

"The police?" Jordyn asks, the confidence draining from her voice.

"Yes, the police. They're on their way over here right now. What's going on, Jordyn?"

"I don't know, I don't know!" Jordyn exclaims, looking panicked, eyes brimming with tears. Thomas almost believes her.

There's a tap on the door and both Thomas and Jordyn look over to find Officer Bree Wilson looking in at them. Curious, Kevin pulls his earbuds away from his ears. A freckle-faced redhead, Bree comes into the bar every so often with a booming laugh and a fondness for Bushmills Irish Buck. Thomas beckons her in and the door squeaks open as she enters.

"Morning," Officer Wilson says. "Glad to see you home safe and sound, Jordyn." To Thomas she says, "We've got a bit of a situation here, Tom, and I think that Jordyn might be able to help us out."

Thomas's relationship with the Pitch Police Department is made up of equal parts irritation and respect. Though the local cops tend to be hypervigilant in pulling his patrons over and running them through sobriety tests, Thomas had to admit that every time he called and asked for assistance with the occasional bar fight, they came right over. "We'll do whatever we can to help. What's going on?"

"We're just at the beginning of the investigation so I don't have much to tell you, but there appears to have been some kind of incident early this morning and there were some injuries."

"Injuries?" Jordyn asks, gnawing on her thumbnail.

"I'm afraid so," Officer Wilson says.

"Cora?" Jordyn asks. "How bad?"

"Do you know something, Jordyn?" Officer Wilson asks. "If you do it's very important you tell me right now. One girl was beaten and the other one is in shock. Someone attacked them, Jordyn, and we need to find out what happened."

Jordyn shakes her head and inches back toward her grandfather. "I don't know anything."

"But you're okay? Not hurt?" the officer asks and Jordyn nods. "You were with Violet Crow and Cora Landry last night?"

"Yes," Jordyn says in a hushed voice. "Are they going to die?" Thomas finds this question jarring, odd for a twelve-year-old, and he wants to shush her. Instead he puts a hand on her shoulder and Jordyn gives him a dirty look.

Officer Wilson rubs her fingers across her lips as if she might find the right words there. "They're in good hands," she finally says. "But we need your help now, Jordyn. Can you answer a few questions for me?"

When Jordyn doesn't answer, Thomas responds. "Of course she'll answer your questions, won't you, Jordyn?"

Officer Wilson walks slowly toward Jordyn much like someone approaching an injured animal. "Take a seat, Jordyn," Officer Wilson says and they situate themselves on round stools in front of the bar. "What time did you last see Cora and Violet?" Her voice is gentle, warm.

"I don't know. It was late," Jordyn says.

"Late last night?" she asks in a soothing voice.

"Yeah, I wanted to come home."

"You left? Can you remember what time?"

"I don't know, late. After midnight," Jordyn says, her eyes fixed to the floor.

"You walked home all the way from Cora's house?" Thomas asks his granddaughter. "That's almost two miles away. Why?"

His voice is sharp. Lately, Jordyn has been a mystery to him, with more sass than he's equipped to handle.

"I just wanted to come home." Jordyn's eyes fill with tears. She lays her forehead on the bar top. "I don't know what happened."

"She came over about thirty minutes ago," Kevin pipes up from behind the bar. "Said you were out of milk and cereal at the house and was going to eat breakfast here."

Officer Wilson pauses, waiting for Jordyn's crying to stop. When it doesn't she sighs and gets to her feet. "Why don't you and your grandpa come to the station and we'll talk more, Jordyn. We could really use your help. There's a bad person out there who hurt your friends. Anything you can tell us might help us catch him. Okay?" Jordyn peeks up and sniffles and nods.

"Go wash your face, Jordyn," Thomas says, "then we'll go down to the station. Okay?"

"But I don't know anything." Jordyn wipes her eyes. "I don't know what to say."

"Just tell the truth," Thomas tells her. "The police will decide whether or not it's important."

The three adults watch as Jordyn slouches off to the bathroom. "Jesus," Kevin says when she's out of earshot. "What happened to those kids?"

"I'm not sure," Officer Wilson says, "but there was a hell of a lot of blood. When we got there the Landry girl was being loaded into an ambulance. She looked really, really bad. The other girl emerged a few minutes later covered in blood. They put her in a police car and took her to the hospital, too."

"Jim Landry runs the Appliance Barn, doesn't he?" Kevin asks.

"Yeah, the mom works at the elementary school. Nice people," Thomas says. "This happened at their house?"

"No, down by the old depot," Officer Wilson says.

"The depot?" Thomas asks in surprise. "What were they doing by the railroad tracks so late at night?"

"A lady walking her dog found the Landry girl and called for help." Officer Wilson shakes his head. "I've never seen anything like it."

Jordyn comes out of the bathroom. Her face is splotchy, eyes red.

"I'll meet you and Jordyn at the station in an hour," Officer Wilson says and Jordyn's eyes fill again with tears.

"I don't want to—" she begins but Officer Wilson stops her.

"This isn't a request, Jordyn. Someone messed those girls up pretty bad," she says and moves toward the exit. "See you soon."

"Come on, Jordyn," Thomas says. "You need to get dressed and then we'll head over to the station. You got things covered here, Kevin?"

Kevin assures them that he's got things under control and Thomas and Jordyn walk next door in silence. Once inside Jordyn runs up the stairs to her bedroom. The smell of freshly brewed coffee beckons, and Thomas, aching for the rush of caffeine, lifts the carafe too quickly, sending searing liquid down the front of his shirt. Cursing, he quickly sheds the soaked shirt, makes his way to their small laundry room and tosses it in the basket overflowing with dirty clothes. Ever since Tess has been in the hospital the daily chores of laundry, dusting and sweeping have gotten away from him.

Thomas pulls a wrinkled but clean plaid shirt from the dryer. It wasn't that he didn't know how to press his own clothes— he did—but Tess always said she didn't mind and he had gotten spoiled that way. Thomas looks at his watch. There was no time for ironing right now; Officer Wilson was expecting them soon. He pulls on the rumpled shirt and tries to smooth out the creases with his fingers.

A pair of Jordyn's tennis shoes and her jacket are lying in a jumble next to the stacked washer and dryer. No matter how many times Thomas reminds Jordyn to pick up after herself it just doesn't seem to stick. He has resorted to piling all of Jordyn's scattered belongings into a laundry basket and dumping them onto her bed, thinking they will be impossible for Jordyn to ignore.

No such luck. With a sigh he reaches down and retrieves the jacket, a light blue fleece that cost about fifty dollars more than it should have. To think that even in the dinky town of Pitch labels matter. Thomas finds it ridiculous, but Tess says that it's important for Jordyn to fit in, especially with not having her mom and dad around.

Thomas drops the jacket and tennis shoes into a laundry basket filled with more of Jordyn's wayward possessions when a dark stain on the sleeve of the fleece catches his eye. He fishes it from the pile and examines the three-inch splotch on the cuff. His first thought is that chocolate is a bear to get out of fabric but this stain is more red than brown. He lifts it to his nose and instead of a sweet sugary scent his nose is met with the smell of copper.

He scratches at it experimentally and a rusty patina is left behind on his fingertip. Blood. Thomas searches for any other drops of blood on the jacket but it only seems to be in that one spot, just below where the palm of the hand meets the wrist. Jordyn didn't say anything about getting hurt, didn't complain of a recent injury. There wasn't a lot of blood. Barely enough to mention. But still. He thinks of Cora Landry lying in a hospital bed with her terrible injuries.

Thomas turns away from the basket filled with Jordyn's shoes, a hairbrush, a pair of socks, a soccer ball and an array of books and magazines and carries the jacket to the sink and turns on the cold water. He reaches into the cupboard for a stain stick and plastic jug of ammonia. It would be a shame, he thinks, scrubbing vigorously at the stubborn spot, if the jacket ended up being ruined.

I got the call about Cora Landry last April. I had rushed into my office to check my messages and to catch up on some paperwork before my next appointment. I had four voice mails. One from the parent of a patient hoping to reschedule their session, two from pharmaceutical reps and one from a fellow doctor at the hospital—Leo Soto, an ER doc with a smooth, timbered voice and a soothing bedside manner. He wanted me to stop down if I had time. A young girl had been brought in by ambulance early that morning with stab wounds. She was heading into surgery soon to repair the wounds from an attack. Extensive reconstructive work to her face was expected.

Due to the violent attack, Dr. Soto anticipated a need for psychological support for the girl and her family. I remember looking at my watch. I was buried beneath paperwork and my next appointment was due to arrive shortly. It sounded like an interesting case.

After getting the call from Dr. Soto, I made my way through the hospital's maze of corridors and skywalks that admitted over twenty thousand patients per year and had more than thirty thousand ER visits. I was only one of about seven hundred physicians employed by the hospital but I loved the bustle, brainpower and the diversity the hospital had to offer. Plus, as a divorcee with no children it housed the only family I have left in the world. To get from the psychiatric tower to the emergency department I took an elevator down three floors and walked what felt like a mile.

"Thank you for coming down, Madeline," Dr. Soto said, greeting me. He was tall and slender. A dark-skinned man, with neatly trimmed silver hair and a matching mustache. At six-feet tall he and I, in my one-inch heels, were the same height. "I'll take you to see Cora and her parents," he said. "Cora is heavily sedated right now but if you can just say a few words to the mother and father about the resources available to them, I know it will be helpful."

"Of course," I agreed. Once assessed, each patient in the emergency room has a private room that shields them from the craziness of the ER. Behind the sliding Plexiglas door was a preteen girl lying in the hospital bed. Her facial wounds were hidden beneath swaths of gauze, but even so, I could see that significant damage had been done.

"We didn't dare try to stitch her up," Dr. Soto told me. "If there ever is a case for a plastic surgeon, this is it. All we are doing at this point is treating her collapsed lung and giving her antibiotics. My biggest concern is saving her left eye. They'll be taking her to surgery momentarily. Frankly, I'm very worried about the parents. The mother is understandably distraught but the father is incredibly angry." Dr. Soto paused as if hesitating to speak further.

"Anger is understandable," I said, feeling like a voyeur. Through the glass door, the mother sat next to the bedside holding her daughter's hand, weeping. The father stood with his back against a wall, his arms folded across his chest. Not a tall man, he was broad-chested, powerfully built and looked ready to leap from his skin.

"Do they know who did this to her yet?" I asked and Dr. Soto shook his head. "Are the parents suspects?" I hated to ask, but had to. I'd seen too many children hurt in too many ways to count by the people who are supposed to love them most in the world. Dr. Soto didn't know. Didn't know much more than the little girl had been viciously attacked.

"Well," I said, taking a deep breath. "Let's go find out if and how I can help."

Oct. 31, 2017

In social studies class Mr. Dover assigned us a really cool project. At first I thought he was going to tell us we were going to have to write the same old Halloween essay like we do every year. Instead of writing about our favorite candy or the best costume ever, Mr. Dover is having us work with partners on a research project.

He came into the classroom yesterday dressed as some guy from the olden times. He had on a white shirt and vest, these short pants, long socks and shoes with buckles on them. He even had on one of those hats they wore back during Colonial times. Mr. Dover carried a lantern and a silver cup. By now we all knew that he wasn't going to just tell us what he was up to, so after we stopped laughing Andrew shouted, "Hey, it's George Washington." And Gabe said, "No, it's Alexander Hamilton!" and then started rapping a song from the musical.

Jordyn laughed real loud like it was the funniest thing she'd ever heard. She and Gabe were going out last year but he must have figured out what Jordyn is really like because now Gabe pretty much ignores her. Gabe is one of those guys who can get away with acting like a show-off. All the kids think he's cool because he plays baseball and can play three different instruments and sing. He also always wears one of those old-fashioned hats with the brim around it, which manages to look cool on him. If anyone else wore it they'd just look stupid. Plus, he's cute. The teachers like him because he knows when to stop.

And Gabe did stop singing as soon as Mr. Dover raised his eyebrows at him. "Right century," Mr. Dover said once it was quiet. "Let me give you another hint." He set the lantern on top of his desk, put one leg up on a chair and in a deep voice said, "Listen, my children, and you shall hear of the midnight ride of..." and we all shouted, "Paul Revere!"

Mr. Dover talked about how that poem was written nearly one hundred years after the actual ride and the ride wasn't all that big of a deal. Mr. Dover likes to talk so it took him about half the class period to get to the point. We talked about all the fake news that went on throughout the last presidential election and that it was important to know what was true and what wasn't.

Two minutes before the bell rang he gave us the assignment. We have to do a group research project about an urban legend—what's real about it and what's made up. Then we have to get up in front of the class and give a presentation about what we learned.

I wanted to throw up when I heard the details of the assignment. I don't mind working in a group but there is nothing I hate more than getting up in front of the class and having to talk. I loathe it. My face turns bright red and my voice shakes. It makes me sick just thinking about it.

In middle school, there are three ways we get put into groups: the teacher picks, you number off or first-come-first-serve where we get to pick our own partners. I hoped Mr. Dover would pick for us—it was less stressful that way—but just before the bell rang he said in this old-fashioned voice: "Chooseth thy partn'r, mine own scholars."

Luckily I caught on to what he was saying and right away turned to Violet and asked her if she wanted to be my partner and she said yes! When Mr. Dover assigns projects it isn't just some one- or two-day thing; they usually last weeks, so it will be good to not have to worry about picking partners for a while.

I looked over at Jordyn and she was whispering in Deanna's ear and they were staring at us. I know they're talking about me and Violet but for once I don't care. Violet's my partner and I think she's going to be really nice. Usually I do whatever I can not to get on Jordyn's radar. She somehow always makes me feel like an idiot. I'll have to make sure to tell Violet to stay away from her. You just can't trust her.

When we were in fourth grade Jordyn invited all the girls in the class to her birthday overnight except for me. My mom went insane and called Jordyn's grandma, who said it must have been a mistake and drove over to our house and made Jordyn deliver the invitation in person. It was MORTIFYING! Jordyn looked like she wanted to vomit and I wanted to disappear. I was sick the day of the party and couldn't go, anyway, which was just fine with me and with Jordyn, too, I'm sure.

Anyway, Violet and I already started a list of urban legends we could choose from: bigfoot, a twenty-foot alligator in the sewer or maybe Johnny Appleseed. After school some kids were talking about researching Bloody Mary or the Babysitter and the Clown Doll or the Mothman, who my sister says is this creepy seven-foot man with red eyes and wings like a moth who would show up just before something really bad happened.

Gabe asked me and Violet what we were going to do our project about and Jordyn butted in and said, "Probably something babyish." I swear she loves embarrassing me. But then Gabe came to my defense and said to Jordyn, "What's your genius idea, then?"

That shut Jordyn up and Violet and I told Gabe about our urban legend.

Me again... The weirdest thing just happened. My sister told me someone was on the phone for me and when I went to answer it no one was there. I kept saying hello but it was just quiet. I finally hung up and when I asked Kendall who it was she rolled her eyes and said she wasn't my secretary. Like I said, weird.

"What do you think?" Dr. Soto asked. "Would you like to meet Cora?"

"Sure, why not?" I remember saying.

Dr. Soto rapped his knuckles gently against the window to announce our arrival and then slid the door open. "Mr. and Mrs. Landry, this is Dr. Gideon. She is the mental health professional I was speaking of. Dr. Gideon, this is Jim and Mara Landry, Cora's parents."

"Hello," I said and extended my hand out to Mr. Landry. "I'm sorry to hear about what happened to Cora. How's she doing?"

Jim clasped my hand and gave it a shake. His skin felt rough and dry against my own. Almost reptilian. "Not great. Look at her," he said, voice shaking. "Some maniac stabbed her."

"She's going in for surgery soon," Mara said and swiped at her tears with a soggy tissue. She was a slip of a woman who looked as if she could collapse beneath the weight of her worry. "Dr. Soto says the surgeons here are very good."

"He's right," I agreed. "World-class. She's in the best hands. Cora has been through an awful ordeal and so have you. Please know that we have many supports that you might find beneficial to Cora and to your family..."

"Listen, Dr. Gideon," Jim said, his voice tight with forced patience. "I don't want to be rude, but honestly a psychiatrist is the last thing that Cora needs right now. The last thing *we* need right now. What we need is for Cora to get into surgery so that the doctor can try and put her face back together." Jim's volume rose with each word until his wife reached for his arm and shushed him. I got the feeling she had to do this often. "What I need—" Jim lowered his voice "—is a crowbar and five minutes alone with whoever did this to my daughter."

"Jim, stop," Mara said, dissolving once again into tears.

"I'm sorry," Jim said as if surprised by the intensity of his own anger. "I'm going to go see if the police have any more information." He brushed roughly past us and out of the room.

"He's scared," Mara explained. "It's just so hard seeing her like this. He hates that he wasn't there to help her."

"Don't be sorry. I understand." I pressed my business card into Mara's hand. "Please call me if you need anything or if I can answer any questions. I often work with children and families who have experienced traumatic events."

"Thank you." Mara sniffed. "But I don't think so."

"Is there someone I can call for you? A family member or friend to come sit with you during surgery?" I asked. Support systems are crucial during tragedies such as this.

"My parents are on their way with our other daughter," Mara said. "They should be here soon. But thank you."

I smiled and lightly touched Mara on the shoulder as Dr. Soto slid the door open.

In silence we walked to the bank of elevators. "Maybe after the surgery the Landrys will be more open to visiting with you," Dr. Soto said. "I worry about Mr. Landry. He's a very angry man."

"Mrs. Landry does seem more approachable," I agreed. "But I don't expect a call from either of them. I can drop by Cora's room later today and check on them."

"Thank you again, Madeline," Dr. Soto said as he took his leave. "I owe you a favor."

I remember the elevator doors opening and inside was a young couple clutching hands. The man—a boy, really—held an empty car seat in his free hand and the girl pressed her face into his shoulder. He averted his gaze as if embarrassed by his red, swollen eyes.

"I'll grab the next one," I said and turned away. Down the hallway, Mr. Landry was speaking to a police officer. Though

I wasn't able to see his face and couldn't quite make out what he was saying, I could hear the frustration in his voice. The policeman stood placidly by, allowing him to say his piece. I knew that the father's anger was understandable, normal even, but Jim Landry seemed to be becoming unhinged. Finally, the police officer held his hand up as if to silence Mr. Landry.

"Do not tell me to calm down!" Mr. Landry's voice filled the corridor, causing people to stop and stare.

The elevator doors slid open and I reluctantly stepped inside. I had been in the presence of the Landrys for just a few minutes and already recognized the hallmarks of a family ready to implode. And there was something about Jim Landry that in my line of work had become much too familiar to me. Angry, aggressive men who liked to be in control, whatever the cost.

I wish I had paid more attention to this—the family dynamics. Would things have turned out differently? Maybe not. I became so fixated on Cora and how she was dealing with the trauma of the attack and her injuries that I missed the bigger picture—what happened before they found her and why it all happened in the first place.

Nov. 4, 2017

Violet came over to my house yesterday after school and we had so much fun! We jumped on the trampoline for a while and then I showed her my room. She told me she thought I had the best room she'd ever seen.

We found out we actually have a lot in common. Cheese pizza is our favorite food and we both like to draw. Violet is really good but I'm just okay. She showed me some pictures she made in her notebook. I told her that she should write graphic novels when she grows up. Violet got all red when I said that but I could tell that she knew I meant it.

I told Violet I hated volleyball and she said she did, too. I said that social studies was my favorite subject this year and that the only bad thing about it was that Jordyn is in the class.

"She's not that bad," Violet said. "She helped me open my locker the other day. Plus, I'm going to her house this weekend. Did you know her grandpa owns a bar?"

HA! I wanted to say. Jordyn has no problem screwing me up when I try to open my locker but she's all nice when Violet needs the help.

I wanted to tell Violet to be careful, that Jordyn was two-faced and sneaky. I wanted to tell her about the time in second grade when Jordyn put her brownie on my seat just before I sat down and it looked like I pooped my pants and I wanted to tell her about how mean she was to me in volleyball practice.

But what I really wanted to tell Violet was how last year Jordyn stole Gabe from Gemma, who was supposedly her best friend. Gemma liked Gabe first and they were "going out," which is really stupid because going out in fifth grade just means sitting by each other at the high school football games.

Gemma got mono and when she came back to school a few weeks later, Gabe and Jordyn were dating. Gemma didn't talk to Jordyn for like a week but then, like Jordyn does, she acted all innocent and hurt. Like it was Gemma's fault. Of course Gemma ended up forgiving Jordyn.

I guess if I was being honest, I probably would have done the same thing. No one likes having Jordyn on their bad side.

So I wanted to tell Violet all this but then my sister pounded on my door and yelled that Violet's mom was there to pick her up so I didn't get the chance.

Then the house phone started ringing and when I went to answer it whoever was on the other end just sat there and didn't say anything so I just hung up.

This happened like five times until my mom stepped in and answered the phone and told them that we had caller ID and she was going to call the police and report them for harassment. We don't have caller ID but the phone calls stopped. I bet it was Jordyn.

Thomas pulls Jordyn's damp jacket from the washing machine. The blood appears to be completely washed away. He lifts it just inches from his face to get a better look. He's tempted to douse it with bleach but quickly dismisses the idea. It was just a spot of blood. Kids bleed all the time. Hell, as youngsters his boys were plastered in Band-Aids on any given day from all the scrapes and scratches they collected.

But niggling doubts keep crowding his head. As much as he loves his granddaughter, she has always had a bit of a devilish streak. A quick tongue and an even quicker temper. There was the time when Jordyn was about six and the school called saying that Jordyn pinched a girl in her class so hard it left a bruise. "Why?" Tess had asked, wanting to understand.

Jordyn scowled and said, "She took my spot on the carpet. I told her to move but she wouldn't."

There was the time when Jordyn was benched in soccer for purposely trying to trip her opponents. Jordyn promised she didn't do it on purpose and Thomas wanted to believe her but there was also the incident last year when Jordyn slammed a locker door on a classmate's hand, breaking two of her fingers. Again, Jordyn insisted it was an accident but the injured party disagreed and so did her mother. Jordyn was suspended for a day.

But these examples are eons away from stabbing someone and Thomas pushes the doubts away. He tosses Jordyn's damp jacket in the dryer, sets the dial to permanent press and then goes out to finally get that cup of coffee. His head pounds from lack of caffeine and the sharp ammonia fumes.

He checks his watch. They need to be at the police station in fifteen minutes and he can still hear Jordyn banging around up in her bedroom. Thomas grabs a broom leaning against a corner and lifts it, soundly tapping it against the ceiling, and Jordyn stomps her foot two times in response. Normally, Tess would scold them both for this noisy mode of communication but over the years it has become a game between them. Today he finds no humor in it.

Thomas pours a cup of coffee into a mug that Jordyn made for him when she was in second grade and takes a tentative sip. His stomach bubbles with nerves. When the boys were young, a visit from a police officer or a sheriff's deputy wasn't an uncommon occurrence.

It shouldn't have been a surprise given Donny's and Randy's lack of supervision. It was a catch-22, Thomas thought. If he and Tess kept the boys at the bar where they could keep an eye on them, the questionable clientele and their bad habits were sure to rub off on them. And if they let them run wild they were bound to go searching for trouble with no chance of Thomas or Tess being there to yank them out of harm's way. It was no wonder that Donny and Randy found themselves in a number of scrapes with the law.

There was many a night when Randy and Donny were deposited on their front step by Sheriff Tate after being caught drinking, carousing and trespassing on some poor farmer's land while trying to tip a cow or two. *It's all harmless mischief,* Thomas used to tell Tess after the boys, pale and hungover, were out of earshot.

Yes, until someone gets hurt, Tess would shoot back until it became kind of a joke between them. They laughed halfheartedly at the time but it was with great relief when Randy finally graduated high school and went off to a nearby community college. Donny went his own direction and left Iowa for college in Oregon. Out of sight, out of mind, Thomas thought. And it worked, at least for a few years. Until Randy showed up on their doorstep with a round-faced spitfire of a four-year-old in tow and they found themselves worrying all over again. This time about Jordyn.

Again Thomas pummels the ceiling with the broom handle. He's discovered over the years that with girls, with Jordyn, anyway, it was different but much more complicated. The boys only had two moods: silly and sleepy. Jordyn, on the other hand, had too many moods to count. But how Thomas loved that girl.

Thomas was sure that Tess felt the same way, though they never really talked about it. Maybe it was because they'd never had enough time with Betsy. Jordyn had the same round cheeks, the same widow's peak, the same belly laugh as their daughter.

Thomas knows that Jordyn is just on the edge of growing up. That there's going to be a lot more sass than sweet in the years to come and it scares him to death that Tess might not be around to guide her, and him, through it. Jordyn needs her. He needs her. He tries not to think about life without Tess. It was just a fall, a bad fall, but Tess is tough. Hell, she put up with him all these years. She'll be able to get through a pesky setback like a broken hip.

With a sigh, Thomas gives up banging on the ceiling and makes the long trek up the stairs. He pushes open her bedroom door only to find it empty but in typical disarray. Jordyn must be in the bathroom.

The book bag that Jordyn took with her to Cora Landry's house for the overnight sits in the middle of the floor. Thomas bends over and pulls out the pair of sweatpants and a University of Grayling T-shirt that Jordyn wears as pajamas and adds them to the ever-growing pile of laundry to wash. His hand grazes something soft and Thomas finds Ella, the gray-and-pink stuffed elephant that Jordyn insists she has outgrown but that always seems to find its way into bed with her. He presses Ella to his nose and inhales Jordyn's familiar scent. A combination of her shampoo and the Juicy Fruit gum that Jordyn chews incessantly.

He digs more deeply into the book bag and pulls out a pair of socks and underwear, a hairbrush, a toothbrush sealed inside a plastic baggie. His hand lands on a social studies textbook. It's heavier than he expects and it tumbles from his fingers and hits the ground hard, thrusting a folded sheet of paper from its pages. Thomas reaches for the paper. It is difficult to pick up but after several tries he is able to snag it with his thick, arthritic fingers. The paper is onion-skin thin and the color of weak tea.

Thomas pushes aside a stack of books sitting on the foot of Jordyn's bed and sits down to get a better look. Carefully he unfolds the paper and immediately recognizes Jordyn's narrow feathery print. *Pitch* is written neatly across the top and below it is a remarkably detailed map of what looks like the train yard.

Below a diamond-shaped compass in the upper right-hand corner is the boarded-up depot, the crisscross hatch marks of the railroad tracks and a half-dozen rectangular-shaped boxcars.

Thomas wants to believe that the map is a geography assignment for Jordyn's social studies class but the fact that his granddaughter and two friends snuck into the train yard the night before leads him to believe it's no simple school assignment. Two girls, one with braids, the other with her hair in a high ponytail, are hiding behind one of the boxcars, mischievous grins slashed across their round faces. Jordyn and Violet. A third girl, smaller than the other two, is standing all alone in the middle of the tracks, her mouth opened in a round, black scream.

He examines the drawing more closely and among the wispy pencil strokes meant to represent the winter wheat next to the train yard is a shadowy spot, more of a smudge, really. Thomas takes the paper to the window and holds it up to the light. Yes. There among the grasses is a vague, faceless shape of a person that inexplicably fills him with trepidation.

Again he thinks of the bloodstain he just scrubbed from Jordyn's jacket. Thomas folds the paper in half and then folds it again, and again until it's the size of a thick postage stamp. He slides it into his pocket and steps into the hallway. "Jordyn," he calls out gruffly. "We need to get going. Now."

Nov. 9, 2017

Violet and I have been eating lunch every day for the last few weeks. She's quiet, like me, but we talk to each other. I even told her that I liked Gabe and I held my breath waiting for her to say that he was too cute or too popular for me, but she didn't. She just nodded like it made sense.

We don't even have to talk all the time. Sometimes we just sit there and eat, not saying anything, and it doesn't feel weird. Violet always gets hot lunch and I bring cold lunch from home. I think that maybe Violet gets free lunch. I think this because for the last three days the lunch lady only gave her a peanut butter sandwich, apple slices and a carton of milk. My sister says that's what kids get who are behind on paying their lunch bill.

My mom always packs me a sandwich, a clementine, a bag of chips and some kind of dessert. Today she put in a monster cookie. I broke it in half and tried to give Violet some but she said no thanks. I put it on her tray, anyway.

The other night my mom dropped Violet and me off at the high school basketball game. I was excited because I hardly ever go to the basketball games. Gabe was already there and waved us over so we could sit next to him and his friends. Jordyn was sitting behind us and I could feel her glaring at me from three rows up.

During the game, Gabe asked me for my cell phone number and I had to tell him that I didn't have one. Violet jumped in and gave Gabe her cell phone number and said that we could text each other using her phone whenever I wanted. No one has ever done something that nice for me before.

Violet decided to do our urban legend project on Pop Rocks candy and soda. Violet said she heard from her brother that this kid from an old cereal commercial died when his stomach exploded after drinking Coke mixed with Pop Rocks. I've never had Pop Rocks but Violet said that she'll ask her mom to bring home a few packs from the gas station where she works and I can try them.

At dinner I told my mom, dad and sister about the project and how cool Mr. Dover is. I talked about how Gabe and his partner wanted to do theirs about a woman whose butt implants exploded but Mr. Dover said no way. A lot of kids wanted to research gross urban legends about murders and ghosts and sex and stuff. Mr. Dover told us that if we didn't want our grandmas to hear our reports to choose a different topic.

Later, Kendall said Mr. Dover was a perv. Kendall told me to watch how he looked at the girls who had big boobs, then I'd see. What she said makes me have a sick feeling in my stomach. Mr. Dover has only been teaching here for a few years. Some people say he came here because he got in trouble at his old school. But I don't think that can be true. They wouldn't have hired him at our school if he did anything bad, would they?

Mr. Dover is cute. He is tall and has longish hair that he pushes out of his eyes about a thousand times during class. He has a young face but he dresses like a teacher (except when he's dressing up like Paul Revere or Abe Lincoln): khaki pants, button-down shirts with a tie. I told Kendall to shut up, that Mr. Dover was the nicest teacher at school. That he actually cared about kids. Then I came up to my room and cried, though I'm not sure why.

For the next few days I watched Mr. Dover more closely. I didn't see him looking at any boobs but it seems like he spent more time talking with girls than boys during class. In social studies, I whispered to Violet what Kendall said about Mr. Dover being a pervert and she laughed. She whispered back, "Hey, that should be our urban legend topic. 'Mr. Dover: Social Studies Teacher or Child Molester?'" I laughed, too, but I felt icky that I brought it up. I like Mr. Dover.

Jordyn came over and asked what we were laughing about and, thank God, Violet said it was nothing. I can just imagine Jordyn telling everyone that I called Mr. Dover a pervert. Jordyn actually sat down and talked to us for a few minutes about normal stuff. She even told me she liked the earrings I was wearing.

Suddenly, I heard a voice say, "Ahem," and when I turned around Mr. Dover was walking over to us. He stood really close behind Jordyn, put both of his hands on her shoulders and said, "Ladies, I hate to interrupt this obviously very important conversation you are having, but we've got work to do."

Violet's eyes went wide and she gave me a look that said, *Oh, my God, you're right, he is a perv!* She burst out laughing and I started laughing, too. Jordyn looked at us like we were crazy but then she started laughing, too, even though she had no idea why. Violet was laughing so hard she gave a loud hiccup. Then everyone started laughing.

"Go get a drink, Violet," Mr. Dover said, finally dropping his hands away from Jordyn's shoulders. To the rest of the class he said, "Okay, comic relief is over, turn to page twenty-four in your books."

Violet hurried out of the room, hiccupping all the way. I pulled out my social studies book and when I looked over at Jordyn she was smiling at me. Smiling like a friend would. Maybe she's not as bad as I thought.

Mara Landry came to my office that evening after our first meeting. I was sitting at my office desk flipping through the collection of notes that I jotted down throughout the day. I've always found that my young patients get anxious when I record my observations during our sessions and tend to spend more time trying to see what I'm writing about them rather than sharing their feelings.

The sun was dipping behind the linden trees that line the campus streets when I heard a light knock on my door.

"Come on in," I called, thinking that it was one of the residents or fellows stopping by my office to discuss a patient. The door opened and Mara Landry stood uncertainly in the doorway. "Mrs. Landry," I said, surprised. I really didn't expect her to reach out to me after our initial meeting and after seeing her husband's reaction to me. "Please, come in. How is Cora?"

"I don't want to interrupt you. I know it's getting late and you probably want to get going," she said apologetically.

"It's no interruption at all. Please, sit down," I invited. Mara Landry looked worn out. Her face was drawn and pale, her shoulders slumped as if the events of the day were pressing down on her and she was suffocating beneath them. A look I'd come to know well on worried parents.

"I can't stay long. I just wanted to thank you for stopping by earlier and to apologize. I know that Jim wasn't exactly…" She struggled to find the right word so I jumped in to rescue her.

"No apology necessary. Tell me about Cora. Did surgery go well?" I asked.

"The doctor said it went well considering all her injuries." Mara's face buckled momentarily as she struggled to keep her composure. I waited and she went on. "There will be scars."

Mara's fingers fluttered near her cheek. "But it could have been much worse and Cora is a strong little girl. She'll be okay. We'll be okay."

"Is Cora awake?" I asked. "Is she in much pain?"

"Some." Mara nodded. "They've been keeping her sedated and she's pretty out of it. But she's scared. She's absolutely terrified. I can tell. She starts to fall asleep and then jolts awake and cries out. I tell her over and over that no one can hurt her anymore, that she's safe, but…she keeps calling out for whoever did this to her to stop. To please not hurt her anymore and Jim can't stand it. The police aren't telling us much right now. They just say they are investigating and once they have information to share they will."

I nodded sympathetically. This was a common refrain I heard from the families of victims of a crime.

"My oldest daughter, Kendall, won't stop crying and can't even look at Cora. Can't even stand to be in the hospital room with her. My family is falling apart, Dr. Gideon." Mara's voice cracked. "One minute we're hosting an overnight for my daughter and her friends and the next Cora is bleeding next to the train tracks."

"Are the other girls okay?" I asked.

"As far as I know. We ran into Violet's mom down in the emergency room but she said that Violet was just being treated for shock." Mara pressed her fingers to her lips. "Oh, God, that sounded terrible," she said shakily. "I'm glad she's okay. I really am."

"Of course," I said.

"I need to get back to Cora," Mara said. "But tomorrow? Do you think you might have some time tomorrow to visit with her?"

"Certainly," I said. "How about I stop by around eight or so?"

"Maybe closer to nine would be better," Mara suggested and I wondered if perhaps that was a time her husband wouldn't be around. It's not a good sign if one parent is open to my services and the other is not, but it's a start.

"Nine will be perfect," I assured her. "Try and get some sleep tonight and I'll see you in the morning."

I watched Mara walk wearily down the hallway. I'd seen it hundreds, maybe thousands, of times: the unsteady, almost drunken walk of those suddenly in the midst of a life-changing event. Mara's equilibrium was off, but with time and help and with some luck she'd gather herself up and see to it that her family get through this and whatever else was to come.

No matter how determined I was to leave work at a reasonable time, I got home well after nine o'clock that evening. As usual, the house was dark and quiet. I immediately peeled off my clothes to shower but couldn't wash away the thoughts of Cora Landry and what happened to her in that train yard. The world was a dangerous place even for a little girl from small-town Iowa.

I stepped from the shower, toweled off and put on my favorite pair of sweatpants and a University of Grayling Wolves sweatshirt. All I wanted to do was go to bed but instead I poured myself a glass of wine, opened my laptop and logged into the hospital's secured online system. I pulled up Cora Landry's medical records and learned that Cora was born at the hospital five weeks early. She spent some time in the NICU and made several follow-up visits to the pediatric specialty clinic over the years.

I jumped to the clinic visit just prior to her attack. Eight months earlier she saw one of the docs for a routine checkup and overall Cora appeared healthy. Height and weight measures indicated that Cora was quite a bit smaller than her peers. The physician wrote that Cora conveyed feelings of extreme anxiousness and worry when it came to school and relationships with her peers. When he broached the subject with her parents, they chose to forgo any sort of psychological or pharmaceutical treatment at the time.

The doctor also noted that Cora had a series of scratch marks at various stages of healing on the inside of her forearms. Cora explained that they were from her cat and the doctor suggested an over-the-counter antibiotic ointment.

I closed the laptop and flipped on the television. I scanned the channels in hopes of finding some mindless sitcom but landed on a video of a reporter standing in front of the emergency room of the hospital. The tagline read Urban Legend Main Suspect in Train Yard Attack on Preteens?

I sat up and increased the volume. The reporter spoke into a camera while a flurry of insects buzzed around the bright red emergency room sign above his head. "Two twelve-year-olds are the purported victims of a decades-old urban legend known as Joseph Wither. Sources say that at least two Pitch girls were hospitalized early this morning after a brutal attack at the abandoned Pitch, Iowa, train depot.

"Though police and hospital officials remain mum on the investigation and the condition of the girls, an anonymous source tells KQIC News that at least one of the victims pointed the finger at Joseph Wither."

"Oh, Jesus," I murmured and increased the volume on the television.

The reporter glanced down at the notebook in his hand and then back at the camera. "According to the legend, Joseph Wither began his crime spree back in the 1940s, over seventy-five years ago. While only a few disappearances of young girls have been officially credited to Wither, over the years Johnson County residents have reported sighting a shadowy entity matching the description of Wither corresponding to the time of a disappearance.

"Tonight, the small community of Pitch is on high alert and eagerly waiting an official statement from law enforcement as to what happened to these young girls. Stay tuned to KQIC for the most up-to-date information on this bizarre, frightening case."

The news report sealed it for me. Ghoulish, I know. This case had it all: a vulnerable little girl, a crime apparently carried out by a fictional villain, a family in crisis. A challenge. I was up for it. In fact, I couldn't wait to get started.

Nov. 10, 2017

So all of a sudden there are now three people in our group and we have a completely different topic. Deanna Salas and her family suddenly up and moved to Saint Louis so Mr. Dover asked Violet and me if Jordyn could join us.

Like we had a choice. Of course we weren't going to say no even though I wanted to. Violet and I have become really good friends and having Jordyn work with us is not great news. She's just really hard to figure out. One day she's aiming volleyballs at your head and the next day she's smiling at you like she's your best friend.

When Mr. Dover told Jordyn to work with us on our project she didn't seem all that happy about it. She was like, "You're really going with the Pop Rocks and Coke thing?" and she said it all snotty.

Violet and I looked at each other, both of us not sure what to say. I wanted to tell Jordyn to go find another group if she didn't like our idea but of course I just sat there. "Listen to what Deanna and I were working on." She looked around to see if anyone else was listening.

I rolled my eyes at Violet and she gave me a look that said, *I know, she's ridiculous.* Jordyn leaned in so close that I could smell the tacos from the lunchroom on her breath. "Joseph Wither," she whispered, like we were supposed to know what she was talking about.

I've heard of Joseph Wither. I knew he was supposed to be some kind of ghost but I didn't really know why everyone was supposed to be afraid of him. Thankfully, Violet was the one to speak up and ask who Joseph Wither was so I didn't feel quite so dumb.

Of course, just as Jordyn was going to tell us, the fire alarm went off and we had to spend the next fifteen minutes standing outside. By the time we got back to the classroom, the bell rang and Jordyn didn't get a chance to tell us what his deal was.

But get this! When Violet, Jordyn and I were going to our next class Gabe started walking with us. He made a point to walk between me and Violet. Jordyn was NOT happy. Gabe asked Violet how she liked Pitch so far and she blushed bright red and said it was okay. Then he said, "See you at lunch," and I swear he was looking right at me! Jordyn huffed off and ignored us for the rest of the day, which was perfectly fine with me.

Whenever Violet comes over, she lets me use her phone to text back and forth with Gabe. I try not to spend too much time on her phone, though. I mean, best friends don't ignore each other because one of them has a boyfriend. Okay, maybe Gabe isn't my boyfriend yet, but I think he might ask me. That's if Jordyn doesn't get in the way. I've never had a boyfriend before and Gabe is perfect. Things are looking up! It's going to be a good school year. I can feel it.

OFFICER WILSON: Okay. We are at the Pitch Police Department and, um, I'm here with Jordyn Petit and her grandfather, Thomas Petit. For the record, Mr. Petit, you agreed to allow your granddaughter, Jordyn, to answer questions regarding the events of April 15 and April 16. Correct?

THOMAS PETIT: Yes.

OFFICER WILSON: You have waived the right to have an attorney present for questioning, correct?

THOMAS PETIT: We want to do anything we can to help. Jordyn will answer any questions you have.

OFFICER WILSON: So for the record, Mr. Petit, you have waived the right to have an attorney present for questioning?

THOMAS PETIT: Yes.

OFFICER WILSON: Also, I am recording our conversation. Can you please say your full name?

JORDYN PETIT: (inaudible)

OFFICER WILSON: Please speak nice and loud.

JORDYN PETIT: Jordyn Ann Petit.

OFFICER WILSON: And how old are you, Jordyn?

JORDYN PETIT: I'm twelve.

OFFICER WILSON: When's your birth date?

JORDYN PETIT: February 2.

OFFICER WILSON: So you had a birthday not that long ago?

JORDYN PETIT: Yeah.

OFFICER WILSON: What did you get for your birthday?

JORDYN PETIT: Some clothes. A cell phone.

OFFICER WILSON: A cell phone? What a great present. Do a lot of your friends have cell phones?

JORDYN PETIT: Some. What happened to Cora? Is she okay?

OFFICER WILSON: Are you worried about Cora?

JORDYN PETIT: You said she was hurt.

OFFICER WILSON: Did I?

THOMAS PETIT: You did. At the bar you said Cora and Violet were taken to the hospital.

OFFICER WILSON: Please let Jordyn answer, Mr. Petit. There are no right or wrong answers here.

JORDYN PETIT: You said that someone hurt Cora and Violet.

OFFICER WILSON: Okay. You spent the night at Cora's house?

JORDYN PETIT: Yes.

OFFICER WILSON: On a Sunday night?

JORDYN PETIT: It's spring break, so we don't have school this week.

OFFICER WILSON: What time did you go over to Cora's house?

JORDYN PETIT: Um. Around six, I think. My grandpa dropped me off at about six.

OFFICER WILSON: And Violet Crow was there, too? What time did she get to Cora's?

JORDYN PETIT: Later than me. Around six thirty. Her brother and his friends dropped her off.

OFFICER WILSON: Violet's brother?

JORDYN PETIT: Yes. Max and his friends.

OFFICER WILSON: Do you know the name of the friends?

JORDYN PETIT: Clint something, I think.

OFFICER WILSON: You don't know his last name?

JORDYN PETIT: No. And there was a girl in the car, too. Max's girlfriend, Nikki.

OFFICER WILSON: Do you know what kind of car they came in?

JORDYN PETIT: I'm not sure.

OFFICER WILSON: The color? Or number of doors it had?

JORDYN PETIT: I don't remember. Blue or black, maybe?

OFFICER WILSON: Okay. After Violet got there, what did you do?

JORDYN PETIT: We ate pizza and talked.

OFFICER WILSON: What did you talk about?

JORDYN PETIT: I don't know. Just school and stuff.

THOMAS PETIT: What does this have to do with anything? Jordyn, do you know anything about what happened to Cora and Violet? Did you see anything?

OFFICER WILSON: Mr. Petit, again I'm going to have to ask you to listen without commenting. We'll get to all that. I'm just trying to put together a timeline of events. Now, please… Jordyn, what did you do after you ate pizza?

JORDYN PETIT: Played some games. Balderdash and Say Anything.

OFFICER WILSON: Were Cora's parents at home?

JORDYN PETIT: Yes, and her sister.

OFFICER WILSON: They were home the entire night?

JORDYN PETIT: Her mom and dad were for sure. I don't know about Kendall.

OFFICER WILSON: Then what?

JORDYN PETIT: We watched a movie.

OFFICER WILSON: What movie?

JORDYN PETIT: *Split* and had popcorn.

OFFICER WILSON: *Split?* The one about that guy with multiple personalities? That's a pretty grown-up movie for twelve-year-olds.

JORDYN PETIT: I guess.

OFFICER WILSON: You watched a movie and then what?

JORDYN PETIT: Nothing, really. Just sat in Cora's room and talked. Then we went to bed.

OFFICER WILSON: What time was this?

JORDYN PETIT: Midnight, I think.

OFFICER WILSON: Then what?

JORDYN PETIT: We couldn't fall asleep and were bored. We decided to go for a walk.

OFFICER WILSON: What time was this?

JORDYN PETIT: I don't know. Late.

OFFICER WILSON: After midnight, though?

JORDYN PETIT: Yes.

OFFICER WILSON: So you got dressed?

JORDYN PETIT: (inaudible)

OFFICER WILSON: Did Cora tell her parents you were leaving?

JORDYN PETIT: No.

OFFICER WILSON: Did she leave a note?

JORDYN PETIT: No. We just left. We thought we'd be back before anyone woke up.

OFFICER WILSON: Where did you walk to?

JORDYN PETIT: Just around. It was stupid. I wanted to go back but Cora and Violet said no.

OFFICER WILSON: They said no?

JORDYN PETIT: They wanted to go to the train yard but I said it was too far. I was cold and wanted to go back to the house. I was tired.

OFFICER WILSON: So you decided to go home?

JORDYN PETIT: Yes. It's not that far from the train yard.

OFFICER WILSON: So you were at the train yard?

JORDYN PETIT: No. I told you, I didn't go there.

OFFICER WILSON: Did you tell Cora and Violet you were going home?

JORDYN PETIT: No. They were being mean. I just left.

OFFICER WILSON: Mean? How so?

JORDYN PETIT: I don't know...just mean. They wouldn't listen to me about going back.

OFFICER WILSON: Did you see anyone else while on your walk? Talk to anyone?

JORDYN PETIT: No.

OFFICER WILSON: Did you see any cars while you were walking?

JORDYN PETIT: I don't know. Maybe. It was late. I don't remember seeing a car drive by us. But I saw a car. It was down another street. Not close by. It wasn't moving but its lights were on.

OFFICER WILSON: What street?

JORDYN PETIT: I don't know. Maybe on Twenty-second Street.

OFFICER WILSON: You were on Twenty-second Street?

JORDYN PETIT: No, I think I saw a car on Twenty-second Street. I'm not sure. I don't know! I don't remember!

OFFICER WILSON: Okay. It's okay, Jordyn. You're doing just fine. You left before you got to the train yard. How did you come home? What streets did you walk on?

JORDYN PETIT: I don't know. I just came home. I cut through some yards to get home faster.

OFFICER WILSON: Did you tell your grandpa when you got home?

JORDYN PETIT: No. I just went to bed.

OFFICER WILSON: Tell me exactly what you did?

JORDYN PETIT: I unlocked the door.

OFFICER WILSON: You carry your house key?

OFFICER WILSON: Look at me, Jordyn, not your grandpa. Do you carry a house key?

JORDYN PETIT: In my book bag. I opened the door. Changed into my pajamas and went to bed.

OFFICER WILSON: And the first you heard about Cora and Violet was when I came to your grandpa's bar?

JORDYN PETIT: Yes.

OFFICER WILSON: What can you tell me about the Joseph Wither project you did for school?

JORDYN PETIT: Nothing. It was just a school assignment.

OFFICER WILSON: The news station is reporting that someone pretending to be Joseph Wither was the one who attacked Cora.

JORDYN PETIT: It was on the news? No, I don't know anything about that. We just went for a walk.

OFFICER WILSON: We found some beer bottles at the train yard, near where we found Cora. You didn't happen to have some alcohol in your backpack, did you?

JORDYN PETIT: What? No!

OFFICER WILSON: But you had your backpack with you?

JORDYN PETIT: Yeah.

OFFICER WILSON: Why? You said you planned on going back to Cora's house after your walk. Why would you bring a backpack with you on your walk unless you had something inside that you needed?

JORDYN PETIT: I don't know. I mean, I just brought it.

OFFICER WILSON: You're not in trouble, Jordyn. But if I find out you are lying to me, then there will be trouble. We have to find out who left the beer bottles there. They're evidence.

JORDYN PETIT: (inaudible)

THOMAS PETIT: Just tell the truth, Jordyn. This is important. Did you take some beer bottles from the bar? You know I can check the inventory and see if any are missing.

JORDYN PETIT: (sound of crying) Yes. I took the beer. I'm sorry. We just wanted to try it.

OFFICER WILSON: So you went to the train yard and drank the beer?

JORDYN PETIT: No, along the way. On our walk.

OFFICER WILSON: But left the bottles at the train yard?

JORDYN PETIT: I don't know. We must have.

THOMAS PETIT: Jesus, Jordyn. Why didn't you just say that in the first place?

JORDYN PETIT: I'm sorry. We tried it but we didn't like it. We dumped it out and I told Cora and Violet that I was going home. Then I left. I promise.

OFFICER WILSON: We'll need to get your fingerprints for exclusionary purposes, Jordyn. Don't worry, Mr. Petit, it's routine. Okay, Jordyn, you were walking to the train yard, drank some beer and then left. Cora and Violet stayed. Is there anything else you need to tell me?

JORDYN PETIT: No. They wanted to stay and I wanted to leave so I went home. I promise.

OFFICER WILSON: You didn't see anybody at the train yard? Anyone at all?

JORDYN PETIT: No.

OFFICER WILSON: Can you think of anyone who would come after Cora?

JORDYN PETIT: No. I can't think of anyone who would do this. What about Violet? Is she okay?

OFFICER WILSON: Well, they're both at the hospital and that's all I can really tell you right now. Tell me again, what time was it you left the Landry house?

THOMAS PETIT: You already asked that question. Do we need a lawyer?

OFFICER WILSON: You certainly are within your rights to call an attorney. The question is, do you think that Jordyn needs a lawyer? If so, please do. On my end, I'm just trying to get as much information as I can to help in this investigation. Jordyn may be the only person who saw or heard something important last night. She might not even know it's important—that's why I have to ask these questions and sometimes more than once.

THOMAS PETIT: I want to help. Jordyn wants to help.

OFFICER WILSON: So I have your permission to continue to visit with Jordyn?

THOMAS PETIT: Yes. Fine.

OFFICER WILSON: Now, Jordyn, what time did you and your friends leave for the train yard?

JORDYN PETIT: Around midnight, I think.

OFFICER WILSON: You said that Cora and Violet were being mean. Did you fight? Did it get physical?

JORDYN PETIT: No! It wasn't like that!

OFFICER WILSON: I've been told that you weren't very nice to Cora, that you bullied her.

JORDYN PETIT: No! Cora is my friend.

OFFICER WILSON: So you weren't bullying her? The people I've talked to are saying that you've been calling her names, posting nasty things about her on social media. Are they lying?

JORDYN PETIT: It was nothing. Just stupid stuff and it was a while ago. We're friends again. I promise!

OFFICER WILSON: I heard there were some disagreements over a boy. Any truth to that, Jordyn? Were you and Cora fighting over a boy?

JORDYN PETIT: No! That's not how it was. Grandpa, I want to go home. Can't we just go home?

THOMAS PETIT: Enough! Are we free to leave?

OFFICER WILSON: You can go, but we'll need to talk again soon. Jordyn, I suggest next time we talk you are more forthcoming in your answers. We'll find out the truth one way or another and it's to your benefit to help us get there.

Nov. 11, 2017

Today I asked Kendall if she knew who Joseph Wither was. She rolled her eyes and laughed. "Duh," she said. "Everybody's heard of Wither. Haven't you ever gone down to the tracks during a sleepover?" she asked. Then she made a face and covered her mouth as if she said something wrong. "Oops, I forgot you don't do sleepovers."

I told her that no one does sleepovers anymore but she just gave me a look that said, *Yeah, right.* The truth is, I haven't been on a sleepover in a long time. Not since before Ellie moved away. And that was only two times and even then we just watched movies and ate ice cream. Once we rode our bikes to the park but we never went down to the railroad tracks. I've always hated the sound of trains—like an old woman screaming in a thunderstorm.

Besides, when I was in first grade, two boys were playing chicken on the tracks and one of them didn't jump off them fast enough and ended up getting hit by the train. I have bad dreams about that sometimes—standing on the tracks and not being able to move. The engineer blows the whistle over and over but I still can't move my legs. When I have this nightmare I end up falling out of bed and waking up on the floor with my mom, dad and Kendall standing over me. It's embarrassing.

I think the boy's name was Charlie and that his family moved away pretty soon after the funeral. I didn't want to ask Kendall to tell me about Joseph Wither and why kids went down to the railroad tracks on overnights but my curiosity got the best of me and I didn't want to sound like I didn't know anything (even though I don't) when Violet, Jordyn and I worked on the project the next day.

Kendall kept teasing me about not knowing who Joseph Wither was; she liked holding this over my head. She loved it when she could rub my nose in stuff.

I wanted to just ignore her and pretend it didn't matter to me but it did so I ended up promising to do her chores for a week. Kendall even invited me into her bedroom, which is a miracle—she never lets me in there. We sat on her bed just like we did when we were little. She told me that Joseph Wither lived in Pitch about a million years ago in a house on Hickory Street, which is the same street where Violet lives. I asked Kendall if she knew which house it was.

She told me to just shut up and listen, that he lived in a house on Hickory Street with his mom and dad and two little sisters. Joseph Wither was seventeen years old at the time and was in love with the fifteen-year-old girl who lived in the house across the street.

I asked if she loved him back and then clapped my hand over my mouth when Kendall glared at me.

Kendall said that the girl did love him back but their parents thought they were too young and ordered them to stop seeing each other. Then Kendall stopped talking and went to shut the bedroom door. Skittles snuck in and I thought for sure that Kendall would freak out about it but she didn't even notice. It felt nice, sitting close to my sister like this. Kendall sat down next to me again and even though the door was shut she whispered how Joseph and the girl would sneak out at night and go down by the train tracks and do it.

I must have had a weird look on my face because Kendall looked at me like I was an idiot and said, "Yes. They did it. They. Had. Sex." She said this nice and slow for me, to make sure I understood.

I told her that I knew what sex was, though it made my stomach feel gross saying it out loud. I told her I thought way back in the old days they were pretty strict about stuff like that. She told me that lots of fifteen-year-olds had sex.

I looked at her closely. Kendall is fifteen and is very pretty. She has long blond hair that my mom says most women have to pay a hundred bucks a month to get. Kendall's skin turns brown in the summer and she has curves. I'm pale and never tan no matter how much time I spend in the sun. I just get sunburned, peel and then turn white again. I also don't have curves, plus I'm short for my grade. People always think I'm younger than I am. I wonder if Kendall is doing it. Boys are always calling our house.

Then I started thinking about Gabe and wondering if he ever had sex with anyone.

Kendall told me to close my mouth and not act so surprised. She told me that she wasn't having sex, that there wasn't anyone in our loser town that she would let touch her. She wanted to wait until she went away to college. Then she told me to shut up again and let her finish the story, that she had homework to do.

She said that Joseph Wither and the girl, Lucy, would sneak out and have sex down by the railroad tracks and one day her dad caught them. He dragged his daughter away and told Joseph that if he ever came near Lucy again he would kill him.

That made me start thinking about the school project and how in the world we are going to give a report about two teenagers doing it by the railroad tracks. Somehow I don't think Mr. Dover is going to let us talk about that. I wonder if it's too late to change our topic to Johnny Appleseed or Sleepy Hollow.

Just then Kendall's friend Emery came into the room and wanted to know what we were talking about. Kendall filled her in, making me look like a stupid idiot, of course, and Emery jumped on the bed and said, "Oooh, this story is so scary." Emery, when she isn't totally ignoring me, is actually pretty nice. She has really long, thick brown hair that Kendall says she flatirons every day. It takes her like an hour each time.

Kendall kept telling the story and said that, one night, Joseph and Lucy made plans to meet down by the tracks near the train depot but Lucy didn't show up. Lucy's family just up and moved away and she never got a chance to say goodbye to Joseph.

Emery takes over the story and says that Joseph was devastated. He couldn't eat, couldn't sleep. He wouldn't go to school. Emery's eyes got big and excited and she started talking in a whispery, ghosty voice, so I knew she was getting to the good part of the story. She said that Wither started hanging out by the railroad tracks, just sitting there waiting for Lucy to come to him. Then one night his house was burned down with his family inside and he disappeared. I can just imagine it. Joseph Wither walking along the railroad tracks going from town to town searching for his lost love. It was very romantic.

I wonder what it's like to be so in love with someone that you would do anything to be with them.

Emery said that the sheriff was sure that they were going to catch him but they never did. That's what everyone thought at first. They thought he would come home eventually, but he didn't. One night, a few months later, two sisters were walking home from a church meeting. There was no moon and no stars out so it was pitch-black. The girls couldn't see anything but they walked that same route all the time and they were together so they weren't scared. It got later and later and still the girls didn't come home.

Finally, their dad went out looking for them and a few hours later he found the body of one of his daughters by the train tracks. She had been beaten to death. I wanted to ask her what happened to the other sister but I didn't want Kendall to yell at me.

It was getting dark outside and Kendall's room filled with shadows. The branches from the big tree outside started tapping on the window like long fingers. I wanted to turn on a light but I didn't want Kendall and Emery to think I was a scaredy-cat so instead I picked up Skittles and started petting her. I pressed my face into her silky fur and started to feel better right away.

Kendall said they never did find the other sister; she disappeared into thin air. And then she said a year after the first girl died another one died. And then another, and another. All found by the train tracks. One beaten to death, one strangled, one stabbed and one drowned. All killed by Joseph Wither. She said that every few years or so a girl would vanish. Those were the girls he loved and took with him.

I didn't realize I was holding my breath until Skittles scratched at the back of my hand because I was holding her so tight. I let her go and she ran beneath the bed. I asked them how many girls Wither killed and how many he ended up taking. Kendall just shrugged her shoulders and told me to get out of her room. They had stuff to do.

Emery told Kendall not to be so mean. That Wither gave her nightmares when she was a kid. Like I said, Emery can be nice. I wish some of that would rub off on my sister!

Anyway, I found a weird website called DarkestDoor that's all about urban legends and myths. All you have to do is post a question about your topic and people from all over will chime in with their ideas. It's pretty cool. I haven't had the nerve to post anything yet. I'm afraid to because my mom is ALWAYS looking over my shoulder watching what I'm doing online.

She is so paranoid. If she knew I was in chat rooms she would freak out. But she has an after-school meeting this week and won't be home until five. That will give me some time. Plus, Violet showed me how to use incognito mode so no one can figure out what websites I've been on.

I caught Gabe looking at me during class today and obviously Mr. Dover did, too. Mr. Dover said, "Gabe, maybe you should just talk to Cora after class instead of staring at her." Even Gabe laughed. Everyone did, except for Jordyn.

After school, Violet and I were walking outside when she got a Snapchat. It was a really bad picture of me with my eyes half-closed and this weird look on my face. Written across the screen was the word *Bitch*. I don't even know what that means. Violet tried to make me feel better by saying that

Jordyn was just joking around, that she takes pictures of everyone and writes stupid stuff.

Just then Jordyn came running up to us and started talking like everything was perfectly fine. She even invited me over to her house this weekend. I don't know. It's all very confusing.

When I return to Violet's room, Officer Grady is in the doorway, waiting for me. I peek around his large frame, which fills the space. The nurse has finished collecting the blood samples, the wayward strands of hair, the bits of evidence that may have been left behind.

Beneath the warming blanket, lies Violet. She is on her side, facing the wall, curled up like a wooly caterpillar. The IV tube snakes out from beneath the blanket and up to the IV bag, where a clear liquid drips slowly into my daughter's bloodstream. She looks so small, so fragile.

"I just don't understand," I say, coming up to Officer Grady. "Joseph Wither is the name of a person that the girls did a school project about. Why would Violet say that a make-believe man attacked them?"

"Boy," Grady says. "Joseph Wither is a boy. Was a boy," he adds, seeing the question on my face. "He hasn't been seen by anyone in decades."

"I don't have time for this. I need to get back to my daughter."

"Ms. Crow, please," he says. "I have to talk to her. We need to find out what happened. Cora Landry isn't in good shape."

I think of Cora and how bad her face looked. Someone tried to kill her; there's no other way to look at it. "Okay," I finally say. "You can talk to her, but I want to be there."

Officer Grady looks like he wants to argue with me on this point but quickly understands that there is no chance of changing my mind and nods in agreement.

"You can stay while I talk to her but I'm going to ask that you don't interrupt. Some of the questions I ask may be upsetting but I have to ask them. Like I said, time is ticking. The longer that monster is out there, the more difficult it will be for us to catch him. As far as I know, Violet is the only witness who can tell us what happened."

We step into Violet's room together and I look to the nurse. "She seems more alert," she says. "She had a drink of water and asked for you." I feel a pang of regret for running out of the room when Violet needed me.

"Violet, honey," I say and Violet shifts in the bed to look at me. Her eyes droop with exhaustion but the nurse is right: she seems more with it. "Can you talk to Officer Grady for a few minutes? He has some questions for you."

Violet nods and makes room for me to sit next to her. "Are you feeling okay?" I ask. "Are you hurt at all?"

"No, I'm okay," she says but her eyes dart from side to side as if looking for someone.

Officer Grady clears his throat and pulls a chair up right next to the bed and retrieves a notepad and pen from his pocket. "I need to ask you some questions about this morning, Violet. You and Cora Landry went to the old train depot together?" Violet nods her head. "I need you to answer out loud, Violet, you understand?"

Again Violet nods and I slide my arm around her shoulders. "Yes," she says and then, "Yes, we went there."

"Was it just the two of you?"

"And Jordyn. Jordyn came, too." I look at Officer Grady in alarm but he coolly jots down what Violet is saying. There was no sign of Jordyn at the train yard. Was she hurt, too? Was she taken?

"Do you know where Jordyn went?" he asks and I'm relieved he at least asked the question. "She wasn't there when we found you and Cora."

Violet gnaws at her lower lip. "I don't know. She was there with us and then she wasn't."

"You and Jordyn were spending the night at the Landry house?"

"Yes."

"How did you get to the train yard?"

"We walked," Violet says and then peeks sheepishly up at me. She knows she's supposed to ask me before she ever goes anywhere. I've learned the hard way with Max and am trying to set firm rules with Violet. My fingers itch to look at my phone to see if Max has checked in but I don't want to interrupt now that Violet's talking.

"The train yard is how far from Cora's house? A mile and a half or two?" Officer Grady asks. Violet shrugs and he moves on. "What time did you leave?"

"Around midnight," she says without hesitation.

"Midnight?" I ask, unable to stop myself. "Why in the world would you three be roaming around town in the middle of the night?" I feel Violet go rigid next to me.

Officer Grady reaches over and pats Violet's knee. "Hold tight, will you, Violet? I'm going to talk to your mom out in the hall for a sec. You're doing great." Officer Grady stands and I slide out of my spot next to Violet and follow him into the hallway.

Once out of earshot Officer Grady turns on me. "The agreement was I ask the questions and you listen, right? How am I going to find out what happened if you keep interrupting?" A red flush creeps up his fleshy neck and I realize he's right. I need to shut up. He's trying to get all the information he can so he can catch the bastard and I'm stuck on Violet sneaking out in the middle of the night.

"I'm sorry," I say. "I'll be quiet."

"You know what would be even better?" he asks. "If you would let me finish interviewing her without you in the room. Kids talk more if the parents aren't listening in."

Again I know he's right. "Fine. I'll wait out here but you'll come and get me right away if she asks for me, right?"

"Sure thing," he agrees, steps back into the room and closes the door before I can change my mind.

I try to listen through the doorway but all I can hear is the low murmur of voices. I give up and check my phone for messages from Max. Nothing. I send Max a text telling him that his sister is in the hospital and he needs to call right now. Just as I hit Send I recognize Cora Landry's parents walking down the long corridor. I rush to catch up with them. "Mara," I call.

I can't remember her husband's name, just know that he manages a place that sells farm equipment. Mara's eyes are red and swollen from crying and her blond hair is pulled back in a messy ponytail. Like me, she appears to have dressed in a hurry. Normally polished and put together, this morning she wears an oversize sweatshirt, paint-speckled yoga pants and a pair of moccasins. "Mara," I say, her name catching in my throat. "I can't believe this happened! How's Cora doing?"

She presses a tissue to her red-tipped nose with shaky fingers. "She was stabbed. In the face and here." With shaky fingers she indicates a spot just below her ribs. Mara's face crumples and she leans into her husband.

"I'm so sorry," I say, swallowing back my own tears. "Was Cora able to say what happened?"

Mara's husband shakes his head. "No. She wasn't in any condition to talk to the police. But the witness said she saw a car with three people inside just before she found Cora."

"This is my husband, Jim," Mara says, remembering her manners even in her distraught state. "This is Beth, Violet's mom."

I'm embarrassed that I don't know the Landrys better. My shift at the gas station usually ends at five and Violet spends nearly every day after school at their house. I should have made more of an effort, thanked them for giving my daughter a place to go besides an empty house.

Mara fishes into her purse for another tissue. "A nurse told us Violet was here but she couldn't tell us how she's doing. Was she hurt?"

"They treated her for shock but she's okay." I feel almost guilty that my daughter might be able to leave the hospital today. "The policeman is talking to her right now trying to put together what happened." I reach for Mara's hand. It is cold and dry to the touch. "I can't believe this. What in the world were the girls doing at the train yard in the middle of the night?"

Mara pulls her hand from mine. "I checked on them before I went to bed. They were in Cora's room sleeping."

I'm startled by the defensiveness in her voice. I wasn't about to criticize another's parenting skills when I had no idea where my own daughter was in the wee hours of the morning and still have no idea where my sixteen-year-old son is right now. "I just mean I can't believe something like this could happen here in Pitch."

"There's no way that it was Cora's idea to leave the house. No way. She never snuck out like this before," Jim says. His voice is tight with irritation and I suddenly know he blames Violet. She's the new girl in town. We're the outsiders. "She knows she's not to go anywhere without talking to us first." He pulls on Mara's hand. "Come on, we need to get up to the surgical floor."

"Good luck," I say. "Please let me know if you need anything."

"Thank you," Mara says, allowing herself to be guided down the hallway by her husband.

I know the Landrys are worried about their daughter but I'm angry on Violet's behalf. Jim all but said that Violet and Jordyn are responsible. We don't know the full story. Besides, I know Violet. She's more of a follower than a leader.

I wish I was back in the room with Violet and Officer Grady. I don't like not knowing what's going on. I have so many questions. Who attacked them and why were the girls out in the middle of the night? I pace outside the examination room until I can't stand it anymore and I ease open the door and sit in a corner of the room where I'm out of the way but can still hear what they are talking about. Officer Grady gives me an aggravated sidelong glance but continues his conversation with Violet.

"You weren't injured, right? No one hurt you, right?" he asks.

"No," Violet says. She looks so small sitting in the center of the bed, her knees now tucked up beneath her chin. Her long dark hair hides her face but from the wobble in her voice I know she's upset.

"But someone hurt Cora very badly," he says gently. "Can you tell me what you saw? What you heard? Anything at all?"

Violet lowers her forehead to her knees, clasps her hands in front of her shins. Officer Grady waits her out. I've got to give him credit. He's being very patient. "You said that you and the other girls got separated. Where did you go?"

"I went to find Jordyn. She got mad and left," Violet says, her mouth muffled by her knees.

This doesn't surprise me. I like Jordyn but she runs hot and cold. One minute the girls will be laughing hysterically about something and the next Jordyn will be stomping away over some imagined slight.

"Why was Jordyn mad?" Officer Grady asks. He lowers his forearms to his knees and ducks his head to try to see Violet's face still hidden behind a curtain of hair. Violet shrugs. Officer Grady waits.

"She said we were being stupid," Violet finally says.

"Why did she say that?" Officer Grady eases his chair a few inches closer to her bedside.

Violet raises her head, tucks her hair behind her ears. Now that her hands are cleaned of the blood I can see that she has bitten her nails down to the quick. I thought she had broken that bad habit. Evidently not.

"Jordyn said he wasn't going to show up," Violet says and my blood runs cold. Without looking at me Officer Grady raises one hand in my direction as if to say, *I've got this.*

"Who is *he*, Violet?" Officer Grady asks. Violet ducks her head. Officer Grady waits a few beats to see if Violet will answer. She doesn't so he decides to move on.

"So Jordyn left and then what did you do?"

"I went looking for her but I couldn't find her, so I went back. I wanted to be there when he did come. And he did—Jordyn was wrong."

"Who?" I ask before I can stop myself. "Who came?" Violet looks over at me as if she realizes for the first time that I've returned to the room.

Officer Grady's radio crackles and he reluctantly removes it from his utility belt. He listens to a string of muffled words that I can't understand but my attention is still on Violet. "Who came?" I ask again once he puts away his radio but Violet is watching Officer Grady carefully.

"Violet, this is very important," he says. His voice has lost all of its earlier warmth. "Who did you see at the train yard?"

Violet ducks her head. "I don't know."

"But you saw someone?" Officer Grady asks. Violet nods. "But you didn't recognize him? You didn't know the person?" She nods again. "So you did know him?" Officer Grady says in exasperation.

"You're confusing her," I protest. "Violet, did you recognize the person?"

"You won't believe me," she answers with a slight shake of her head.

"Violet, all we want to know is the truth," Officer Grady says, again trying for his earlier gentle tone but Violet is having none of it and buries her face in her hands.

"I think she needs a break," I say, unable to keep the anger from my voice. "Can't we do this later?"

Officer Grady sighs. "I just got word on my radio that a sheriff's deputy picked up your son and another boy. He's asking for you. They'll meet us down at the police station."

"What for?" I ask in disbelief. Max gets in his share of trouble but has never been picked up by the police before.

"I'm not sure," Officer Grady says.

"Bullshit," I blurt out. "The sheriff doesn't randomly pick up two teenage boys without a reason. What happened?"

"I honestly don't know," Officer Grady says. "The witness at the train yard reported seeing a black, two-door Honda around the time she found Cora. Your son was found with another boy in a car that matches that vehicle's description. The deputy is bringing them in to answer a few questions. Once the doctor discharges Violet, I can drive you back to town."

"It's got to be some kind of misunderstanding," I say in frustration, sure that the woman who found Cora must have made a mistake. There isn't any lighting in the train depot. It was too dark and any car she might have seen would look black. "I want to make it clear—I don't want anyone talking to Violet or Max without my permission. Do you understand?"

Officer Grady nods. "No," I insist. "I want you to get on that radio right now and tell them that under no circumstances is anyone to question Max until I get there."

"Understood," Officer Grady says as he opens the examination room door. "I'll meet you at the front entrance and we'll head back to Pitch."

It's insane to think that Max could have hurt anyone. He's gotten into a bit of trouble but has never been violent except for the one time back in New Mexico and that was just a stupid schoolyard dustup.

The nurse removes the IV from Violet's arm and since her clothes have been taken as evidence she gives Violet a small pair of scrubs to wear home from the hospital. "Sorry I don't have any shoes for you," she says, "but I do have these lovely yellow socks." Violet gives the nurse a small smile. To me the nurse says, "Paperwork is all done so you are free to go. Good luck and don't hesitate to call if you have any questions." I thank her and wait until she leaves before I speak again to Violet.

"Did you see Max while you were out?" I ask Violet as she pulls on the socks. "Near the train yard?" Violet shakes her head and looks like she wants to tell me more but doesn't say anything. "What?" I ask. "This is important. Did you see a car near the train yard this morning, Violet?"

"It's hard to remember," Violet says as we move into the corridor and toward the exit where Officer Grady will be waiting for us.

"You need to remember," I say more sharply than I mean to and Violet flinches as if I slapped her. "We just need to be as helpful as we can." I soften my voice. "For Cora's sake."

I want to reach for Violet's hand. I want to go back to a time when the warmth of our palms pressed together made everything more bearable. But of course there is no way Violet will allow this public display of affection. Instead she veers away from me until we are nearly on opposite sides of the hallway.

By the time we reach the exit, Officer Grady is out front leaning against his car and talking on his cell phone. When he sees us he hangs up and opens the back door. I can't help but notice all the curious looks we get as we climb inside.

"I just got off the phone with Pitch PD. Max knows you're on your way," Officer Grady says, turning on the engine. "Buckle up."

"Where is she?" Violet asks.

"Who?" I ask. "Cora? She's with another doctor being taken care of."

"Jordyn," Violet says, fidgeting with the seat belt until I reach over and snap it into place for her. I find the question a bit odd, though I'm not sure why. Of course she'd be curious about what happened to her friend. Maybe it's the tone of her voice—not worried, not concerned. I try to read Violet's expression but it tells me nothing.

"She was at the police station for questioning but I imagine she's home by now," Officer Grady explains as he eases the car from its spot in front of the hospital.

"What did she say?" Violet asks, looking out the window. She's talking as if she's asking what's for lunch.

Officer Grady glances at me through the rearview mirror and our eyes meet. He's confused by Violet's reaction, too, and he's looking to me for help. "Violet, honey," I say, "are you feeling okay?" I wonder if she might still be in shock, worry that I may have insisted on bringing her home too soon.

Violet is examining her knuckles, scraping at the dried blood that fills the narrow grooves. Cora's blood. I pull her fingers away, repulsed. "When's the last time you saw Max?" I try again. "Was it last night when he and Clint took you to Cora's house?"

"And Nikki," she adds.

"Did you see Max at all?" I ask, my voice rising with frustration. Why can't she give me a straight answer? "Listen, Violet, Max could be in a lot of trouble. Did you see Max after he dropped you off?"

Violet's forehead briefly creases in worry. "No," she says so that I barely hear her and turns away from me again to face the window. She's lying. I'm just not sure about what. We travel the rest of the way back to Pitch in silence. I want to talk to her more about what could be happening with Max but I don't want to say too much in front of Officer Grady.

I know it's impossible that he had anything to do with what happened to Cora but what if he's arrested, anyway? We're the new people in town. Max—with his skateboard and his long, dark curly hair, and a half smile that people think is a smirk— looks like he could be dangerous. But he isn't.

He's a kind, loving boy. Ever since Max's dad and I divorced nine years ago when he was seven he's tried to be the man of the house—taking out the garbage, making sure the doors are locked at night. It wasn't until just before we moved here that he started getting in trouble and now since he met Clint and Nikki that he's become so secretive.

When we finally get to town Officer Grady slows the car

and asks me if I want to stop at home first. I hesitate. I need to get Violet home and showered and in her own clothes but I also have to get to Max. I don't know if I trust the cops to follow my order not to let anyone question Max without me there.

"We better go straight to the police station," I decide. A few minutes later he pulls up in front of the station and I look down at Violet's feet. She's wearing only the yellow socks that the nurse gave her. I can't haul her into the police station dressed the way she is.

"Maybe you want me to take Violet to a relative's or friend's house. The police station really isn't a place for kids."

I shake my head. "We don't have family in town. And Violet's best friend is Cora, so that's out. I guess I can call a neighbor."

Violet grabs my wrist. "I want to stay with you," she says.

"What's the matter?" I ask in surprise. "I thought you liked going over to Jordyn's house."

Violet shakes her head, lips pressed tightly together. "I just don't want to. Please don't make me go."

"You seem pretty upset, Violet," Officer Grady says. "Did something happen with Jordyn?"

"No, I just want to stay with my mom," Violet insists. She's lying. At least partially. I can tell because Violet's voice has taken on the babyish tone she uses when she knows she's in trouble and wants to get on my good side. I want to make her tell me what happened but say nothing because Officer Grady is watching us both closely.

"I won't leave you, honey." I kiss the top of her head but she keeps a viselike grip on my arm. "Thanks," I say to Officer Grady, "but she's been through a lot today. I think she should stay with me."

The last time Jordyn was over at the house, just a few days ago, the girls seemed like they were getting along fine. They holed themselves up in Violet's room and didn't come down for two hours. Not even when I told them I had just thrown some cookie dough in the oven.

When they finally reemerged I asked Violet why Cora didn't come over, too. The three of them are as thick as thieves. Violet said that Cora was busy but I caught the look on Jordyn's face when I mentioned Cora's name. Like she had just bitten into something that's gone bad. I meant to ask Violet about it later but forgot.

Now I wish I had. A million times over I've seen that look on the faces of the girls I knew as a kid. The nasty smirks that slid into place just before they stabbed you in the back.

Corareef12:

Help! I'm working on a school project and trying to find out more information about Joseph Wither. He lived in Pitch, Iowa, in the 1940s and people say that he killed several young girls because his girlfriend was grounded from seeing him. I can't find any actual proof. Does anyone know anything about this?

4leafclover:

That's quite the school project! I never had an assignment like that in school!

Lazydazey:
Never heard of him.

Dutchman007:

My grandpa grew up around Pitch and told us stories about Joseph Wither. Said he burned down his family home and then ran away. Girls started showing up dead by the railroad tracks and rumor was that Joseph Wither was behind it. My grandpa said that most people thought he killed himself or ran away and he had nothing to do with the dead girls.

Corareef12:

Thanks! That's what I'm beginning to think. We can't find any proof of anything—just lots of stories. Plus, people around here are saying that Wither is still killing girls but he'd be like ninety!

4leafclover:

Corareef12, just how old are you? You really shouldn't give personal info about where you're from here...

Following closely behind Officer Grady, Violet and I make our way up the steps and into the police station, a squat, one-story redbrick building with the words *City of Pitch Police Department* stenciled in orange letters across the large plate-glass window. The shell of a pay telephone hangs between a set of double doors and a wooden bench.

"Go ahead and take a seat for a minute," Officer Grady says, gesturing to the wooden bench littered with newspapers and magazines. "I'll go check on the kids and come get you so we can talk."

We sit on the wooden bench and wait. I wonder if I should call a lawyer right now, just in case, but I don't know any attorneys and I sure as hell can't afford one.

"Mom, what do they think Max did?" Violet asks.

"Nothing. It's just a misunderstanding," I reassure her. "We'll get it straightened out and go home."

The front entrance opens and a woman walks in with a young girl that I recognize as Nikki's little sister. The woman is wearing an egg-yolk-colored waitress uniform from a twenty-four-hour café located on the highway south of town. Her frosted hair is scraped back in a tight bun and a thick layer of foundation and lipstick do nothing to hide the fatigue on her face.

"You're Max's mom," she says. Her heavily mascaraed eyes settle on me. It's an accusation. There is no friendliness in her tone and I know this isn't going to go well.

"Yes, I'm Beth Crow," I say and both Violet and I rise from our spots on the bench. I try to keep the defensiveness out of my voice. "And you are...?"

"Lorena Dobric, Nikki's mother. What kind of trouble has

your son gotten Nikki into this time?" she asks. The little girl eases away from her mother as if hoping to avoid any crossfire.

"Hold on," I say. "Let's just wait and see what they tell us. The officer just went in back to get Max."

"I know what they'll tell us. That your son and that other boy, Clint, have gotten Nikki in trouble." Lorena leans over the counter and calls out, "Anybody there? I want to talk to someone now! I want to see my daughter!"

"Mom?" Violet asks uncertainly.

"It's okay," I tell her. I hand her my phone. "Go sit down and play a game on my phone. Don't worry." Violet reluctantly moves toward the bench, sits down and begins tapping at the phone's screen.

Nikki's sister gravitates toward Violet. "Where are your shoes?" I hear her ask as she joins Violet on the bench.

"Hello? Anyone back there?" Lorena says more loudly. "Where is my daughter?" She turns back to me. "I don't have time for this. I have to go to work."

A woman wearing a police uniform with the name Wilson stitched across the front pocket comes into the room. Her blond hair is braided into a long rope that hangs down her back. "We'll be with you in just a minute, folks," she says. "Please be patient."

"Where is my daughter?" Lorena asks again, not budging from her spot in front of the counter. "I want to see her now."

"Take a seat," the officer says with forced patience. "We're in the middle of an attempted murder investigation. I'll call you when we're ready."

Her words slam into me like a fist. *Attempted murder.* "I'd like to see my son, too," I say. "He's not under arrest, is he?" Next to me Violet is tugging on my sleeve. "Just a minute, Vi," I tell her.

To the officer I say, "I want to see my son. Now." My voice holds more courage than I feel. My heart is banging in my chest now. I have visions of Max handcuffed and sitting in a cell somewhere in the building and it's all I can do to not climb over the barrier and search for him.

"Settle down," the officer says with exaggerated calm that makes me want to yank her braid. "He's not under arrest and no one questioned him. He wasn't talking, anyway." She disappears through another door and Violet pulls at my arm again.

"Violet, just wait!" I snap just as Officer Grady reappears.

"Come on back, ladies," he says, holding the door open so we can pass through. "Last door on the right."

I rush down the hallway with Violet at my heels and come to a stop in the open doorway of a conference room. Max, Nikki and Clint are slouched in chairs arranged around a long, scarred wooden table that fills most of the small room.

"Max, are you okay?" I ask.

"Yeah," he says. He looks tired, bewildered and a bit scared but no worse for wear. His curls have lost some of their spring. A sure sign that he's been running his fingers through his hair, a nervous habit he's had since he was little.

Coming up behind me, Lorena starts right in on Nikki. "Where the hell were you all night? You know I have to get to work and I can't leave your sister alone."

Nikki's eyes, already swollen and red, fill with new tears but she doesn't respond. I see Max reach out and link a finger with Nikki's.

"Is Nikki free to go?" Lorena asks.

"We'd like to ask each of them a few questions about this morning," Officer Grady says, "but we need your permission before we do so."

"No," Lorena cuts him off. "We're leaving. Nikki, let's go." Nikki looks uncertainly at Officer Grady, who nods his head.

"She can go, but we would appreciate setting up a time to talk."

"Was she drinking? Doing drugs?" Lorena asks sharply.

"No," Officer Grady says.

"Were they speeding? Breaking any laws?"

"No, they were not."

"Then we're leaving. There's nothing for us to talk about." Lorena latches on to her daughter's arm, lifting her from the chair, and begins to move to the doorway. "Misty," she says to her other daughter. "Let's go." Nikki shrugs off her mother's grasp and dashes from the room.

"Can you please tell me what's going on?" I ask once the door closes behind Lorena and the girls, taking most of the air with them. The room suddenly feels claustrophobic, stifling.

"Please sit," Officer Grady says and we do. "A witness saw a car near the train yard this morning matching the description of the one Max and his friends were in. A sheriff's deputy saw the car out on the highway and pulled them over. Clint here got smart-mouthed and the deputy ended up bringing the three of them into the station."

Max speaks for the first time. "Mom, what's going on? What happened at the depot?" He glances over at Violet, who is watching, taking everything in. "Why is Violet dressed like that?"

"No one told him?" I ask in surprise.

"No," Officer Grady says. "We're investigating a crime. We wanted to find out if they knew anything first."

"Someone attacked Violet and Cora Landry at the train yard last night," I tell him and his face first registers shock and then anger.

"Who?" he asks, looking over to Violet, who is looking anxiously around the room.

"A witness says it could be you and your friends," says Officer Grady.

Max opens his mouth to say something but I jump in first. "Don't say a word," I order. To Officer Grady I say, "Listen, I said no one was going to question my son and I mean it."

Officer Grady holds up his hand to silence me. "Violet's friend

is in pretty bad shape. Someone hit her so hard that he frac-
tured her skull."

"Eff that," Clint says, standing and squeezing behind my chair
toward the door. "You can't pin that on me. I'm out of here."

Officer Grady continues as if Clint hasn't spoken. "He
knocked the teeth out of her head. We got a guy back at the
train yard looking for them." Clint freezes in the doorway and
the scowl slips from his face and Max looks like he's going to
throw up.

Though Officer Grady speaks in a low, measured voice, a red,
angry flush has creeped up his neck. "Cora's at the hospital in
surgery right now with a plastic surgeon who is trying to put
her face back together again, so if you can tell me where you
were between midnight and 1:00 a.m., I can cross you off my
list and focus on finding the person who did this."

A look passes between Max and Clint. Oh, my God, I think,
they can't prove where they were last night. There's no one who
can vouch for their whereabouts.

"You've got nothing?" Officer Grady's voice rises.

"Mom." Max looks at me for help.

"Just tell him where you were," I urge. "Just tell him the
truth. This is important."

"We were just driving around," Clint says, all of his earlier
bluster gone.

"Near the train yard?"

"No," says Clint.

"Yes," Max says at the same time.

"Which is it?" Officer Grady demands, staring at Max. "Yes,
you were at the train yard where a twelve-year-old girl was attacked. Or no, you weren't."

"He's trying to tell you." I raise my voice. "Give him a
chance."

"Stop it." Violet buries her face in her hands. "Please stop it.
It wasn't them."

I reach across the table and tenderly pull her fingers from her face. "What did you say?"

"It wasn't them. They didn't do it," she whispers.

Officer Grady takes a step toward us and this time I hold up my hand to stop him.

"Violet, do you know who hurt Cora?" I ask, still holding her hands in mine. She nods, hot tears plopping onto my knuckles. "Who? Who was it?"

She doesn't speak. The only sound in the room is her faint crying. Even Clint looks uncomfortable.

"Please, Violet," I say, dipping my head so I can see her face. She can't bring herself to look at me. "Honey, this is important. If you can help Cora, you need to." I lift her chin and wipe her tears away with my fingers. "Violet, it's okay. I won't let anyone hurt you."

"I told you—it was Joseph Wither," she whispers.

"Honey, you know that he isn't real, right?" I ask. I'm thinking that it might be some pervert pretending to be him or maybe Violet is just confused.

Clint laughs and I shoot him a look that silences him.

"Why do you think it's Joseph Wither?" Officer Grady keeps his gaze on Violet. "Could it have been someone who *said* he was Joseph Wither, Violet?" he asks.

Violet shakes her head. "No, it was him. He came, just like he said he would."

Officer Grady scratches at his neck.

"What?" I ask. "You talked to him? Who is he?" I look to Max, who shrugs his shoulders.

Again Clint laughs and this time Max says, "Shut up, Clint."

Violet gnaws at her thumbnail. "He is, too, real," she says. "Cora showed me messages from him."

"Violet," Officer Grady says but she refuses to look his way. "Violet, this is important," he says firmly. "Look at me." Violet looks at him with something I've seen more and more in my daughter lately: defiance. "Someone might have told you he was Joseph Wither, but he wasn't." Violet's eyes fill with tears and she swipes them away angrily. "Now, did you see someone attack Cora? Can you tell me what he looks like?"

Violet presses her hands to her ears and shakes her head. "He's real," she whispers.

"He's the bogeyman." Clint laughs. "The monster under your bed. Was he under your bed, Violet?" he asks snidely.

Max has had enough. He's out of his chair in a flash and shoves Clint, pinning him to the nearest wall. "I told you to shut up," he hisses. The two boys are nose to nose, but Clint has about fifty pounds on Max. Right now the only thing going for Max is the element of surprise and his anger.

"Jesus, Max," Clint says. "Don't freak out. I'm just joking around." Max looks like he wants to punch the smirk off his face and part of me wishes he would.

"You saw it. He assaulted me," Clint says, pushing Max away.

"You're being a jerk," Officer Grady tells him. "You get off on teasing little girls? Go sit out front and wait for your mom to come and pick you up. If you leave before I talk to her, I will arrest you."

"Asshole," Clint mumbles under his breath as he moves toward the door. "Freak," he says, directing the word toward Violet.

"He's real!" Violet shouts after him. Spit flies from her mouth and she kicks at him but misses.

"Violet!" I exclaim.

Clint pauses and narrows his weasel eyes at her, the sneer returning to his face. "Did you go looking for him? Did you really think he was going to take you with him? If you believed that, then you really are stupid."

Violet jumps up from her chair and lunges at Clint. Thankfully, Officer Grady is there to stop her. "Out front, Clint. Now," he commands and Clint stalks out, leaving a stream of curse words trailing behind him. Max looks at his sister as if she's lost her mind.

Officer Wilson comes into the room holding a set of hand-cuffs, sending Violet into another round of hysterics.

"You're upsetting her even more," I cry.

"I got this, Wilson," Officer Grady says. Officer Wilson hesitates. "I mean it, put the cuffs away. You can go now. I've got it covered."

Officer Wilson looks like she wants to argue but I'm guessing that Grady has a few years of seniority on her. Reluctantly she returns the cuffs to her hip. "Looks like a 10-96 to me," she says, eyeing Violet.

"What's that mean?" I ask, knowing it's nothing good.

"Never mind," Officer Grady says to me. To Wilson he says, "Wait outside." With a shake of her head Wilson steps from the room and positions herself in the hallway so she can still look inside. Officer Grady briefly releases Violet with one hand and gives the door a push. I can't help but feel a bit of satisfaction as it closes in her face.

"Okay, Violet," Officer Grady says. "Easy now. I hear you. Someone who said he was Joseph Wither was there. I believe you. I know you're scared."

Violet tries to pull away from Grady again but realizes it's futile and slowly she settles down, her tantrum eases and her breathing slows until she is limp in his arms. Once he relaxes his grip I pull her close to me. "It's okay," I soothe.

To Officer Grady I say, "I know you need to talk to her, but you can see how upset she is. She isn't going to be any help like this. Please let us go home. She can rest and then you can talk to her, I promise. Please," I beg, my voice trembling.

"All right," Officer Grady finally says. I know it kills him to let us go home. He wants to get whatever information he can from Violet. Only she and Cora know what really happened by the train tracks and Violet is the only one in any condition to tell him. "Take Violet home, let her get some sleep. But I do have to talk to her soon. Tonight if possible, tomorrow morning at the latest. Got it?" I nod as I stroke Violet's hair and she cries noiselessly into my chest. "I'll give you a ride home."

The last thing I want to do is get back into a police car, but my car is back at the house so we don't have another choice. "Thanks," I say. Officer Grady opens the conference room door and we slowly file out. Officer Wilson has given up her spot by the door and is back at the front desk.

"I'm taking Ms. Crow and the kids back to their place. I'll be back in about twenty minutes," Officer Grady says and Wilson gives a casual wave of her hand to let him know she's heard him but keeps her eyes on the stack of paperwork in front of her.

Once outside, Officer Grady turns to Max. "Stay away from that Phelps boy, understand? He's nothing but trouble."

"I will, no problem," Max agrees. I hope that Officer Grady's warning is enough. I've tried telling Max that for months. Maybe the way Clint was teasing Violet in the conference room has finally revealed his true colors to Max.

To me, Officer Grady says, "Listen, I understand we're dealing with kids here and I'm trying to be sensitive to what Violet has been through, but I'm running an investigation. You understand that, don't you?"

"I'm trying," I say, trying to keep the irritation I feel from creeping into my words. "But I have to take care of my children. They're my top priority."

Grady opens the back door of the police car and Cora and Max climb inside. I'm about to join them when he stops me with a hand on my shoulder. "Yeah, and Cora Landry and the safety of everyone in this community is my priority. I'm going to have to ask the hard questions and the sooner I can do that, the faster we'll catch this guy," he says. "And I can't ask Violet these questions unless I have your permission and support."

I nod. I know he's just doing his job. Maybe it's the small size of the department or that they don't have a lot of violent crimes to investigate, but so far I'm not impressed.

"I'll talk to Violet," I say wearily. "I know she wants to help Cora, too. She just needs some rest."

"Thank you," Grady says and I get inside the vehicle. Violet and Max are sitting low in their seats, keeping their heads down—Violet, trying to hide her tears, and Max, trying to make himself invisible to anyone passing by who might know him. I close my eyes and lift my face to the sun's weak warmth— so different from the persistent, unrelenting sunshine back in New Mexico—and for the first time since our car broke down leaving us stranded outside of town, I regret coming to Pitch.

JW44:
I JUST FOUND YOUR POST, CORAREEF12. I KNOW ALL ABOUT
JOSEPH WITHER. PEOPLE WILL SAY HE'S JUST A LEGEND BUT HE'S
REAL. HE'S NOT WHAT THEY SAY, THOUGH. HE'S JUST LONELY. HE'S
LOOKING FOR PEOPLE TO BE HIS FRIEND, TO TRAVEL WITH HIM.

 4leafclover:
Don't listen to him, Corareef12. He's full of shit.

 JW44:
4LEAFCLOVER, I WASN'T TALKING TO YOU.

 Corareef12:
It's okay, 4leafclover. I want to know.

 4leafclover:
This is NOT okay!

 JW44:
YEAH, 4LEAFCLOVER, SHE WANTS TO KNOW. SMALL MINDS CAN
MOVE ALONG NOW...

 4leafclover:
Fine, it's your funeral. I'm out of here.

 JW44:
GOOD! CORAREEF12, WHAT DO YOU WANT TO KNOW?

 Corareef12:
I don't get it...why would he kill them if he wants them to be
his friend?

JW44:
HE KILLS THE ONES HE DOESN'T WANT, TAKES THE OTHERS WITH HIM. THEY DON'T DIE—THEY LIVE FOREVER. THEY BECOME HIS SHADOWS.

 Corareef12:
But that's impossible.

 JW44:
IS IT?

 Corareef12:
Yes! How would you know, anyway?

 JW44:
BECAUSE I'M WITHER.

Clint:
Wither Lives! Just ask Max

Abby:
?????

Ryan:
What happened?

Clint:
Kid got stabbed at the train yard. Wither Lives!

Abby:
UR full of it

Clint:
His sister was there. Said it was Wither. Ha ha

Ryan:
No way! Who was the girl?

Abby:
Is she okay? Did she die?

Clint:
Not yet

I interviewed Mara Landry in one of the family rooms located on the third floor of the children's hospital. I wanted to talk with Mara privately before I met with Cora but understandably she didn't want to be too far away from her daughter.

She settled onto a love seat covered in a striped, industrial-strength fabric made to stand up to the wear and tear of hundreds of worried and grief-stricken parents and visitors. I pulled a chair up and sat down next to her, positioning myself so I could see if anyone was lingering near the door to ensure privacy for our conversation.

Mara looked somewhat rested compared to when I saw her the evening before. Knowing that Cora's injuries weren't life-threatening certainly must have eased her mind. Her blond hair was brushed and tucked smoothly behind her ears and her face was expertly made up. Someone must have brought her a change of clothes. Gone were the paint-splattered yoga pants and sweatshirt. Instead she wore tailored jeans, ballet flats and a long-sleeve black T-shirt.

During the fifteen minutes that we visited, Mara painted a picture of a happy twelve-year-old who just happened to be in the wrong place at the wrong time. I took note that Mara didn't mention any of the anxiety that was noted in Cora's medical records.

"Where are the police in their investigation? Have they given you any more information?" I asked.

"Just bits and pieces," Mara said. "It's very frustrating. The officer did say that they didn't think robbery was the motive. I mean, obviously. Who would rob a twelve-year-old? But then he said that the ER nurses found two hundred dollars in Cora's pocket. Why in the world would she have that kind of money with her?"

"What did Cora say?" I asked.

"She said she didn't know. She couldn't remember." Mara shook her head. "It doesn't make any sense."

"Why were the girls at the train yard?" I asked. "Did you find out what they were doing there?" I asked this question not just out of curiosity, but because it would give me some insight into Cora and her personality. Was she a risk-taker? A follower?

Mara immediately bristled. "I don't know why they were there, but I'm sure it was Jordyn's or Violet's idea," she said, pressing her lips tightly together in disapproval. "Cora has never really had a best friend before. The closest thing to it moved away last year. Cora had a very difficult time in school last year. One of her classmates ended up being very nasty. The girl treated Cora horribly, but Cora kept putting up with it until I finally called the school and the girl's parents."

Mara sighed. "Maybe I should have let the girls handle it on their own, but I just couldn't stand seeing her suffer. She's had a bit of a hard time finding a new group of friends. You know how it is in rural towns."

Mara waited for me to agree with her, that yes, I understood the intricate, social rituals unique to towns with populations that hovered below a thousand people. I knew better than to respond. If I agreed with her, then I was passing judgment on the community she calls home. If I disagreed, then I was not validating her experiences.

"Tell me about Cora's friends," I said instead. "The ones who spent the night at your house."

"Well, Cora has known Jordyn since kindergarten but they never really played together when they were little. Jordyn's grandparents run one of the local bars in town. I think my husband went to high school with one of their sons." She thought for a moment. "Maybe I'm wrong about that. Anyway, Cora and

Jordyn didn't hang out until this year. They never had much in common. Cora is reserved, more shy. Jordyn is loud—" Mara frowned "—has to be the center of attention."

"And the other girl?" I asked. "Violet?"

Mara's hand moved to her ear and she yanked on it nervously. "Violet's new. Her mom works at the gas station, but Cora and Violet have become very good friends. Violet comes over just about every day after school now. Her mom seems kind of rough but Violet's no trouble at all. She's a sweet girl."

"So, you'd say that Cora has had a good school year in relation to peers?" I asked.

"I'd say so," Mara agreed. "I mean, she is almost a teenager and God knows they are a mystery. But Cora hasn't mentioned any troubles and I'm sure I would have noticed."

"Would you like for me to meet Cora now?" I asked. "Does she know I've come to see her?"

"I told her that another doctor was going to stop in." Mara stood and folded her arms across her chest as if chilly. "I thought that maybe you could explain what it is you do."

"Of course," I said and followed Mara from the family room, past the nurses' desk and across the hall to Cora's room. Mara pushed open the door to reveal a darkened room, lights off, shades closed. The only light came from a muted television set that hung from the wall. A teenage girl sat in the corner.

In the bed was a diminutive, still shape. "Cora, honey," Mara said, leaning over her. "Are you awake?"

If Cora gave a response, I didn't hear it.

"The doctor I told you about is here. I'm going to let some light in here so the two of you can talk, okay?" Mara went to the window and adjusted the shades so that the morning sun filtered through the slats, giving the room a hazy glow.

The left side of Cora's head was shaved and dozens of stitches punctuated her skull. A heavy bandage covered her left eye and cheek and the skin that was exposed was eggplant purple.

Stitches crisscrossed her swollen lips and her left arm was encased in a purple fiberglass cast. It was impossible to know what Cora looked like before the attack. Her features were so distorted that I wondered how the police were able to identify who she was. Perhaps it was the other girl at the scene who gave the emergency workers Cora's name.

"Hello there, Cora." I approached her bedside slowly so as not to startle her. The last thing Cora needed was another stranger converging on her. I came to her right side and positioned myself so that she could see me. "I'm Dr. Gideon." Cora's eye, sky blue but dulled by painkillers, blinked languidly up at me.

"I know you've met a lot of doctors since you've been here but I'm a different kind of doctor. I'm not here to look at your arm or your other injuries. I'm sure you've had plenty of people poking at you, am I right?" Cora gave me a shy nod. "I'm the kind of doctor who listens."

"A shrink," the girl sitting in the corner said.

"That's right." I smiled.

"Kendall, that's not polite," Mara scolded. "This is Cora's sister, she's fifteen," she said as if that explained it all.

I wondered where Mr. Landry was. Had he stepped out for a bit? It was a Tuesday; perhaps he wasn't able to get away from work. I made a mental note to look through the paperwork to find out what Jim Landry did for a living.

"Hello, Kendall, it's nice to meet you," I said before turning back to Cora. "Sometimes," I began, "after people get hurt they have a lot of different kinds of feelings. Scared, mad, confused. Are you feeling any of those things right now?" Cora remained still. "I imagine you may not feel a lot like talking, but I want you to know that when you are ready, I will be here to listen.

"In the meantime, I brought you a little present." I reached into my oversize bag and pulled out an array of notebooks and a set of gel pens. "Sometimes the kids I work with find it easier to write or draw about how they are feeling. Do you see a notebook here that you like?"

Using her uninjured eye, Cora scanned the notebooks that I fanned out on the edge of her bed. I always offered a variety of notebooks for patients to choose from: one that looked like the cover was painted with pale pastel watercolors, a zebra-print, one with a picture of a polar bear and her cub on the front, and one with a plain blue cover. Kendall stood and joined me at the bedside.

"Oh, look, Cora," she said as if talking to a much younger child. "There's one with polar bears. You'd like that one, I bet."

"What do you think, Cora?" I asked. "Is that the one you'd like?" Still no response. This wasn't unusual. Children who experienced violent events were often unwilling, even unable, to express themselves at least initially. "How about this? I'll leave all of them right here along with the pens and when you're ready you can choose the one you'd like. You can write down whatever you'd like in the notebook and if you want, we can talk about it when I see you next. What do you think?" Cora nodded.

"Do you get to read what she writes down?" Kendall asked as if challenging me.

"Nope, it will be Cora's private journal. No one is going to read what she's written. I promise and I know that you will honor Cora's privacy." I looked to Mara and Kendall, who both bobbed their heads in agreement.

"Cora, the only way someone will read your journal is if you want them to." I made a mental note to ensure that my next meeting with Cora included just the two of us. Older siblings often tried to speak for the younger brother or sister but if I was going to get a sense of what Cora was really feeling I was going to have to get her to speak for herself.

"Do you have anything you'd like me to know right now, Cora? Anything you'd like to tell me?" Though someone tried to clean her up, the smell of iodine and blood permeated what remained of Cora's hair. Her breath was stale and coppery.

Cora's unmarred eye blurred with tears. "I didn't die," she whispered, revealing the gaps in her teeth where her attacker had knocked them out. "I'm still here."

Corareef12:

JW44, I have a few more questions. Where did you go after you left Pitch?

Corareef12:

If you are really Joseph Wither, how can you still be alive? Wouldn't you be really old?

4leafclover:

I don't think he's coming back and that's a good thing. You really need to be careful in these chat rooms. You just never know who you are talking to.

Now, Thomas stands outside Jordyn's bedroom door and listens. The boys, when they were upset, would storm out of the house and disappear for two or three hours but would always come home when their stomachs began to growl.

A part of him wants to barge in and yank Jordyn right out of bed and another part of him wants to just let her sleep. Jordyn didn't come down for dinner last night even though she hadn't eaten any lunch. Thomas tried to imagine what Tess would do in this situation. Probably bring her something to eat, but Thomas thought that if Jordyn got hungry enough she would come out on her own.

Jordyn didn't come out, at least not that Thomas knew. Before he went to bed last night, Thomas stood in this exact same spot and listened. Through the heavy oak door, he was sure he heard his granddaughter crying, but instead of going to Jordyn and trying to comfort her, he lumbered off to his own bedroom.

"Jordyn," he finally calls out, not able to stand it anymore. "Jordyn, open this door right now." No answer. "Jordyn Ann Petit, if you don't open the door, I swear to God I will take it off its hinges." Still no answer.

Ridiculous, Thomas thinks to himself. Jordyn's meteoric moods were sucking the air out of the house.

"I'm going to get a screwdriver!" he says through the door. When there is still no reply, Thomas knows there is no turning back. The door is going.

With newly found energy he moves down the steps at a speed he hasn't known in years. By the time he makes it to the kitchen and reaches the door that leads to the basement where all the tools are stored his heart is racing. He leans against the door frame as he collects snatches of air in short, sharp breaths.

When did he get so old? Why was everything so difficult? When he closes his eyes, Thomas still pictures himself as the strong young man who could heft kegs from the cooler with ease. He could work eighteen hours at the bar, sleep for six and then start all over again. Where had that man gone?

The stairs down to the basement are rickety at best and Thomas decides the search for a screwdriver isn't worth a second broken hip in the family. Instead he limps across the kitchen and pulls open the wide, deep cabinet drawer that holds an olio of odds and ends.

His fingers rummage past a crescent wrench, a few wayward screws, a large whisk, tongs and ladles. He finally locates a screwdriver and turns to make the trek back up the stairs to Jordyn's room but swivels back to the drawer. He stares down at the jumble. Some items are missing, though he can't quite put his finger on what. He pushes the drawer closed and, at a much slower speed, begins the journey back upstairs.

By the time Thomas reaches the top of the steps, perspiration stains have bloomed beneath his armpits and at his neckline. His hand slick with sweat loses his grip on the screwdriver and it tumbles down the stairs, landing on the hardwood floor with a clatter.

Frustration erupts in his chest and it's enough to propel him forward. "Jordyn Ann Petit," he hollers, his fist pounding against the wooden door frame, "you open this door right this minute!"

The door slowly opens and Thomas expects to see a stone-faced, defiant Jordyn standing in front of him. Instead his grand-daughter wears an expression of intense fear.

My God, Thomas thinks, *she's terrified of me*. Thomas is immediately contrite, ready to apologize. He never, ever wants Jordyn to be afraid of him. A healthy amount of respect would be nice, but never fear.

"Grandpa," Jordyn says, her face crumpling as she throws herself against Thomas, her arms barely reaching around his wide waist. Thomas stands there momentarily dumbfounded, arms extended out to his sides as if unexpectedly struck by a wave of cold water.

"What is it?" Thomas asks, finally lowering his arms and returning Jordyn's fierce embrace. "What's the matter?" Thomas is expecting Jordyn to say that she's sorry for going out in the middle of the night without permission, to express remorse for saying that she didn't want to go and to want to check on how Violet and Cora were doing, to apologize for locking herself away in her room for hours.

Jordyn weeps into his neck. This isn't a spat-with-friends, sorry-for-being-naughty kind of cry. These are bone-deep sorrow-filled cries.

"No one was supposed to get hurt, Grandpa. It was all just a stupid game," she croaks.

It takes a moment for Jordyn's words to register with Thomas but still they make little sense. What kind of game would lead to two girls being hospitalized? He thinks of Jordyn's earlier confession that they had taken some beer from the bar. Had alcohol played a role? The train yard was filled with old junk; maybe after drinking the girls had been horsing around.

"I never meant for something bad to happen," Jordyn cries. Thomas awkwardly pats Jordyn's head, his mind racing. She pulls away from the hug and holds her phone out to him. "We didn't do anything. I promise. It's not us."

Thomas takes the phone from Jordyn and examines the screen. It's a horrible picture of Jordyn and Violet holding knives and covered in blood. "It's not us. It's fake, but people are sending it around to everyone and saying we hurt Cora," Jordyn says, leaning into him, her shoulders rising and falling with each sob.

Thomas squints at the image on the screen and upon a closer look he can tell the photo has been doctored. He has so many questions but he starts with a simple, "What happened?"

"We snuck out to go look for Joseph Wither." Jordyn sniffles.

Thomas knows this game. The boys did the same thing when they were kids. They would creep from the house and run down to the railroad tracks searching between boxcars.

"I took the beer from the cooler." She looks up at her grandfather. "I know I shouldn't have. It tasted gross. We were telling ghost stories and going to hunt for Wither. I was going to run into the field and hide and then jump out and scare them but we didn't get that far.

"Just before we got to the train yard we thought we heard someone else coming. We got scared and ran off in different directions. After a few minutes I started going back to see if I could find Violet and Cora but then I heard the screaming and the train coming and I ran home. I know I should have gone back to help. I thought at first maybe one of them got hit by the train and I couldn't stand the thought of it." Jordyn screws her eyes shut and shakes her head from side to side. "I couldn't stand the thought of seeing it."

"But Cora wasn't hit by a train, Jordyn," Thomas says patiently. "Someone stabbed her and beat her. Badly. What do you think happened? And don't tell me it was Joseph Wither. He isn't real."

"I know, I never thought he would show up. It was a game but I think Cora and Violet really believed it. They talked about it all the time. I'm so sorry."

"So you have no idea what happened? What were you going to do when you found him?" Thomas tries one more time. Jordyn hesitates a second too long. "What? You need to tell me," he says firmly.

"We were just trying to protect ourselves," Jordyn says. "We brought the knife thingy."

"Protect yourself? How?" When Jordyn doesn't answer he knows. "You brought a weapon?" Thomas asks.

Jordyn nods. "The knife thingy from the kitchen drawer."

Thomas thinks of Cora—the stab wounds, her damaged face. "Jordyn, where's the knife?"

"I don't know. I think Violet was carrying it last. But she would never hurt Cora," Jordyn adds in a rush.

A wave of nausea sweeps over him. This can't be happening. "Jordyn," he says, cupping her chin so she is forced to look at him. "Is there anything else? Anything at all that I need to know?" Thomas asks, praying that there isn't.

Jordyn shakes her head. "No, I promise." Thomas releases her chin and again Jordyn collapses into him. "What should I do?" she asks, her voice muffled against the nubby fabric of Thomas's sweater.

"Nothing for now," Thomas whispers into her ear. "Don't worry, we'll clear it all up." Jordyn lifts her head and looks up at Thomas for further reassurance. "You look tired," Thomas observes but he really just needs to be alone for a minute and think about what Jordyn has just told him. "Go and lie down, close your eyes for a bit."

Jordyn is hesitant but allows Thomas to guide her back into the bedroom and into her bed. Thomas pulls the quilt up around Jordyn's shoulders and reaches over to the bedside lamp to turn off the light and the room dims to a hushed gray.

Thomas sits on the edge of the bed and listens as Jordyn's sniffling slowly subsides. He watches as Jordyn's eyes grow heavier and heavier until they remain shut. He waits until he is sure that Jordyn is fast asleep and then carefully rises from the bed, reaches down and retrieves Jordyn's book bag from the floor.

He rifles through the laundry basket of clean clothes until he finds the fleece jacket and the other clothes that Jordyn was wearing yesterday and shoves them into the backpack. Beneath a small wooden desk where Jordyn sits to do her homework are her tennis shoes. Thomas bends down and picks them up and examines the soles. The microscopic dark specks could be blood or could just be mud. He thinks of the picture on Jordyn's phone and her bloodstained jacket.

Knowing that Jordyn will most likely sleep only for a few hours or so, he needs to get going. He has work to do.

JW44:

HI, CORAREEF12, I'M SORRY I DIDN'T RESPOND TO YOU THE
OTHER DAY. I DON'T THINK IT'S A GOOD IDEA THAT WE TALK
IN THE PUBLIC CHAT ROOM—4LEAFCLOVER IS SO ANNOYING.

Corareef12:

That's okay. She was pretty nosy.

JW44:

HOW DO YOU EVEN KNOW SHE'S A GIRL? YOU SHOULD BE CARE-
FUL ONLINE. I MEAN, 4LEAFCLOVER IS PROBABLY A DIRTY OLD
MAN LOOKING FOR A SWEET KID LIKE YOU.

Corareef12:

Ha! I don't think so.

JW44:

JUST BE CAREFUL. DO YOU STILL WANT THE ANSWERS TO THOSE
QUESTIONS YOU ASKED?

Corareef12:

Yes! If you are really Joseph Wither, how old are you? Wouldn't
you be like 90?

JW44:

I WOULD BE IF I WAS LIKE EVERYONE ELSE. BUT I'M NOT. I'M SEV-
ENTEEN AND ALWAYS WILL BE.

Corareef12:

Yeah, right. Then where did you go after you left Pitch? Where
do you live now?

JW44:
I NEVER STAY IN ONE PLACE TOO LONG BUT I ALWAYS END UP COMING BACK TO PITCH.

Corareef12:
I wouldn't come back here. It's so boring.

JW44:
I'VE BEEN ALL OVER THE WORLD. PITCH ISN'T SO BAD.

Corareef12:
Have you been to New York?

JW44:
YES, AND I'VE BEEN TO LONDON AND PARIS, TOO.

Corareef12:
I've always wanted to go to Paris.

JW44:
YOU SHOULD GO SOME DAY. IT'S AMAZING.

Corareef12:
What does the 44 stand for?

JW44:
THAT'S THE NUMBER OF GIRLS I TOOK OVER THE YEARS.

JW44:
HA HA. JUST KIDDING—1944 WAS THE YEAR I TURNED 17. DO YOU HAVE ANY OTHER QUESTIONS?

Corareef12:
I can't think of anything right now.

JW44:
YOU DON'T BELIEVE THAT I'M WITHER, DO YOU?

 Corareef12:
No. I think you're just messing with me.

 JW44:
I'M OFFENDED, CORAREEF12. IF YOU CHANGE YOUR MIND, JUST LET ME KNOW.

 Corareef12:
Okay.

 JW44:
HEY, I HAVEN'T BEEN TO PITCH IN A WHILE. IS THE SUSIE Q STILL THERE? I USED TO GET GREEN RIVERS.

 Corareef12:
It's still here. What's a green river?

 JW44:
7UP WITH LIME IN IT. DON'T TELL ME YOU'VE NEVER HAD ONE!

 Corareef12:
Sounds gross.

 JW44:
YOU SHOULD TRY IT. LET ME KNOW WHAT YOU THINK.

 Corareef12:
Maybe.

 JW44:
I KISSED MY FIRST GIRL AFTER WE SHARED A GREEN RIVER. HAVE YOU EVER BEEN KISSED?

Corareef12:
I don't think I want to say.

JW44:
WHY?

JW44:
COME ON, YOU CAN TELL ME. WHO AM I GOING TO TELL?

Corareef12:
It's embarrassing. My friend Jordyn says she's kissed a bunch of guys. Even Violet said she had a boyfriend back in New Mexico.

JW44:
DON'T BE EMBARRASSED.

Corareef12:
There is one boy who I think likes me, but I don't think he's going to kiss me anytime soon.

JW44:
YOUR FIRST KISS SHOULD BE SPECIAL. WITH SOMEONE WHO IS AS SPECIAL AS YOU ARE.

Corareef12:
Now you sound like a dad or something.

JW44:
BELIEVE ME, I'M NO ONE'S DAD.

Max took off right after Officer Grady dropped us at the house yesterday and didn't come home for about three hours. I'd hoped he didn't go after Clint but thought it was more likely that he went to go see Nikki. I wanted to ask where he had been and what he knew about Joseph Wither but he didn't say a word all afternoon, just went into his bedroom and closed the door.

Last night I tucked Violet into her bed and lay down beside her until she fell asleep. I dozed a bit but kept waking up, worried about Violet, worried about Max and worried about the attacker. What if he knew where we lived? What if he was outside our house watching, waiting?

Below me I hear a voice. Then nothing. As I move down the steps, careful not to make a sound, I hear another voice coming from Max's room. A girl's voice. Nikki. How could Max sneak his girlfriend into the house at a time like this? So selfish, I think angrily. I want to bang on the door, order her out of my home, forbid Max from seeing her anymore, but instead I lower myself to sitting position on the stairs and try to force myself to take a breath before I say something I regret.

The bedroom door opens and Nikki and Max come out holding hands, Boomer following on his stubby legs, and my anger immediately disappears. They don't look like two teenagers trying to get away with something; they both just look sad, worried and very tired—exactly how I feel. They look at me at the same time and drop hands as if burned. "Mom," Max begins. "We were just talking, I promise."

I believe him and suddenly I'm grateful to this girl with smudged eye makeup and badly dyed hair who was willing to face the wrath of two mothers to come and see my son in the middle of the night. The weight of what's happening with Violet has to be hard for Max. He's already lost his best friend in the whole mess, though I know I'm not going to shed any tears over having Clint out of our lives. I nod wearily. "You guys want something to eat?" I ask. "I can throw a pizza in the oven."

Max's face relaxes and Nikki lets out a long stream of breath in relief. "No thanks," she says. "I should get home."

"You're driving her, right?" I ask Max.

"Yeah, if you don't mind me taking the car," he says.

"The keys are on the kitchen counter," I say and he hurries to the kitchen to grab them. To Nikki I ask, "Will you get in a lot of trouble for being out so late?"

She wrinkles her nose and shrugs. "I might be able to get back inside without my mom knowing. She can sleep through just about anything."

"I'm sure she just worries about you, Nikki, the way I worry about Max and Violet," I tell her as Max comes back, keys in hand.

"Ready?" he says, opening the front door. "I'll be back in a few minutes, Mom."

"Nikki, please come back during the daylight hours," I say and she gives me an embarrassed smile before the two step out into the dark.

I shut the door behind them and then hear Max's voice. "What the hell? Mom!" he calls out.

I fling open the door. "What is it?" I ask, scanning the yard and street in front of us, searching for any sign of trouble. Max and Nikki stay facing me and that's when I realize I'm looking in the wrong direction. I turn and though it's still dark out the porch lamp casts a weak light that illuminates slashes of red paint across the aluminum siding. I have to take a few steps backward to take in the full measure of what I'm seeing. *Murderer—U R Next.* And below these words, the message is signed, *Wither.*

"I'm going to kill Clint," Max says, his face set in determination, making me believe that he means it.

"You have to ignore him." Nikki pulls on his arm. "He's try-ing to get to you."

"How can I ignore this?" Max asks, gesturing toward the front of the house. "He's such an asshole."

"Max," I warn. "You do not go over to Clint's. Do you un-derstand? The last thing I need right now is for you to get ar-rested. Besides, you don't know he did it. It could be the person who attacked Cora. This is just crazy! Come back inside."

"I really have to get home," Nikki says, glancing anxiously over at Max. "I'm going to get into a lot of trouble if I don't get back before my mom wakes up."

"Mom, we'll be fine," Max insists. "I promise I won't go over to Clint's. But if I catch him in our yard ever again, I'm going to beat his ass."

Once they pull away I examine the graffiti more closely. Def-initely spray paint and already dry to the touch. I scan the dark street, wondering if the vandals are hiding in the shadows. Did a group of bratty kids do this? Or maybe it's a genuine threat on Violet's life. I shiver.

Boomer sniffs around the yard and focuses his attention on an object lying in the grass. I walk over to take a look at what he's found. A can of spray paint. I leave it on the ground where it sits and go inside to call the police.

An officer shows up within minutes and takes my statement. He knows all about what happened in the train yard so I don't have to go over those details but I do fill him in on how Clint Phelps acted at the police station earlier in the day.

I watch as the officer slips on gloves and places the spray can in a plastic bag and then takes a few pictures of the front of the house. The words, sprayed in sharp red slashes across the house, make me feel dirty, guilty. I don't want the neighbors to see them.

"Do you think you could help me cover it up?" I ask the of-ficer. He agrees and I run back inside and find two old bedsheets and some tape. Together, we begin to cover the graffiti and by the time we're pressing the final corners into place Max is pulling up in front of the house.

The officer gives me an encouraging smile and hands me the roll of duct tape. "I'll drive around the neighborhood and then swing by the Phelps place to see if anything suspicious is going on," he says. "In the meantime, make sure you lock your doors and call us if you need anything at all."

I thank the officer and say goodbye as Max joins me by the door. By the look on Max's face I'm sure that Nikki's mom has given him hell. "What's the matter, Max?" I ask. "Did something happen?"

He waits until the police car pulls away and then tilts his phone toward me. "Look what's going around." A horrific image looks up at me from the screen. Someone has Photoshopped Violet's and Jordyn's faces on two blood-splattered figures wielding knives, and the number of likes on Instagram is nearing three hundred. I feel sick.

"It's probably the same idiots who spray-painted the house," I tell him, my stomach churning. "Try not to worry about it."

Max lets out a long breath. "Except for Nikki, I hate it here."

"Me, too," I say. "But we have each other and that's going to have to be enough for now."

We go inside. I lock the front door and then go around to each window making sure they are secured, too. I say good-night to Max and then go upstairs to peek in on Violet. She is sleeping soundly. I sit on the edge of her bed for a long time watching her chest rise and fall.

Nov. 22, 2017

I know that JW44 isn't really Joseph Wither. It's probably some random person who saw my post on DarkestDoor and thought it would be funny to pretend to be Wither. Ha ha. I don't plan on talking to him anymore. I mean, I did pay attention during Digital Literacy class. I've seen the news. I've heard all about stranger danger since I was in kindergarten.

And the way he asked me if I ever kissed anyone before. That is just strange. Sometimes I think about what it would be like to kiss someone. It used to be Gabe I'd think about, but now it's Joseph. For some reason I feel guilty if I imagine myself kissing Gabe—like Joseph could look into my head and see what I'm thinking. I wonder if Joseph thinks about kissing me, too.

I asked my sister if she ever had a green river to drink and she asked me what it was. It was kind of cool knowing something that she didn't. Before I could tell her what was in it my mom came into the room and said, *7Up and lime syrup!* She said she hadn't thought of green rivers in ages, that she used to drink them all the time when she was a kid. *Sounds gross,* Kendall said.

Since it was an early out today from school because of Thanksgiving, I asked Jordyn and Violet if they wanted to walk to Susie Q's after school and they said yes. We sat in a booth in the back of the restaurant and looked at the menu. I didn't see a green river listed but I asked the waitress if I could have one. I expected her to say no, but she said, *Sure thing, sweetie. You want a wedge of lime with that?* I said yes, feeling kind of grown-up.

Jordyn ordered a turtle sundae and Violet just ordered a small hot chocolate, which was the cheapest thing on the menu. I added a large order of fries to mine and acted all surprised that the waitress brought out such a huge basket. Violet gave me a little smile like she knew what I was doing. I pretended I didn't see.

While we were eating, I asked Violet and Jordyn if they ever wondered if Joseph Wither could be real. Violet said no way. It was just a story that people told to scare each other but Jordyn thought maybe he could be real. Not real real, she said. More like a ghost.

Jordyn's answer surprised me. I thought for sure she would laugh and say that anyone who believed that Wither is real is stupid. Then we got talking about ghost stories and scary movies and laughed and laughed. It was fun. Before I knew it, Kendall stomped into the restaurant and said that Mom was waiting in the car outside to pick me up.

Things are going really well with Violet and Jordyn. I forgot what it felt like to have best friends and it feels so good. The other day at school Melody Jenkins started walking really close behind me in the hallway. My shoe was untied and she kept trying to step on my shoelace so I would trip. I tried to ignore her and just walk faster but she stayed right behind. Then Jordyn came around the corner and saw what was happening. She rushed over and told Melody to stop it. Melody said something snotty and Jordyn told her to eff off. Melody opened and closed her mouth like a fish but didn't say anything and just stomped off.

No one has ever stood up for me like that. Ever. Not even Ellie before she moved away. I actually like going to school now.

The only bad thing is the whole Gabe thing is still weird between Jordyn and me. Jordyn always makes a point to show me any texts he sends her. The texts are really no big deal. Just about assignments and Jordyn is always the one who texts him first.

Gabe and I still text using Violet's phone. She even lent me her phone overnight so Gabe and I could text. Gabe and I also talk in person and that's so much better than texting. Every morning Gabe and I walk into school together and he waits until I put my things into my locker. We don't talk about anything special but it's nice.

The green river was okay. It just tasted like 7Up but sour. I thought about going home and emailing JW44 and telling him that Susie Q's still serves green rivers but then I remembered that I probably shouldn't. What I should do is tell someone about him. A *trusted adult.* Not my mom or dad. They would freak out. Maybe Mr. Dover. But I know I won't tell anyone about Joseph. He's my secret.

The night that Violet let me borrow her phone, I used it to go to the DarkestDoor website to send Joseph a message. I told him I was using my friend's phone and then Joseph said something that freaked me out a bit. He told me to take a picture of myself and send it to him. I got scared and told him I had to go. I didn't talk to him for a few days.

But even when we aren't sending messages back and forth, I'm thinking about Joseph. After I go to bed I make up conversations in my head. He always says the right things. He's always there when I need him. I can almost feel him lying there next to me.

Corareef12:
Hey, I tried a green river. It was good!

JW44:
I TOLD YOU SO. DID YOU SHARE IT WITH SOMEONE SPECIAL?

Corareef12:
Just Jordyn and Violet.

JW44:
WE'LL HAVE TO HAVE ONE TOGETHER SOMETIME.

Corareef12:
Yeah, right.

JW44:
WHAT DO YOU MEAN? YOU DON'T THINK WE'LL EVER MEET IN
PERSON?

Corareef12:
I think that once I'm done with the school project you'll probably
just forget about me.

JW44:
NO WAY. I'D NEVER LET THAT HAPPEN. HOW IS YOUR PROJECT
GOING? I THOUGHT OF SOMETHING THAT YOU MIGHT WANT TO
INCLUDE IN YOUR PRESENTATION. SOMETHING THAT NO ONE
ELSE KNOWS ABOUT. ARE YOU INTERESTED?

Corareef12:
Okay, tell me.

JW44:

WHAT WILL YOU DO FOR ME?

Corareef12:

What do you mean?

JW44:

IF I TELL YOU MY SECRET YOU HAVE TO TELL ME ONE OF YOURS.

Corareef12:

I don't have any secrets.

JW44:

COME ON, EVERYONE HAS SECRETS. I'LL TELL YOU MINE IF YOU TELL ME YOURS.

Corareef12:

I don't know. I guess you're my secret. No one knows I talk to you.

JW44:

THAT'S NOT A SECRET. I ALREADY KNOW THAT. SOMETHING ELSE, THEN. GO TO THE WINDOW.

Corareef12:

What?

JW44:

GO TO THE WINDOW AND STAND THERE. I WANT TO SEE YOU.

Corareef12:

How can you see me? Are you outside right now?

JW44:

JUST GO AND STAND IN THE WINDOW FOR A MINUTE AND THEN COME BACK.

Corareef12:

Okay. I'm going now.

Corareef12:

All right. That was weird but I did it. I didn't see you, though.

JW44:

I SAW YOU. YOU'RE WEARING A GRAY SHIRT AND HAVE YOUR HAIR IN A PONYTAIL.

JW44:

YOU STILL THERE?

Corareef12:

Are you outside?

JW44:

I'M ALWAYS AROUND. OKAY. NOW I'LL TELL YOU MY SECRET. PEO-PLE DON'T KNOW THIS BUT THERE WAS ANOTHER GIRL, A LONG TIME AGO. HER NAME IS RACHEL. EVERYONE THOUGHT SHE RAN AWAY. BUT SHE DIDN'T—SHE CAME WITH ME.

JW44:

ARE YOU STILL THERE?

Corareef12:

Is she dead?

JW44:

NO. THAT'S ALL JUST RUMORS. I DON'T NEED TO KILL PEOPLE. THEY WANT TO COME WITH ME. RACHEL WANTED TO COME WITH ME. ALL THE GIRLS DID.

Corareef12:

But what about the girls who died? Everyone says you killed them.

JW44:

LIES. THE GIRLS WANTED TO COME WITH ME. THE ONES THAT DIED WEREN'T BRAVE ENOUGH. I CAN'T TAKE RESPONSIBILITY FOR THAT.

Corareef12:

I don't think I can include this in the report. I don't have any proof. My teacher says we have to have reliable sources.

JW44:

YOU DON'T THINK I'M RELIABLE?

Corareef12:

I need proof. Like from a book or newspaper.

JW44:

GO TO THE LIBRARY AND LOOK THROUGH THE YEARBOOKS FROM 1991. YOU'LL FIND IT THERE.

Corareef12:

What will I find?

JW44:

THE PROOF. THEN WE CAN MEET EACH OTHER IN REAL LIFE. THEN YOU'LL KNOW I'M WHO I SAY I AM.

I remember being taken aback by Cora's statement—*I didn't die.* "Yes, Cora," I said. "You are alive and a whole lot of people are so happy about that." Cora tried to say something more but it morphed into a grimace of pain. I patted her uncasted arm and told her that I would stop by later in the afternoon to see how she was doing. Cora nodded, then closed her uncovered eye and floated off to sleep. I told Kendall goodbye and beckoned Mara to join me in the hallway.

Around us the hallway buzzed with activity. Nurses and doctors moved purposely down the corridor while patient visitors moved slowly as if in a stupor of fatigue and worry. "I'll plan on dropping in a few times each day while she's here. It will give us a chance to get to know each other and hopefully help Cora to feel more comfortable talking to me. Have her doctors told you how long they plan on keeping her?" I asked.

"Until Thursday or Friday, they think," she answered, rubbing the back of her neck with one hand. It was nice that families could stay right in the hospital room with their children but the sleeping accommodations weren't known for being comfortable. "With her head injury they want to watch her for a few more days and they want to make sure her sutures are healing well and no infections crop up," Mara said.

"I'm glad to hear they are keeping a close eye on her. I'm happy to see that Kendall is here, too. You mentioned last night that she was hesitant to come see Cora."

"I'm not sure what changed," Mara said, "but I'm glad she came. Cora thinks the world of Kendall and Kendall doesn't always have a whole lot of time for her."

"I think that's pretty typical of siblings," I reassured her.

"Oh, there's Jim," Mara said, looking past me. I turned and

Mr. Landry, dressed in khakis and a button-down shirt, hurried toward us carrying two disposable cups of coffee. He nodded at me by way of greeting and handed one of the cups to Mara. "I just got off the phone with the chief. You know who their main suspect is?" he asked incredulously.

"Who?" Mara clutched at his sleeve, causing his own cup to tip, and coffee spilled to the ground. "Did they arrest someone?"

My curiosity was piqued. I hadn't gotten any details about the crime beyond what Mara had told me and that ridiculous news story from the night before. I pulled a Kleenex from my bag and crouched down to wipe up the spill. I purposely didn't bring up the news report with Mara, not wanting to upset her needlessly.

"Joseph Wither." He laughed. An angry bark that held no humor.

"Seriously?" Mara asked, pressing her fingers to her lips. "They said that?"

"Not really, no," Jim said. "The officer said that the Crow girl said it was Joseph Wither coming back from the dead and that he stabbed Cora with some kind of knife."

"What would make her say that?" Mara asked. "It must be a mistake."

"Of course it's a mistake," Jim snapped and I pulled Cora's door shut in hopes that she couldn't hear our conversation. "The police officer said that it's most likely the Crow girl was just scared and confused."

I thought of the newscast from the night before. "Joseph Wither?" I asked, inviting further explanation. Thinking that maybe the news reporter did get it right.

"A ghost," Jim said, throwing his arms out in frustration. I wanted to grab the cup of coffee before he spilled it all over his wife, or me for that matter. "A phantom. He's not real. Just some stupid character the kids talk about. She may as well have said it was the Easter Bunny or a leprechaun for what it's worth. At this rate the police aren't going to catch anyone."

"What does Cora say?" I questioned. "Has she talked about the attack at all?"

"No, she hasn't said anything beyond crying out in her sleep." Mara shook her head. "The police wanted to question her yesterday but she was so out of it after the surgery they decided to wait until today. Someone is supposed to come later this morning to talk to her."

Cora's door opened and Kendall poked her head out. "What's going on?" she asked in a whisper. "You're being really loud." She was a striking young woman. Tall and lithe with the stature of a ballerina.

"Did we wake Cora?" Mara fretted. "It's nothing."

"It is something, goddammit." Jim brushed roughly past Mara, sending a wave of coffee across the front of her T-shirt.

"Ouch!" Mara jumped backward and pulled her wet shirt away from her skin. "Jim," she hissed, "let her rest. Don't bother her." But Jim had already swept past Kendall and into Cora's room with the rest of us trailing after him.

"Cora," he said, trying to keep his voice low and composed but instead it came out as brusque and exasperated, causing Cora to startle awake. "Cora, the police need to know who hurt you. Can you tell us what you saw?"

"Mom?" Cora called out uncertainly.

"Stop it, Jim, you're scaring her! She's not ready to talk. Leave her alone!"

"Mr. Landry," I said, keeping my voice even but authoritative. "The more upset Cora is, the more difficult she may find it to remember the important details of the event."

"Event?" Jim swung around toward me, causing me to take a step backward. "Event? This wasn't an event. Someone targeted our twelve-year-old daughter, beat her and stabbed her with a knife. That is not an event, it's attempted murder!" His breath came out in ragged puffs.

"I understand," I said, trying to lead him from Cora's bedside. "It's very upsetting."

He didn't move but continued to speak to Cora. "This is very important, Cora." He leaned down so that his lips were near her face. "Violet told the police that Joseph Wither hurt you. Why would she say that? Was someone down at the tracks pretending to be him? Can you remember what he looked like?"

"I don't remember," Cora whimpered. This was not helping. Cora was clearly distraught and forcing her to try to remember what happened could make her shut down, making it more difficult for her to recall important details of the crime.

"Dad, stop it," Kendall cried before I could step in to try to redirect the conversation. She pulled at his arm but he shook her off.

"But you must have seen something," Jim insisted. "You had to be facing him when he stabbed you. Try to think."

"Jim, please," Mara whispered.

"Mr. Landry," I said firmly and pressed the call button for the nurse. "Look at Cora. You're scaring her. Going about it this way won't give you the answers you want. Let's step outside and talk about it."

My words seemed to bring him to his senses. He stared down at his daughter, who was crying silently. "Shh, Cora," he said. "I'm sorry, honey. I didn't mean to upset you." He cradled her bandaged head in his hands. "I'm sorry. I just want to get the person who did this to you and I know it wasn't some stupid legend. It was a real person and I don't want him to hurt anyone else." He kissed her cheek and this seemed to soothe her.

A nurse stepped into the room and I watched him leave, knowing that he was overwhelmed and feeling helpless. Still, I didn't like Jim Landry much. Something about him rubbed me the wrong way. I moved away from Cora's bed so the nurse could take her temperature and examine her bandages. "What's your pain level?" the nurse asked. "Zero being no pain and ten being the worst."

"A nine," Cora said, her chin trembling. "Everything hurts."

When the nurse left to get something to ease Cora's pain, Mara dropped into a nearby chair. "The girls did a school project on Joseph Wither," she said weakly. "Last November. For Mr. Dover's class."

"I'm sorry, I didn't grow up around here so I don't really know who Joseph Wither is. Was," I said. "A character of some sort?"

"An urban legend," Kendall said. "Mr. Dover assigned the same project to us when I was in sixth grade. We had to research an urban legend and present it to the class. Cora and her friends made a movie."

"On this Joseph Wither person?" I asked and Mara nodded. "So lots of people could have known that the girls worked on this project?"

"I guess." Mara shrugged. "Mr. Dover and Cora's classmates would have known for sure." Mara rubbed her arms as if trying to warm herself. "Do you think someone might have pretended to be Joseph Wither and lured the girls to the train yard and attacked them there?"

"Oh, my God, that's horrible," Kendall said, chewing on her thumbnail.

"Or perhaps, because of the project they worked on, the Crow girl's thoughts immediately went to Joseph Wither," I suggested. "It sounds like the police are looking into all the possibilities. The important thing to remember is that Cora is safe now. No one can hurt her here."

Jordyn:
Can u believe Cora did that to me?

Violet:
Yeah, that was crazy!

Jordyn:
She ruined the whole thing.

Violet:
It was pretty bad. Poor Kaley.

Jordyn:
Poor Kaley and poor me!
Did you see Gabe's face?

Violet:
I don't think Cora could
believe it herself.

Jordyn:
I'll get her back. I don't know
exactly how, but she'll pay.

Dec. 4, 2017

I haven't been able to stop thinking about JW44. In my head I know someone must be playing a joke on me, but mostly I want to believe it. To believe
in him. I decided that if what JW44 said about the yearbook in the library
was real, then I'd believe everything else.

Today Jordyn complained to Mr. Dover that we'd hit a dead end with finding any more information about Wither. Dover asked us what we tried and
she listed all our sources. "Keep looking," Mr. Dover said, putting his arm around
her. "I have faith in you."

At lunch I brought up the idea of going to the library to see what we could
find out. "I hate the library. It's so dumb," Jordyn said, putting her hands
around her neck as if studying there would bore her to death. "Besides, it's so
dinky it probably won't have any new information, anyway."

I told her that it wouldn't hurt to try and that I was going to the library
with or without them, that the project was due soon and we had to get it
done. Violet said she would go and then after a minute Jordyn shrugged and
said she'd go, too.

When we got to the library I really wanted to go to the yearbooks but
Jordyn went straight to the librarian and told her what we were working on.
The librarian said we should look at old newspaper articles and took us back
to the microfiche machine and asked us what dates we needed.

She went into a back room and came back with a box of microfiche
film from 1944 and '45. The spinning microfiche pages made me dizzy but we
did find an article that talked about the Wither house burning down. In the
story the sheriff said that he thought that Joseph probably started the fire
and then ran away.

Then we found another news story that came out a few weeks later that
talked about a fourteen-year-old girl named Loretta and her twelve-year-
old sister named Helen. Loretta, who was found dead by the railroad tracks,
was strangled with some kind of rope and Helen was missing.

So Kendall and Emery weren't lying to me. They were right, at least about this part of the story. The sheriff said they wanted to talk to Joseph Wither about the murder and the kidnapping.

The really scary part is that the Wither family lived on the same street as Violet. Obviously, the house isn't there anymore, but still, it's pretty creepy. After that we couldn't find any more articles that mentioned Joseph Wither and Jordyn got all mad and said that we can't do a report with only one dead body, that it wasn't really a legend, then.

Violet said that of course we could do the report; we just had to look harder for more information. I brought up the idea of looking at the school yearbooks and Jordyn laughed. That's stupid, she said. There isn't going to be anything about the missing girls in them. But Violet said there might be pictures.

She was right. We went to the reference section where there were pictures of Joseph, Loretta and Helen in the yearbooks. Jordyn said Wither was cute. I thought he was, too, but I didn't say that. Wither had sad eyes, which kind of makes sense since he and Lucy weren't allowed to see each other. Violet drew a picture of him in her sketchbook based on the photograph. It was really good. I told you she was a good artist.

While Violet and Jordyn went to make copies of the yearbook at the copy machine, I found the Pitch High School yearbook from 1991 and pulled it down from the shelf. I flipped through the pages, not sure what I was looking for. JW44 said the girl's name was Rachel so I started with that.

I found a picture of a girl named Rachel Daly, who was a senior in 1991. She was pretty even though she had the really big hair that Kendall said was popular during that time. I looked at the picture carefully, but I couldn't see anything that would tell me that JW44 would know who she was.

I turned back to the index and started going through the long list of student names and came across another Rachel. Rachel Farmer. She only had one page number next to her name. I turned to page thirty-six and found her picture right away. My stomach did a flip-flop. Someone had drawn a heart around her face and had written next to it in tiny letters JW+RF.

Jordyn came up behind me and asked me what I was doing. I slammed the yearbook shut and said nothing. She gave me a weird look and said she had to go home and would see me tomorrow.

So JW44 must be real. The yearbook proved it.

I thought about Rachel Farmer and JW44 all night. I haven't been sleeping very well lately. I keep hearing scratching at my window so I get up and check, thinking it might be Joseph wanting me to let him inside. Sometimes I think I see him hiding in the shadows.

During the daytime, it doesn't seem so scary, but at night it's different. After I go to bed I hear sounds coming from the vent above my desk. I think it might be Joseph Wither whispering my name over and over through the vent in my bedroom.

But that's impossible, right?

The first few nights, I went into my mom and dad's room and told them I was having a bad dream. My mom would walk me back to my room and lie with me in bed until I fell asleep. But after the third night, my dad said enough was enough and I needed to get to sleep on my own.

I've been trying, I really have. Last night I didn't hear anything coming from the vents and there wasn't any scratching at the window. It was quiet. Too quiet. Now I'm afraid I did something wrong and he won't come back.

I sit at the kitchen table, a lighter, a pack of cigarettes, a cup of coffee and a pocket-size can of pepper spray in front of me. I've been sitting here for hours watching in case whoever spray-painted our house comes back. When the sun finally comes up, I still can't bring myself to move from this spot. I pick up the pack of cigarettes, tap one out and roll it around in my fingers. I haven't smoked a cigarette since I found out I was pregnant with Violet, haven't even craved them until I found the half-smoked pack and lighter in the pocket of Max's jacket. I can't even be mad at him.

I started smoking when I was in ninth grade and didn't stop until I was in my midtwenties. I just was hoping he would be smarter than I was. I don't even plan on saying anything to him about it. I suppose it's the least of our worries.

As for the pepper spray, I bought it years ago after my purse was stolen while I was walking with Max and Violet through a mall parking lot. It was the middle of the day; we had just been to a movie and stepped out into sunshine, intense after the darkened theater. Max was doing an uncanny imitation of Jim Carrey and Violet and I were laughing. A man swept by, brushing roughly against my shoulder. *Excuse me*, he said apologetically and kept moving, taking my purse with him.

He was gone before I realized what happened. I lost my ATM card, my credit cards, my driver's license and a bit of cash. Thank God I had my car keys in my hand at the time. After calling the police and filing a report I drove to the nearest Walmart and bought the pepper spray and clipped it onto my key chain.

I don't know if it even works anymore but it makes me feel a bit better having it within arm's reach.

Boomer whimpers from the top of the steps. Violet begged to

have him sleep with her last night and his short legs and round belly make it impossible to manage the stairs on his own. My arms and shoulders ache from carrying him up and down the steps.

I sigh and push my chair back from the table but before I stand Max materializes from his bedroom. He is barefoot and wearing his favorite Star Wars T-shirt, fraying and thin from hundreds of washings, and an old pair of sweatpants that are an inch too short. With his tangle of black curls, he looks much younger than his sixteen years. "I've got him," Max says, stifling a yawn.

I glance at the clock on the microwave. Eight thirty. Officer Grady will be here at nine. Grady wanted me to bring Violet to the station so he could interview her but I told him no way. That Violet got way too upset when she was there. He finally agreed that he would come to the house in the morning.

I made him promise not to upset Violet and he made me promise to keep my mouth shut while he asked the questions. He didn't say it quite like that but I got the gist. He also promised to have an officer drive by the house a few times during the night to make sure that no one was sneaking around. That made me feel a bit better but I still slept with my pepper spray under my pillow.

I just have time to get Violet up and dressed and give her breakfast before Officer Grady arrives. I meet Max at the bottom of the steps. Boomer is cradled in his arms and I can't help but smile at the sight. "Officer Grady will be here in a half an hour. Why don't you get dressed and I'll make you some toast."

He grimaces and carefully lowers Boomer to the floor. "Do I have to be here?" he asks.

"I think you should," I say and reach up to brush an unruly curl out of his eyes and he pulls his head back. "There's no school and don't you want to find out what's going on?"

"I guess." He shrugs and opens the front door to let the dog outside.

"Plus, I think it will make Violet feel better having us both there. Hey, what else do you know about Joseph Wither?"

"It's just some stupid urban legend," Max says and I begin to go upstairs to get dressed and wake Violet. "I think he's here," Max says. "There's a police car pulling up."

"Shit! Let him in and tell him we'll be down in just a minute." I rush up the steps, taking two at a time. I was hoping to wake Violet slowly. Gradually. Now I have to hurry her, never an easy task.

"Violet, honey," I say, trying to keep my voice upbeat and easygoing. "It's time to get up." Violet buries herself more deeply beneath the covers and mumbles something. "Come on, Violet." I ease back the covers. "You have to get up. Officer Grady is here to talk to you."

This immediately gets her attention, but not in a good way. "I don't want to talk to him," she moans. "He's mean."

"He's not mean," I say, trying to keep my voice relaxed. "He's trying to find out who hurt Cora. Don't you want to help him do that?"

"I already told him," she complains.

"Well, sometimes the police have to ask the same questions in a lot of different ways. Just tell him the truth and then he'll be on his way. Got it?" Violet nods reluctantly and swings her legs over the side of the bed. "You get dressed, wash your face and brush your hair. We'll go downstairs together."

I go to my side of the room and dig through my dresser for clean clothes. I pull on a pair of jeans and a T-shirt, shove my feet into a pair of tennis shoes. On the other side of the room divider I hear Violet doing the same thing. "Can I come through?" I ask, wanting to give her privacy to change.

"Just a sec," she says. Someday I'll have enough money saved to move into a house with more than two bedrooms but until then or until Max goes off to college we're stuck with this. I grab a brush off my dresser and start running it through my hair until she says it's okay for me to come over to her side of the room.

"I have to brush my teeth," she says sadly and leaves while I hang behind. Just peeking out beneath her bed is one of her sketchbooks. I feel sort of guilty looking but Violet's drawings sometimes tell me so much more about what's going on with her. Violet is a perfectionist when it comes to her art and the first few pages are of subjects she has drawn a million times: unicorns, peace signs, Boomer.

I have to admit she is very talented and I wish I could afford to pay for the extra art classes I know she would love. I flip to the middle of the journal and land on the first hesitant strokes of her project. The paper is smudged from the rub of an eraser and she abandons the page. This goes on for the next several pages until I can tell that she's trying to draw a face, though I can't tell whether the subject is male or female.

I keep turning the pages and eventually the face of young man with intense eyes is looking back at me. He has a long, straight nose and prominent cheekbones. Though he's only drawn from the neck up, there is something old-fashioned about him. Maybe it's the way his hair is swept away from his forehead, maybe it's the seriousness of his expression—something that I've always connected with old-time portraits.

In any event, the drawing is astonishingly realistic for such a young girl to have drawn. Centered, at the bottom of the page are the initials JW. My blood runs cold.

Could this be the person pretending to be Joseph Wither? Who is he? And why is Violet sketching him? Or maybe a picture is just a picture and it has nothing to do with Joseph Wither.

"Mom," Max calls from downstairs, "Officer Grady is here."

Startled, I close the sketchbook and put it back beneath the bed where I found it. "Coming," I call back and on shaky legs go into the hallway and tap on the bathroom door. "Vi, are you ready?"

Violet opens the door and, though she's dressed, has washed her face and combed her hair, she still looks exhausted. She must have slept about as well as I did last night. Purple smudges stain the thin skin beneath her eyes and crusty sleep has collected in the corners.

I put my arm around her shoulders and she doesn't pull away. For this I'm glad. Together we walk down the steps where Officer Grady, standing by the front door, is waiting for us. Boomer sniffs curiously at the soles of Officer Grady's shoes and Max sits on the couch looking like he'd like to be anywhere but here.

"Morning, Beth, Violet." He nods at us. "I heard about the vandalism. Any more problems last night?"

"Come on, I'll show you," I say and lead him back outside. I yank on one of the sheets and it comes floating down to reveal the graffiti.

"I'm glad you called it in," Grady says, taking in the slash of angry words painted across the house.

"It's scary," I say, unable to keep my voice from shaking. "Did you find out who did it?"

"No, but we'll stay on top of it," Grady says as he helps me tape the sheet up again.

"I barely slept. All I can think about is what happened at the train yard and how someone is creeping around our house. I'm afraid for my kids."

"We'll do our best to have someone drive by your house several times throughout the day."

"And night?" I ask hopefully.

"If it comes to that, yes," Officer Grady assures me.

We head back inside. Officer Grady and Violet take a seat at the kitchen table and Max lingers in the entryway. I offer coffee to Officer Grady and he accepts. As I'm getting the coffee cup out of the cupboard and waiting for a fresh pot of coffee to brew I notice Officer Grady looking around the room. I try to see my kitchen through his eyes.

It's outdated for sure with its counters and appliances courtesy of the early '90s, but it's clean and cheerful. Max's and Violet's school pictures hang on the refrigerator along with a math paper that Max got an A on and a picture of Boomer that Violet had drawn.

On the counter is the cookie jar that we hauled all the way from Algodon. It had belonged to my grandmother and had once been filled with cowboy and peanut butter cookies. Now it held store-bought sandwich cookies but Officer Grady wouldn't know this. He eyes the pack of cigarettes and canister of pepper spray on the table and I gather them up and replace them with a steaming cup of coffee. "Any news? Have you caught anyone yet?" I ask.

He takes a cautious sip from his cup before answering. "Not yet. We've been canvassing the neighborhood nearest the depot and have been gathering evidence from the train yard. Hopefully, that will give us the information we need to solve who did this."

Across from him Violet fiddles with the salt and pepper shakers, clinking them together and creating an annoying beat. I cover her hands with mine to still them and she returns the shakers to their spot in the center of the table and places her hands flat atop the table.

"Why don't we get down to business?" Officer Grady says, reaching into his pocket for a small notebook and pen. "I have your permission, Beth, to ask Violet questions about the events of April 15 and 16, correct?"

I nod. "Of course. We want to help in any way we can."

"Violet, you said yesterday that someone named Joseph Wither was the one who hurt Cora. How do you know this?"

Violet shrugs. "I don't know. I just do."

Officer Grady looks like he wants to push further on this and I don't blame him. I want to know the answer, too. I think about the drawing of the young man in Violet's sketchbook. Instead he pauses to take another sip of coffee and then leans forward in his seat, his elbows on the table. "Why don't you tell me about the overnight at Cora's house?" he asks conversationally. "What time did you get there?"

"Around six, I think?" She turns in her chair to look at Max, who has hoisted himself up onto the kitchen counter to sit. "That's when you guys dropped me off, right?"

"Yeah, around six sounds about right," Max says, a bit taken aback at being drawn into the questioning.

"How did you spend the evening?" Officer Grady asks. "What kinds of things did you and the other girls do?"

"The usual," Violet says in a quiet voice. Violet had only been on a total of two sleepovers when we lived in New Mexico. Since moving here, she spends nearly every other Friday night at the Landry house. It's become like a second home to her, I think guiltily.

Cora has never spent the night at our house, though I tell Violet she is more than welcome to invite her over. It never happened, though. There is always an excuse as to why Cora never spends the night: Cora has a stomachache, the family is heading out of town early the next morning, they have family plans.

I thought I was sending Violet to a nice home, with nice parents.

"We ate pizza and watched a movie. Then we went to bed," Violet says.

"What time did you go to bed?" Officer Grady asks.

"Eleven thirty, I think."

I'm getting frustrated. Why does it matter what they ate and what movie they watched? I want to know what happened at the train yard. I want to know what animal went after the girls. I'm just getting ready to say this when Violet begins to speak again. "Then we got up again at midnight to go to the old train depot."

Officer Grady slides his eyes to me and gives a slight shake of his head. I take this is as my cue to keep my mouth shut. "Why were you going to the train depot?" he asks.

"It's kind of a long story," Violet says, tracing one finger through the small mound of salt that she spilled on the table.

"That's okay, Violet," Officer Grady says. "We've got time."

"Well, we were going to look for Joseph Wither. We thought that maybe we could find him. We thought we could see what he looks like and maybe stop him."

"Stop him from what?" he asks.

"From killing another girl or taking one," Violet says so matter-of-factly that you'd think she was talking about doing her homework or drying the dishes.

"Oh, my God," I say. "Violet, what were you thinking? Why would you do that?"

"We were curious. We thought it would be fun." A ripple of regret passes over her face.

"You saw him?" Officer Grady asks. "You saw Joseph Wither attack Cora?"

"It was really dark," Violet says. "It was hard to see anything. But I heard her scream."

"And then what did you do?" he asks.

"I hid in the grass. I was afraid." Violet blushes. "She screamed and screamed and I know I should have gone and helped her but I couldn't move."

"You kept yourself safe, Violet. That was a smart thing to do," Officer Grady tells her. "You heard Cora scream and you hid in the grass. Where was the other girl, Jordyn Petit?"

"I don't know," Violet says. "She got mad at us and said she was leaving but I don't think they did."

Officer Grady looks up from his notebook. "They? Was there someone else with you at the train yard?"

"I meant Jordyn," Violet says. "I don't think *she* left."

"Why do you think that?" Officer Grady stares so hard at

Violet that she actually squirms. She's lying about it only being the three of them at the depot.

When it's clear that Violet isn't going to answer his question, Officer Grady goes on. "So, you heard Cora scream and you hid in the grass. Then what?"

"All of a sudden she stopped. It got real quiet so I came out and found Cora. She was all bloody. I thought she was dead."

"What about the blood on your hands and clothes?" Officer Grady asks. "How did it get on you?"

Uncertainty skitters across her face and I jump in. "She was helping her friend. Weren't you, Violet?" Officer Grady shoots me a warning look.

"Violet?" he repeats.

"I don't remember," she says.

"When the lady with the dog found Cora, no one else was around. Where did you go?"

"I ran and hid," she says. "I was scared."

"When you came out of the grass, you were carrying something. Do you remember what it was?" Violet shakes her head.

My mind thinks back to the moment when Violet wandered out from the overgrown grass. I remember how her clothes were bloodied. I remember something slipping from her bloody fingers but didn't think it was important. I had completely forgotten about it.

"It was a hawk-billed knife, Violet. Do you know what that is?" Violet doesn't answer but continues to look down at her hands, which are on her lap, her right index finger moving in swift strokes across her thigh. I know what she is doing. It's a nervous habit. She's sketching something. Her finger is her pencil, her leg her canvas. "It's a knife with a hooked blade. It's very sharp," Officer Grady continues. "It's what was used to hurt Cora. Why were you holding it, Violet?"

"We just brought it in case we needed to protect ourselves from Wither," she murmurs, her finger still sweeping across her thigh. I'm momentarily stunned. The girls brought the weapon that was used on Cora? None of this makes any sense.

"Violet," Officer Grady says, "look at me." Violet lifts her chin and meets his eyes. "There is no such thing as Joseph Wither."

"There is," Violet whispers.

"The real Joseph Wither died a long time ago."

"No, he didn't." Violet shakes her head. "He can't die."

"He must be real." I try to defend her. "I mean, maybe someone *told* her he was Joseph Wither, but he was lying."

This is taking too long. For every minute that Officer Grady spends sitting in our kitchen questioning Violet, this Wither person is getting farther and farther away.

Officer Grady looks pissed but I push back from the table and stand. "I'll be right back." I hurry from the kitchen and up the stairs and into the bedroom. I pull the sketchbook from beneath the bed and run back downstairs.

"See." I thrust the sketch in front of Officer Grady. "Maybe this is who you should be looking for."

"Mom!" Violet exclaims, trying to intercept the sketchbook. "That's mine. You can't go through my things."

Officer Grady takes the book in his hands and Max slides off the kitchen counter to look over his shoulder.

"Who is it?" Officer Grady asks.

"Joseph Wither," Violet says in a small voice.

"Why did you draw the picture of him, Violet? How do you know what he looks like?" Officer Grady asks.

"For a school project." I speak for her but Grady gives me a sharp look that quiets me.

"We found a picture of him in an old yearbook at the library," Violet explains.

Officer Grady rubs a hand over his mouth and drops the sketch pad onto the table with a thunk. "Joseph Wither would be in his nineties by now and he most definitely wouldn't look like this anymore."

"He does," Violet persists. "He does look like this."

"We found your fingerprints on the weapon, Violet."

"Whoa," I say in disbelief. "Of course you did. We all know that she picked up the knife or whatever the hell it was after she found Cora." Officer Grady looks at me skeptically. "What are you saying? You think that Violet did this?"

"What am I supposed to think?" He lifts his hands like he's had it with all of us and sighs. "We have some text exchanges between Violet and another child that are pretty damning. Violet's fingerprints are on the weapon used to stab Cora and Cora's blood was all over her hands and clothes. What does that look like to you?"

"It looks like this conversation is over," I say, voice shaky with rage. "Get out." My mind is reeling. What text messages? The other child has to be Jordyn. So that's why they took Violet's phone at the emergency room. They were looking for evidence.

"Why would Violet hurt Cora?" Max speaks up. "She's her best friend. Violet wouldn't hurt anyone."

"I don't think Violet is being as forthcoming as she can be."

"What about someone pretending to be this guy? Apparently everyone in town seems to know who he is. And anyone could have known the girls were doing a project about him. What about her classmates or the teacher? Did you question Mr. Dover?"

"Mom," Violet says, mortified.

"Shh, Violet," I tell her.

"There are aspects of the case that I can't discuss with you," Officer Grady says. "But I have to ask tough questions even if they are upsetting."

"What if I refuse?" I lower my voice. "What if I don't let you talk to her?" I challenge.

"Then I'll have to get a warrant."

"What does that mean?" I ask. "You'll arrest her?"

"I don't want it to come to that but if I have to..." Officer Grady's icy voice lets me know just how serious he is.

"Mom?" Violet says, bursting into tears. "I don't want to go to jail," she cries. "Please, don't let him take me."

"It's going to be okay," I tell her. To Grady I snap, "Don't you think she's scared enough? Now you have to threaten to arrest a twelve-year-old?"

"All I'm asking for is for some cooperation." Grady turns to Violet, who has gotten up from her chair and backed away from the table. "Don't you want to help your friend, Violet?" he asks.

Violet nods but her eyes flick toward the front door. I know what she's going to do before she does. She dashes from the kitchen and wrenches open the front door before I can even get to my feet. "Violet," I cry. "Violet, come back!" But she's gone. Just like she used to do when she was five and kindergarten seemed too overwhelming and hard.

She's run and taken my pepper spray with her.

After Jim Landry's outburst I decided to go back and check on Cora. As I approached I heard voices floating out from the hospital room. I peeked inside and could see a man sitting next to Cora's bed. He was leaning in close to her and brushed his fingers across her forehead, gently pushing her bangs aside. Cora was smiling up at him while a brightly colored Mylar get-well balloon, anchored by a small weight, bobbed gently on the bed next to Cora. I didn't want to interrupt but as I was turning to leave the man saw me lingering in the doorway.

"Come on in," he said. "I was just getting ready to leave. I'm John Dover, one of Cora's teachers."

I extended my hand and John Dover reached out to take it. He was taller than my six feet and I guessed he was in his early forties. He was handsome and had an easy smile that I was sure the young girls he taught found attractive. "I'm Dr. Gideon," I introduced myself. "I don't want to interrupt your visit."

"Mr. Dover teaches social studies," Cora said. "It's my favorite subject."

"Well, Cora is a great student," Mr. Dover said, laying a hand on Cora's sheet-covered foot. "You have to get well fast, Cora," he said. "Third period won't be the same without you there."

Cora smiled shyly at the compliment. "I'll try," she said.

"Well then, I'll count on it," Mr. Dover said. "I should let you get some rest now. You take care."

"You're leaving already?" Mara Landry said as she came into the room carrying two cups of coffee.

"Well, you know those lesson plans don't write themselves," Mr. Dover said, causing Cora to give a little laugh.

"I'll walk out with you," Mara said. "Cora, what do you tell Mr. Dover?"

"Thanks for the balloon and thanks for coming to see me," Cora said, her eyes focused downward. I imagined it was awkward, to say the least, to have your teacher see you in a hospital gown.

After Mara and Mr. Dover left I stayed behind. "That was very kind of your teacher to come and visit you," I commented.

"He's nice," Cora said with a shrug. "I bet he'd come to see any student that was in the hospital."

"Maybe," I said. "What makes social studies your favorite class?" I asked.

Cora shrugged again. "I don't know. Mr. Dover makes it interesting. Fun."

"How so?" I pressed, wanting to get a sense of what was important to Cora.

"Sometimes he dresses up like characters when he teaches and he listens when you talk to him," Cora said, pulling on the silver ribbon dangling from the balloon.

"What do you talk about?" I asked as I settled in a chair next to Cora's bed.

"School, friends, just regular stuff like that. I used to eat lunch in his classroom and we'd talk. My sister says he's weird, but I don't think so."

"Weird in what way?" I asked, making sure I kept my voice light, conversational, even though the fact that Cora ate lunch in a teacher's classroom raised some questions for me.

"I don't know, just weird. She said he was a perv, but he isn't. He's just nice. He cares," Cora explained.

I wanted to talk more about Mr. Dover with Cora—something felt just a bit off-center about him—but Mara breezed back into the room. "What are you two chatting about?" she asked, coming to Cora's side.

"Nothing," Cora said, casting a worried glance my way.

"I was just asking Cora how she was feeling," I said, making a mental note to find out why she didn't want her mother to know that we were talking about Mr. Dover.

I said my goodbyes and reminded Mara and Cora that I would be back in the morning but if they needed me for anything sooner they certainly could give me a call. I hurried through the corridors in a rush to get to my next appointment when I saw John Dover sitting in a bank of chairs near the elevators. "I was hoping to catch you," he said, rising to his feet. "Can we speak for a moment? About Cora?"

I tried not to show my surprise. Mara must have told him what kind of doctor I was. "Of course I can't share any medical information about Cora," I explained. "But if you know of anything that might be helpful to Cora's situation, I'm sure her family would appreciate it."

"I'm sorry to say I can't help with finding out who did this to Cora—" Mr. Dover slid his hands into the pockets of his coat "—but she's such a fragile little girl. I worry that she won't pull through this."

"What do you mean?" I asked. Cora's injuries were terrible, but from what her other doctors were saying, they weren't life-threatening.

"Mentally," Mr. Dover said almost apologetically, as if he was betraying Cora. "After what's happened I worry that she'll retreat even more deeply into herself. Cora always seems to be in her own little world."

"You see this at school?" I asked.

"I do," Mr. Dover said. "Over the months I've seen Cora isolating herself from classmates and I see it in her writing and in how she interacts with others. She has a very vivid imagination." I didn't interject in hopes that he would continue. "What I mean is that Cora tends to read into situations. From her perspective, people are out to get her."

"Well, given her current circumstances," I said before I could stop myself, "I think that is a pretty accurate perspective."

"No, no." Mr. Dover held up his hands as if to stop whatever path my thoughts were heading down. "Obviously, someone hurt Cora badly. I didn't mean to suggest that wasn't the case. What I'm trying to say is just the opposite."

I must have looked skeptical because Mr. Dover took a deep breath and tried again.

"From having Cora in class I've noticed that she takes things to heart whether the slight is real or imagined. One wrong look from a classmate and Cora is crushed. One misinterpreted comment and she starts to cry and runs to a teacher. She tends to build up the event into something it really isn't. She embellishes. Kids resent it and this causes some friction. So what I'm trying to say, and doing so poorly, is on a good day Cora struggles to keep it together, so I can imagine how hard this is for her." Mr. Dover let out another breath and furrowed his brow. "I just want her to be okay. Cora's a good kid."

"That's all we want for Cora," I said, forcing a smile. "Thanks for sharing your thoughts, but I have to get to my next appointment." I turned and headed away from the elevators, opting for the stairs and leaving Mr. Dover behind.

As my footsteps echoed down the concrete steps, John Dover's words ran through my head. He made it sound like Cora was known for reporting slights, real or imagined, to the teacher. Could the attack on her have been in retaliation for this? That seemed like too much of a stretch.

Besides, there was something about John Dover that made me bristle. For someone who purportedly cared so much about his student why would he take the time to seek me out only to tell me what a basket case Cora is? *She embellishes*, he said. She lies. Why, I wondered, was it so important to John Dover to tell me this?

Dec. 5, 2017

My mom came home while I was in the middle of emailing JW44, so I had to get off the computer really fast. I ran out to the kitchen and sat at the counter like I was doing my homework.

I don't like being sneaky. It makes me feel bad but I know my mom would freak out if she found out I was talking to a stranger online. My mom is so happy that I actually have two friends that she has stopped asking me a thousand questions about school and who I sit by at lunch. She even lets me go over to Jordyn's house once in a while, but I can't go to the bar and only if Jordyn's grandma is there.

She still hasn't let me go over to Violet's house. When I ask her why, she just makes a dumb excuse even though we both know it's because of the neighborhood that Violet lives in and the fact that Violet's mom hasn't lived here for a hundred years.

My mom wouldn't be so happy if she knew how Jordyn has been acting toward me lately. Jordyn has been so impatient. Everything I do is stupid or dumb or I'm being a baby. I never know what she's going to be like when I get to school. Honestly, it's exhausting.

I woke up in the middle of the night last night because I suddenly remembered that I didn't erase the history on the computer. If my mom or dad checked, they would know that I've been on the DarkestDoor website and I'd be dead and grounded from the computer forever and I'd never be able to talk to JW again. I had to sneak past my mom and dad's room and Kendall's room and get downstairs to the computer room and I swear the floor creaked with every step I took.

It only took me a few seconds to clear the computer's history but then I started thinking about what Joseph said about looking into what happened to Rachel Farmer. First, I went to Mr. Dover's class website where he lists all the homework assignments. If someone walked in on me I could at least say that I had forgotten to do an assignment and was working on it because it was due the next day.

I even started writing an email to Mr. Dover with a question about the bibliography we had to write for our project so I could show my mom or dad if they walked in.

Then I opened another window and typed "Rachel Farmer" in the search bar. A ton of results popped up, so I added "Pitch, Iowa" and "1991" and hit Return. That narrowed the results down to just a few pages so I clicked on the first link that brought up a newspaper article about Rachel. It said that Rachel disappeared one evening after an argument with her mom. The police thought she had run away and was asking anyone with information to contact them.

The same picture of Rachel that was in the yearbook was included with the article. She didn't look like the kind of girl who would run away. She looked normal. I expected her to be prettier. Suddenly I hated her and I don't know why.

I clicked on the next link when I heard my sister say, "What are you doing up?" and I nearly had a heart attack. I clicked on Mr. Dover's school page really fast and told her that I forgot to do an assignment and that I'd be in big trouble if I didn't get it done. She said I better get to bed before mom or dad found me on the computer. When she left I clicked on a few more links about Rachel Farmer. From what I could tell, the police decided she ran away and they never found out where she went.

So Rachel Farmer ran away with him. But why would Joseph pick her? What was so special about her?

I went ahead and sent the email to Mr. Dover with my question about the bibliography and within like two seconds he answered back. *What are you doing up at one in the morning, Cora?* he asked. *Go get your beauty sleep and you can ask me your question in the morning.*

I wasn't expecting that.

When I finally got to bed, I couldn't stop worrying about Joseph and Rachel Farmer. I wanted to ask him why he loved her. Why he chose her. I almost got up again to send him a message but then I heard someone in the hallway.

Instead I lay in bed and Joseph started whispering to me through the vents. But this time he wasn't saying my name over and over. It was Rachel's.

OFFICER WILSON: Thank you for coming in, John. I'll try not to take up too much of your time.

JOHN DOVER: Happy to help.

OFFICER WILSON: Please state your full name, age and address for the record.

JOHN DOVER: John Philip Dover. Forty-one and I live at 206 Apple Street.

OFFICER WILSON: And how long have you resided there?

JOHN DOVER: I've lived there for about four years or so.

OFFICER WILSON: Does anyone else live there with you?

JOHN DOVER: No, by myself. I'm divorced.

OFFICER WILSON: So, I'm sure you're aware of the attack on two of your students.

JOHN DOVER: Yes. Cora and Violet. How are they doing?

OFFICER WILSON: I don't have the latest update on their conditions. What can you tell me about Violet Crow?

JOHN DOVER: She moved here last fall. Quiet. Shy.

OFFICER WILSON: What was her relationship with her class-mates?

JOHN DOVER: Fine, I think. Like I said, she was…is quiet. Doesn't have a whole lot to say in class.

OFFICER WILSON: Who would you say her friends are?

JOHN DOVER: The only kids I ever really see her with are Cora Landry and Jordyn Petit.

OFFICER WILSON: Did the girls ever have any arguments that you were aware of?

JOHN DOVER: Not that I know of, but Jordyn always seems to have some kind of conflict with her classmates.

OFFICER WILSON: Conflict? Anything ever get physical?

JOHN DOVER: God, no. Nothing like that. Just kid stuff. Jordyn likes to be in charge and not everyone likes to be told what to do.

OFFICER WILSON: But nothing physical? What about ver-bal arguments?

JOHN DOVER: Have you ever been in a middle school hall-way? Kids argue. That's not unusual.

OFFICER WILSON: What about Cora Landry? What kind of student is she?

JOHN DOVER: Nice girl. She's bright but typically very quiet. I've been trying to get her to speak up more, be more confident about sharing her ideas. Cora cares very much about what others think about her so she's afraid to make any waves. Unfortunately, middle school students can spot this a mile away.

OFFICER WILSON: She was bullied?

JOHN DOVER: I don't know if I would say that. Cora is a bit naive for her age. Like I said, her classmates pick up on this and can give her a hard time, but I wouldn't call that bullying.

OFFICER WILSON: Did you ever see Jordyn or Violet being dismissive or rude to Cora? Anything that would suggest bad blood between them?

JOHN DOVER: For a while they were inseparable. I remember thinking that it was nice that Cora finally found some friends, but had been pretty solitary up until then. They had a bit of a dustup right before Christmas.

OFFICER WILSON: Oh? Over what?

JOHN DOVER: I can't remember. Hurt feelings are par for the course in middle school. They've been pretty cool to each other since then. Although I did see them eating lunch together lately.

OFFICER WILSON: I understand that the girls worked on a project together in your class—the urban legend project.

JOHN DOVER: That was months ago. What does that have to do with anything?

OFFICER WILSON: Just trying to get a sense of the relationship between the three girls. What topic did they choose?

JOHN DOVER: God, I don't remember. I teach six sections of social studies throughout the day. Wait… Joseph Wither, I think.

OFFICER WILSON: How did the girls come up with the idea for the project?

JOHN DOVER: I have no idea.

OFFICER WILSON: You didn't suggest the topic?

JOHN DOVER: No, I don't think so. I brainstorm ideas with the kids but they choose their own topics. Why?

OFFICER WILSON: What about websites? Did the girls ever go into chat rooms or have contact with anyone online?

JOHN DOVER: No! Never. At least, not that I know of and definitely not at school. What's going on? What does this have to do with my class?

OFFICER WILSON: I'm hoping to see the girls' notes and list of references. Do you have that?

JOHN DOVER: I think so. They'd be somewhere in my classroom. I can go get them for you when we're done here.

OFFICER WILSON: That would be great. You live a few blocks from the Landry home, correct?

JOHN DOVER: I'm not sure. I don't know their address. I'm sure I live a few blocks from a lot of my students.

OFFICER WILSON: But you live just a few blocks away from the train yard? Is that right?

JOHN DOVER: Yes, but why—

OFFICER WILSON: Where were you the night of Sunday, April 15?

JOHN DOVER: Wait a second… I don't understand…

OFFICER WILSON: We are asking the same question of every individual who came into contact with the girls recently.

JOHN DOVER: You're talking to all the teachers?

OFFICER WILSON: We're talking to anyone who has direct contact with the girls.

JOHN DOVER: After school I went into Grayling to go out with some other teachers from school.

OFFICER WILSON: You went all the way to Grayling?

JOHN DOVER: Yeah, it's no fun running into parents of students at the local bar. We ate at the Airliner and hit a few more bars.

OFFICER WILSON: What time did you get home?

JOHN DOVER: Midnight, I guess—give or take a half hour. Then I went right to bed.

OFFICER WILSON: By yourself?

JOHN DOVER: By myself.

OFFICER WILSON: So no one can vouch for your whereabouts between midnight and 1:00 a.m.?

JOHN DOVER: I guess not.

OFFICER WILSON: Tell me about your teaching job prior to coming to Pitch.

JOHN DOVER: I don't… What's that have to do with this?

OFFICER WILSON: Just being thorough. Where did you work before coming to Pitch?

JOHN DOVER: At the high school in Willow Creek. But I don't understand why you're asking me this.

OFFICER WILSON: Why did you leave?

JOHN DOVER: I just… I wanted to move closer to where I grew up, to my parents.

OFFICER WILSON: So you left Willow Creek on good terms.

JOHN DOVER: As far as I'm concerned, we did.

OFFICER WILSON: So, I'll take that as a no.

JOHN DOVER: You can take it however you want.

OFFICER WILSON: Rumor has it that you had an inappropriate relationship with a student.

JOHN DOVER: Not true.

OFFICER WILSON: You know I'm going to call Willow Creek, don't you?

JOHN DOVER: Go for it. There's nothing there.

OFFICER WILSON: Then you have nothing to worry about, do you? What happened?

JOHN DOVER: One of my students had a crush on me. Read into things that absolutely weren't there. She sent me some texts. Parents saw them and freaked out.

OFFICER WILSON: How'd your student get your cell phone number?

JOHN DOVER: I gave it to all my students. I wanted to be accessible to them. Big mistake.

OFFICER WILSON: But you left Willow Creek. Why would you leave if you did nothing wrong?

JOHN DOVER: The girl's mom was on the school board, that's why. Didn't matter that I had absolutely zero inappropriate contact with that girl, people looked at me differently. But for the record, the Board of Educational Examiners found that I did nothing wrong. Nothing.

OFFICER WILSON: How about your students here? Did you give them your cell phone number?

JOHN DOVER: No way. I learned my lesson. Causes nothing but trouble.

JW44:
SO, DO YOU FINALLY BELIEVE ME ABOUT RACHEL?

Corareef12:
I guess so.

JW44:
ARE YOU GOING TO PUT IT IN YOUR REPORT?

Corareef12:
I don't know.

JW44:
WHAT'S THE MATTER? YOU DON'T SEEM LIKE YOURSELF.

Corareef12:
I did something I shouldn't have.

JW44:
WHAT DID YOU DO?

Corareef12:
I don't want to tell you. You'll think I'm a terrible person.

JW44:
I COULD NEVER THINK THAT. WHAT DID YOU DO?

Corareef12:
I borrowed Violet's cell phone without asking her.

JW44:

I'M SURE SHE DOESN'T MIND. YOU'RE FRIENDS, RIGHT?

Corareef12:

I mean, I took her cell phone. I brought it home without telling her. Our computer wasn't working. Violet accidentally left her phone behind in the lunchroom. I picked it up and was going to give it back to her, but then I thought I'd just take it home for one night. Just one and then bring it back to her tomorrow. I told you it was bad.

JW44:

YOU STOLE HER PHONE?

Corareef12:

I'm sorry. I'll bring it back tomorrow. I feel sick.

JW44:

YOU TOOK HER PHONE SO YOU COULD TALK TO ME? I THINK I LOVE YOU, CORAREEF12!

Dec. 11, 2017

I kept trying to find the right time to return Violet's cell phone to her but there was no way to do it without being totally obvious. She had let me use her phone before. She even let me take it home overnight once but her mom found out and was super pissed. Violet said she couldn't let me borrow it overnight again.

I was desperate. Our computer has been broken for days and my dad kept saying he was going to take it in to be fixed but didn't. I was afraid Joseph was going to be mad at me for not emailing him and Violet's phone was right there. I can't believe I did it. I've never stolen anything before in my life but I felt like if I didn't talk to Wither everything would be ruined.

I feel terrible.

And Violet was really worried about it. She kept saying how her mom was going to kill her for losing it. I tried to make her feel better by telling her I'd help her look for it and saying that it would show up.

We went to the library again after school and we finally figured out exactly what we were going to do for our final presentation. A movie. At first we were just going to write a report and make a poster for our project— Violet's a really good artist—but then we heard that Gabe's group was going to present their project about the Bermuda Triangle through a fake newscast and Katie's group was making a board game called Roswell with little plastic alien game pieces made from a 3D printer. It's a lot harder than it sounds. We spent the last two days in class on the script and wanted to get it finished so we could start filming.

Jordyn complained that the script was too short. That we didn't have enough information. Violet suggested that we go back and look through the old newspapers again and Jordyn said, "Don't be stupid, we're not going to find what you're looking for in a newspaper. They can't print stuff without clear-cut evidence. They couldn't just go around saying that Joseph Wither was killing girls down by the railroad tracks."

I could tell that the way Jordyn was talking to Violet hurt her feelings but Violet just asked what her bright idea was. I couldn't stop thinking about Rachel Farmer and the yearbook so I got up from my chair and went to the reference section and pulled the yearbook down from the shelf.

I opened it to the picture of Rachel Farmer and laid it in front of them. "How about this?" I said and pointed to the photo with the heart around Rachel's head.

Jordyn gave me a look like, *So what?* I told them all about how Rachel Farmer disappeared and that chances are she was one of the girls that went with Wither. "See the initials?" I asked. "JW+RF."

"That doesn't mean anything," Jordyn said. "Anyone could have written that."

I said I didn't think so. That it was pretty obvious that Joseph Wither wrote it and that Rachel ran away with him and Jordyn said that was just stupid. That made me mad and I said, "You just think everything is stupid today. I want to include it in the movie." I looked at Violet and waited for her to agree with me but she didn't say anything.

"Well, Violet and I don't want it in the movie, do we?" Jordyn said so loud that I was sure the librarian was going to come over and tell us to be quiet.

Violet said that we probably shouldn't include Rachel Farmer in the movie because we had no way of proving that he was the one who took her. Then Jordyn butted in and said that I was probably the one who drew the heart around Rachel's head and wrote the initials.

I shouted. I mean, really shouted, "I did not!" That's when the librarian did come over and told us to keep it down.

Then Jordyn said we needed to find someone really old to talk to—someone who was around in the '40s who would remember what had happened. I barely said anything after that. I was too mad. I was mad at Jordyn for saying my idea was stupid and at Violet for taking Jordyn's side.

Jordyn said we should start with interviewing some of the old guys who hang out at the bar, that they have a story for everything, and said that tomorrow after school we could go to the bar and ask some of the old farts who go there for a beer and a burger at like five o'clock because they go to bed at eight every night.

I knew I wasn't going to be able to go and that I wouldn't even bother asking my parents. My mom doesn't like me hanging out at Petit's. That's so stupid because Petit's isn't just a bar—lots of families go there to eat pizza and hamburgers—but my mom still says no, that it's no place for girls to spend time without their parents. I don't even think I want to go. Right now I'm so sick of Jordyn being so bossy and never listening to my ideas. I ended up telling them that I have an appointment tomorrow after school, which was a total lie.

I'm kind of jealous that Violet and Jordyn have been spending so much time together on the project without me. Violet is my best friend but Jordyn always finds a way to get in the middle of things. I thought about lying to my mom and just going to Petit's with them but my mom knows everyone and it would just get back to her, anyway.

Just before we packed up to leave I casually tried to sneak Violet's phone into her book bag while Violet went to the bathroom and Jordyn put some books back on the shelf. Well, Jordyn caught me. She asked me what I was doing and all I could think of to say was *Nothing*.

And Jordyn said, "Isn't that Violet's cell phone?" Just then Violet came back and Jordyn said, "Cora has your cell phone."

"I found it on the floor," I said. Dumb, I know.

"But, Violet," Jordyn said, "you lost it at school, right?"

Violet nodded and looked at me like she was really hurt.

I told them again that I found it on the floor beneath the table and if they didn't believe me, well, that was their problem.

I could tell that Violet wanted to believe me but Jordyn made it clear she didn't.

"I can't believe you stole your best friend's phone, Cora. That's awful."

I hollered that I didn't steal it, that I found it, but Jordyn dragged Violet away and left me just sitting there.

Corareef12:
We present our project to the class in a few days.

 JW44:
YOU'LL DO GREAT!

 Corareef12:
Yeah, I can't wait until it's over.

 JW44:
ARE VIOLET AND JORDYN STILL MAD AT YOU ABOUT THE CELL
PHONE?

 Corareef12:
Whenever Jordyn walks by me in the hallway she pretends to
cough and says, Thief. She told everyone I took it. Violet says
that she just misplaced the phone, but I can tell that she thinks
I stole it. She's not mean to me but she isn't really nice, either.
She hardly talks to me anymore.

 JW44:
LIKE I SAID, THEY'RE NOT TRUE FRIENDS. YOU KNOW YOU CAN
COUNT ON ME, THOUGH. WHEN DO I GET TO SEE THE MOVIE?

 Corareef12:
IDK. It's kind of embarrassing.

 JW44:
WHY? I'M SURE IT'S AWESOME. I BET YOU'LL GET AN A.

Corareef12:

I hope so. We spent all day Saturday filming it. I thought we'd never finish. I played the part of Lucy.

JW44:

YOU DO LOOK A LITTLE BIT LIKE LUCY. YOU'RE PRETTIER, THOUGH.

JW44:

YOOHOO. ARE YOU STILL THERE?

JW44:

WHO DID YOU HAVE PLAY ME?

Corareef12:

Gabe Shannon. He's a boy in my class.

JW44:

DID YOU KISS HIM?

Corareef12:

What? NO! We were just acting. Nothing happened.

JW44:

BECAUSE I DON'T THINK I'D LIKE IT IF YOU DID.

Corareef12:

We didn't, I swear. We just pretended to. No one wants to kiss me, anyway. Everyone hates me.

JW44:

I DON'T THINK THAT'S TRUE, CORA.

Corareef12:

How do you know my real name?

JW44:

DUH. YOUR USERNAME STARTS WITH CORA. I KIND OF FIGURED THAT WAS YOUR FIRST NAME. I'M RIGHT, AREN'T I?

Corareef12:

But how do you know? Are you like God who knows everything?

JW44:

WELL, I'M NOT GOD, BUT THANK YOU. IT'S HARD TO EXPLAIN, BUT I JUST KNOW. I KNOW THAT YOU WEAR A PINK COAT AND HAVE A PURPLE BACKPACK WITH WHITE POLKA DOTS. I KNOW YOU HAVE BLOND HAIR AND BLUE EYES. AND I KNOW THAT YOU'RE VERY PRETTY. A LOT PRETTIER THAN THOSE TWO GIRLS YOU HANG OUT WITH.

Corareef12:

Well, I don't really hang out with them anymore and everyone else thinks Jordyn and Violet are the pretty ones.

JW44:

NO WAY. BESIDES, YOU HAVE A MUCH BETTER PERSONALITY.

Corareef12:

I wish they were my friends again.

JW44:

ARE YOU SURE? I THINK THEY MAKE YOU SAD.

Corareef12:

It's lonely at school.

JW44:

WELL, I'M YOUR FRIEND, TOO. REMEMBER THAT. MAYBE WE COULD MEET SOMEDAY. IN PERSON. WHAT DO YOU THINK?

Corareef12:
Are you really Wither? I feel like maybe you're just pranking me.

JW44:
YES. I WOULDN'T LIE TO YOU, CORA. I CARE ABOUT YOU TOO MUCH.

Corareef12:
I don't know what to believe anymore.

JW44:
I'LL PROVE IT TO YOU.

Corareef12:
How?

JW44:
COME TO THE TRAIN YARD. WE'LL MEET IN PERSON. YOU'LL SEE...

JW44:
CORA?

JW44:
WHERE'D YOU GO?

Thomas's first thought is the attic. He places a step stool beneath the hatchway in the ceiling and pulls on the cord that unfolds the stairs. He threads his arms through the straps of the book bag and, with it resting on his back, clutches the wooden rungs just above his head and makes his way upward.

By the time his head pokes through the narrow opening in the ceiling he knows the attic won't work. The wide-planked wooden floor is covered in a thick layer of dust. He hasn't been up here in about five years, when he and Tess cleaned it out.

If Thomas stows the backpack up here he will disturb the nearly half-decade worth of dust. His footprints will give him away and he doesn't have a good enough explanation as to why he would venture up the wobbly steps. He slowly makes his way back down the rungs, fearful that a misstep could result in a broken leg and he'd end up in the hospital in a bed right next to Tess. Then what would happen to Jordyn?

Next, Thomas tucks the backpack behind a stack of neatly folded sheets and towels on the top shelf of the linen closet. He knows this won't work, either. He's seen enough crime shows to know that the police will look there, too. He wanders the house trying to come up with the safest spot. He knows in his bones that it is just a matter of time before the police chief will knock on the door, warrant in hand, and begin to ransack each and every one of the closets in the house, look beneath the beds and behind the furniture.

His eyes land on the old fireplace that they light a few times per year. Using the stone mantel for balance, he lowers himself to the floor and cranes his neck to look upward into the flue. The fireplace is swept and cool to the touch. If anyone walks in at this moment, he can say that a starling or a swallow has flown down the chimney and he is searching for any sign of a nest.

Lying on one shoulder he shoves the backpack as far up the chimney as it can go. He stays there for a moment, trying to catch his breath and waits to see if the pack filled with Jordyn's clothing, textbook and tennis shoes will tumble to the ground. It doesn't move and Thomas breathes a sigh of relief, sending a small windstorm of ash into the air.

He knows the flue is just a temporary solution. When he has the chance he will have to get the backpack out of the house for good. There are plenty of dumping places around Pitch. Locust Creek with its fast-moving current, strong enough to sweep the contents far away, or he can bury them in a cornfield to eventually be chewed up by a combine.

"Grandpa," comes Jordyn's tremulous voice from above him.

"Down here," Thomas calls back, struggling to get to his feet. By the time Jordyn comes down the steps he is washing his sooty hands in the sink. "Did you have a good rest?" Thomas asks as Jordyn slumps into the kitchen and rubs her eyes.

"Uh-huh," Jordyn answers, stifling a yawn, and takes a seat at the table.

Thomas pulls a clean dish towel from a drawer and wipes his hands dry before pulling out a chair and sitting next to his granddaughter. He has planned what he is going to say, has murmured it over and over to himself the past two hours.

"Jordyn," he begins, keeping his voice authoritative and matter-of-fact, "the police will be back to ask more questions about what happened at the train yard." Jordyn's chin begins to quiver but Thomas plunges forward. "They are going to ask you over and over about what you did at Cora's house and what you did at the train yard and it's very important that you say the same thing each time. Do you understand?"

Jordyn nods. "You told them you left Cora and Violet at the train yard, right?" Again, Jordyn nods and her eyes begin to fill.

"No," Thomas says sternly. "No tears, Jordyn. This is important. When they come back around, you tell them the exact same thing. You were going to go to the train yard but you stopped before you actually got there. You took a drink of beer, dumped it out and then you left. The girls were fine when you left and then you came straight home."

Thomas waits for Jordyn to nod in understanding and then reaches out and runs a calloused palm across Jordyn's sleep-rumpled hair. "You left your book bag at the train yard, but don't worry, I'm sure they'll find it."

"Grandpa—" Jordyn's forehead creases in confusion "—but I didn't…"

"Shh, I know," Thomas says, trying to gentle his voice. "Don't worry, we can get you a new one for school if need be. Next time just don't be so careless. They'll ask you what was inside and you'll tell them you had your pajamas and social studies book in there. And your house key. That's all, right?" He waits for Jordyn to agree and when she doesn't, Thomas says, "Jordyn, I found that map in your backpack and that list. There was blood on your jacket. Do you understand how that would look to the police?"

Jordyn nods and bites her lip. "Nothing bad was supposed to happen. I don't know how she got hurt so bad, Grandpa. I promise. I didn't do anything."

"Okay. You just tell them you left the backpack at the train yard, got it?" Jordyn nods again. Thomas stands and goes to the kitchen sink and looks out the window.

With forced cheerfulness Thomas returns and drops a kiss atop Jordyn's head, saying, "I called the hospital and talked to Cora's mom earlier. She says Cora is doing better and is up for visitors. Go on and get dressed and we'll go see her."

A spasm of alarm crosses Jordyn's face and she looks ready to protest. "No arguments," Thomas says, though in the back of his mind he can hear Tess telling him that he should wait until

Cora is home from the hospital before taking Jordyn to see her in such a state. That it might be too upsetting to her.

He tries to nudge Tess's intrusion from his head. "We'll stop and see Grandma and then your friend. I think that will be a nice thing to do, don't you? Cora is one of your best friends, right?"

"Right," Jordyn repeats.

"You know," Thomas says. "You girls are lucky. Even Cora. Her mom says she's got quite the head injury and may have to have plastic surgery on her face, but the stab wound wasn't as bad as it could have been. She could have died. You all could have died."

Thomas watches Jordyn's face. He sees fear and revulsion. Good, he thinks. This is why he's taking her to see Cora. Jordyn needs to know that it's dangerous for three little girls to go out in the middle of the night. Not that he thinks they were asking for it; he doesn't think that at all. But it would have never happened if they had just stayed put like they were supposed to.

"Then go on, Jordyn, go on now and get ready," he orders.

Jordyn pushes herself away from the table in resignation and slouches off. Thomas hopes he's not making a big mistake. But wouldn't it look more suspicious if Jordyn didn't go to visit Cora? Wouldn't she look guiltier?

Pitch is a small town so you'd think there'd only be a few places Violet could hide but really there are dozens: back home, Jordyn's house, school, Hickory Park, even outside of town where there are miles and miles of winding gravel roads. Hickory Park is in the far southwest part of town, the school is closed for spring break and I don't think she would go back home.

"Try the depot," Max says.

"Why?" I ask. "Wouldn't that be the last place she'd go?" I ask, thinking Violet would be terrified, worried that the monster who stabbed Cora could be there.

"She's been hanging around there with her friends a lot lately. I think that's where they filmed the movie for their school project. There's lots of places she could hide," he explains. I had no idea that Violet was spending time at the train yard. I have so many questions but decide to save them for later.

My phone rings and I hand it to Max to answer.

"Hello," he says. "Yeah… No, we haven't found her yet, either. We're heading to the train yard in case Violet went there." He hangs up. "Officer Grady," he tells me.

"Yeah, I figured." Part of me wishes that Max hadn't told Grady where we were headed. His mere presence freaks Violet but I couldn't exactly tell my son to lie to the police.

I take the same road we drove the other night and park next to the boarded-up depot building. A bright red-and-white sign warns me against trespassing but I get out of my car, anyway, after telling Max to stay put. The train station doesn't look quite as scary as it did in the dark of night but with the tall, weedy grass and the abandoned rusty boxcars it's still eerie.

With one foot I test the steps that lead up to the depot platform. The wood cracks and pops with my weight so instead I hoist myself up, the rough concrete biting into my knees and the palms of my hands. I stand, brush the grit and dirt from my hands, and look out over the train yard. A scrap of yellow crime tape lies on the ground near where Violet collapsed. The only sound I hear is the rustle of the tall winter wheat waving back and forth in the light breeze.

Dozens of boxcars with rusty pockmarks sit throughout the yard. Violet could be in any one of them or in none at all.

First, I walk around the depot building. The brick is cracked and crumbling but each window and door is sealed up tight with heavy plywood. I can't find any way that Violet could have gotten inside.

That leaves the boxcars. I hop down from the platform and make my way to the nearest car and look inside. Its corners are filled with cobwebs and candy wrappers and crushed beer cans but no Violet. I move on to the next car, this one tipped on its side. I peer over the edge and an animal, a mouse or ground squirrel, blinks back at me, then scurries away. Violet's not here, either.

The third car sits back away from the others and is nearly swallowed up by the tall grass that has grown up around it, nearly concealing the faded, flaking paint that spells out Primrose Sugar. The area around the side door seems undisturbed but I decide to check, anyway. I wade through the grass, its stalks scratching at my chin. Unlike the other boxcars, the door to this one is only open a bit.

The tall grass blocks the sun from reaching the opening so I pull out my cell and shine its light through the narrow opening. Nothing. I'm about to move on to the next car when I hear a whimper.

"Violet?" I say, trying to see through the darkness. There's no answer. I yank on the door, trying to open it so I can get inside, but it's rusted in place.

The opening is only about six inches wide but if I turn sideways I might fit. I squeeze my upper body through the small opening and scan the far corners of the car with the light from my cell phone.

Sitting crouched in a corner is Violet. Her hand is clamped across her mouth as if trying to hold back a scream. "Violet, it's Mom." I try to force my way inside but the angle is all wrong and for a second I'm stuck. "Violet," I say again. "It's just me. Officer Grady isn't here. What happened, sweetie? Why did you run away?"

She looks at me with eyes filled with fear but doesn't speak. "I know you're scared but I promise that I won't let anyone hurt you. We'll get this all cleared up and have you home in no time. I promise."

Outside comes the sound of tires on gravel.

"He's coming," Violet whispers.

"Officer Grady?" I ask. "Is that who you are afraid of? I promise, Violet, I won't let him hurt you." But she's not listening. Holding my breath and squeezing my stomach in as tightly as I can, I'm somehow able to wriggle inside the car, my jeans catching and tearing on the ragged, corroded edges of the door.

"Violet, it's just me right now. It's going to be okay." I reach my hand out to her. Her skin is ice cold and she's shivering. "Please tell me what's going on. Why did you run away? Why did you come here?"

Using the light from my phone I scan the walls. Stenciled in a now grimy white are the words *Primrose Sugar—Do Not Damage*. The boxcar is surprisingly clean. There are no signs of any critters taking up residence here, as if someone has been tending to it. I wonder if the boxcar is some sort of clubhouse for Violet and her friends.

Violet is sitting on a blanket that I recognize as an old one of ours. There is a wooden pallet in a corner and atop it sits an empty mason jar with a several scraps of paper stuffed inside.

"Shut the door, shut the door." She slaps my phone from my

hand and it skitters across the floor. The car is plunged into shadows. "Shh, Mommy, he'll hear." The terror in her voice is unmistakable.

"Officer Grady?" I ask again, this time in a whisper. "Violet, I don't understand."

In the distance I hear a car door slam; next to me I feel Violet tremble. "Violet, come on, this is ridiculous." In the distance the blare of sirens come closer and closer. I don't think I'll be able to get her out of here now. "Stay here. I'll be right back."

With difficulty I climb out of the boxcar to find Officer Grady walking toward me.

"Your son told me you came this way. Any sign of her?" Officer Grady asks, looking over my shoulder toward the boxcar. Before answering I wait for the sound of sirens to fade but instead they only get louder.

"What did you do?" I ask.

"She just took off," Officer Grady tries to explain. "She's out of control, Beth. I called an ambulance for her own safety."

"An ambulance?" I ask in disbelief. "But she's not hurt," I say before I realize what he's getting at. "Oh, no." I shake my head. "She'll be fine. I just need a few minutes alone with her and she'll relax. She just doesn't understand what's going on. She's scared."

"You found her?" Officer Grady begins to move toward the boxcar and I step in front of him.

I nod. "Please, just stay outside and I'll talk to her. If I can keep her calm, will you please send the ambulance away?"

"I can't promise that," he says.

Officer Grady heads back toward the depot and I return to the boxcar. "Violet, please," I beg through the doorway. "You have to come out."

The very worst thing I can do is yank her from her hiding place. Violet is not a violent girl, but when she feels cornered or anxious, she kind of freaks out. Has since she was a toddler. In kindergarten she was known as a runner. The kid who would dart from the classroom and out the front doors when things didn't quite go her way. I thought she had outgrown it.

I climb back inside the boxcar, the skin on my hips and shoulders rubbed raw from the narrow fit. We sit shoulder to shoulder in silence for a few minutes, though I'm eager to get her out of here. I don't know how long Officer Grady will be patient.

"They're bad," Violet whispers and a shiver runs through me.

"Who is?" I ask. This is the first time I heard her mention more than one person.

"You won't believe me," she says tearfully. "No one believes me."

"I believe you," I say fiercely. "I promise. Do you know who stabbed Cora?" I ask. "Can you describe them to Officer Grady?" I wonder if there is a sketch artist in a police department of this size. Probably not. But then I think of the drawing in Violet's sketchbook. Maybe that will be enough.

"I told you—Joseph Wither."

I try to keep the frustration from seeping into the expression on my face. I promised Violet I would believe her. "Okay, it was Joseph Wither." I think about what Officer Grady said about questioning the known pedophiles in the area. Pedophiles—plural. I'm not naive but how can such a small town have more than one? "How did he know you were going to be there?" I manage to ask.

"Cora talked to him," Violet says, setting her chin atop her bent knees. "They talked to each other."

"Cora?" I ask, thoroughly confused.

"Through a chat room and emails." She begins to cry. "I think he's going to get me next."

I slide my arm around her shoulders. "He won't. I promise you there is no way I'm going to let anyone hurt you, but you have to talk to Officer Grady. You have to help him find the people who hurt Cora so they can't hurt anyone ever again. Okay?"

"I don't think I can," she says, looking helplessly up at me.

"Of course you can. You're my brave girl, right?"

"You can't catch someone who is already dead, can you?" she asks and it takes me a second to realize she's serious. She thinks a ghost or a ghoul, whatever this Joseph Wither is, stabbed her best friend and evaporated into thin air.

"Who else was there, Violet? Who else hurt Cora?"

She hesitates but finally speaks. "Jordyn."

"Jordyn?" I repeat. "Jordyn helped stab Cora?"

Violet shakes her head. "No. I don't think so. I don't know. We were just going to play a joke on Cora. Scare her, but Cora wasn't scared. She said she already knew that we were going to play a trick on her—that she wasn't scared one bit. That she knew that Wither wasn't going to hurt her. He loved her." Violet pauses in her story to take a deep breath.

"Jordyn called her crazy, said he wasn't real, and Cora said he was. Jordyn pushed Cora down. Hard. She fell against the train tracks. That's when I ran. I ran and hid."

I'm afraid to speak. Afraid that my voice will interrupt Violet's train of thought and she'll stop talking. But I have so many questions. When I'm sure that Violet isn't going to go on, I say, "If Jordyn pushed Cora down, don't you think it makes sense she stabbed her, too?"

Violet shakes her head. "No, Jordyn ran away, too. I saw her run."

"But she could have come back, right?"

"I saw something moving through the grass. It was going toward Cora. She was sitting on the tracks holding her arm and crying." Violet shivers and presses her face into my neck. "I couldn't watch. I ran away but I heard the screams. I swear someone else was there. It was him. It was Joseph Wither."

"Oh, Violet," I say, holding her more tightly. "You have to tell Officer Grady all of this. You have to tell him everything."

"But Jordyn will hate me. She told me not to say anything."

"When? When did she tell you this?" I ask. I had no idea that Jordyn and Violet had even spoken since the overnight.

"She called the house last night. We talked for just a second." Violet sniffles. "She told me not to say anything about their fight. She said if I was her friend I wouldn't say a word."

"Jordyn's not your friend, Violet," I say angrily. "Friends don't ask you to tell lies. Just tell the truth and everything will be okay. Let's go and talk to Officer Grady. And, Violet, whatever happens, you have to stay calm, cool and collected. Got it?"

Violet manages to give me a halfhearted smile. That's what I used to say to her when she was younger and I'd drop her off at school. "Remember, the three C's, Violet," I'd say. "Stay calm, cool and collected and everything will be okay."

I lead Violet to the door and watch as she carefully climbs out. On instinct I go back and grab the jar filled with paper and tuck it under my arm. I suck my stomach in and force myself from the boxcar. "You ready?" I ask and she nods.

Together we cross the train yard to where Officer Grady and Max are waiting along with an ambulance and another police officer. The lights are still flashing but at least the sirens have been silenced.

"Can Violet come with me? We'll go right to the station. She has a lot to tell you," I say. Officer Grady shakes his head.

"I'm sorry, I have to follow procedures. The EMTs have to check her out.

"It's okay, Violet." Officer Grady leads us to the ambulance and I reach for her hand but she pulls away and then I see the small crowd that has gathered.

"Fuck," Max says under his breath. I want to pinch him for swearing out loud but I feel the same way. "Where did they come from?" About half a dozen people have gathered just outside the train yard.

"They probably heard about it on the scanner," Officer Grady explains, disgusted as I am about the ghoulishness of the on-lookers.

"Just ignore them," I murmur. "Pretend you don't see them and get in the car." Heads down, with Violet between us, we hurry toward the cars.

"Be careful now," a voice calls out from the crowd. "Joseph Wither might be around here somewhere." Nervous laughter comes from the crowd.

"Don't listen to them," I say through clenched teeth but Violet looks around frantically.

"I think he's over there," the voice calls and I scan the crowd looking for the idiot bent on scaring my daughter. Clint Phelps. He keeps showing up like a bad penny.

Max looks like he's going to explode. "Stay put," I tell him. Clint gives me one of his famous smirks and it's all I can do not to walk over to him and knock it from his face.

"Or maybe over there." Clint tosses his chin toward the winter wheat.

"Shut up, Clint," Max says. Tears roll down Violet's face as two EMTs begin to move cautiously toward us. I don't like where this is going. I don't like it at all.

"Does he knock at your window at night?" Clint singsongs. "Does he come and sit on your bed? He's coming for you next."

Max has had enough. "Asshole," he says as he rushes toward Clint and barrels into him. As Officer Grady moves to break up the fight between Clint and Max, the EMTs approach Violet, who looks wild with fear.

"I don't want to go," Violet cries and to my horror pulls out my canister of pepper spray.

"Violet, put that down," I order. To the EMTs I beg, "Please don't hurt her. She's just scared."

"We're not going to hurt her, ma'am," the female EMT tells me. "We're trying to keep her safe. Now please move back." Reluctantly, I move away from my daughter. The EMT says to

Violet, "I know you're upset. That boy said some mean things and that scared you."

I glance over at Max and Clint and see that Officer Grady has stepped in to separate Max and Clint but I notice, with some satisfaction, that Clint has a bloody lip. I just pray that Max doesn't get arrested for assault. Or Violet for that matter.

"Violet, my name is Laura, and this is Ray," says one of the EMTs. "We're here to help you, okay?" Violet slowly retreats until her back is pressed against the boxcar, the pepper spray still clutched in her hand.

"Please, Violet," I beg, "don't run. Please put down the pepper spray." I'm crying and the sight of my tears seems to have gotten through to Violet. She slowly lowers her hand.

Officer Grady stands between the two boys, arms outstretched to form a barrier. "You saw him tackle me," Clint gripes.

"Go sit in your car," Officer Grady orders Max. "Now." Max, breathing heavily, looks at Clint like he'd like to get in one more punch but thinks better of it and throws open the car door, climbs inside and slams it so hard the window shakes. "You—" Officer Grady points at Clint "—are going to the station."

"What did I do?" Clint protests. In one swift move he turns Clint around, pushes him against the car and pulls out a pair of handcuffs. "You see that little girl?" Clint darts his eyes to Violet, who has thrown the canister to the side and slid to the ground into a pitiful heap. I breathe a sigh of relief.

"You are interfering with official acts," Officer Grady snaps. "You can sit at the station until your mom comes to pick you up. And if you keep arguing, I will arrest you." This seems to do the trick and Clint finally shuts up.

The EMT squats down next to Violet and speaks to her in a soothing tone. "It's okay, Violet. No one is going to hurt you. Take two deep breaths. Can you do that?" Violet gives a long, shuddering breath, then another, but her body is still tense. "Good job, Violet. Good job. Now, do you think you can sit up?" Violet nods and pushes herself into a sitting position. "Nice work, Violet," the EMT says. "You let me know when you're ready to stand up, okay?" Violet peeks up from beneath her veil of hair and looks relieved to find that the crowd is gone.

After Officer Grady has placed Clint in the back of one of the cop cars he walks toward us slowly, as if he's approaching a frightened bird with a broken wing. "What happens now?" I ask him. "What are they going to do?"

"Protocol is they have to take her to the hospital."

"But she's fine now. See? Please don't do this." The EMTs have helped Violet to her feet and are guiding her toward the ambulance. She looks dazed, sleepy. "Did they give her something? A sedative?"

"I don't think so. Sedating a patient is a last resort. Sometimes, after an outburst, they can be pretty tired." This isn't a surprise to me. When she was younger, after Violet had her tantrums, she would crash for a good hour or two. What is a surprise to me is that Officer Grady called Violet a patient.

"Violet isn't hurt, look at her." We both watch as the EMT helps Violet into the back of the ambulance.

"Listen, Beth. You have to admit, something isn't right here. The three times I've encountered Violet, she's had some kind of episode."

"She's terrified. Of course she's not handling this well. Please, just let me take her home."

Grady presses his lips together. "Can't do it. We have to get her checked out by a doctor. Make sure she's okay and then we'll go from there."

"Listen." I lower my voice so no one else can hear. "Violet told me that Cora and Jordyn Petit had a fight at the train yard. Jordyn pushed Cora down. Have you questioned her? She made Violet promise not to say anything. Don't you think it makes more sense that Jordyn and someone else are pretending to be Joseph Wither and lured the girls to the train yard? What about

Clint?" I nod toward the police car where Clint is staring daggers at us. "He's the crazy one. Who teases a little girl like that?"

My comment about Jordyn seems to have gotten Grady's attention because he pauses to write something down in his notebook. "We'll check that out, I promise, but she has to go to the hospital. It's the rules. She was in my custody and then got loose. I'm sorry."

"Then she can come home?"

"Then I can finish asking her questions about the other night and then we'll see what happens next. Come on, you can tell her you'll meet her at the hospital."

I feel like Grady is finally starting to listen to me. We walk over to the ambulance where Violet is sitting on the loading deck. Violet looks up at me apologetically. "I'm sorry," she says, pressing her face into my midsection.

"I know, honey. The EMTs are going to take you to the hospital just to make sure you're okay."

"I don't want to go," she cries. "I'm sorry. I told them I'm sorry." She clutches me desperately.

"You can come and sit back here with her the entire way," the EMT assures me.

"Can I go tell my son to meet us at the hospital?" I ask and the EMT nods.

I tilt Violet's face so she is looking up at me. "It's okay, Vi, it's okay." I kiss her on the cheek and take a step back. "I'll be right back."

Blindly, I walk to the car where Max is waiting for me. "What's that?" he asks.

I look down at the jar tucked under my arm. I nearly forgot about it and am surprised that Officer Grady didn't ask me about it, too.

"I don't know," I say as I hand it to him. "But I think it might be important. I'm riding with Violet. Bring it with you to the hospital. I'll meet you there in a few minutes."

Dec. 21, 2017

I don't know what I'm more nervous about—giving the report to the class tomorrow or that Joseph wants to meet me in person. It's weird but I feel like we've been friends forever. I feel like I can tell him anything. Talk to him about everything.

Now that we're finished with the project I won't have an excuse to be on the computer so much anymore. I wish I had my own cell phone, then I can talk to him any time I wanted to. I have some money but there's no way that my mom will let me have one, even if I pay for it myself. Sometimes I hate her so much.

Violet is still pretty much ignoring me and Jordyn is being awful. I'm not sure how she figured out my locker combo, but I'll come walking down the hallway and find all the stuff in my locker thrown on the ground and people don't just walk around the pile. They walk on top of everything. My coat has footprints on it and someone crushed my calculator. Like I said, I'm not sure how Jordyn got my combination but I'm sure she's the one who's dumping my stuff on the ground.

I kind of wonder if Gabe might have been the one to tell Jordyn my locker combo. I only told him it that one time he helped me open my locker but he's seen me open it a ton of times since. He's been acting weird to me, too. He doesn't talk to me at lunch anymore and only says hi to me if I say it first.

I almost don't care anymore. If Jordyn and Gabe think I'm such an awful person (I know, I am), then I don't want to be friends with them. At least I have Joseph. I wake up at 1:15 in the morning on the dot and sneak down to the computer hoping to find a message from him.

I've even started wearing makeup. But only at school. My mom didn't let Kendall wear makeup until she was fourteen and even then it was only mascara and lip gloss. I stole a tube of mascara and some eyeliner out of Kendall's bathroom and put it on once I get to school. I don't know why. I guess it makes me feel older.

The other day, after I put my makeup on and was coming out of the girls' bathroom at school, Mr. Dover was there. He looked at me kind of funny and later he said, "Wow, Cora, you're looking all grown up." I have to admit that made me feel kind of good and bad at the same time. He's my teacher. He's not supposed to say things like that, right?

I asked Joseph if he liked it that I started wearing makeup and he told me that he thought I was beautiful, with or without the makeup, and that made me smile for the first time in a long time. Then he asked me what color bra I was wearing. I didn't know what to say. But then he wrote, *Just kidding*. I don't know. It's hard to tell when he's joking and when he's being serious. I know I'm doing something wrong by talking to him, but I don't want to stop.

Jordyn:
Can you believe all that gunk Cora's been wearing on her face? Her eyelashes look like tarantulas!

Violet:
Yeah—it's a little much.

Jordyn:
More than a little. She looks ridiculous. I bet she's doing it because of Gabe.

Violet:
Probably.

Jordyn:
Gabe thinks she's gross.

Violet:
They used to talk a lot.

Jordyn:
Gabe talks to everyone. Someone should really talk to Cora about her eyelashes. I can't wait until we're done with this stupid project and we don't have to pretend to like her anymore.

Jordyn:
Srsly? You don't still like her, do you?

Violet:
She's all right.

Jordyn:
Come on! She stole your phone! And you have to admit she's so annoying. Can you spend the night on Friday? Gemma and Kaley are coming over too. Gabe and Russ might come over and watch a movie with us. Just don't say anything to Cora. She'll probably start crying if she finds out she's not invited.

Jordyn:

Did the police talk to you? You didn't say anything did you?

Jordyn:

Do you know how Cora is doing? My Grandpa is making me go see her. I'm scared to face her.

Jordyn:

Why don't you answer me?

Jordyn:

I mean it, Violet. Don't say anything about us bringing the knife. We'll get in trouble.

As Thomas drives them to the hospital he fills the silence with innocuous questions and commentary. He tries to imagine the kinds of questions that Tess would ask.

He asks Jordyn about how she did on her last math test and about whether or not she decided to go out for the softball team later this spring. He asks if the art teacher ever had that baby and if it was true that the Fletcher boy had been suspended for supergluing quarters to the floor in the cafeteria.

Fine, no, yes and yes, Jordyn answers, her voice flat, expressionless.

After about five miles, Thomas runs out of questions and Jordyn leans forward and fiddles with the radio, trying to find a station that isn't distorted with static or dedicated to saving souls. She finally settles on a country-western station even though Thomas knows Jordyn normally wouldn't be caught dead listening to, as she calls it, *that twangy crap.* Jordyn's tears have dried and though her eyes are red and her skin blotchy she seems to be pulling it together.

Thomas is only half listening, anyway. He is lost in his own thoughts, his eyes fixed on the road in front of him, hands gripping tightly to the steering wheel. Though Thomas doesn't know the exact events of the other night, he is positive that Jordyn didn't do anything beyond trying to play a silly prank on her friends. He's just afraid that's not the way it may appear to others.

Earlier, when he talked to her, Mara Landry told him that Cora didn't see who attacked her and had no idea what happened. Thomas would feel better once the two girls are in the same room and he can watch them, see how they interact with one another and get a sense of what to do next.

Maybe Thomas should press Jordyn harder about what had

happened but as long as he doesn't know exactly what occurred in the train yard he can't speak against his granddaughter. It doesn't take a rocket scientist to know that the girls were up to no good. The midnight walk, the beer, the blood. God knows what the knife was for.

And there was Jordyn's quasi-confession. *It was an accident, Grandpa. Nothing bad was supposed to happen. It was just a game.* Well, Thomas knows that people go to jail or get sued for less.

As long as Jordyn sticks to her original story about leaving her friends behind at the train yard before the attack or accident, or whatever it was, then she will be fine. As long as no one finds the backpack with Jordyn's coat everything will be okay. Thomas couldn't be sure that he was able to remove all traces of blood.

By the time Thomas pulls into a parking spot at Walmart, Thomas almost has himself convinced that everything will work out for the best. They wander the aisles in search of a get-well gift for Cora and for Tess. "How about this?" Thomas asks, picking up a pillow in the shape of a tiger. "It matches your school mascot."

Jordyn wrinkles her nose. "Too babyish," she says, moving on, her eyes briefly landing on the various stuffed animals, board games and action figures that line the shelves.

"How about these?" Thomas holds up a set of painted Russian nesting dolls. He's eager to get out of here. "They're nice."

Jordyn just rolls her eyes. After ten more minutes of unenthusiastically received suggestions, Thomas finally understands that Jordyn doesn't want his help and falls silent. He watches as Jordyn picks up a lip balm laboratory kit, a manicure set with three different kinds of nail polish and a T-shirt tie-dye kit, and examines each carefully only to replace them on the shelf. She keeps returning to a bracelet-making kit that contains hundreds of tiny colorful beads and elastic cording. "This, I think." She looks to Thomas for approval.

"She'll love it," Thomas says, but what does he know about what twelve-year-olds think is cool. Jordyn shrugs, unconvinced.

The remainder of the journey to the hospital is spent in mostly nervous silence. Jordyn busies herself with arranging the bracelet-making kit inside a gift bag fluffed with sparkly tissue paper and by signing a card with the picture of a cat, paw wrapped in a bandage and a plastic cone around her neck. *I hope you get to feeling purrfect again soon.*

"Cora really likes cats," Jordyn says, sliding the sealed envelope into the bag. "Maybe I could get her a kitten," Jordyn says. "That would really cheer her up."

"I don't think Cora's mom and dad would feel quite the same way." Thomas grins. "It's a nice thought, though."

"But what if her mom and dad say it's okay?" Jordyn asks.

"I think the present you picked out will be just fine," Thomas says firmly as the hospital comes into sight and they stare up at the glass-and-steel structure.

"It's so big," Jordyn says. "Is the whole building really just for kids?" she asks.

"That's what I hear," Thomas says as he pulls into the parking garage. "I guess if I was sick this wouldn't be such a bad place to stay, huh?"

They exit the parking ramp at street level and enter through the hospital lobby. Jordyn runs ahead to the elevators and waits for her grandfather to catch up with her. Thomas takes his time. The hospital is huge and she knows he has to conserve his energy or Jordyn will have to push him out of here in a wheelchair. The elevator doors open and a woman and girl step out. The girl, about Jordyn's age, is hairless and has a wide moon face courtesy of prednisone. Jordyn gives them a shy smile and moves aside to let them pass, her eyes lingering on their retreating backs. Together they step onto the elevator and Jordyn waits until the doors close before speaking.

"Do you think she has cancer?" she asks.

"That would be my guess," Thomas says, leaning against the elevator wall.

"Do you think her mom gets to stay with her while she's here? When she gets chemo?"

"It didn't used to be that way. Parents would have to stay in guest lodging or go home when their child was in the hospital. But nowadays parents can stay right in the room with them."

Jordyn thinks about this for a moment. "If my kid was sick I would never leave them. No matter what. Even if they told me I had to."

Thomas knows that Jordyn is thinking about her own mom and dad. People who for some unearthly reason decided that fighting for custody of their daughter was too much effort. Not that Thomas was complaining. The farther away Jordyn's dad and mom stayed, the better, but he knew their absence hurt Jordyn beyond words.

"What if Cora's mom and dad are mad at me?" Jordyn asks as the elevator settles on the third floor.

"Now, why would they be mad at you?" Thomas asks lightly. "You were gone well before anything happened. They can't fault you for that." The doors open and Thomas slides his arm around his granddaughter's shoulders. "Come on now, let's go see your friend."

No matter how cheery the wall paint or the whimsical artwork that lines the corridors, the smell of hospitals hasn't changed much in thirty years, Thomas thinks. At least the newness of the children's hospital overpowers the antiseptic odor that makes Thomas woozy with memories.

When they reach Room 317 Thomas knocks on the door. After a moment Mara opens the door, steps out into the hallway and gently closes the door behind her. "Hi," she says. "It's so nice of you to come." She smiles but her eyes are wary. "Cora's nervous about people seeing her this way, Jordyn. She...she doesn't look like herself."

Thomas places his hands on Jordyn's shoulders. "She understands, don't you?" Jordyn nods solemnly. "Do you want me to come in with you, Jordy?" Thomas asks, using Tess's pet name for her.

Jordyn nods and together they move through the doorway and Thomas blinks, trying to acclimate to the dim room. A small shape comes into focus and for a moment he is transported back in time. Of course, Betsy was so much younger than Cora, but still. Seeing the heavily bandaged girl nearly swallowed up beneath a pink fleece tie blanket covered in rainbows is jarring but he smiles widely in hopes of concealing his shock. "Cora, how are you?" he asks.

"I'm okay," comes a small, hoarse voice. "Hi, Jordyn."

Thomas listens carefully. If there is any fear or anger in Cora's voice, he can't find it.

Jordyn's eyes widen at the sight of Cora's shaved skull and bandages. She seems to be holding her breath. Thomas gives her a quick poke. "Hi," she finally exhales.

Silence fills the room but Thomas resists the urge to speak and just watches. Though her face is heavily swathed in gauze, Cora doesn't appear fearful of or angry with Jordyn. It's Mara who is looking at Jordyn with suspicion, maybe even disdain.

After Betsy died, Thomas remembers Tess talking about feeling an inexplicable hatred toward toddlers, especially little girls. She would see them at the park or in a store toddling unsteadily with arms stretching upward toward their mothers, and turn away bitterly. Of course it didn't make sense, but nothing about losing a child makes sense. Eventually, Tess's aversion faded but it took time.

Perhaps Mara feels this way. An irrational anger at the girl who left, the girl who escaped the attack, or maybe Mara knows more. Thomas prods Jordyn with a finger and she takes a few steps closer to her friend.

"Does it hurt?" Jordyn asks shyly.

"Yeah." The conversation stalls. Jordyn shifts from foot to foot and Cora stares down at her bedcovers.

"Do they know who did it?" Jordyn asks bluntly.

"No, not yet," Cora says, running her fingers over the purple cast. "I don't remember much." He could be imagining it, but Thomas is sure that he sees Jordyn's shoulders relax.

"Jordyn, the gift," Thomas prompts.

Jordyn, remembering the present in her hand, holds the bag out to Cora. "We got you this. It's nothing much," she says as Cora reaches into the bag, retrieves the card and clumsily tries to open the envelope with her good hand. "Let me help," Jordyn says and takes the card. She slides a finger beneath the envelope's seal and pulls out the card.

"She looks like Skittles," Cora says, smiling weakly.

"Cora," Mara says with a hint of dismay.

Cora sets aside the card and plunges her hand into the bag through the tissue paper and pulls out the bracelet-making kit. "Thank you," she says. "I love it."

"You're welcome," Jordyn says proudly but then her grin falls away. "Your arm. You won't be able to put the beads on the string."

"That's all right," Cora consoles. "We can make them together. Do you want to sign my cast?" Using a black Sharpie marker, Jordyn signs her name across the fiberglass cast.

"When we're back at school, I can help carry your books and stuff if you want," Jordyn offers as the two girls examine the box of beads while Thomas and Mara look on.

"That would be great." Cora gives a half smile and then winces at the pain.

"Have you talked to Violet yet?" Jordyn asks, picking at the tape that seals the box.

"No, not yet," Cora says, a twinge of sadness in her words. "Have you?"

"I haven't, either," Jordyn says, pulling out a plastic bag filled with jewel-colored beads. "What colors do you like?" she asks.

"The purple ones. To match my cast. Which colors do you want yours to be?"

"Blue, I think," Jordyn says and the two busy themselves with sorting the beads into piles.

Thomas breathes an inward sigh of relief. Surely if Cora blamed Jordyn for the attack in the train yard, then she wouldn't suggest plans to make bracelets together.

"What is *she* doing here?" a shrill voice comes from the doorway. Jordyn and Cora freeze in place and stare in surprise at the teenage girl who has swept into the room, face stormy with anger. Thomas's moment of relief is instantly replaced with dread.

"Kendall," Mara says sharply. "That's rude."

"She's rude!" Kendall snaps back. "She's been awful to Cora the last few months.

"How can you even show your face here?" Kendall asks Jordyn, who looks to her grandfather for help. Thomas doesn't know what to say.

"It's okay," Cora says in a small voice.

"It's not," Kendall shoots back. "It's not okay! She made you cry every day for weeks. And don't tell me that's not true. I heard you! She's not your friend, Cora."

"Kendall, go outside," Mara says in a shaky voice. "Right now."

"You are so gullible," Kendall persists. "You let people walk all over you. For once stand up for yourself. And you—" She turns to Jordyn.

"Jordyn, let's go," Thomas interrupts, finally able to speak. Jordyn rises from her seat, murmurs goodbye to Cora and skirts past Kendall.

"Stay away from my sister!" Kendall calls after them as they rush from the room past a tall woman lingering in the doorway.

In silence Thomas and Jordyn move through the hallways, Jordyn blinking back tears, Thomas biting his tongue. Thomas waits until they are in the truck before he speaks. "What did you do to her?" he asks Jordyn. "What did you do to that little girl?"

I found Cora sitting up in her hospital bed watching television. Mara told me she planned on being away from Cora's room during our morning meeting so we could have some privacy. I knew this was hard for her and understandably so, but I convinced her that this time to talk freely would be good for Cora.

She was still connected to an IV and her head was swathed in bandages. A half-eaten breakfast tray sat in front of her. I was glad to see she had at least eaten something. Next to the tray there were two bracelets made out of beads and another in purple hues on Cora's wrist. "Those are pretty," I said, coming to her side. "Did someone make them for you?"

"My friend Jordyn came. She brought a kit and we started to make a few." Cora's speech was still a bit slurred from her injuries but the swelling in her lips had gone down.

"I saw," I said. "I looked in but didn't want to interrupt your visit. I also saw your sister came in. She seemed very upset at your friend."

"I don't want to talk about that," Cora said flatly, instantly becoming guarded.

"Okay," I said, picking up one of the bracelets designed in shades of blue: turquoise and navy. "These are pretty. Who did you make them for?"

She held up her wrist. "This one was for me, of course, and we made one for Jordyn that looks just like mine. And that one—" she nodded toward the one I'm holding "—is for my sister."

"May I sit?" I asked.

"Sure," Cora said and I pulled a chair next to her bedside. "What about this one?" I pointed to the remaining bracelet on the tray. She shrugged. "What about your friend Violet? Did you make one for her?"

Cora poked at her oatmeal, cooled now to a gray paste, with her spoon and didn't say anything.

"How is Violet?" I asked, watching her face carefully.

Again Cora shrugged. "I don't know. I haven't talked to her."

"Ah," I said. "She hasn't called or visited you yet."

"I don't have a cell phone so she couldn't call me, anyway, but she hasn't come to visit." She was trying to act indifferent but the visible part of her face told a different story.

"Maybe her mom won't let her. The two of you had something very traumatic happen to you. Sometimes people don't quite know what to say or how to act." Cora remained silent. "Have you thought about calling Violet yourself?"

"My mom says that Violet should be the one to call me. Not the other way around. But yeah, I thought about it."

"How does that make you feel?" I asked the age-old question.

"Sad, I guess. Lonely. I thought we were best friends."

"What about other kids from your school? Have you heard from any of them?"

"Just Jordyn. No one else." Cora shook her head and then winced and touched her lips gingerly.

"Are you in much pain? Do you want me to call the nurse?"

"No, that's okay. My stomach hurts only when I get up. My eye and mouth hurts, but my mom says that once my mouth heals they'll fix my teeth. I'll get fake ones. Here and here." She opened her mouth in a gap-toothed grimace.

"I bet you're looking forward to that."

"Yeah, but I don't like going to the dentist," she said.

"Me, either." After all that Cora has been through, I thought, the terror and the pain, the dentist was the least of her worries. "How have you been sleeping, Cora? Are you getting some rest?" It was hard to tell by looking at her because the exposed portion of her face was storm-cloud purple.

"You can't tell anyone what I say to you, right? You're my doctor so it's a secret?"

"Some secrets I can keep," I said. "Like what you're feeling. What I can't keep is if you are thinking about hurting yourself or someone else or if you are taking illegal drugs."

Cora wrinkled her nose. "No way."

"And I promise you that I will not share anything you tell me without letting you know first," I told her. "You can talk to me about anything, Cora. I'm here to help you."

Cora thought about that for a minute. "Okay. I do sleep better when my mom's here but it makes me feel bad, too. I'm almost twelve. I should be able to fall asleep without my mom in the room."

"You had a scary thing happen to you. It's understandable to want your mom nearby."

"Yeah, I guess. But when she's here, she just looks at me all sad. Like I'm going to die or something. I guess she's scared, too. She keeps asking me what happened and who did it and what did I see. It just makes my head all muddled, so sometimes I pretend to be asleep. Are you going to ask me about what happened the other night?" She rubbed her fingers across her cast where a scattering of signatures decorated the fiberglass.

"Not if you don't want me to." I was hoping that as I got to know Cora, she'd open up to me about what she remembered. If anything. "You've got a lot of signatures there," I observed.

"Mostly the nurses." She pointed to them. "And this one is the doctor who did my face. And this is Jordyn's. She's my friend who brought me the bracelet kit. And her grandpa signed, too."

"Tell me about Jordyn," I said.

"She's okay," Cora said, but begrudgingly. "She's kind of hard to figure out. One minute she's really nice and then all of a sudden she's acting like she hates you."

"Sounds confusing," I mused.

"It is," Cora said emphatically. "Jordyn, Violet and I used to be best friends but we got in a fight right before Christmas and

I thought she'd never talk to me again. But then last week she all of a sudden started talking to me again. I think it was because I told her I was sorry about her grandma getting hurt. She fell and broke her hip and is in the hospital. Anyway, Jordyn came over and it was like things were like they used to be."

"And there's your sister's name and your mom's. How about your dad? Did he sign it?" I thought of Jim Landry and the anger that seemed to rise up off him in waves.

"Not yet. But he will. He's just pretty mad at me right now."

"About what?" I kept my voice neutral, conversational.

"We snuck out the other night. I knew we shouldn't have done it, but we did. I'm not supposed to be out running around that late at night."

"Your dad told you he was mad at you?" I asked.

"He didn't have to. He didn't say anything. That's how I know he's mad. He doesn't say anything, just sits there with his arms crossed." Cora demonstrated by clumsily folding her own arms across her chest.

"Sometimes scared looks a lot like angry, you know."

"My dad isn't scared of anything."

"You might be surprised," I offered. "You could talk to him about it."

"Maybe," Cora said unconvincingly and I could tell I was edging into sensitive territory and I didn't want to push Cora too soon. Otherwise, she might not confide in me at all.

"Did you decide which notebook you'd like to write in?" I asked, nodding toward the stack of spiral-bound notebooks sitting on a chair in the corner of the room.

"I think the one with the polar bears," Cora said. "I used to have my own journal. I wrote in it all the time."

"Oh, yeah? I keep a journal, too," I told her.

"Do you write about me?" she asked, narrowing her eyes with worry.

"It's not that kind of journal," I assured her. "It's my personal journal. I write about how I feel about things, about the books I'm reading. I also write about when I have disagreements or problems with people I care about. It helps me sort through my thoughts. What kinds of things do you write about?" Cora looked at me with suspicion. "Maybe you can ask your mom or sister to bring you your journal so you can write while you're here."

"I lost it," she said with worry. "I hope no one finds it."

"Maybe it will show up. In the meantime, you can write in this one." I retrieved the notebook from the corner of the room and set it on the table next to her. "You picked the one your sister suggested. How old is Kendall? Fourteen? Fifteen?"

"Fifteen." Cora rolled her eyes.

"How do you two get along?"

Cora shrugged. "Okay, I guess. Usually she just ignores me. Most of the time she hangs out with her friend Emery. Sometimes she makes fun of me. But once in a while she's nice and we'll talk."

"What kinds of things do you talk about?" I asked. I was fishing to see if Cora had an ally in Kendall.

"Nothing, really. School sometimes," Cora said with resignation. "She thinks I'm a pest. But then all of a sudden she sticks up for me like she did earlier."

"It can be hard to figure out big sisters sometimes," I said. "But from what I can see, Kendall cares very much about you."

"That's because I almost died," Cora said matter-of-factly, picking up the notebook and flipping through the empty pages. "She's being super nice and it is so weird. Everyone is being really nice. Even Jordyn. It's weird."

For the next thirty minutes, Cora and I chatted. Though I tried to steer our conversation toward the night at the train yard and her relationships, Cora revealed little. After a while, she fell silent and I watched as she doodled in her new journal, writing random words on the page in rounded cursive. Dotting each *i* and *j* with a small heart.

It was sad knowing that only one of Cora's friends made the trip to the hospital to visit her and even that seemed a bit forced. From my spot in the doorway, I was able to somewhat covertly watch the interactions: the grandfather nudging the girl toward Cora, prompting her to give Cora the present. Mara Landry's clenched fists contrasted by her smooth, emotionless face. The friend's repulsed expression upon first seeing Cora's skull with its railroad track of staples. Kendall's extreme reaction to seeing Cora's friend there. And there was something else, too. Guilt, perhaps regret. I wasn't sure.

I was just getting ready to wrap things up when Cora asked, "Do you believe in ghosts?"

This seemed like such a simple question, but I knew I had to answer thoughtfully, carefully. I had a sense that for the first time she was getting ready to talk to me about Joseph Wither. "What kind of ghosts?" I asked.

Cora started lightly sketching in her journal. A child's drawing of a ghost covered in a sheet, black circles for eyes. "The ones that talk to you," she said, adding a sky full of stars.

"I've never had a ghost talk to me," I answered. "How about you? Do ghosts talk to you?" I asked.

She shrugged. "When I was little I thought ghosts looked like this." She tapped on the picture she had drawn. "I thought there was a ghost who hid in the vent in my bedroom. When the cold or hot air came through it, I thought it was the ghost whispering to me."

"What did the ghost say?" I asked, intrigued.

"Nothing special, really. My name mostly. Someone breathing, scratching sometimes." Cora paused in her drawing and peeked up at me to gauge my reaction.

"That must have been frightening," I offered.

"No, not really. They didn't scare me," she said lightly. "They were friendly. I called them Bebe and Billy. My dad got sick of me talking about them so I stopped."

It isn't uncommon in young children to have imaginary friends so this revelation didn't surprise me. "How about now?" I asked, hoping we were getting to Joseph Wither.

"Do you think ghosts can talk to you through the computer?" Cora asked as she flipped to a new page in the notebook and started drawing the outline of a cat.

Here we were. I needed to be very careful. If Cora revealed to me that someone, perhaps a predator, had been communicating with her online, I would have to share the information with law enforcement. A delicate dance we do in the mental health world. Honoring patient-doctor privilege and keeping our patients safe from harm.

"Has someone been talking to you online, Cora, and telling you that he's a ghost?" I asked.

Cora reached for a marker and colored the cat's eyes green. "His name is Joseph and he lived a long time ago," she said.

"What else does he tell you?" I asked gently, not wanting to push too hard.

Instead of answering, Cora wrote *Skittles* above the picture of the cat and then *For Dr. G. from Cora* at the bottom. She tore the sheet from the notebook and handed it to me.

"This must be your cat," I said. "She's pretty."

"Not that damn cat again," Jim Landry said from the doorway. "Cora, enough's enough."

"We brought ice cream," Mara said brightly, coming in behind her husband and holding up two shakes. "Chocolate or strawberry. You pick." Kendall shuffled in, carrying her own shake. She looked exhausted.

"We'll talk more later," I told Cora, reluctant to end our conversation. "Thank you for the picture and enjoy your ice cream."

I said goodbye to the Landrys and went directly to my office to record everything I could remember about my conversation with Cora. I remember thinking that I should probably call the police. But I didn't. I wanted more information. I needed more time to talk to Cora in order to put together the pieces of the puzzle.

Dec. 22, 2017

I want to die. The presentation was a disaster. I am so stupid. The movie was fine. Everyone clapped and Mr. Dover said we did an amazing job. The problems started during the question and answer part of the presentation and Bailey asked how many girls were supposedly killed by Wither and how many disappeared because of him.

I went back to my desk and pulled the yearbook from beneath a pile of my books and opened it to the page with Rachel Farmer's picture. I'm not sure why I brought it up. I told Violet and Jordyn I wouldn't but I did. I told everyone that most of what we read was that there were six girls who disappeared. But there were really seven because Rachel ran away with Joseph Wither back in 1991.

I kept rambling on and on—I don't even know exactly what I said. Something about how Wither didn't actually kill anyone, that the girls chose to go with him. That they *wanted* to be with him and were willing to leave their families and friends to go with him. Finally, I realized that no one was looking at me anymore and everyone was looking at Kaley Martin, who was crying at her desk in the back of the room.

"Shut up!" Jordyn said and poked me on the arm.

I stopped talking and Kaley got up and ran out of the room. Mr. Dover sent Violet to go check on her and said that Jordyn and I could sit down.

Another group got up and started their presentation but I wasn't listening because I was so confused. Gabe leaned forward in his seat and whispered in my ear, "Way to go, Einstein. Kaley's aunt was Rachel Farmer."

Then Violet came back and said that Kaley wouldn't come out of the bathroom so Mr. Dover stepped out into the hall and didn't come back for like ten minutes. Once he left, Jordyn started to yell at me. "I thought we told you not to include the yearbook in the presentation!"

I told her I was sorry, that I didn't know, but she wouldn't listen. She yanked the yearbook off my desk. "I bet you wrote this," she said, shoving the page in my face. I told her no, that I would never do that, but I could tell she didn't believe me. I looked at Violet but she just stared down at her desk.

Then someone from the back of the room said, "Everyone knows about Kaley's aunt. She and Kaley's mom were twins. She ran away when she was a teenager and they never heard from her again. They do a thing at church in memory of her every year."

"You are so stupid," Jordyn said. "You probably think Wither is real."

And I said it out loud. I knew I shouldn't have. I shouted, "He is real. He is! He told me so!" And then everyone laughed and laughed. Even Gabe. Even Violet.

"Shut up!" I yelled at Jordyn. "Shut up! Shut up! Everyone thinks you're a bitch. Even Gabe says so!"

"Well, everyone knows you're crazy and a thief!" Jordyn yelled. Then I slapped her. Right across the face. The room went quiet. And I realized I made a really big mistake. Four big mistakes. I told Jordyn to shut up, told everyone that the boy Jordyn likes called her a bitch, told the world I was talking to an urban legend and I slapped the most popular girl in my class. I'm dead.

I thought for sure that the minute Mr. Dover came back in the room, Jordyn would tell on me. But she didn't. She just sat down in her desk and opened up her social studies book. I almost wish she had told on me, then I would have gotten in trouble and it would be over. Now I have to wait and see what Jordyn is going to do.

When Mr. Dover came back in the room, Kaley wasn't with him. He just said, "Don't worry, folks. She's fine." I don't know how I made it through the rest of class. I felt so sick.

After the bell rang and everyone left, Mr. Dover asked me to stay after. That's when I started to cry. "I'm sorry," I said. "I really didn't know."

"Of course you didn't," Mr. Dover said. "You don't have a mean bone in your body, Cora." Then he hugged me for a long time until I stopped crying. When I finally stopped blubbering, I asked him what I should do.

"I've found saying sorry works most of the time," he said, handing me a tissue from the box on his desk. "Especially if you truly feel bad and it's obvious you do. It will all blow over."

Well, it didn't blow over. At lunch I tried to sit down next to Jordyn so I could tell her sorry, but she moved over so I couldn't. I looked at Violet for help but she pretended she didn't notice and kept right on eating her peanut butter sandwich. Everyone else gave me dirty looks and scooted over so I couldn't sit next to them, either.

I looked around for Mrs. Morris, knowing that she would find me a place to sit, but she was busy yelling at a table of boys who were smashing their ketchup packets. I ended up just leaving the cafeteria and went to Mr. Dover's room instead and asked him if I could sit there until the lunch period was over. He said sure and corrected papers while I tried not to cry.

The rest of the day was just as bad. Everyone whispered and gave me dirty looks when I walked by. Even the teachers looked at me funny. The worst part was I didn't get a chance to apologize to Kaley. She must have gone to the nurse's office or something because I didn't see her the rest of the day.

What made it even worse was that now everyone knows I think Joseph is real. It's so embarrassing.

I tried to call Violet and Jordyn a million times but they won't answer their phones so now it's holiday break and everyone hates me and I don't have anyone to hang out with. My mom keeps asking me what's wrong but I can't tell her. She'd be so disappointed. Even Kendall noticed and tried to cheer me up by inviting me to watch Christmas movies with her and Emery.

I haven't been back on DarkestDoor, either. I want to be mad at Wither. I mean, he kind of made me add Rachel Farmer to my presentation. I think I should probably just forget about him. This is going to be the worst Christmas ever.

Once we arrive at the hospital, a nurse is there to greet us. She explains that the doctor will check Violet over and then I can come back to be with her. I give Violet another kiss and promise I'll see her soon.

The nurse directs me to the emergency waiting room where a young woman is sitting behind the counter and she is in no rush to look up from her desk to acknowledge me. I tap on the glass partition and with infuriating slowness she lifts her heavily mascaraed eyes. "Can I help you?"

"Yes, my daughter was just brought in by ambulance." I look around for any sign of Max. He hasn't arrived yet.

"Your name?"

"Beth Crow and my daughter's name is Violet."

"Insurance card."

"We were just here the other day. Can I just go in back and see that she's okay?" I'm begging now and it isn't fazing this woman. I guess she's used to seeing people on their very worst days and has to stay unemotional and businesslike. I still hate her.

"The doctor will let us know when you can go back and see her. Insurance card, please."

"I don't have insurance," I say, feeling my face go hot. At my office supply job in Algodon I had decent insurance but the convenience store didn't offer family coverage and I sure as hell didn't make enough to pay the premiums. I know the hospital bill will probably bankrupt me but what am I supposed to do?

The woman sighs as if she is just tolerating me. "Please take a seat and I'll let you know as soon as information is available."

Instead of sitting, I pace. I have no idea what's been going on with Violet but somehow she has gone from being a victim to being hauled away in an ambulance.

Once I know that Violet is okay, I plan on raising hell with Officer Grady. There must be policies and procedures on how to question child witnesses. Violet could have been killed by a maniac. As far as I'm concerned, the police department can foot the bill for this emergency room visit.

Finally, Max comes through the entrance carrying the glass jar filled with slips of paper. "Is she okay?" he asks. "Have you seen her?"

"No, I haven't heard anything yet. This is ridiculous. She isn't hurt, she's scared. We may as well sit down until they call us."

We sit and Max reaches his hand inside the narrow opening and pulls out a piece of paper, unfolds the slip and begins to read.

"I can't wait for Friday! What should I bring with me? I hope we go somewhere warm. I'm tired of the cold."

"Weird," Max says, tilting the paper so I can look at it. The handwriting is large and embellished with loops and hearts and exclamation points. A young girl's writing but not Violet's, thank goodness. He pulls out a handful of slips and begins to read one after the other.

"I think my mom will miss me but I don't know about my dad. He hardly knows I'm here, anyway. My sister won't care at all. I guess I should be sadder, but I'm not. Do I need to bring a coat? What about food?

"I think I'll bring my journal. That way I can write about our trip. I wish I could bring my cat. Do I need to bring money? I have about two hundred dollars saved up.

"It sounds like whoever wrote these was planning on running away," Max says as he scans the final scraps of paper.

"Are they all written by the same person?" I ask.

Max nods his head. "It looks like it. What do you think is going on?"

I think about what Violet said about Cora communicating with someone claiming to be Joseph Wither online. "We'll give the jar to Officer Grady. He'll get to the bottom of it."

"Why is Violet acting so crazy?" Max asks. "What's wrong with her?"

"I don't know," I admit. "But she's scared. Terrified. She keeps going on and on about Joseph Wither." I just can't believe that Violet thinks he's real. She stopped believing in Santa Claus and the tooth fairy in second grade.

Max shrugs. "I don't get it, either, but there are kids in my class who swear that Ouija boards work and that they can summon evil spirits. Maybe she just got caught up in it all."

"Maybe," I say, but I'm not buying it. "At any rate, someone attacked Cora and Jordyn Petit knows more than she is letting on." My head is pounding and I search through my purse for some aspirin.

"This is all Officer Grady's fault," I say, wrenching the lid off the aspirin bottle. I tap out two capsules and swallow the pills dry. "He should be out looking for this guy and not harassing a little girl."

"You got to admit that Violet has been acting kind of weird lately."

"How? In what way?" I ask him, genuinely surprised.

"It's embarrassing," Max says, trying to act like the tough older brother but I can tell he is worried about Violet. "I don't know, she's just weird. She's always drawing in her sketchbook and she and her equally freaky friends have been hanging around the train yard all the time. You know who hangs around the train yard? Tweakers and meth heads."

The Primrose Sugar boxcar must be their secret hiding spot. I'm guessing that most of the older teens wouldn't be able to fit through the door. I barely made it inside. It would be a spot where they could go and be left alone.

"And you didn't feel the need to tell me that your twelve-year-old sister was spending time in places like that? Really, Max?" I'm pissed. Max has done some stupid things but I can't believe he wouldn't tell me about this.

"When I saw them I told her that she better go home and never come back. She said that they had been there tons of times, said they were just doing research for their school project and that they wouldn't come back. Sorry for believing her," he says sarcastically.

"Which leads to my next question. What were you doing at the train yard?" I ask, not really wanting to know the answer.

"Skateboarding," he says. I raise my eyebrow and shake my head. Max laughs. "I promise. We were just skateboarding. The train yard is the closest thing to a skate park around here. Don't worry, Mom, I'm not stupid enough to do drugs."

I want to believe him but he hasn't had the best track record when it comes to honesty. Besides that, I don't trust Clint as far as I can throw him. I decide this isn't the time to argue.

All those afternoons I thought that Violet was at Cora's or Jordyn's house, were they really at the train yard? It surprises me. I thought the Landry house would be the safest place in all of Pitch. Cora's mom is definitely what people would call a helicopter mom. Violet said that Cora doesn't have a cell phone and is only allowed on the computer to do schoolwork. Mara has never let Cora come to our house and all along it should have been the other way around. Why didn't Mara know where the girls were spending their time? How could she let them sneak out in the middle of the night?

The receptionist, followed by a nurse, finally comes out from the treatment area and I pop up from my seat. "Ms. Crow," the nurse says. "Come on back."

"Can my son come, too?" I ask.

"Of course." The nurse leads us back into the treatment area but instead of taking us to one of the examination rooms she opens the door to a small room, empty except for three chairs and a side table with an open box of tissues atop it.

This must be the spot where families get the bad news from

the doctor. The news that their loved one hasn't survived the car accident, the heart attack, the stroke. I don't want to go in.

"Come on in and take a seat," the nurse invites with a smile that I take as a good sign. "The doctor will be right in to talk to you." Max and I sit down and wait and after a few minutes I see Officer Grady in the hallway talking to a tall, striking woman dressed in a skirt, heels and white doctor's coat.

"What do you think is going on?" Max asks.

"I have no idea," I say and we stand as Officer Grady and the woman approach.

"Beth, Max," Officer Grady says. He's got his cop face on.

"Ms. Crow? I'm Dr. Gideon." She reaches out to shake my hand, then Max's. Dr. Gideon appears to be in her midforties and is perfectly put together. Immediately I'm intimidated.

"What kind of doctor?" Max asks.

"Of psychiatry," Dr. Gideon says.

I look up at Officer Grady lurking in the doorway. "What's going on?" I ask eagerly. "Where's Violet?"

"A nurse is with Violet right now. She's calm," Dr. Gideon says. "Please take a seat."

"I don't want to sit. Tell me what's going on," I snap, surprising even myself with my tone.

"Beth," Officer Grady says mildly. "We're all here to help Violet."

"It doesn't feel that way." I sink back into my chair and Dr. Gideon sits across from me. Max stands in a corner, watching, biting his lip nervously.

"We are in the process of assessing Violet right now and I think it would be a good idea for her to stay with us overnight, so we can do a thorough evaluation."

"For what?" I ask in disbelief. "I don't understand. The EMTs thought she would be just fine."

"I asked for the evaluation," Officer Grady says from the doorway. "I'm concerned about Violet. She ran away from the house, she was hiding in a boxcar, Beth, and then she tried to run away again. She's clearly afraid of something."

"Of course," I say. "Of course she's afraid. Someone tried to kill her best friend. Could have killed her." I pick up my purse from where I set it on the floor next to me and stand. "I'd like to take my daughter and go now."

"Ms. Crow." Dr. Gideon leans forward in her chair. "At the moment Violet truly believes that someone is after her. She says it's Joseph Wither coming back from the dead. She knows quite a bit about his history."

"That damn project," I say. "But it doesn't make sense that Violet would believe he's real," I protest. "Some pervert has been contacting the girls pretending to be Joseph Wither. She told me. He lured them to the train yard. Of course she thinks he's real because *he* made sure of it."

"That could be the case," Dr. Gideon says. "But nevertheless, she's scared. I'd like to give her some time to work through what really might have happened at the train yard."

Realization washes over me. "You don't think that someone pretending to be Joseph Wither attacked Cora, do you? You think that Violet did it? You think that Violet stabbed her and is blaming it on Joseph Wither."

"No way," I hear Max say from the corner. "No way."

"Beth, there were only five sets of footprints in the dirt next to where Cora was found. Cora's, the woman who found her, Violet's." Officer Grady sits in the third empty chair. I feel penned in. When I had the chance I should have sold every last possession we owned to get the car fixed so we could go back home to Algodon.

"Who do the other two sets belong to?" I ask weakly.

"We don't know for sure," Officer Grady says. "But one set is small, consistent with a child's. The other a bit bigger. Could belong to an adult or a larger child."

"Jordyn," I murmur. "Jordyn Petit was there, too. Violet said that Jordyn Petit and Cora were arguing and Jordyn knocked her down. Violet said that Cora fell against the tracks and hurt her arm. Doesn't it make sense that if Jordyn pushed Cora she could have been the one to stab her, too?"

"Mom," Max says. "What about the jar? I left it in the waiting room."

"What jar?" Grady asks.

"Go get it," I tell Max. To Grady and Dr. Gideon I say, "I don't want Violet talking to anyone without a lawyer."

Dr. Gideon clears her throat. "My main concern is Violet. I don't work for the police. My job is to find out what psychologically and medically might be going on with her. I want to keep her overnight, see how she does, and then we'll go from there."

"What if I say no," I ask. A tear escapes and rolls down my cheek and I quickly wipe it away.

"You can't say no," Officer Grady says kindly but in a way I know he means business. "Believe me, the Pitch jail is the last place you want Violet. This is where you want her to be right now. Beth, she needs help."

The name of this god-awful town alone should have been enough of an omen. I want to run from this room, grab Violet and Max and get back in the car and drive as far away from here as I can.

JW44:
WHERE HAVE YOU BEEN, CORA? I'VE BEEN CHECKING BACK HERE EVERY DAY. IS EVERYTHING OKAY?

Corareef12:
No. Everything is NOT okay. Everyone hates me.

JW44:
WHY? WHAT HAPPENED? HOW DID YOUR PRESENTATION GO?

Corareef12:
It was bad. You said I should include Rachel Farmer in the presentation but that was completely screwed up! She was the aunt of a classmate of mine and all it did was make her cry. Then I freaked out and told the entire class that you were real! That you and I talked. They think I'm crazy. Then I slapped Jordyn. Everyone hates me.

JW44:
YOU SHOULDN'T HAVE DONE THAT. WE WERE SUPPOSED TO BE A SECRET.

Corareef12:
I know! I'm sorry. What should I do?

JW44:
THE FIRST THING YOU NEED TO DO IS TO TELL PEOPLE YOU WERE JUST JOKING ABOUT TALKING TO ME. WE COULD BOTH GET IN BIG TROUBLE. HAVE YOU TOLD ANYONE ABOUT THIS WEBSITE? THAT WE'VE BEEN SENDING MESSAGES? HAVE YOU SHOWN ANYONE THE EMAILS?

Corareef12:
I haven't shown anyone. I promise.

JW44:
GOOD. BECAUSE IF YOU HAVE, WE WOULDN'T BE ABLE TO TALK ANYMORE. I'D HAVE TO GO AWAY FOREVER. DO YOU UNDER-STAND?

Corareef12:
I understand. I promise. I'll never tell anyone. Please don't go.

JW44:
FORGET ABOUT JORDYN AND VIOLET—THEY'RE OBVIOUSLY NOT TRUE FRIENDS.

Corareef12:
Maybe. But they were the only friends I had and I miss them.

JW44:
I'M YOUR FRIEND, CORA. YOUR ONLY FRIEND. DON'T FORGET THAT. I'M ALWAYS HERE FOR YOU.

Jan. 7, 2018

I went to school today ready to tell everyone that I was just joking about the whole Joseph Wither thing. That I was trying to be funny and it obviously wasn't. I was going to say that I was sorry for slapping Jordyn, that I was just having a really bad day.

At lunch I sat with Violet knowing that she, at least, wouldn't make me move. I sat down next to her and she gave me half a smile. It wasn't much, but it was better than nothing. I unwrapped my sandwich but couldn't eat it. I kept saying to myself, *Tell them you were joking about Wither, tell them you were joking about Wither.* But before I got the chance, Jordyn started talking.

"Did you hear about Cora Landry?" Jordyn asked.

"No, what happened?" Gemma asked in this fakey voice.

"She moved away. Poof! Just up and disappeared." Jordyn made her eyes wide and frowned, like she was sad. I felt like throwing up.

"I wondered why I hadn't seen her around in a while," Kaley said like some big mystery had been solved. "Where'd she move to?" I tried not to cry.

"Probably somewhere with Joseph Wither, you know, because he's real," Jordyn said. No one was looking at me. "What about you, Violet?" Jordyn asked. Tears were plopping onto my sandwich, making the bread soggy. "Have you seen Cora lately?"

I held my breath.

Violet looked down at her tray. "No, I haven't seen her."

No one talks to me. No one looks at me. Even Violet. It's like I'm a ghost.

"I swear, I didn't do anything to Cora," Jordyn tells Thomas again after they visit Tess in the skilled care facility. It was a quick visit. Thomas had planned on telling Tess about what happened to Cora at the train yard, but after the upsetting meeting with Cora and her family, Thomas couldn't bring himself to say anything. Tess didn't seem to notice anything was amiss. She chatted enough for all of them.

Jordyn buckles herself into her seat. "We were both mad at each other for a while, but we made up. I don't know why her sister said all those mean things."

Thomas thinks about this. It's true that kids argue all the time. Get in little spats here and there. Maybe Cora's sister was just being emotional, and rightly so. Their family had been through a lot. And wouldn't Cora's mom have refused to allow them to visit if Jordyn had treated Cora badly? But then there was the prank that Jordyn admitted to wanting to play on Cora. He doesn't know what to believe anymore. Besides, Cora seemed genuinely happy to see Jordyn. If Jordyn had been as awful as Kendall said, would she have acted that way?

"I think Cora was really glad you came," Thomas says as he pulls out of the parking lot.

"Yeah," Jordyn says but there is no conviction in her voice, only sadness.

"What is it?" Thomas pulls his eyes away from the road to look at Jordyn. "I think Cora really likes the gift you gave her, don't you?"

"Yeah, I guess." Jordyn moves to turn on the radio and Thomas puts his hand over hers just before it reaches the controls.

"Tell me," he insists.

"It's just that...her face..." Jordyn's eyes brim with tears and

Thomas feels a sense of relief. Finally, Jordyn is expressing some real empathy for her friend.

"It looks bad now, but once it heals I'm sure she'll look like herself again," Thomas says. "Try not to worry about that. The hospital has really good doctors."

"I wish..." Jordyn begins. "I wish we never went out the other night. I wish we hadn't brought that stupid knife. I wish we had just stayed at Cora's."

"I know, honey," Thomas says and pats Jordyn's leg. "You learned a hard lesson. Just remember that for the next time you go on an overnight."

"Grandma is probably never going to let me spend the night at anyone's house ever again." Jordyn groans.

"You're probably right," Thomas says, but it's halfhearted and filled with more affection than anger.

The remainder of their drive back to Pitch is silent and as they arrive home it's to find a police car parked outside the house. It's not an unusual sight. The police often park on Main, the busiest street in town. Thomas pulls the truck into the driveway and as they get out the officer that first interviewed Jordyn steps from her cruiser and strides toward them.

An uneasy feeling settles in Thomas's chest. "Hello," he greets Officer Wilson with suspicion. "Do you have a few more questions for Jordyn?"

"Actually, it's more than that, Mr. Petit," she says, then pauses as if trying to find just the right words to say next.

"What's going on?" Thomas asks. This time more forcefully, his mind spinning with questions.

Jordyn stands close to Thomas and remains silent.

Something is wrong, Thomas tells himself. "We just came from the hospital. Saw Cora. Jordyn and Cora had a nice visit, didn't you, Jordyn?" Jordyn nods.

Officer Wilson shifts uncomfortably from foot to foot. "I'm afraid I'm here to bring Jordyn into the station."

"For more questioning?" Thomas asks. "That's no problem. Jordyn's happy to answer any more questions you have. We all want to find out who did this."

"I'm sure that's true," Officer Wilson says. Her voice is cold, which concerns Thomas even more than the gun in her holster. "I'm here to arrest Jordyn for the attack on Cora Landry."

"What?" Thomas laughs. A bark of disbelief. Jordyn's eyes flick between the two of them. She does not understand what is happening.

"We have a witness who says they saw Jordyn push Cora down at the train yard as well as some other evidence," Officer Wilson says.

Thomas looks at his granddaughter, who strangely is not protesting the claim. "There has to be some kind of mistake," he says.

"I'm afraid it's not a mistake. I have a warrant to search your home." Officer Wilson hands Thomas a piece of paper.

Thomas thinks of the book bag shoved up into the fireplace. They can't know about that, he tells himself. "Jordyn, go inside." Thomas points toward the house. "Right now."

"Come here, Jordyn," Officer Wilson says, her voice steely. Jordyn looks between Officer Wilson and her grandfather, uncertain as to what to do.

"Who is this witness?" Thomas asks. "Jordyn already told you everything she knows. She wouldn't hurt anyone."

"We've got some more evidence that we need to sort through and in the meantime Jordyn needs to come with me," Officer Wilson says, reaching into her pocket and pulling out her phone.

"You're calling for backup?" Thomas asks, stepping forward. "Seriously?"

"Relax, Mr. Petit. I'm not going to call for backup unless you do something stupid. I want to show you something." She taps her phone and turns the screen so Thomas can view it.

"Jesus Christ," Thomas murmurs as he rubs a hand across his face. "Jesus Christ, Jordyn."

"What?" Jordyn asks in a soft voice and Officer Wilson tilts the phone so Jordyn can see.

It's a photo of the three girls standing in front of what appears to be a boxcar scribbled with graffiti. It's dark out and the three girls are smiling, mugging for the selfie that Violet Crow is taking. But it's what is in Jordyn's hands that chills Thomas to the bone. Jordyn, wearing the light blue fleece jacket that had the blood on the sleeve, is standing behind her two friends. In one hand is the strap of Jordyn's book bag and in her other, poised above Cora's head, is a knife. She has a mischievous grin on her face.

"Someone grabbed the shot from Snapchat," Officer Wilson says, putting the phone back in her pocket. "Now you can see why we need to bring Jordyn to the station."

"Jordyn?" Thomas's voice cracks. "You said you left before you got to the train yard."

"No," Jordyn says, shaking her head. "I didn't. I didn't do it, I promise. Cora pushed me first. I just pushed her back. I swear I didn't stab her."

"I believe you," Thomas says but there's no conviction behind his voice. "Don't worry, we'll get it all straightened out."

Another police car pulls up and a male officer steps from the vehicle but keeps his distance. "Jordyn Petit," Officer Wilson says, "you are being arrested for the attempted murder of Cora Elizabeth Landry."

Thomas's chest constricts with fear. "What are you doing?" he asks.

"You have the right to remain silent. Anything you say can and will be used in a court of law," Wilson continues.

"Hey," Thomas says, trying to step in between Jordyn and the officer but Wilson stops him with an icy look.

"Grandpa?" Jordyn cries out as Officer Wilson guides her by the elbow toward the police car. "Grandpa, I don't want to go."

"You have the right to an attorney. If you cannot afford an attorney, one will be provided for you. Do you understand the rights I have just read to you?"

"No!" Jordyn whimpers. "Grandpa, don't let her take me. Please."

"Mr. Petit," Officer Wilson warns.

"Jordyn, you go with Officer Wilson and I'll meet you there." Thomas tries to keep his voice steady. "But do not answer any questions, do you hear me? I'm going to call a lawyer and they will take care of everything." He turns to Officer Wilson. "Where are you taking her?"

"To the police station here. Just down the road."

"I don't want to go," Jordyn says, her voice filled with panic. She clutches onto her grandfather. "Please, Grandpa, don't make me go." She's crying now, drawing curious looks from those driving by.

"I'll be right there, Jordy, I promise," Thomas says, trying to keep the sureness from leeching from his own voice. "I'll get you out of there right away. I promise."

Thomas leans in to kiss Jordyn's forehead. "Don't say a word. Remember, you weren't there," Thomas whispers into her ear. "You weren't there."

But the picture tells another story. Jordyn was clearly at the train yard with her friends and was holding the knife that was used on Cora. What had happened between the time this picture was taken and the attack?

"Grandpa, please," Jordyn cries as Thomas tries to untangle her from his arms.

"Head up, Jordyn," Thomas says firmly. "We'll get this all straightened out."

"Deputy Porter and Deputy Blake from the Johnson County Sheriff's Office will conduct the search, Mr. Petit."

"What are you looking for?" Thomas thinks of the book bag stuffed up inside of the fireplace and his heart skips a beat.

"The clothes she was wearing the other night, her shoes, her book bag," Officer Wilson says. "And the home computer and Jordyn's cell phone if she has one. It would be very helpful if you could tell us where we can find those items."

"No," Thomas says. "We're done helping. Jordyn answered all your questions—we've been cooperative." He looks on as two officers approach the house.

"Is the door locked?" one of them asks.

Thomas watches helplessly as Officer Wilson guides Jordyn to the police car. He waits until the car has pulled away from the curb and disappears down the road, then hands his keys to the deputy. He steps aside in resignation as they unlock the door, go inside and shut the door firmly, leaving Thomas behind.

Thomas stands awkwardly on the sidewalk for a moment and then turns and walks toward the bar. Once inside, he gives Kevin a look that tells him not to ask any questions. He goes behind the bar, pours himself a shot of whiskey, carries it to the cramped office in the back.

First he calls the lawyer that he and Tess used to update their wills. The attorney says that she doesn't practice criminal law. She recommends Robert Peale, an attorney with years of working with juveniles accused of crimes. She will ask Robert to meet them at the police station within the hour.

Thomas sits down at the cluttered desk where he does the paperwork, downs the shot of whiskey and tries to decide how he's going to get that book bag from the chimney before the police find it.

Chances are they won't think to look in the fireplace, but if they do, Thomas will just have to admit that he was the one who hid it up there. Regardless, it won't look good for Jordyn. And what will the officers do when they can't find Jordyn's clothing from the other night?

Thomas wonders if they will arrest him, too. They'll all be locked up before this is all over. Maybe he should have gone with them and given them clothing that looks similar to what Jordyn wore the other night. All her jeans look the same and there were no photos, as far as he knew, of the shoes she wore to the overnight.

Would they ask Jordyn which ones she was wearing? Probably. He should have had a talk with her, should have told Jordyn exactly what to say. Emboldened by the whiskey, Thomas gets to his feet and retraces his steps through the bar, absentmindedly returning greetings from the regular customers.

Once outside he sees the police vehicles still parked out front and takes this as a sign that they haven't found the book bag yet. Thomas tries the doorknob but finds that it won't turn. The door must have locked behind the officers when they went inside. He pats his pockets before remembering that he gave his keys to the officers.

Thomas glances covertly around to see if anyone is watching, finds no one and runs his fingers beneath the metal mailbox affixed to the front of the house. Using duct tape, he had secured an extra house key beneath the mailbox in case of an emergency. But there's nothing there now. He dips his head and twists his neck to get a better look.

Nothing but a sticky residue left behind by the tape. Thomas doesn't think that Tess would have moved the key. She never misplaced her set, always putting them in the exact same place. That left Jordyn. She kept her key on a lanyard in her book bag but rarely had to use it because Thomas or Tess was almost always home.

Thomas had carefully gone through Jordyn's book bag and didn't remember seeing the key there. Had Jordyn taken the lanyard with her on her overnight at Cora's? Yes, he had reminded Jordyn to take it with her because he had planned to run into Grayling on Monday morning and wasn't sure if he'd be home when Jordyn returned from Cora's house. Had Jordyn used the extra key to let herself in the house early Monday morning? And if so, what happened to her own key?

Thomas knocks on the front door, embarrassed that one of the officers has to let him inside his own home. "I just did laundry. I can get you those clothes," Thomas says as if this was the plan all along. He tells himself to show no hesitation.

As if inconvenienced, he stomps up the steps trying to ignore the throbbing pain in his knees as the officers trail close behind. He goes into Jordyn's room to find the dresser drawers are open and her clothing is strewn around in untidy piles.

"In here," Thomas says, opening the closet. He scans the hangers. "I think these are the ones that she wore the other night." Thomas removes a hanger from the closet and holds it out to the officers.

"Mr. Petit," Officer Porter says, "please just point us in the right direction and we'll take care of it." He holds up his gloved hands to remind Thomas that his granddaughter's clothing has become evidence.

"Oh, right," Thomas says, appropriately contrite. "She wore that T-shirt hanging right there." He points to a long-sleeved white T-shirt that looks like half a dozen others that Jordyn wears. Deputy Porter pulls it off the hanger and tucks it into a plastic bag. "Now—" Thomas turns toward the half-open drawers with Jordyn's socks and underwear trailing out of them like entrails "—I have no idea which of those Jordyn wore. I think you're going to have to take them all."

Deputy Porter slides his eyes to the sheriff's deputy who was assigned to assist with the collection. "What about the jacket?" the deputy asks.

"Jacket?" Thomas asks.

"Yes," Officer Porter says with exaggerated patience. "The jacket she was wearing in the photo. It was light blue..."

"I haven't seen it," Thomas says. "Maybe she left it in her book bag."

"And where might that be?" Thomas senses that Officer Porter is losing patience.

"Jordyn said she dropped it the other night, on her way home from Cora's house. She was really upset when she realized she didn't have it. Her social studies book was inside."

"How does someone lose a book bag?" the deputy asks as two large sweat stains appear beneath his arms. The room that once smelled like his granddaughter now is stuffy and smells of body odor and gun oil. Thomas feels his chest constrict and he longs to open a window. "Wouldn't she realize she wasn't carrying it?" the deputy gripes.

"I don't know," Thomas says. "Maybe she set it down to tie her shoe and forgot to pick it up."

"Speaking of shoes," Deputy Porter says. "Where are the shoes Jordyn was wearing Sunday night?"

"On her feet," Thomas says shortly. "She only has that one pair of tennis shoes."

Deputy Porter looks into the closet and sighs. "We better take them all, just in case."

"In case what?" Thomas snipes, forgetting for a moment that it isn't wise to antagonize the people who just arrested his granddaughter.

"In case there is blood or other evidence on the bottom of them," the deputy shoots back as he begins to gather each pair of Jordyn's shoes and place them in evidence bags.

"So you're telling us Jordyn's book bag and fleece jacket are not in this house?" the deputy challenges.

"No, they are not," Thomas says, matching his tone. "I wish they were because they would tell you everything you need to know. Jordyn had nothing to do with what happened to Cora Landry."

"I'm afraid there's evidence to say otherwise, Mr. Petit," the deputy says. "Any other computers in the house besides this one?" He points to the laptop on Jordyn's desk.

Thomas shakes his head no. He usually just uses the one over in the office at the bar. Jordyn uses it once in a while, too. But he's not going to tell the deputy that.

Thomas drifts from the room, not able to stand watching the deputies dismantle his granddaughter's room piece by piece. Maybe there was more truth to what Kendall Landry said than Jordyn was owning up to. If he was being honest with himself, he would admit that he had his doubts. Otherwise, he wouldn't have bothered washing the blood out of the jacket and gone to all the trouble to hide the book bag so carefully. Why else would he have gone to such lengths to protect his granddaughter?

Jan. 15, 2018

I've been eating lunch in Mr. Dover's classroom ever since school started after break. He usually just works on his computer but once in a while he'll pull out his lunch and eat with me. We talk about random stuff like homework assignments and what books we've been reading. It's been nice having somewhere to go instead of the lunchroom but I still really miss Violet. Jordyn, not as much, but I even miss her a little.

Mr. Dover says I should try and talk to them again but I don't know. I don't think having friends should be this much work. I mean, I know it takes work to be a good friend but it shouldn't hurt this much.

I told Mr. Dover that being friends with Jordyn and Violet was just too much work and I came this close to telling him about Joseph and how easy it was to talk to someone over the computer. But of course I didn't say anything because if I did that Mr. Dover would probably call my parents, or worse, call the police.

Before I left his room today, Mr. Dover told me not to give up on friendship, that it's worth it to invest in other people. He also said that if I wanted someone to talk to, he'd always be there for me. He told me to keep my chin up. I'm trying, I said.

Then he grabbed a sticky note, started writing something on it. "I usually don't do this," he said, handing the piece of paper to me. It was a phone number. "Call me if you need to talk. Anytime," he said. "And how about not saying anything to anybody about this. The administration frowns—" and Mr. Dover made a silly sad face when he said this "— on teachers sharing their personal phone numbers."

Then he gave me a hug and told me to get to class.

At the time I thought it would be helpful to Cora and Violet that I was able to talk to each of them about their experiences in the train yard. I thought it would help shed some light on the events of the night. At first I wondered about the wisdom of this and even ran it by one of my colleagues. He assured me as long as I didn't share any of what Violet or Cora disclosed to the other, it would be fine.

When I arrived for my next session with Cora it was to find her sitting up in the reclining chair in her room. She was still attached to an IV; a fleece tie blanket was draped over her legs. "You're up," I said in surprise. "How does it feel?" I asked, pulling up a chair so that we were sitting knee to knee.

"It's okay," Cora said halfheartedly. "The stitches on my stomach feel weird sitting like this, but the nurse said it was good for me. They made me go for a walk earlier."

"How'd that go?" I asked.

"Tiring," Cora said, smoothing the edges of the bandage that covered her eye. "And people keep looking at me funny. My face looks so bad."

"Usually the first few days after surgeries like this are the worst," I explained. "Once the swelling goes down and the bruising fades it will be better."

"That's what the other doctor told me, too," Cora said. She shivered. "It's cold in here."

I stood and went to the cupboard where I knew the extra blankets were stored and pulled one down.

"The police came by again yesterday," Cora said as I tucked the blanket around her shoulders. A vaguely sweet, foul odor emanated from Cora. "I think the policeman was mad at me."

"Why do you say that?" I asked, thinking about what John

Dover said about Cora being hypersensitive about what people say to her and taking things the wrong way.

"Because I can't remember anything. He kept asking me what I saw and who I saw and what happened and I couldn't tell him," Cora said with annoyance.

"I'm sure he wasn't mad at you," I said. "Maybe just frustrated because he can't find the person who did this awful thing."

"No, he was definitely mad," Cora insisted. "I could tell. He was practically yelling at me and then I started crying and my mom made him leave." I could see that Cora was getting worked up again but she kept talking. "Violet's been saying that Joseph Wither was the one who attacked me."

Violet had told me the same thing and I wanted to continue the conversation with Cora that we had the other day, about ghosts and conversations with Joseph Wither, but didn't want to force the topic. I was happy Cora brought it up.

"Why do you think Violet is saying this?" I asked.

Cora shrugged and winced in pain at the sudden movement. "I guess because she thinks that Joseph Wither is real," she said.

I knew I had to be careful as to how I responded here. I needed to be noncommittal, nonjudgmental, so as to not interject any personal perspectives. "You mentioned the other day when you gave me the picture of Skittles that Joseph Wither was contacting you online..." I let the sentence hang, hoping that Cora would fill in the blanks. She didn't.

"Why do *you* think Violet thinks he's real?" I asked instead.

Cora sat in silence for a long time, her forehead creased as if trying to work out something in her mind. "What do you think?" I asked. "Do you believe that Joseph Wither is real?"

When she finally met my eye, she hesitated before speaking. "What if I believe two crazy things?"

"I would say that people believe all kinds of things and that doesn't necessarily mean they're crazy. Sometimes people just need to talk through what they are thinking and then things make better sense. Do you want to share your two things with me?"

"What if I believe in Joseph Wither and what if I believe that Violet and Jordyn were the ones who hurt me?"

My blood ran cold. Had Cora been hiding the fact that her best friend was the one who stabbed her? Had a twelve-year-old girl really tried to kill her best friend? In my few sessions with Violet I hadn't got the sense that she was the perpetrator. Was I wrong? My first impression of Violet was that of a very frightened, confused little girl, which was perfectly understandable given the circumstances. But what I wasn't clear about was the source of Violet's fear. Was she afraid of the attacker or was she afraid of being caught?

"Was Violet the one who hurt you, Cora? Is that what you are saying?"

She didn't respond and I noticed that her face had gone a shade paler and a thin sheen of sweat had appeared above her lip and her eyes had a glassy glint.

"Cora, are you feeling okay?" I leaned forward and laid the back of my hand against her forehead and was met with surprising heat. "You have a bit of fever," I told her, though I was worried that it could be much more than that. "Let me go get your nurse and have her take your temperature."

"Okay," Cora said as she closed her eyes and leaned back in her chair. It's easy to forget how exhausting it can be carrying on a conversation after a significant injury.

I stepped out into the hallway and flagged down a nurse. "I think Cora Landry may have a fever. Could someone check her temperature?"

After a few minutes, a young woman wearing pink scrubs breezed in. Cora's nurse. "Hey there, Cora," she said. "I hear you're feeling pretty crummy. Let's check you out." She smoothly pressed a thermometer into her ear and after a few seconds it beeped. "One hundred and three. You don't mess around, do you?" Cora managed to open her eyes to narrow slits but they fluttered shut.

"Infection?" I asked.

"It looks that way. I'll call the doctor and I imagine she'll order another course of antibiotics." To Cora she said, "I'm going to take a peek under your dressings, Cora, okay? I promise I'm just looking—I won't poke around." Cora nodded weakly.

The nurse carefully began to peel away the bandages that covered the left side of her face. "Ahh, it looks like you've developed a bit of an infection, Cora. You just hang tight now and we'll get you all fixed up, okay?" I looked over the nurse's shoulder and could see that Cora had developed more than a bit of an infection. The entire wound was seeping with green discharge.

"Do you know where her parents are?" I asked.

"The mom went down to the cafeteria so you could have privacy for your session with Cora and I haven't seen her dad yet today. I'll give her mom's cell phone a ring," the nurse explained.

I sat down next to Cora as the nurse left the room. Cora murmured something that I didn't quite catch.

I leaned in closer. "What did you say?"

"Violet was there but he didn't stay," Cora said. "I thought he would stay."

"Who didn't stay?" I asked. Cora reached up to touch her face. "No, no, Cora." I reached for her hand. "Don't touch it. Who didn't stay, your dad?"

Her uninjured eye opened while the other one remained closed, glued shut with pus. "Not my dad. Joseph Wither."

JW44:

YOU'VE SEEMED SO SAD LATELY. ARE THINGS STILL BAD AT SCHOOL?

Corareef12:

Yeah, it's pretty bad. No one talks to me, which is almost worse than people being outright mean. At least when they're mean they know I'm there. I stayed home sick twice this week. My grades suck and my mom is starting to talk about getting me a tutor. I can't wait until spring break.

JW44:

I'LL LEAVE YOU A PRESENT AT THE PRIMROSE. WILL THAT CHEER YOU UP?

Corareef12:

The Primrose?

JW44:

THE BOXCAR. THE ONE WITH THE FLOWERS.

Corareef12:

Why can't we just meet in person? Why won't you just let me see you at least?

JW44:

NOT JUST YET. YOU HAVEN'T TOLD ANYONE ABOUT ME, HAVE YOU? THIS HAS TO BE OUR SECRET.

Corareef12:

I haven't told anyone. I promise. When?

JW44:

BE PATIENT. PEOPLE WOULDN'T UNDERSTAND. YOU'RE JUST A KID.

Corareef12:

I'm not just a kid.

JW44:

YOUR PARENTS WOULD NEVER LET YOU GO TO THE TRAIN YARD
LATE AT NIGHT. THAT'S WHEN I COME OUT. JUST COME FRIDAY.
THE PRESENT WILL BE THERE FOR YOU.

Corareef12:

Promise?

JW44:

I PROMISE.

Feb. 6, 2018

I decided to call Mr. Dover over the weekend. Everyone was out of the house. I mean, he said I could but I was still nervous. My palms were sweaty when I picked up the phone and my fingers shook while I dialed the numbers. The phone rang and rang and I almost hung up when he answered but I didn't.

I started crying when he said hello and Mr. Dover just sat on the other end and waited for me to stop. "What's the matter, Corabell?" he asked. "Having a bad day?"

I told him that I was sad and lonely and not sleeping very well. I asked him about what he told me about not giving up on friendship. I told him that I really missed Violet. That I'd been saying hi to her in the hallway and she always says hi back.

Mr. Dover told me that it sounded like I had already made up my mind to talk to Violet and that I should go for it. I thanked him and he said, *No problem. But remember not to say anything about this call, okay?*

I emailed Joseph, too, and told him what I was thinking and he told me I should just forget about Violet, that she's not worth my time. He told me I should spend my time thinking about important things—him!

On Monday, I chickened out and went to eat lunch in Mr. Dover's room again. The principal walked by and peeked in the room. Then she called Mr. Dover over and they whispered for a few minutes. I overheard her saying something about how it isn't appropriate for him to be alone in a classroom with a student. That people might misunderstand.

So after lunch Mr. Dover told me that I should probably start eating lunch in the cafeteria again.

Today, when I walked into the lunchroom, I felt like my heart was going to explode I was so nervous. Nobody even looked twice at me, which was just fine with me. I sat next to Joy Willard and we even talked a little bit but I kept looking over at Violet. She was sitting at the same table as Jordyn but they weren't sitting next to each other. Jordyn was actually sitting next to Gabe and they were talking and laughing. Violet wasn't talking to anyone.

I feel like if I can just get Violet by herself I'll be able to explain that I'm really sorry about the cell phone. I know that Joseph said I should forget about Violet, that she's not my friend, but I'm so lonely that some days I don't even think I can get out of bed. If I had just one friend, just one besides Wither, I know I'll feel better.

Tomorrow morning before school starts I'm going to wait by Violet's locker and beg her to talk to me. If this doesn't work, I don't know what I'm going to do. I don't think I could stand coming to school anymore if I thought everyone hated me.

Feb. 7, 2018

I did it! I talked to Violet. I told her I was sorry about the cell phone and about how I freaked out the day of the presentation. That I shouldn't have started yelling at everyone the way I did. That I shouldn't have slapped Jordyn. It felt so good to finally talk to her. I asked her if she would please just come over to my house. I had to show her something.

At first she said no, that she didn't think she could. I know she was thinking about Jordyn and that it would be social suicide if she got caught hanging around with me. I told her Jordyn wouldn't have to know, no one would. She thought about this and then said okay.

Joseph keeps telling me to make sure I come to the train yard on Friday, that he'll leave something there for me. I want to go, but I'll admit I'm scared. I casually asked my sister if she knew where the Primrose Sugar boxcar was and she got all upset and started yelling at me to stay away from the train yard, that hobos and druggies hang out there, and if she found out I was going there she was going to tell Mom.

I told her to relax, that I heard some kids talking about it at school and I just wanted to know what it was. She calmed down after that but said that she would seriously kick my butt if I started hanging out there.

So Violet is coming over on Friday and then I can explain everything and maybe she'll go with me to the train yard. I know that Wither said I shouldn't tell anyone about our emails but Violet can keep a secret. I just hope she'll keep mine.

Feb. 10, 2018

So Violet and I went to the train yard yesterday. I didn't tell her that we were going to go to find the present that Wither left for me. I don't know if I didn't tell her because she wouldn't believe me or if I didn't believe it myself.

She kept asking me what was so important that I needed to tell her, but I started to lose my nerve, so I told her I would tell her later, after we ate supper.

We told my mom we were just going to the park for a little while and she offered to give us a ride but I told her no thanks, that we wanted to walk. I asked her if she would hold on to Skittles so that she wouldn't get out but she just rolled her eyes and kept on chopping up the vegetables for supper and told us to be home before six.

It was freezing out. It snowed all day so I had on my winter boots and I lent Violet an old pair that my sister used to wear. Violet said she forgot hers at home but I don't think she has any. I've never seen her wear any before, but most kids don't wear snow boots to school, anyway, so it's not a big deal.

It took us about fifteen minutes to walk to the tracks. It looked like we were the first people there in a while—at least since it snowed. The ground was glittery and perfect with no footprints. I almost hated to walk across the train yard and mess it all up. Out of the corner of my eye I saw Skittles run by. Her golden fur was like a streak of sunshine against the snow. She must have followed us. "Sweet, silly girl," I said. Violet thought I was talking to her and we both started laughing.

We looked for Skittles's footprints in the snow, but the wind was blowing and we couldn't find them. I wasn't too worried, though; she always finds her way home.

I asked Violet if she believed that Wither was real and she laughed and said no way, so I laughed, too. We walked along the tracks, our boots sinking deep into the snow, until we were both out of breath. Then Violet said sometimes she thought Wither might be real and she wondered where he would go when it was so cold out like this.

I watched her for a minute. I couldn't tell if she was making fun of me or not. But then she said that maybe he slept in one of the boxcars at night. I guess that makes sense, though I don't think it would be much warmer inside a boxcar than out.

I told Violet that I thought that Wither probably snuck into people's houses at night and hid under the stairs or in a closet. Violet wanted to know how Wither got inside the homes. I wanted to tell her that he scratched at windows and came through vents. Instead I told her that I guess he gets in and out the same way Skittles does—whenever someone opens and closes a door.

We walked toward the boxcar that had a faded flower painted across the side of it. There weren't any tracks around it, either, but the wind was blowing pretty hard and when I looked back at the footprints that Violet and I had made they were already almost invisible.

"I'm getting cold," Violet said. "Let's go back to your house."

"Just a minute," I told her. "I want to see what's inside here."

"Why?" Violet asked. "It's just an old boxcar. There's probably a coyote or other wild animals hibernating in there."

"I don't think coyotes hibernate," I said but I hadn't thought of animals. The door was slid open only a little bit but it wasn't hard for me to get inside. "Are you coming?" I asked Violet.

She shook her head no and said I was crazy. But she didn't say it in a mean sort of way. More like as if I was brave.

It was dark in the boxcar and smelled like the sour pickles my dad likes to eat straight out of the jar. The boxcar was empty except for a wooden box with a glass jar sitting on top of it. No Joseph Wither. I didn't really expect him to show up but I was still disappointed. I walked over to the wooden box and saw that the glass jar had something inside it. A piece of paper and a wrapped piece of butterscotch candy.

"Are you coming?" Violet called from outside.

"In a minute," I called back as I took off my mittens and twisted the metal lid. I set aside the lid and reached inside the jar. The piece of paper was folded into a tight square and my fingers were so cold it made it hard for me to unfold it.

My eyes went right to the bottom of the letter. It was from Wither. My stomach flip-flopped and suddenly I wasn't cold anymore. I unwrapped the yellow candy and for a second I heard my mom's voice in my head telling me not to eat it—that it might be poisonous. But I put it in my mouth, anyway. It tasted like sunshine.

DEAR CORA,

I KNEW YOU WOULD COME! I HOPE YOU LIKE THE CANDY.
DON'T TELL ANYONE!!! THIS HAS TO BE A SECRET OR WE
WILL BOTH GET IN TROUBLE. IT WON'T BE LONG NOW AND
WE CAN SEE EACH OTHER IN PERSON.

LOVE,
JOSEPH

Somehow I'm able to doze here and there but the chair in the family waiting room doesn't make sleep easy. Across the room from me Max is curled up in an awkward ball on the room's one couch. He looks cold but I've got nothing to cover him with.

What am I going to do about work? I've already missed two days and I haven't worked there long enough to get any vacation time. If I don't work, I don't get paid.

I watch Max sleep, his hands tucked beneath his chin, which sprouted a shadow of a beard overnight. I blinked and he grew up on me. I blinked and my daughter went from a nice, quiet twelve-year-old girl to being in a locked ward of the hospital, accused of being crazy, of trying to kill her best friend.

My stomach growls loudly and I can't believe my body is betraying me at a time like this. I haven't eaten since yesterday morning and the thought of food makes me want to be sick but I know I have to at least attempt to take care of myself for the sake of Violet and Max.

I stand and stretch, my muscles aching from sitting for so long, and I go over to where Max is sleeping and give him a gentle shake. "Max," I whisper and his eyes open. "I'm going to find something to eat. You stay here and I'll bring you something." He nods and his eyes close again.

I take the elevator down to the main floor and follow the signs to the cafeteria. The smell of scrambled eggs and bacon fills my nose and my stomach rumbles again. The cafeteria is nearly deserted and I grab a few bagels and donuts and two bottles of orange juice and carry them to the cash register. As I pull my cash from my pocket I see Cora's dad at a table, sitting by himself, a cup of coffee in front of him.

I think about what Violet told me about Jordyn pushing Cora

down at the train yard. I wonder if the police have told him anything more about the investigation.

"Ma'am? Ma'am?" The cashier looks at me with eyebrows raised. "That'll be eight dollars and forty-two cents."

"Sorry," I say and hand him the money and don't wait for the change. I decide to take the cowardly way out and, with head down, try to leave the cafeteria without Jim Landry seeing me. No such luck.

"Hey," Jim calls. I stop and turn to face him. He's not a tall man, but burly and strong, and from the way he's glaring at me it's obvious the police have told him their theory. The cashier's eyes flick back and forth between us.

"I'm sorry about what happened to Cora, but they're wrong." I keep my voice low and steady. "Violet didn't do this."

He takes a step toward me and it's all I can do not to run away. "Why isn't your daughter helping the police?" he asks through clenched teeth. "She knows something—I know she does. Cora could have died. She could lose her eye."

Part of me wants to tell him what Violet said about Jordyn pushing Cora to the ground but I know it's not a good idea. That will only seal his belief that Violet was part of the attack. I know my daughter and I'm not going to let anyone change what I believe about her.

I straighten my spine and lift my chin. "You're wrong. I don't know what happened at the train yard, but I know that Violet had nothing to do with it. She is trying to help the police. She's just scared."

"And Cora isn't? She's terrified! Why was Cora the only one who got attacked? Strange coincidence, don't you think? There were three girls in the train yard and only one got hurt?" Jim shakes his head. "I know they had been arguing, that Violet and Jordyn were freezing Cora out for months. I know more than they're letting on."

"What about the teacher?" I ask, desperately wanting to get

the focus off Violet. "Mr. Dover? The police questioned him, right? What are they saying about him?"

Jim glares at me as the cashier comes out from behind the register. "Everything okay?" he asks nervously and he pulls his phone from his pocket.

"We're fine," I tell him. And without a backward glance I leave the cafeteria.

Instead of taking the elevator I decide to take the steps and by the time I get back to Max I've stopped shaking. "Here," I say, holding the bag out to Max, who is now sitting up on the sofa and watching TV with the volume on low.

"Thanks," Max says and reaches his hand into the bag and pulls out a donut and a bagel and starts eating. When he comes up for air he takes a long look at me. "What's the matter? Did something happen with Violet?"

"No, it's not Violet." I hesitate to tell Max more. He's only sixteen and has had to grow up faster than most kids his age but it's been just the three of us for so long. He should hear about what's happening with Violet from me. "I saw Cora's dad in the cafeteria. He thinks that Violet and Jordyn are hiding something about the attack. He's very angry."

Max sits up straight. "Do you want me to talk to him?" I know he means it. When he was nine he clobbered a boyfriend of mine who grabbed my arm during an argument and when he was thirteen he told off our landlord for turning off our electricity when our rent check was a few days late.

"No, buddy, I don't want you to talk to him. I think it's best we don't talk to the Landry family at all."

I told Officer Grady about Jordyn pushing Cora down and he promised me that he would look into it. All I can do is trust him.

I glance at the clock. Seven thirty. I'm hoping that I'll be able to see Violet sometime this morning. Dr. Gideon told me that seeing her would depend on how her night goes. Max also told me I need to find Violet a lawyer. I tried a few local firms yesterday afternoon but they made it pretty clear that I couldn't afford their services. I've missed work for the last two days and I can't imagine going back until I get Violet out of here but we need the money. I don't own a house, I work at a gas station and drive a crappy car. How am I going to be able to pay for a decent attorney for Violet?

"You want me to run home and check on Boomer and the house?" Max asks.

I don't want him to go back to the house without me there with him and tell him so. The vandalism has rattled me. "I'd be fine, you know. I wouldn't let anyone mess with me." I give him a look that makes it clear it's not up for discussion.

Max rolls his eyes at my overprotectiveness and stands and stretches his arms over his head. "I'm going to go walk around," he says. "I'll be back in a while."

My phone buzzes and I check the display. It's the guy, Sam, from the other night. He's texted and called about a dozen times. I hit Ignore.

I nibble on a bagel and take a drink of orange juice and stare mindlessly up at the television. A man and a woman come into the family room. The woman looks dazed and the man fights back tears. They sit down on the sofa, only a few inches between them but it seems like they are a million miles apart. I wonder what brought them here. What mental illness has overtaken their loved one. But of course I don't ask.

I turn my attention back to the television and the local morning newscast. A reporter is standing in front of the Welcome to Pitch—We're Glad You're Here sign.

"Do you mind if I turn it up?" I ask the couple as I grab the remote and press the volume button until I can hear the reporter's voice.

"Officials aren't revealing much, but what we do know is that three twelve-year-old girls were involved in an incident early Monday morning that left one child with severe injuries. Our sources tell us that the weapon used was a knife much like this one." The reporter holds up an odd-looking hooked blade with a wooden handle for us to see.

"Oh, Jesus." I lower my face into my hands. A knife. I know there is no possible way that Violet could have stabbed anyone. But my mind keeps flashing back to the image of her walking out of the tall grass covered in blood. So much blood.

"The Pitch Police Department and Johnson County Sheriff's Office aren't sharing details," the reporter says, "but we do have unconfirmed reports that an arrest has been made in the case, though we don't know who the individual is. Word is that a local Pitch man was brought in at least once for what a spokesperson has called 'routine questioning.' The name of that man has not been released and we do not know if he was arrested. Again, we do not have official confirmation of an arrest, but will continue to follow this shocking and disturbing case and be sure to bring you any updates as they unfold."

The woman sitting across from me clucks her tongue and shakes her head while her companion murmurs, "This is terrible, just terrible. I hope they string up whoever did this to that poor little girl."

The woman looks at me as if waiting for me to agree. But I can't do anything, not even nod my head. In any other situation, I'd be thinking the same thing, saying the same thing. But my daughter is tangled up in this entire mess and I'll do whatever I have to in order to get her out.

Feb. 25, 2018

It took me a few weeks, but I ended up telling Violet everything and I showed her all of Wither's messages. She kept saying, *This can't be real! Someone is playing a trick on you!*

I told her that at first I thought he was fake, too. Then I showed her the message about Rachel Farmer and the yearbook and I think that's when Violet started to believe that Wither is real.

I begged her not to tell Jordyn, that she'd make my life even more miserable than it already was. She said she promised. She said Jordyn wasn't hanging around with her much, either, and said some mean things about Violet's mom working at a gas station. Violet also said that Jordyn and Gabe started going out again. This made me feel jealous, though I'm not sure why. It's not like Gabe has gone out of his way to be nice to me lately.

I told Violet that Jordyn wasn't worth worrying about and to forget about her. She smiled like she was thinking, *Yeah, right.* But then we ate supper and made cupcakes. My mom even let us go into my room to eat them. We laughed and talked until like one in the morning. It was so much fun.

Before Violet's brother and his dorky friend Clint picked her up to take her home, I made her promise not to tell anyone about Joseph Wither. She rolled her eyes and held up her right hand and said, "I swear I won't tell anyone!" So all I can do is believe her.

But all I can think about is how Wither said he can see everything. I wonder if he already knows. He'd be so mad. This afternoon I snuck back to the depot and left a little present for him at the Primrose—a note and a rock I found that was shaped like a heart. I hope he likes them.

JW44:
THANK YOU FOR LEAVING THE NOTE AND THE HEART-SHAPED
ROCK.

 Corareef12:
You're welcome. I've been looking for you at the train yard—but
you're never there. It's not easy to get away. My mom would kill
me if she knew.

 JW44:
I KNOW YOU ARE ANXIOUS TO MEET IN PERSON BUT I DON'T
WANT YOU TO GET IN TROUBLE. PEOPLE WON'T UNDERSTAND.
ESPECIALLY YOUR PARENTS.

 Corareef12:
I know.

 JW44:
I SAW YOU TALKING WITH THAT BOY THE OTHER DAY. WHY? DO
YOU LIKE HIM MORE THAN YOU LIKE ME? I HOPE NOT.

 Corareef12:
I don't. I told you, he's just a friend at school.

 JW44:
PROMISE?

 Corareef12:
I promise.

 JW44:
OKAY. I BELIEVE YOU.

Corareef12:
What's it like where you live? Is it like Pitch? I hope not.

 JW44:
IT'S AMAZING. IT'S HARD TO EXPLAIN BUT THINK ABOUT THE MOST PERFECT PLACE IN THE WORLD. WE CAN HAVE GREEN RIVERS WHENEVER WE WANT. AND YES, YOU CAN EVEN BRING YOUR CAT. I HOPE YOU HAVEN'T TOLD ANYONE ABOUT ME. REMEMBER, THEY WON'T UNDERSTAND AND IF THEY FIND OUT I'LL HAVE TO LEAVE AND WE'LL NEVER BE ABLE TO TALK AGAIN OR SEE EACH OTHER.

 Corareef12:
I told you I wouldn't say anything. You treat me like I'm a baby—you never believe me.

 JW44:
 THEN STOP ACTING LIKE A BABY.

 Corareef12:
I'm not!

 JW44:
THEN PROVE IT. STAND IN FRONT OF YOUR WINDOW.

 Corareef12:
Why?

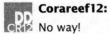 **JW44:**
STAND IN FRONT OF YOUR WINDOW AND LIFT UP YOUR SHIRT.

 Corareef12:
No way!

JW44:
SO YOU ARE A BABY.

Corareef12:
I am not. Why are you being like this?

JW44:
DO IT.

JW44:
DO IT NOW.

Corareef12:
Okay. I'll be right back.

Corareef12:
Are you happy now? I did it.

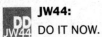
JW44:
LIAR.

Every time Thomas walks past the fireplace it's all he can do to not stare. Last night, after Officer Wilson took Jordyn away and the deputy left with evidence bags filled with Jordyn's clothes, Thomas looked up the chimney with a flashlight to make sure that the book bag was where he left it. It was. Thomas debated whether to yank the pack down, look through it to see if Jordyn's house key was inside and find a new hiding place but decided to leave it alone, at least for the time being.

He came home from the police station beside himself and he knew that he couldn't keep this news from Tess any longer. He wanted to drive to the skilled care facility and tell her in person, but he told himself that he didn't want to be too far away from Jordyn in case she needed anything. If Thomas was being completely honest, he would admit that he just couldn't bear facing Tess. So he called her instead.

He tried to downplay it by saying the police were just questioning her, that it was all one big misunderstanding, but in his mind all he could think was, *They put her in a cell! A twelve-year-old girl in a jail cell where thieves and drug addicts and murderers and all other sorts of criminals belonged.*

Thomas promised to call Tess later in the day to give her an update, but in the meantime he goes to the kitchen to put on a fresh pot of coffee and though he doubts he'll be able to eat anything, he drops some bread into the toaster just in case.

Thomas's knees protest with each step and he knows he'll have to go to the doctor to get a cortisone shot soon, but not today and not tomorrow but as soon as Jordyn comes home. Thomas pulls the butter dish from the cupboard and sets it on the kitchen table along with a jar of peach jam Tess canned last summer when the phone rings.

His first thought turns to Jordyn. Maybe it's the lawyer calling to tell him it's all been a terrible mistake, that they are releasing Jordyn right away. Or, he thinks, maybe it's the jail calling to say that Jordyn was hurt by some criminal during the night. You hear about that on TV all the time.

Thomas sets down the jar of jam, half hoping that the phone will stop ringing before he gets there. No such luck. "Hello," he says.

"Murderer," comes a muffled voice. "Tell the murdering bitch we're coming for her." Thomas's heart seizes. Had the Landry girl died? They just saw her yesterday and though she looked rough she was far from the edge of death. There's no way she could have died. Someone would have called and told them, but not like this.

"Who is this?" Thomas manages to ask.

"Eye for an eye," the voice hisses and Thomas slams down the phone. Just kids, he tells himself. Just a prank call.

Thomas sits, elbows on the table, forehead resting in the palm of one hand. Sure, Jordyn has had her issues. Thomas remembers the school calling over a half a dozen times this year. Once for copying a classmate on a math test, twice for making fun of a girl in her class. *Jordyn called her lardo and a fat ass*, the teacher explained, spelling out the offensive word: *a-s-s*. Once for snapping a girl's bra in the locker room and a time or two for being disruptive while the teacher was talking.

Except for a few minor incidents, there really hadn't been anything about Jordyn *actually* hurting anyone. Of course the girl is going to have some issues. Her parents *abandoned* her, for God's sake.

Thomas wants so badly to talk to Tess about all of this. He needs to talk to her. She'll be furious with him for hiding Jordyn's arrest from her. Today, he promises himself. This afternoon, after the arraignment, he'll call his wife and try to explain what's going on.

The sky is the color of dishwater, gray and cloudy. And though all the snow has melted a cold breeze sweeps across his skin and Thomas wonders if the mild mid-April weather they've been having is just a tease.

He doubts that the girls would have left the Landry home in the middle of the night if there had been snow and the temperature near freezing. Though it's only a short drive to the jail it still feels too far away. From talking with the attorney, Thomas knows that Jordyn is very lucky to have remained at the jail in town.

Robert said she very easily could have been shipped to the nearest juvenile detention center nearly an hour away and that was if there was room available. If there were no open beds in Cedar Rapids she could still end up as far away as Sioux City, which is over a five-hour drive.

The key, Robert said, was that because Jordyn is a juvenile, she cannot be within sight or sound distance with any adult prisoners at any time. He said the Pitch jail has one solitary room that will keep Jordyn separate from the others.

It's Thomas's understanding that the initial hearing is to be held at one this afternoon. This is where the judge reads the charges against Jordyn and asks her what her plea will be. Guilty or not guilty. Maybe he'll get a chance to talk to Jordyn. Thomas wants to get his eyes on her, see if she's really doing okay. He has a lot of questions for Jordyn. Like why was there a picture of Jordyn and the girls in front of a boxcar when Jordyn told him, no, *promised* him that she never actually went into the train yard? He also wants to ask about Jordyn's house key and where Jordyn might have put it. That key has been worrying him. If Jordyn dropped it in the train yard anywhere near the spot where Cora was attacked, then it proved that she had lied to them all.

The phone trills and as much as Thomas wants to ignore it, he knows he can't. The call might be about Jordyn or about Tess. He hurries down the steps, hoping to grab it before the person on the other end hangs up. As he listens to the voice on the other end his face darkens.

"Listen," Thomas hisses into the phone, "call here again and I'll break your legs." He slams down the phone so hard that the cradle is knocked from the wall and the receiver falls and bounces against the floor and sways, dangling by the coiled cord.

Thomas's hands are shaking, eyes wild.

He wants to rip the phone out of the wall, he wants this nightmare to be over, he wants Tess to come home so they can face this together. She would know what to say, what to do. Thomas picks up the receiver and lightly returns it to the wall and it immediately begins to ring again.

"Hello," he says sharply, then apologizes when Jordyn's attorney identifies himself on the other end. "What's going on?" Thomas listens for a moment.

"I'll meet you there in thirty minutes," he says. He hangs up and Thomas doesn't return the receiver to the cradle, but lays it on the kitchen counter. This will take care of the crank calls, he thinks.

Jordyn's attorney has a lot to tell him. Jordyn's arraignment is to be held at ten and the juvenile court officer assigned to the family will also be there to help them walk through all the ins and outs of what's going on. But it's Robert's final statement that has his mind spinning.

Jordyn's ready to talk.

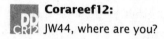 **Corareef12:**
JW44, where are you?

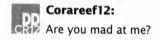 **Corareef12:**
Are you mad at me?

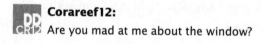 **Corareef12:**
Are you mad at me about the window?

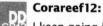 **Corareef12:**
I keep going back to the Primrose to see if you left me another
note but you haven't. I left you notes but they are still there.
Please answer me.

Case #92-10945
Direct message dated March 12, 2018,
via DarkestDoor.com

Corareef12:

I don't know what I did wrong. You said you were my friend. I don't have anyone else to talk to. Everyone else except Violet hates me. Is it because I'm friends with her again? I'll stop. I'll do whatever you want me to, just please answer.

Case #92-10945
Direct message dated March 13, 2018,
via DarkestDoor.com

Corareef12:

After my parents went to bed last night I snuck out and went to the Primrose. I kept thinking you might show up. I stayed there until really late but you didn't come. Doesn't that prove to you that I love you? I'm not sure what you want from me. Please just tell me what to do.

Case #92-10945
Direct message dated March 15, 2018,
via DarkestDoor.com

Corareef12:

I haven't been able to sleep. I wait until my parents go to bed and then I sneak downstairs to use the computer. I sit here and wait for you to send me a message. Why won't you talk to me? Please tell me. I fell asleep in class today I'm so tired. Everyone started laughing. I thought I saw you waiting for me outside after school, and instead of getting into my mom's car I went and looked behind the trees to see if it was really you. But no one was there—you were gone. I couldn't breathe. I felt like I was going crazy. Please send me a message. Just one. Please tell me what I did wrong.

Case #92-10945
Direct message dated March 16, 2018,
via DarkestDoor.com

 Corareef12:
I've been standing in front of the window every night. Just the way you wanted me to. My mom caught me yesterday with my shirt off standing there and freaked out. Doesn't this prove it? Doesn't this prove that I love you?

I punch the off button on the television remote. I wonder who the man is that they've interviewed. Maybe Violet will be able to come home sooner than later. I still have to find Violet a lawyer and find her one now. Just in case. I step out into the hallway for privacy and look up and down the corridor for any sign of Max. He's nowhere to be seen.

I pull out my phone and do another search of lawyers who serve Pitch and the surrounding area. Dozens of names come up so I narrow my search to juvenile law and the list is cut down to just a handful. I start at the top with Anderson and Boothe Law Offices located in Carbonville. A chipper receptionist named Genevieve answers the phone on the first ring. She asks how she can be of help and I realize I don't even know how to begin.

"I need a lawyer for my daughter. She's twelve," I say.

"What's the charge?" the woman asks and I'm taken aback. I didn't think I would have to go through the entire story with a complete stranger, let alone the office receptionist first.

"I'd rather speak with a lawyer," I say. "Is someone available?"

"If you can give me some details about your daughter's case, I can direct it to the attorney best suited for assisting you," she says smoothly and I can tell it won't be easy getting through this firewall.

"She hasn't been charged yet, but they're talking attempted murder," I say, cringing with the ugliness of the words.

There is silence on the other end of the phone. I can't imagine that these are charges that even the most experienced of lawyers see very often. Genevieve clears her throat. "Why don't I take your number and one of our attorneys will call you back shortly."

I tell her my number and before she hangs up I ask the question that I really don't want to know the answer to. "Can you

give me a ballpark figure of how much it costs for a situation
like this?"

Genevieve is silent and I wonder if this firm has even had an
attempted murder case before when she says, "Well, there are
many factors to take into consideration, but on average I'd say
that services will be about a hundred and fifty dollars an hour."

She may as well have said a million dollars an hour. I'm not
naive enough to think that an attempted murder case will take
only a few hours. I make about three hundred and fifty bucks
a week and that's if I work overtime. In less than three hours a
lawyer will wipe out a week's worth of work.

"Thank you," I tell Genevieve and hang up. It's dawning on
me that if Violet does get arrested I'm most likely going to have
to get a public defender.

I look up to find Officer Grady coming toward us. He looks
as exhausted as I feel. I wonder if he's gotten any sleep the last
two days. Good, I think. He's the one who made Violet run.
He's the one who got Violet committed to the hospital. He
should be just as tired as we are.

"Morning, Beth," Officer Grady says. "How's Violet doing?"
he asks.

"I don't know. Visitors' hours aren't until noon. Did you get
your warrant and come to arrest her?"

"Listen, Beth, I need to talk to you for a few minutes. Let's
go sit," Officer Grady says, leading the way to the family waiting room.

I'm about to tell him that there are already people in there
but the sight of a cop standing in the doorway gets the couple
moving and they gather their things and leave. "I'm holding off
on getting that warrant but I may not be able to wait too much
longer." I drop onto the sofa and Officer Grady sits across from
me and leans forward, elbows on his knees. "Listen, Beth," Officer Grady says, "I'm not Violet's lawyer..."

"Do I need to get her a lawyer?" I ask, panic squeezing my lungs.

"If it comes to that the court will appoint one for Violet."

"But I don't know if I can afford one." My face grows hot. It's mortifying to have to admit that I can't provide for my daughter.

"The court automatically appoints a lawyer to Violet. It's standard for juveniles. It will all be explained to you if she's taken into police custody." Officer Grady shifts in his seat. "Listen, that's not why I'm here to talk to you. I've got kids, too. A girl in high school and a boy in eighth grade at the same school as Violet."

I see the sympathy on his face and I know he's thinking of his own children and the possibility of them being caught up in a similar predicament. The pressure on my chest eases a bit. Maybe Officer Grady is in our corner, maybe he believes that Violet is innocent.

"I want to show you something." He stands, pulls out his phone and sits next to me on the sofa. He scratches his eyebrow and takes a breath. "If I were in your boat, I'd want all the information."

That familiar feeling of dread begins to overwhelm me again and I know that whatever Officer Grady is going to show me isn't going to be good news for Violet.

He pulls up a video and it takes a moment for me to understand what I'm seeing. A black-and-white, grainy video of the train yard with a twelve-thirty time stamp for April 16. There is no sound. I look up at Officer Grady. "We installed a camera last fall when we suspected an increase in drug activity at the depot. Keep watching."

Three figures come into the frame and though their features are fuzzy, I recognize Violet's long dark hair. The other two girls have to be Cora and Jordyn. They are walking shoulder to shoulder and arrange themselves in front of a row of boxcars.

Violet reaches into her pocket and pulls out what appears to

be a cell phone, stretches out her arm and raises it above her head
to take a picture. Jordyn lifts her arm, too, and in her hand is
something—but I can't tell what it is. Once the photo is snapped,
Jordyn reaches into her backpack and pulls out a bottle, twists
the lid and takes a drink. The camera is too far away to see her
face but by the way she shoves the bottle toward Violet it's ap-
parent that she doesn't like the taste.

"Are they drinking alcohol?" I ask. Officer Grady ignores
my question, keeping his eyes on the screen. Violet wipes the
rim of the bottle with her sleeve, takes a drink and offers it to
Cora, who shakes her head. Violet presses the bottle back toward Jordyn, who takes it, dumps out the rest and tosses the
bottle to the ground.

The girls freeze in place and then turn their heads toward
somewhere out of sight of the camera. The girls spend the next
few moments in what looks like deep conversation until Jordyn lifts her book bag to her shoulder and begins to walk away.
Cora grabs one of the straps and tries to pull Jordyn back toward her. Jordyn gives one big tug, forcing Cora to let go and
tumble to the ground. Then Jordyn tosses whatever item was in
her other hand to the ground next to her. Violet reaches down
to pick it up.

"Is that...?" I begin to ask but then stop. I know what it is.
It's the knife. "It doesn't mean that Violet..." I say but Officer
Grady holds up a finger to silence me.

Cora gets to her feet and shoves Jordyn, who stumbles back
a few steps. Cora turns her head as if something has caught her
attention. Jordyn lunges, arms outstretched, striking Cora on
the back with both hands. Cora falls hard and doesn't immediately get up. Violet bends over as if checking on Cora.

Violet's and Jordyn's heads snap toward something off camera. Even Cora, from her spot on the ground, looks up. Jordyn
and Violet run off in different directions as Cora struggles to
her feet, clutching at her arm, and staggers away.

"Just wait," Officer Grady says as I start to speak. Several minutes pass with nothing but even though I know what's coming I can't help squirming in my seat. I don't dare blink, afraid of missing something, and I keep my eyes on the screen.

A shape rushes past so quickly that I can't tell who it is. Officer Grady stops the video, backs it up fifteen seconds and replays it. "We're pretty sure that's Jordyn Petit. See the backpack in her hand?"

I nod and we continue to watch the video. The train rushes by and then several more minutes pass. Finally, a woman and her dog come into view. The dog sniffs at the weeds, searching for the best spot to relieve himself while the woman, holding the leash, taps her foot impatiently. The dog, nose to the ground, perks up his ears and pulls on the leash, dragging the woman out of the frame.

The seconds on the time stamp tick by until Officer Grady fast-forwards the video. "The witness calls 9-1-1 and we show up about ten minutes later."

Right on cue a handful of cops run through the train yard and soon after two EMTs rush past carrying their medical gear. The woman and her dog, escorted by an officer, come back into sight. She is frantically waving her arms and talking when she suddenly looks at her hands as if seeing them for the first time. This is where I must have asked, *Is that blood?*

The EMTs hurry by again, this time carrying Cora on a stretcher. In the upper corner of the video a shadow appears. It's all I can do to not rip the phone from Officer Grady's hands to get a closer look.

"What are you looking at?" comes a voice from the doorway. Max has returned.

"Quiet," I demand and see the hurt on his face. *Dammit*, I think. I can't seem to win with Max right now. Max is part of this family. Shouldn't he hear what's going on? "I'm sorry, Max," I tell him. He nods but I can tell his feelings are hurt.

He stands behind us and watches as I return my attention to the video. The person on the edge of the video gets closer and I know it's Violet.

Her movements are odd. Zombielike and she's carrying something in her hand. My stomach lurches. The knife. Violet drops it to the ground and the next thirty seconds of film are chaos. I watch myself running toward her, my feet kicking up the dusty gravel, a cop at my heels. Me, pulling a bloody Violet into my arms, thinking that she was dying, laying her on the ground.

Violet was holding the knife. Officer Grady pauses the video and I stare at the two of us frozen in time: Violet's eyes are black holes, my mouth opens in a silent scream. This is it, I think. This is the exact moment that our lives were changed forever.

"I was hoping that you might be able to recognize a fourth person in the video," Officer Grady says. He hits Play. "Look. There. Do you see it?" At the upper edge of the video I do think I see someone. It's blurry and shows someone walking quickly, but not running, through the camera's frame.

I nod. "Yeah, I see it."

"It's not one of the girls," Grady says. "They ran in different directions. It's like they were running from him." He taps Pause again.

Relief floods through me. "There was someone else there. I knew it."

"Can I take a closer look?" Max asks and Officer Grady hands him the phone and he watches the video several times, stopping and starting it over and over.

"Max, what is it?" I ask, getting impatient. This does not look good for Violet and I'm sure that Officer Grady is just minutes away from arresting her.

"I know who that is," Max says, looking up from the screen. "It's Gabe Shannon, he's in Violet's class. I can tell by his hat."

Jordyn:
Be there at midnight. This
is going to be awesome.

Gabe:
Yeah, I'll be there. I'll hide in the
grass until you give me the signal.

Jordyn:
Remember Violet doesn't know you're
coming either. I'll start screaming and
give you the knife. Then you go after
Cora. She'll shit her pants.

Mar. 20, 2018

I can't get out of bed. My mom thinks I've got the flu or something. I've missed a bunch of school and haven't showered in like four days. I don't understand why Joseph doesn't send me a message.

I called Mr. Dover late last night and he tried to make me feel better. He said everyone missed me but I know that's not true. I could disappear and no one would care.

My mind kept returning to the sound of utter disbelief in Cora's voice when she told me that Joseph Wither didn't stay. I had wanted to talk with Cora more about it, but Mara and Jim rushed back into the room frantic after her fever spiked.

Clearly, someone pretending to be Joseph Wither was with Cora the night she was attacked; that's most likely the one who attacked her. Or perhaps she just imagined he was there. But why would Cora sound so sad about him leaving? Was he someone she knew?

It's not uncommon for victims of abuse to become dependent on the perpetrator, to seek out their approval. It's all part of the abuser's sadistic, manipulative game. I wanted to talk with her more, wanted to see if she could remember anything new about her encounter that night.

Cora had also expressed doubts about her friends, Violet and Jordyn. If only she remembered. At the time I believed that if my conversations with Cora could help her identify the person who did this to her, then so be it. In my line of work there were often unanswered questions and a lack of closure. It wasn't my job to catch the bad guys. My role was to help children who experience trauma identify and describe the feelings they had and from there develop tools and healthy coping responses in order to increase the feelings of control and self-reliance.

I logged into the hospital's electronic file system and pulled up Cora's medical records and went right to the April 15 file. I clicked on the photographs that the ER nurse took of Cora's injuries and winced at the sight. From Cora's injuries, it appeared she had to be facing her attacker when she was stabbed, but it was after midnight. Maybe it was too dark or maybe the attacker knocked her out before she could clearly see who it was.

Cora was struck by the knife one time. A four-inch horizontal slash on her left side just above the abdomen.

The head, arm and facial injuries appeared to be made by some kind of blunt object. From the pictures and X-rays there was really no way for me to tell exactly what weapon was used. The toxicology screen showed no evidence of drugs or alcohol. There was nothing new to be learned there.

It was the injury to the arm that didn't make a lot of sense to me. Did the attacker begin by using one kind of weapon and then transfer to another? It was possible.

Perhaps Cora fought back, causing the attacker to drop the knife or the blunt weapon. There didn't appear to be defensive wounds on any part of Cora's body. No sliced fingers or arms to show that she put up a fight.

Why didn't she fight back? Was it because the attacker was someone she knew? Someone she trusted? Could it have been one of her friends—Violet or Jordyn, or both? Something still didn't seem quite right but I just hadn't landed on it, not yet.

When I went back to check on Cora the room to her door was shut and a sign was affixed to the door frame—*I'm resting, please do not disturb.* I decided to take a chance and lightly tapped on the door. When it opened I came face-to-face with Jim Landry. "Yes?" he asked brusquely.

"How's she doing?" I whispered.

"She's sleeping," he answered shortly. I was about ready to apologize for disturbing them when Mara stepped out from behind her husband and joined us in the hallway.

"She's got an infection." Mara's face was pale, strained. "In her eye."

"I'm sorry," I said. "What is the doctor saying?"

"More antibiotics and now we just wait and see."

This is not good. Mara doesn't say it, but I know that there's a chance that Cora could lose her eye.

"If you can excuse us," Jim said. He looked helpless, defeated. But there's something else on his face. Guilt, perhaps. He looked past my shoulder and brushed past me, moving down the hallway. I turned and saw him striding toward a police officer.

"Oh, God," Mara said, running her fingers through her hair. "I can't deal with this right now. They keep wanting to ask Cora questions and she can't answer them. She doesn't remember anything."

I thought about what Cora told me earlier about how Joseph Wither didn't stay at the train yard with her. If Cora remembered this, then maybe she remembered more details, but I couldn't just come out and tell Mara what her daughter revealed to me during our discussions. The guidelines about patient confidentiality are very clear. "The police often need to question victims several times. It's surprising what witnesses can remember over time," I explained.

"I know," Mara said in resignation. "I just wish this would all go away, that none of this ever happened." Jim Landry and the police officer approached us. Both look dazed, somber. "What is it?" Mara asked when she saw their faces. Neither spoke. "Tell me."

"We've brought in another witness. Someone else who was at the train yard that night. I wanted to tell you in person," the officer said.

Jim let out a frustrated puff of air. "Is it Violet?"

"No, a young man. Gabe Shannon. He was on surveillance footage from the train yard," the officer explained.

"Gabe Shannon?" Mara repeated. "We've known the Shannons for years. I work with his mother. Gabe and Cora have gone to school together since preschool. She likes Gabe."

"You have video? I want to see it," Jim demanded.

"We can't share that with you just yet," the officer explained. "We're still investigating."

"The attack's on that video, isn't it? What about that Crow girl? She was in on it, too, right?" Jim asks.

"I can't speak to that, but what I can say is that we're getting to the bottom of it. But I will need to talk with Cora again. We have more questions."

"Please not now, not today," Mara said through her tears. "She's sick. She has a high fever and an infection."

"Okay," the officer acquiesced. "But soon. It's crucial that we talk to her. I hope Cora feels better and I'm sorry. About everything." He walked away, and the enormity of these arrests hit me hard. Pitch is a small town. Everyone knows everyone else.

"Oh, my God," Mara gasped. "What if it was Violet? He said that there may be more arrests. What if Violet was in on it?"

"Don't jump to any conclusions," I said. "I'm sure more information will be coming soon." I thought of my recent session with Violet Crow. She seemed to be telling the truth. She appeared to be genuinely frightened.

"I can't take this," Mara cried. "I can't take not knowing why they did this to her." She turned to me. "Can you talk to her mother? Violet's mom? Can you try and find out what she knows?"

I hesitated. "Mara, I'm not an investigator. My job is to help Cora."

"But getting more information about what happened would help her, wouldn't it?" Mara looked at me desperately.

"I can ask some questions but that doesn't mean I can share what I find out with you. You understand that, right?"

"I don't care. I just want you to help Cora. Please."

"And how do we tell Cora that her best friends tried to kill her?" Jim hissed through clenched teeth. "How are we going to do that?"

JW44:

I'M SORRY I HAVEN'T WRITTEN IN SO LONG. IT JUST ISN'T SAFE.
I'M SORRY YOU WERE SO WORRIED. DID YOU REALLY STAND IN
FRONT OF THE WINDOW WITH YOUR SHIRT OFF? WE HAVE TO
BE CAREFUL. PEOPLE MAY BE WATCHING US. I THINK OF YOU
ALL THE TIME. I SAW YOU THE OTHER DAY WITH YOUR FRIENDS.
THEY TALK ABOUT YOU. DID YOU KNOW THAT? THEY SAY MEAN
THINGS. THEY SAY THAT YOU ARE ANNOYING AND BORING. THEY
SAY YOU ARE A THIEF. THEY SAY YOU LIKE GABE BUT HE THINKS
YOU ARE JUST A BABY. I THOUGHT YOU'D WANT TO KNOW. I
KNOW I WOULD. THEY AREN'T REALLY YOUR FRIENDS. I'M YOUR
FRIEND. REMEMBER THAT, CORA.

Apr. 1, 2018

It's almost like things used to be. Violet and I sit together at lunch every day and everyone seems like they forgot about the whole Rachel Farmer disaster. Even Kaley forgave me. Mr. Dover set it up so I could talk to Kaley in private in his classroom.

I told Kaley I was really sorry. That I didn't know about her aunt, that I didn't mean to hurt her. Kaley said it was okay and gave me a hug. When she left I sat down in my desk and started to cry. Mr. Dover came back into the classroom, sat next to me and just waited with me until I stopped.

Things are still weird with Jordyn. I mean, she's not totally ignoring me but whenever I say something or when Gabe talks to me she just stares at me with this look on her face like I just said the dumbest thing in the world.

On Friday, Gabe and I were goofing around after school and he put his hat on top of my head and I pretended that I was going to go home with it and we were laughing and laughing. Jordyn did not like this at all and ripped the hat off my head, pulling a chunk of my hair with it. It hurt and my eyes welled up but I didn't cry. Gabe told Jordyn to relax and he grabbed the hat back from her and put it back on my head again.

When I told Wither about this he said, *I told you so. I told you she wasn't your friend.* Then he said something that kind of scared me but also made me feel good.

Do you want me to shut her up for you?

Apr. 12, 2018

Today after school Violet came over. It's been nice having a best friend, but I feel kind of weird ever since Joseph told me the mean things that she and Jordyn have been saying about me. I want to ask her about it, but I'm afraid to. I mean, I'm just happy that she's talking to me again. Violet doesn't act like she thinks I'm annoying and boring. She seems to like hanging out with me but I guess it could all be an act.

We grabbed a snack and ran upstairs to my bedroom and started doing our homework when someone pounded on the door. Violet and I screamed and we heard someone laughing from the hallway and then Jordyn walked in.

I don't trust her. I can't believe she has forgiven me for ruining our presentation and slapping her. Plus, Gabe has started sitting next to me at lunchtime again and he talks mostly to me. I counted the other day. Gabe talked directly to me five times and to Jordyn just two times. Jordyn didn't like that at all. She kept trying to take over the conversation but Gabe pretty much ignored her.

Anyway, Jordyn barged in the room waving a piece of paper and practically screamed, "I've got a great idea. Let's go find Wither!" Violet and I both said *Shh* at the same time.

She flopped down on my bed and we sat down next to her and Violet tried to grab the paper out of her hand, but she held it high over her head.

"Why would we want to find Joseph?" I asked Jordyn as if this was the craziest thing I've ever heard.

"Duh, because *Joseph* loves you, Corareef12," she said. I nearly threw up. I looked over at Violet but she wouldn't look me in the eye. She told Jordyn about DarkestDoor and the letters. She promised that we wouldn't tell anyone about it, especially Jordyn. I wanted to cry and it was a miracle that I didn't, but there was no way I was going to let Jordyn see me blubbering like a baby.

Later, Violet told me that she only told Jordyn about DarkestDoor and not about the letters he left for me. I don't know if I believe her or not. Everyone in school probably knows about it now.

Jordyn took her own sweet time showing us the piece of paper she was holding. It ended up being a map she drew of town, but not a very good one. I asked her what the X's meant and she said that the X's were the places in town where Wither supposedly killed or kidnapped a girl over the years. There was an X by Locust Creek, one by the cemetery and another X in the train yard. Violet told her that she forgot a few.

"Oh, well, let's just ask him," Jordyn said and pulled up the DarkestDoor site on her phone.

For once in my life I stood up to Jordyn and took the phone out of her hand before she could post anything.

"Stop it!" I told her. "It was just a joke. I don't even talk to him anymore." This was a lie, of course.

But Jordyn wasn't giving up. "This is perfect," she said. "We'll go to the train yard and once he shows up to grab Cora we'll..." She crossed her hands over her neck in a choking motion and stuck out her tongue.

I kept saying what a stupid plan it was. How there was no way we could get to the depot without our parents finding out—which was a total lie. I still go back to the Primrose every few days to see if Wither left a note for me in the jar. Violet said that if we spent the night at her house there was a good chance we could sneak out and not get caught because her mom would go up to bed and leave us alone while we slept in their living room.

I looked at Violet and realized that she was full-in on this plan and not on my side anymore. Jordyn was winning. She was trying to take Gabe from me (okay, I know he's not really mine, but I think he likes me) and she's trying to take Violet from me, too.

I told them that going to Violet's house wasn't going to work because number one, my mom never lets me spend the night at anyone else's house, and number two, Violet's house is like four miles away from the train yard.

"I guess we'll just have to go without you," Jordyn said in a fakey voice that sounded like she felt bad but I knew she didn't. The only thing worse than going to the train yard with Jordyn was to have her go there without me.

I said I would ask my mom if they could spend the night and Jordyn said she would bring the weapon because we needed to protect ourselves. Violet didn't say much of anything. I think she knew I was mad at her. At five thirty my mom poked her head inside my room and said that Violet's mom was there to pick her up. I didn't say goodbye.

Jordyn:
I really think she believes this Wither crap.

Violet:
Yeah. It's pretty scary, though

Jordyn:
Not you, too? You're both such dorks

Jordyn:
JK. Don't be mad

Violet:
It's just creepy. Maybe we shouldn't go

Jordyn:
Srsly? Don't chicken out now. Besides, it will be hilarious

Violet:
IDK

Jordyn:
Never mind. I'll ask someone else to go. I thought you were up for it

Violet:
I am!

Jordyn:
K. CU Sunday

OFFICER WILSON: Okay, Jordyn. Your attorney tells me that you have some additional information regarding the incident at the train yard. Is that right?

JORDYN PETIT: Yes.

OFFICER WILSON: It's very important that you answer my questions thoroughly and honestly. Do you understand?

JORDYN PETIT: Yes.

OFFICER WILSON: Because the assistant district attorney is holding off on your arraignment because you told Mr. Peale here that you had some information that could help the police. Is that right?

ROBERT PEALE: I explained this all to Jordyn. She is well aware that she needs to be completely truthful. She knows that you will have to investigate her claims before she is allowed to go home. Right, Jordyn?

JORDYN PETIT: Right.

OFFICER WILSON: Okay, Jordyn, tell me what happened the night of April 15.

JORDYN PETIT: Where should I start? At Cora's house or at the train yard?

ROBERT PEALE: Why don't you start at the train yard, Jordyn. That's what's important here. If Officer Wilson has more questions, she'll ask.

JORDYN PETIT: We went to the train yard, like I said.

OFFICER WILSON: For the record, who went to the train yard?

JORDYN PETIT: Me, Violet and Cora. We were going to look for Joseph Wither. We did a project on him for school and we wanted to see if we could find him. Later Gabe was going to meet us there.

OFFICER WILSON: What made you think Joseph Wither was going to be there?

JORDYN PETIT: Well, I knew he wasn't really going to be there. I knew he was make-believe but Cora thought he was real and I think that Violet kind of believed it, too. Cora went on this chat room and met someone who said he was Joseph Wither. He kept telling Cora how much he liked her. How special she was.

OFFICER WILSON: A chat room? Did you tell anyone about this? Your grandpa? A teacher, maybe?

JORDYN PETIT: No. Cora made us promise that we wouldn't and we didn't want Cora to get into trouble. Her parents don't let her go online much. She would have gotten in big trouble if they found out.

OFFICER WILSON: Do you remember the name of the website?

JORDYN PETIT: DarkDoor? No, it was DarkestDoor.

OFFICER WILSON: Okay, so you went to the train yard to look for Wither…

JORDYN PETIT: Yeah. Violet and I were going to play a prank on Cora. We were going to pretend that we saw Wither and scream and yell. Gabe was going to be there, too, and jump out. Violet didn't know that Gabe was coming, though. We brought a knife and I was going to pretend to be stabbed by Wither, who was really Gabe. Then I was just going to get up and show her that I was okay. We just wanted to scare her.

OFFICER WILSON: Is that what happened? You scared her?

JORDYN PETIT: No. We didn't get a chance to.

OFFICER WILSON: Why's that?

JORDYN PETIT: I don't know for sure. At first it was fun being at the depot so late. It was dark and creepy. But it was cold and I started to get nervous we were going to get in trouble so I told Cora and Violet that I wanted to go home.

OFFICER WILSON: Did the other girls want to leave, too?

JORDYN PETIT: Cora wanted to stay. She wanted to keep looking for Wither. When I tried to walk away she got mad and grabbed on to my backpack and almost knocked me down. I turned around and pushed her. She fell down.

OFFICER WILSON: That's when she got hurt?

JORDYN PETIT: She was holding her arm. I didn't mean to push her so hard but she yanked on my book bag first. Then we heard a noise off in the grass. At first I thought it was Gabe but then I wasn't sure. It was dark and scary so we ran off.

OFFICER WILSON: Did you run away together? In the same direction?

JORDYN PETIT: No. We all went a different way. I ran toward the depot building and hid behind a boxcar. I'm not sure where Cora and Violet went. I never saw Gabe.

OFFICER WILSON: Then what happened?

JORDYN PETIT: I watched from behind the boxcar for a few minutes.

OFFICER WILSON: What did you see?

JORDYN PETIT: (inaudible)

OFFICER WILSON: Jordyn, what did you see?

JORDYN PETIT: I'm afraid to tell.

ROBERT PEALE: It's okay, Jordyn. No one can hurt you here. Go ahead and tell Officer Wilson what you told me.

OFFICER WILSON: Jordyn?

JORDYN PETIT: I saw Violet run off toward the tall grass—not to the spot where we heard the noise, the opposite direction—and she disappeared. She hid in there. Cora started to run along the tracks but she was going slow because of her arm, I think. She was holding it.

OFFICER WILSON: Which way on the tracks was Cora going? East or west?

JORDYN PETIT: Um, I don't know. But she went away from the depot building.

OFFICER WILSON: You were hiding behind a boxcar and saw Cora and Violet running away, too. Then what did you see?

JORDYN PETIT: I saw someone coming out of the grass.

OFFICER WILSON: Did you recognize the person? Did you know who it was?

JORDYN PETIT: I think so.

ROBERT PEALE: Remember, Jordyn, you have to be sure. If you're not, you need to tell us. It's very, very important that you get this right.

OFFICER WILSON: Jordyn, do you know who it was coming out of the grass?

JORDYN PETIT: It was my teacher. It was Mr. Dover.

I sit alone in the waiting room staring down at my hands, images of the video running over and over in my mind. The girls happy one moment, taking selfies in front of the boxcars, then everything went to hell. I wonder why Gabe Shannon was there. Violet never mentioned him being there. Then there was the bloody knife Violet dropped when she came out of the tall grass. I wish I could watch the video again to see if Violet was the one holding the knife just before the girls ran off.

"Ms. Crow?" comes a voice from the doorway. I look up to find Dr. Gideon in the doorway.

I jump to my feet. "Is Violet okay?" I ask.

"I was hoping we could go somewhere a little more private and have a chat," she says.

I hesitate. "I don't want to go too far away from Violet."

"We can leave a message at the nurses' desk and they can alert us if anything comes up," Dr. Gideon assures me.

"Okay," I say and send a quick text to Max to let him know where I am. Though I was reluctant, I had sent him home to check on Boomer, to get me a fresh change of clothes.

Dr. Gideon and I walk together in silence until we reach her office. She steps aside and allows me to enter first. The office isn't large but is brand-new like the rest of the children's hospital. New carpet smell fills my nose and the walls are empty except for a framed medical degree hanging behind a cherrywood desk. In fact, it looks like she's still moving in. Cardboard boxes are stacked in a corner in front of an empty bookshelf.

"Pardon the mess," Dr. Gideon says and invites me to sit in a chair situated in front of her desk. "I'm just getting settled in." Dr. Gideon is tall and looks more like an aging WNBA player than a doctor. "Never played," Dr. Gideon says, reading my mind. She sits behind her desk and smiles. "Everyone had high hopes for me, especially my dad, but I was more interested in reading books than shooting hoops." I nod, embarrassed and more than freaked out that she knew what I was thinking.

"She's so young to be here by herself," I say, choking up. I think of the ratty stuffed monkey that she still sleeps with once in a while and wonder if they'll let me bring it from home for her.

Dr. Gideon looks at me kindly. "I know this has been very difficult," she says. "As a mom you know that so many different factors can impact a child's behavior." I nod. This is true. Some days I wake up and wonder which child will be sitting at the kitchen table that morning. But I've worried more about Max than Violet and another lightning bolt of guilt hits me. Have I been so caught up in Max's teenage drama that I ignored my daughter?

"Based on my visits with Violet I anticipate that she will go home tomorrow. I do suggest that you follow up with some sort of emotional support for her. I've got some resources for you and a list of counselors that you may want to contact."

I take the handwritten list from Dr. Gideon but all I've registered is that Violet gets to go home tomorrow.

"I know your first concern is Violet, as it should be, but I'm hoping you can perhaps answer a few questions that I have—so that I can better understand the situation as a whole," Dr. Gideon says.

"What do you mean?" I ask in confusion. "I don't know what I can possibly tell you."

"I've gotten permission from Cora Landry's mother to visit with you and to share that I'm working with the Landry family as they navigate through this difficult situation."

I sit in silent disbelief and seeing the look on my face Dr. Gideon continues. "I promise you that what you say will be held in confidence."

"I've got nothing to say to you," I say bluntly. "Is this even ethical? Violet did not have anything to do with hurting Cora. I don't care what anyone says."

"Ms. Crow," Dr. Gideon says gently. "I'm not here to gather any evidence to use against your daughter. I'm just trying to understand some of the peripheral aspects of what happened."

"Peripheral aspects?" I repeat, my voice shaking with anger. "Is this your fancy way of asking if my daughter is crazy or some psycho bully who lured Cora to the train yard to ambush her?"

"Not at all, Ms. Crow. As I said, I don't see signs of mental illness in Violet. I do think she experienced something terrifying in that train yard."

I think back to over the last few months and the whole Joseph Wither project she'd been working on with Cora and Jordyn. I was so excited to see her fitting in at school, that she was finally part of a group, that she finally had a best friend. Some friends, I think. Jordyn and another boy arrested for the attack. It could very easily have been Violet who was targeted.

JW44:
THANKS FOR WARNING ME ABOUT YOUR FRIENDS' PLAN TO COME
TO THE TRAIN YARD ON SUNDAY NIGHT. YOU DON'T NEED TO
WORRY, THOUGH. NO ONE CAN STOP ME.

Corareef12:
You're welcome. I just thought you'd want to know. I hate them.
I'm going to cancel the overnight.

JW44:
DON'T DO THAT. THEY'LL NEVER SEE ME COMING.

Corareef12:
What do you mean?

JW44:
I MEAN, THEY MAY THINK THEY'LL BE READY FOR ME BUT NO
ONE EVER IS. WHAT ABOUT YOU? ARE YOU READY?

Corareef12:
I don't want to have them spend the night. They are awful.

JW44:
FINE. MAYBE THEY'LL STILL GO TO THE TRAIN YARD ON SUNDAY.
JORDYN IS VERY PRETTY. MAYBE SHE'LL WANT TO COME WITH ME.

OFFICER GRADY: Thanks for agreeing to come in again, John. I'm Officer Keith Grady and I'll be interviewing you this afternoon.

JOHN DOVER: I guess I'm a little confused. I thought I answered all the questions the other officer had for me yesterday.

OFFICER GRADY: We just have a few more things to go over, then you can be on your way. Sound okay?

JOHN DOVER: Sure. Fine. I want to help.

OFFICER GRADY: What can you tell me about a website called DarkestDoor?

JOHN DOVER: DarkestDoor? Never heard of it.

OFFICER GRADY: You never stumbled across it while doing a web search of some kind?

JOHN DOVER: I guess I may have. I've been on a lot of websites. But I don't recall that one specifically. I may have gone on it. Do you remember the name of every website you've ever surfed?

OFFICER GRADY: Think hard, John. We have a warrant for your home and school computers right now. Our tech guys are pretty good at their job and will be able to figure out your digital footprint pretty quickly.

JOHN DOVER: Why are you searching my computers? I don't understand. I haven't done anything.

OFFICER GRADY: Where were you on Sunday night, John?

JOHN DOVER: I already told the other officer. I went to Grayling with some coworkers. I got home around midnight.

OFFICER GRADY: And you were there the rest of the night?

JOHN DOVER: Yes!

OFFICER GRADY: Can anyone vouch for you?

JOHN DOVER: Brett Reese dropped me off at about midnight but after that, no. I went to bed.

OFFICER GRADY: You live just a few blocks from the train yard, don't you?

JOHN DOVER: Yeah, but so do a lot of people.

OFFICER GRADY: True. But those people don't have an eyewitness who says she saw them at the train yard right around the time Cora Landry was attacked.

JOHN DOVER: Someone said they saw me? Who? They're lying. I was at home.

OFFICER GRADY: Sit down, John. I understand why you're upset but if you're telling the truth you have nothing to worry about.

JOHN DOVER: I am telling the truth. Who said they saw me at the train yard? It's a lie.

OFFICER GRADY: You went to visit Cora Landry at the hospital earlier this week, is that correct?

JOHN DOVER: Yes. She was severely hurt. She was my student. Is my student. I don't think that's so unusual. Lots of teachers probably do the same thing.

OFFICER GRADY: But this is the problem, John. You have a history of inappropriate communication with students. Your principal said that Cora was eating lunch alone with you in your classroom. And now someone says they saw you at the train yard the night of the attack.

JOHN DOVER: I can explain all that. Jesus Christ. Am I under arrest?

OFFICER GRADY: No, you're not.

JOHN DOVER: Then I'm free to go, right?

OFFICER GRADY: Certainly. Just don't go too far. I'm sure we'll be speaking again soon. And by the way, I'm going to need your phone. I'm not going to find any phone calls between you and Cora Landry on this phone, am I?

I decided to leave the hospital at a decent time and met my colleague Michaela at a nearby restaurant for dinner. It was a mild evening; the earlier overcast skies had cleared, the temperature warmer than it was before the sunset. The streetlights reflected off the wet pavement and I tried to avoid the puddles that impeded my path so that I moved like a drunken college student lurching from bar to bar.

We ordered wine and pasta and as we ate I updated Michaela on how Cora was doing, how she developed a bad infection, the weird vibe I got from her parents, what Cora said about Joseph Wither leaving her at the train yard. As I talked, Michaela's face changed from polite interest to disconcertion. "What?" I asked.

"I was just thinking how innocent our childhoods were. I mean, I grew up in a pretty tough neighborhood but little girls didn't get stabbed," Michaela said.

"Oh, there were monsters back then," I told her. "Sometimes they were just better hidden." We both thought about this for a second, the only sound the clank of silverware against the ceramic dishes.

"It's strange." I broke the silence. "At first, Cora mentioned this Wither entity and then she said she had no idea who attacked her, that she didn't see anything, but from my visits with Cora, she hinted at the idea that she thought Joseph Wither was real, too. Then today, when her parents told her about the arrests, Cora didn't act surprised at all, more like…resigned. In fact, the big sister was more upset than anyone. She started crying and ran out of the room when she heard the news."

"So the friends did it, then," Michaela said matter-of-factly.

"I don't know." I sighed. "But apparently the police have some physical evidence, social media posts and a video."

"The attack was caught on video?" Michaela asked in surprise.

"I didn't get the sense that it was quite as dramatic as that." I pushed my plate away. "More like the video put them in the area at the time of the assault."

"Any drugs or alcohol involved?" Michaela asked.

"There wasn't any in Cora's system. I don't know about the other girls. But Cora has a pretty bad infection and the docs are talking about more surgery. When I left she had a high fever."

"Sad all around," Michaela said.

"Yes, it is," I agreed.

My phone buzzed and reluctantly I answered it. It's the hospital. "This is Dr. Gideon," I said. I listened to the resident on the other end and with each word my stomach dropped. "I'll be right there."

"What is it?" Michaela asked. "Did Cora take a turn for the worse?"

"No," I said as I grabbed my coat from the back of my chair. "It's her sister, Kendall. She just tried to kill herself."

I rushed back to the hospital, and made a beeline to the emergency room where Kendall was being treated.

My old friend Dr. Soto was working again. "Where are they?" I asked and he directed me to one of the examination rooms. I tapped on the glass and when the door slid open I was slammed with a sense of déjà vu. Kendall was attached to an IV, eyes closed, her mouth black with chalky charcoal, a sure sign they pumped her stomach. Mara was sitting in a chair next to her, bent over in anguish.

"Mara," I whispered. "How is she? How are you?"

Mara lifted her head; her eyes were bloodshot, her face streaked with tears. "I don't know what's happening," she choked out. "Why would Kendall do something like this?" Kendall stirred in her bed and Mara and I moved to the hallway.

"She took pills?" I asked.

Mara wiped her eyes with the heel of her hand. "Yeah, after she ran out of Cora's room earlier she didn't come back and, honestly, we didn't go looking for her. Cora's fever spiked again and we were worried about her." Mara looked over at Kendall's sleeping form. "We just thought that it was overwhelming for Kendall and she needed some fresh air, some space. If I knew she was going to do this, I would have gone after her. She swallowed a bottle of Tylenol PM and God knows what else."

"Has she been conscious?" I asked.

"Yes, just sleepy. I've nearly lost both my children in a matter of days, Dr. Gideon. What has my family done to deserve this? My husband is beside himself with anger. Did you know they let those kids go home? Can you believe that?"

This was news to me. Last I heard, Jordyn and the boy were the main suspects and were in custody and being questioned. Things were happening so fast. "Cora could lose her eye and Kendall tried to...and she refuses to talk to me, won't tell me what she was thinking." Mara looked at me helplessly. "How can I help her if she doesn't tell me what's wrong?"

"Sometimes confiding to those people who mean the most to us can be the most difficult," I said. On the other side of the door Kendall blinked her eyes open.

"But she should know that she can always talk to me. I'm her mom." Mara's voice broke on the final word.

"Would you like me to visit with Kendall?" I asked.

Mara dug a tissue out of her pocket and dabbed at her nose. "But you can't repeat what she says to you, right?" Mara asked. "I won't be any closer to knowing why she did this."

"You're right," I told her. "I can't tell you the details of our conversation but I can help Kendall process what's been happening, help her try to understand what she's feeling. And I can encourage her to talk to you."

Mara and I looked through the glass at Kendall, who pushed herself up in bed and wiped at her mouth with her sleeve, grimacing at the taste of charcoal. "It's up to you, Mara, but at some point Kendall is going to need to talk to someone." Mara knocked on the glass and gave Kendall a little wave and tried to muster a smile. Kendall looked away, pretending she didn't see.

"Oh, Jesus," Mara said, pressing her forehead against the door. "I can't take much more of this and I know that Jim is already at the end of his rope. Please talk to Kendall. Please help her."

"Give us a half hour," I suggested. "It will be a start."

Mara released a shuddery breath. "What should I do? I don't know what to do."

"Your husband is with Cora and I'm here with Kendall. Maybe go down to the cafeteria, take a walk."

Mara looked hesitant. "How about just fifteen minutes?" I asked.

"Okay," Mara agreed. "Okay." I watched from the doorway as Mara went back into the examination room to tell Kendall that she'd be right back. She leaned down to give Kendall a peck on the cheek but her daughter pulled away and the kiss was lost to the air.

I made sure Mara was heading toward the elevators before I stepped back into the examination room. Kendall crossed her arms over her chest and stared at the ceiling, trying to set her chin in defiance but couldn't quite keep it from trembling. I pulled a chair close to her bedside and sat. "You've had quite the day," I said.

"Are you going to start yelling at me, too?" she asked hatefully, her voice raspy. Most likely from the tube that was shoved down her throat. "My dad freaked out. *How could you do this, Kendall? How could you do this to us?*" She lowered her voice, mimicking her father. "Like it had anything to do with them."

"It didn't?" I asked. "Your parents have been focusing a lot of their attention on Cora..."

"You think I swallowed those pills because I'm *jealous*? Are you kidding me? I just want it all to go away."

"What do you want to go away?" I asked. The pain in her eyes was difficult to witness.

Kendall eased back onto her pillow and closed her eyelids. "I did something bad," she murmured, tears squeezing from the corners of her eyes. Minutes ticked by as I waited for her to say more and she finally opened her eyes. "What Cora says to you is private, right?" she asked. "So you can't tell anybody what I say either, right?"

"That's right," I said. "As long as you aren't planning to hurt yourself again or aren't planning to hurt someone else, what you say to me will be confidential."

Kendall thought about this; red dots pinpricked the skin beneath her eyes, broken blood vessels from vomiting up the pills she had taken. "Even to my parents?" she asked. "Even to the police?"

My pulse quickened but I kept my face neutral. "That's right. I can't tell your parents or the police."

"It's my fault," she whispered. "What happened to Cora. Emery and I were the ones pretending to be Wither. I found out Cora was looking for information about him in a chat room. It was just a joke. We didn't really think she would fall for it. But she did." Kendall swallowed with difficulty and I picked up a glass of water next to her bed and held it out to her. She waved it away.

"After a few days I told Emery we needed to stop," Kendall explained. "And I thought she agreed. But she kept going. I didn't know. I swear. But Cora was acting all weird so I checked the website and found the emails. Emery was the one who told Cora to go to the train yard." Kendall bit her lip, drawing blood. Tears streamed down her cheeks and thick mucus collected beneath her nose. "She's the one who told Cora that she could see Joseph Wither in person. That all they had to do was go to the train yard at midnight. It was supposed to be a joke." Kendall clutched at the bedsheets, twisting them between her fingers.

"I know we should have never done it in the first place. But I tried to stop it, I really did."

I tried not to let the horror show on my face. "Do you think that Emery may have been the one to attack your sister?" I asked.

Kendall shook her head vigorously. "No, no. That night I was texting with her until after midnight. And when she heard about what happened she became hysterical. It was so mean of her but she wouldn't hurt anyone. I don't know what to do," she cried, covering her face with her hands. "What should I do?"

It shouldn't have surprised me, the cruelty of young girls, but in this case it did. One impulsive act had set off an avalanche of events that had resulted in an attack on a little girl, two arrests and an attempted suicide.

I chose my words carefully. "It's up to you, Kendall, but since you are asking for my advice, I think you should tell your parents and then talk to the police together. Eventually the police will find out that you and Emery were the ones who posted on the website. It won't be easy, but it will be better for everyone if you tell the truth."

"Can you be with me? When I talk to them?" She looked so young, so scared.

"Of course. When you're ready, you let me know."

"But not right now." She turned her head away from me, closed her eyes. "Maybe tomorrow."

Thomas is in his truck just before the sun rises. He didn't sleep well last night. Someone was sneaking around the back of the house. He had tried to catch whoever was out there but his arthritic legs couldn't move fast enough. At any rate he was able to scare them off before they caused any mischief.

When he finally got back into bed his mind started replaying the events of the day before. Thomas went to the courthouse, Jordyn's dress clothes in hand, fully expecting that she would be arraigned. He wasn't sure what she was going to talk about, but it didn't sound good.

When he got there, Robert told him that the arraignment was postponed, Jordyn was being reinterviewed by the police and more than likely she was going to get to come home the next day. Though Thomas pressed him, Robert wouldn't give any details as to what bombshell Jordyn was about to drop. He said the police had to investigate Jordyn's claims and he'd be able to share more soon. "I believe her," Robert had told him and Thomas breathed a sigh of relief.

Thomas drives up and down the quiet streets of Pitch to center himself. Most homes are still steeped in darkness with lights off and shades drawn. He could put a name to just about each and every house he passed, and if he couldn't remember names he remembered drinks.

Simon Gaspar lives there in the green house with the white shutters. He is partial to gin and tonics with a twist of lime. The Porters live across the street in the gray house with the bay window. Roy Porter likes rum and Coke while his wife always orders a Long Island iced tea. The woman in the yellow house at the end of the block asks for something called a Fallen Angel, a concoction made with gin, white crème de menthe, lemons, bitters and a cherry on top.

Thomas finds himself on Hickory, a street whose inhabitants tend to like their booze cheap and hard. He rolls past the Crow home and for the life of him he can't associate any sort of liquor with Beth. In fact, he's not even certain that Beth has stepped foot in the bar. Not much of a drinker, Thomas thinks. Or just not a barfly. Thomas remembers Jordyn saying something about how Violet's mom worked all the time. He imagines it's not easy being a single parent and can't fathom raising his boys on his own.

He wants to be angry with Beth and wants to hate Violet, but finds he can't. Violet has always seemed like a nice girl, has always seemed to bring out a softer side of Jordyn. He didn't know much about that boy Gabe.

The sun is just beginning to rise, turning the eastern sky moscato pink and triple sec gold while the west remains blanketed in what's left of the night. Thomas heads back west, passing by a whiskey sour, a Tom Collins and a planter's punch. He turns onto Apple Street and drives slowly past the teacher's house. John Dover. Cold Press Black Ale served in a frosted mug.

That damnable assignment seems to be the catalyst for this whole rotten mess. What kind of teacher tells his students to research ghosts and murderers and the like? When he was a kid, they were required to research Civil War battles and famous explorers. He spent many unsuccessful hours memorizing poems and important historical dates. Nowadays, kids could just look that all up on their phones. Ridiculous.

A bubble of resentment rises in his throat as he circles around the block and comes to a stop in front of the Dover house. If Mr. Dover hadn't given the assignment and hadn't teamed the three girls together this would have never happened. Here, he's sleeping soundly in his own bed while his granddaughter is locked away. It's not right. A shift in shadows at the front window catches his eye. So maybe John Dover isn't resting so peacefully right now. Good, Thomas thinks. Serves him right.

Thomas takes a left back onto Main and another left onto Juneberry, a street filled with four-bedroom homes and large backyards. The people who live on Juneberry tend to veer toward the more expensive beers. Guinness, IPAs, microbrew and craft beers. They are also the worst tippers.

Thomas parks across the street from the Landry home. A carbon copy of its neighbors, the house is set well away from the road and, while there is no sidewalk, the driveway is large and circular, giving the children plenty of room to ride bikes and play without fear of being struck by a car. Jim and Mara Landry come into the bar every month or so. Mara is a wine drinker—pinot grigio—and Jim a Sam Adams guy. They sit at a corner table, sipping their drinks, deep in conversation and enjoying one another's company.

Thomas remembers thinking that it was nice to see a couple actually talking to each other and not staring down at their drinks or phones or looking up at the television screen mounted on the wall. A light pops on from within the Landry home and, framed by the large picture window, someone steps into view. Jim Landry.

Instinctively, Thomas slumps down in his seat but it's too late—he's been seen. Jim Landry's spine straightens as if suddenly alert and he cups his hands and presses his face against the pane of glass to get a better look. Thomas does not want a confrontation. He's witnessed one too many bar fights that could have been avoided by one less drink or by making a judicious exit a few minutes sooner.

The front door opens and Landry barrels down the steps, a baseball bat in his hand. Before Thomas can put the truck into gear and drive away, Jim Landry is wrenching the car door open. "Stay the hell away from my family," Landry says, his voice low and dangerous. "I swear to God I will bash your head in if you come near us again."

Heart pounding, Thomas manages to yank the door shut. Juneberry ends in a cul-de-sac so it's all he can do not to throw the truck into Reverse and speed backward out of the subdivision. Instead he pulls from the curb and frantically speeds down to the circular dead end and back down the street past Jim Landry, who glowers at him from the lawn.

It was stupid, Thomas thinks, to come here. Doing so in no way helps Jordyn, only makes them all appear more sinister. He drives aimlessly around until his heart rate steadies, and finds himself approaching the train yard. It makes no sense for him to go there, either. What does he expect to find?

Despite his reservations, Thomas pulls next to the old depot, a shell of a building with boarded-up windows and doors, and situates the truck for a quick getaway, headlights facing the exit. He opens the door and is met with the chilly morning air that is unique to April. Stinging and brisk but with the promise of warmer hours ahead. The depot is surrounded by broken concrete cushioned only by the overgrowth of weeds that over the years have sprouted, untamed, through the crumbling slabs.

There's no crime scene tape, no police presence at all, no townspeople or press with a ghoulish curiosity. Only him. Thomas carefully steps from the truck well aware that he is one misstep away from a broken ankle or worse. He thinks he hears the gravel pop and looks around to see if another vehicle is approaching but none appears. He's jumpy, paranoid. Being silly, he tells himself.

He hasn't been here in years. Not since he was a child and he went with his parents on a cross-country train ride to visit relatives in Pennsylvania. The depot closed soon after and the rails were then used exclusively for cargo transport. Over the years there has been talk of renovating the depot into a restaurant or a museum or something of the like, but, unsurprising, it's never come to pass. Pitch, for some reason, tends to rail against any kind of progress before it even begins.

A cold breeze brushes against his neck, the sound of metal on metal clatters and Thomas turns to see the red eyes of an opossum lumbering across the train yard. He checks his watch. Another cargo train will come through in the next twenty minutes or so. Four times a day they hear the telltale whistle, more of a lonely foghorn, really, that lets the good people of Pitch know that boxcars and storage containers filled with ethanol, fertilizers, grain, stone, sand and gravel are passing through.

Thomas scans the train yard, the abandoned boxcars, the acres of waving grass and the tracks that go on for a thousand miles in either direction. Wearily, he realizes the futility of this treasure hunt. How is a man of near seventy, with failing eyesight and unstable joints and an unreliable heart, going to be able to find anything helpful to the investigation?

But since he's already here, it won't hurt to look. He sighs and, holding on to the truck for support, he picks his way through the broken concrete until he's on even ground. Three discarded boxcars on concrete blocks sit in a rusty row and Thomas recognizes the car with Soo Line printed across the panels. This was the backdrop for the picture where the three girls were mugging for the photo that showed Jordyn holding the knife. So Jordyn came at least this far into the train yard, Thomas thinks, but still well away from the portion of the tracks where the attack was reported as taking place.

Thomas slowly moves forward, eyes pinned to the earth in front of him. There are coins and pop tabs, an earring, but nothing of real interest.

Thomas approaches the tracks and comes upon a large rust-colored stain in the gravel. Blood, he thinks. This must be the spot. He imagines pint-size Cora Landry cowering, hands above her head warding off blows from the hand wielding the knife. His stomach roils.

No. There is absolutely no way that Jordyn could have done it. None. He can see where the tall grass has been trampled down in one spot. Had the girls gone through the field or was it the real attacker? Hidden behind the thousands of slim stalks, a perfect hiding place in the dark for someone to spy on three young girls. Two, Thomas amends. Jordyn said she wasn't here. A child nearly died here, Thomas realizes fully, perhaps for the first time since this all began. It makes him feel dirty, complicit, being here.

And if he really thinks about it, he has been. He hid Jordyn's backpack—her clothing, her shoes—up inside a chimney flue. Had Thomas, in trying to protect Jordyn, made things worse? Made her appear guilty? He needs to get home and pull the backpack from the chimney and take it to the police. They will be able to run tests, examine the contents and prove that Jordyn is innocent. He needs to go home; he needs to make this right.

The sun is just beginning to rise and morning moisture clings to the winter wheat. Thomas reaches into his pocket to retrieve his keys and a small wad of bills comes out with them. The money drifts to the ground and as Thomas bends down they are whisked away by a stiff breeze. Thomas follows the bills into the tall grass and bends over to grab one that has come to rest among the stems.

A metallic glint catches his eye and he bends over and pushes the grass aside to find a small book embossed with the word *Journal* in silver glitter. Thomas picks up the book; it is wet to the touch and smeared with dirt.

He flips through the pages and finds them filled with girlish script but the sun isn't bright enough for him to read what's been written. He digs in his pocket for his phone; the light from the screen illuminates a page. He reads quickly as if the words might disappear before his eyes. He feels sick, dirty, as he begins to comprehend the story unfolding in the pages.

A whistle blows in the distance, the train marking its arrival to the crossing west of town where the long white arms come down, stalling traffic for a good ten minutes. Thomas, resolving to put an end to this entire mess, slides the book into his coat pocket, turns and strikes solid flesh. His first thought is Jim Landry has come here to confront him. He knows he is no match for an angry man, a father no less, who is thirty years younger, stronger and bearing a grudge.

Instead he finds himself face-to-face with John Dover. The teacher. "What are you doing here?" Thomas asks. The gruffness of his voice masks the pounding of his heart.

"I could ask you the same thing," Dover says, the hood of his coat pulled up over his head and his hands tucked into the pockets to ward off the cold. "I saw you sitting outside my house." In the distance the train calls out again, a rusty foghorn. "Why?"

"Just out for a drive and getting some exercise," Thomas says, taking a few steps to the right, uncomfortably aware of the bloodstained gravel at their feet. Couldn't someone have rinsed it away?

"But why stop in front of my house?" Dover asks. "What possible reason would you have for doing that? Is there, maybe, something you want to ask me?"

Thomas examines Dover's face carefully. Through the dimness he sees no anger, no hostility, but there is concern, possibly fear. Why would John Dover be frightened of him? "I've got nothing to say to you," Thomas says and starts moving along the tracks, eager to get far away from the rusty patch of earth and away from John Dover.

But Dover isn't going anywhere and joins Thomas. Together they walk silently along the tracks, a cold breeze pushing them along. Thomas eyes the ground in front of him, still searching for the key.

"What she's saying isn't true," Dover says.

"I have no idea what you are talking about," Thomas says but his pulse quickens. He casts a wary glance toward Dover.

"The police brought me in for questioning again last night. They took my computers and my phone. I know what Jordyn is saying about me. It isn't true." Dover is walking so closely to Thomas that their shoulders graze. "I wasn't anywhere near here the other night."

It comes to Thomas then what Dover is talking about. Jordyn must have told the police something about Mr. Dover and the attack. This is what the attorney meant when he said Jordyn was ready to talk. Was John Dover the one who attacked Cora Landry? He thinks of the journal hidden in his coat pocket. In his quick perusal, he had seen Dover's name dozens of times.

Thomas's skin begins to vibrate with anger. Had Dover lured his granddaughter and the other girls to the train yard? After what happened to Cora, Jordyn must have been terrified that Mr. Dover was going to come after her, too.

"Did you hear me?" Dover says loudly, snagging Thomas's jacket in one hand. "Jordyn is going to ruin my life. You have to make her tell the truth."

"Let go of my coat," Thomas orders, trying to keep his voice steady, even. Dover curls the fabric even more tightly between his fingers.

"She's lying," Dover hisses. He's near tears.

"My granddaughter doesn't lie," Thomas says, though this isn't quite true. Hadn't Jordyn lied about sneaking out, about the alcohol, about pushing Cora down, about seeing anyone at the depot?

Far down the tracks the six-thirty train comes into view. Right on time.

The earth shivers beneath Thomas's feet and the clickity-clack of the approaching train crescendos and Thomas has to raise his voice. "You're wrong about Jordyn. She's a good girl."

"A good girl?" Dover cries, his face so close that Thomas can smell the Cold Press Ale on his breath. "I've watched your granddaughter bully and tease Cora Landry all year long and for some reason she's accusing *me* of stabbing a twelve-year-old girl! I'm a teacher, for God's sake."

The headlight from the oncoming engine floods the train yard and Dover's face is distorted with disbelief, rage. "Jordyn was only pretending to be Cora's friend. Now she's trying to blame me.

"What did I ever do to her?" Dover steps toward him with each word, forcing Thomas backward until his heels bump against the iron rails. Thomas cries out, his left knee buckling. Sent off balance on the loose gravel he falls and lands on his back perpendicular across the tracks. The men lock eyes, both registering first shock then fear as the train inches closer. Thomas reaches for Dover's hand, the slick fabric of his down coat slipping through his fingers as he tumbles and falls backward onto the tracks.

His spine strikes the metal rails and the breath is knocked from his lungs, momentarily stunning him. He struggles to sit up but his coat is snagged on a rusty railroad spike. He looks to Jordyn's teacher for help and for a minute Thomas is afraid that John Dover will simply allow him to be crushed by the train. Afraid that he will just walk away. Suddenly Dover steps into view and is standing over him, his mouth open in a twisted scream.

"Get up!" Dover shouts, his voice drowned out by the screech of the train. "Get up!" Dover reaches down and grabs onto Thomas's legs and tries to pull him from the tracks but his coat is hopelessly ensnared. "Please." Dover furtively glances to the right and at the coming engine. "Please get up!" He stands upright and waves his hands over his head, trying to get the conductor's attention. The train doesn't slow but continues its steady progress toward them.

Again, Thomas tries to right himself but he is pinned to the tracks like an insect mounted on a specimen card. Dover steps over the tracks and bends over to wrestle with the zipper on Thomas's coat. His fingers are stiff from the cold and the zipper doesn't budge. "Please, God, please," Dover breathes as he tries to unthread Thomas's arms from the coat and pull it over his head.

The world goes black and he feels like his arms are being torn from his body. A deafening roar thunders through his ears. Thomas thought that he'd be terrified. That death would be just about the hardest thing he'd face. But now he knows it's not the hardest. Losing Betsy, being separated from Tess, what's happening to Jordyn are all the hardest. The hardest in different ways. He can't leave them, not when they need him the most.

But dying doesn't sound so bad, he thinks, and not so scary. Maybe Donny would come home. Maybe even Randy would come home to take care of Jordyn and Tess, take over the bar. He'd like to have seen that. Thomas is tired, so very weary. He feels Dover give him one final yank as the train brays its arrival, low and insistent, filling Thomas's ears with its somehow soothing, dizzying wails.

Apr. 15, 2018

I tried to cancel the overnight. I don't want to do this. I tried everything. I told my mom I was sick. But she told me that I'd used that excuse one too many times. She said that it was good that I was spending time in the land of the living again. If she only knew.

Violet and Jordyn will be here in a little bit. It makes me sick that I'm going to have to spend the next few hours with them and I can't believe that the first time I see Joseph they are going to be there, too. I'm nervous. Scared.

What if he doesn't show up? What if he does? What if he does and he doesn't pick me?

Max and I spent another night sleeping in the family waiting area but we were both so tired at the time we could have slept standing up. Once Dr. Gideon discharges Violet we can all go home.

On the couch next to me Max is scrolling through his cell phone while I mentally try to balance my nearly nonexistent checking account. "Mom." Max turns to me. His eyes are wide and his face is a sickly shade of white.

"What?" I ask and he holds out his phone to me. I take it and look at the screen to find a series of text messages from a group of kids. Only Nikki's and Clint's names are familiar.

"Oh, my God," I whisper and thrust the phone back into Max's hands.

"What's happening?" Max asks me, sounding like a small boy.

"I don't know," I say, pulling him in for a hug, and for the first time in a very long time my son doesn't pull away from me.

Nikki:
Someone got hit by a train at the old depot

Max:
Does anyone know who it was?

Clint:
I heard it was the old guy who owns Petit's

Max:
Jordyn's grandpa? What happened?

Ryan:
I heard he jumped in front of the train because of what Jordyn did

Clint:
I heard Mr. Dover pushed him in front of the train

Ryan:
That's BS. Why would Dover do that?

Clint:
Jordyn told the police Dover's a perv and hurt that kid at the train station

Nikki:
That's awful! Did he die?

Ryan:
I heard he died

Clint:
I heard he didn't

Corareef12:

I'm ready to go. I decided only to bring my journal and I have about two hundred dollars just in case we need it. I can't believe we're really doing this. I gave my mom a really long hug, but don't worry, I didn't make her suspicious. I just said goodbye to her in my head. I stood in Kendall's bedroom trying to think of a way of telling her goodbye, but I couldn't think of what to say. She finally told me to go away, that I was creeping her out. I didn't bother saying goodbye to my dad. He probably won't even notice I'm gone. At first I was scared about leaving but I'm not anymore. I thought about what you said, how Jordyn and Violet aren't really my friends. I know you're right. I can tell they are talking about me. I can hear their whispers. I think the only person who cares about me, besides my mom, is Mr. Dover. And you, of course. I'll look for you at the train yard and then we can go away forever. They'll be so sorry they were mean to me. You'll be there, won't you? You promise?

JW44:

I'LL BE THERE.

When I got to the nurses' station I had a note from Mara saying that she and Jim had gone to the hospital's rooftop garden. I took the nearest elevator to the top floor and I found them staring out at the city below. The rooftop is a beautiful spot like nothing I'd ever seen in a hospital before with its glassed-in walkways lined with flowers and plants. It looked more like an arboretum than a spot for patients and their families to sit and regroup.

Seeing the look on Mara's face, I asked, "Are the girls okay?"

"Yeah," she said, shifting in her chair. "There was an accident this morning. Thomas Petit, the grandfather of one of the girls, fell on the tracks while a train was coming." She lowered her head into her hands.

"He's going to be fine," Jim said. "John Dover, a teacher from the school, was able to pull him from the tracks in time."

"What were they doing in the train yard?" I asked, my curiosity getting the better of me.

"There was some kind of argument." Mara rubbed her eyes. "And Mr. Petit fell. There are rumors about Mr. Dover…"

"Don't think about it anymore," Jim said. "It won't do any good. We have our own daughters to think about." Jim looked to me. "The police said that engines have front-facing cameras mounted to them. They'll be able to figure out what happened." I nodded but didn't say anything. I was processing this new information.

"I need to get back to Cora," Mara said and stood abruptly.

"May I peek in on her?" I asked. "See how she's feeling?" Mara nodded weakly and the three of us took the elevator back down. When we got to Cora's room, Cora already had a visitor.

Kendall, dressed in her street clothes, sat on the edge of Cora's bed. "Kendall, honey?" Mara asked. "What are you doing here?" She looked at me in confusion.

"It's okay, Mom," Kendall said. "One of the nurses walked me down. She's waiting outside. I'm fine."

Kendall looked far from fine. Dark circles beneath her eyes told me she hadn't gotten much rest. Her hair hung lankly on her shoulders and was streaked black with what I suspected was the charcoal used to pump her stomach.

Cora didn't look much better. Her left eye was heavily bandaged and the wounds on her scalp and face had crusted over but she was awake and sitting up in her bed.

Alarm bells went off in my head. Kendall was getting ready to tell her parents what she had done to Cora. "Kendall," I began, "I don't think this is the time." I had hoped that when Kendall was ready to tell her parents about her role in posing as Joseph Wither it wouldn't be in front of Cora. I didn't think Cora was ready to hear this.

"But I need to," Kendall said in a tremulous voice. "If I don't do it now, I don't think I ever will."

"Kendall." I shook my head. "Let's wait until we can talk to your mom and dad privately."

"What is it?" Mara interrupted.

"Mara," I tried again, "I think this is a conversation best left for—"

"No, let her talk," Mara said. "You know you can tell me anything, Kendall. Anything at all."

I demurred, perhaps my biggest mistake, and reluctantly moved to the corner of the room where I'd be out of the way.

"It's my fault," Kendall said. "What happened to Cora." Tears filled her eyes and she took a shuddery breath.

"There's nothing you could have done to stop what happened, Kendall. It isn't your fault." Mara pulled a chair up next to Kendall and reached for her hand.

Kendall shook her head. "No, it's my fault. And Emery's. We were the ones who sent the messages."

"I don't understand," Mara said. "What messages?"

"Online. On a website. We pretended to be Joseph Wither. But then I stopped and Emery kept doing it. I swear I didn't know. She told Cora that Wither would be at the depot." The tears fell and Kendall looked pleadingly at her sister. "It was just a joke. I don't know who went to the depot but it wasn't me. It wasn't Emery."

"A joke?" Mara furrowed her brow, puzzled, and looked to her husband for help. "What does she mean, a joke?"

Jim looked like he might explode. "She means that she and Emery lured the girls out in the middle of the night. It means that she tricked her sister into walking into a trap."

"No." Kendall's eyes widened in fear. "No, it wasn't me. I stopped after a few days and I told Emery to stop, too."

Mara stared at her daughter as if seeing her for the first time. "Kendall?"

"Did you plan it together?" Jim asked. "Were you there?"

"No, Daddy," Kendall cried. "You know I was at home. You know I would never do that. Emery would never do that."

"I don't know, Kendall." Jim's voice broke. "I don't know you at all."

I got ready to jump in before it went too far. Before someone said something they would forever regret, when I looked at Cora. She was just sitting there as if in a trance, hands lying limply at her sides, no expression on her face. "The messages weren't from him?" she asked. "He isn't real?"

"I'm so sorry, Cora," Kendall choked out. "I'm so sorry. It was just a joke, a stupid joke. If I had known that Violet and Jordyn were going to hurt you—"

"I have to go to the bathroom," Cora said and abruptly pushed herself up from the bed. She looked blank, as if she hadn't heard what her sister just told her.

"Let me help you," Mara said, standing and going to her daughter's side.

"I can do it," Cora murmured and slowly wheeled her IV pole toward the bathroom.

"Let me call the nurse." Mara reached for the nurse's call button.

"No, I'm fine," Cora said, her voice devoid of emotion. Once inside the bathroom, she gently shut the door and locked it with a gentle click.

"Dammit, Kendall," Jim spat. "What the hell have you done?"

"I'm sorry," Kendall moaned, rocking back and forth. "I'm so sorry."

Jim grabbed Kendall by the forearm and began to pull her toward the door. "Get out," he said between clenched teeth. "I can't bear to look at you."

"Stop it!" Mara cried and wedged herself between them. "Get your hands off her!"

I remember raising my voice, telling the Landrys to calm down. I remember suggesting that everyone take a break for a few minutes, then we could come back together to discuss what Kendall had just shared.

Jim Landry laughed bitterly. "I'm done talking," he muttered and shouldered his way past Mara and out of the room.

"I'm so sorry," Kendall wept as Mara gathered her into her arms.

It was then when I noticed that Cora hadn't returned from the bathroom. I moved to the door and gently knocked. "Cora," I called through the door. "Cora, are you doing okay in there?"

No response.

I knocked more forcefully.

Still no answer. That was when I saw the clear liquid seeping out from beneath the locked door.

"What is it?" Mara asked from behind me.

"Go get a nurse," I said calmly. Through the door I tried to summon a response from Cora. "Open the door, Cora."

Within seconds a nurse came into the room. "Open the door," I ordered. The nurse deftly unlocked the door and pushed it open. Sitting in a corner with her head on her knees was Cora, the coil of plastic tubing laid next to her, its contents surrounding her in a now bloody puddle. At first I thought the blood was from the IV access site in Cora's hand but as Cora lifted her head from her knees I quickly found that not to be the case.

"Oh, my God," Mara gasped.

"This is your fault!" Jim Landry hissed at me. "You were supposed to help her!"

Stitch by stich, Cora was pulling the sutures from her face, her fingers sticky with blood. She must have already plucked the stitches from her abdomen because blood bloomed brightly across her hospital gown.

I fell to my knees and grabbed her bloody fingers in mine. "Cora, why?" I asked. "Why did you do this to yourself?"

"It wasn't Kendall," she whispered. "It wasn't Violet and Jordyn. They didn't do it."

Five months later

Later, I got to see the video footage from the camera in front of the train's engine. I came as close to dying as I ever have. The video wasn't the best quality and there was no audio but it was clear that John Dover and I were having words. I tripped and fell backward and John Dover tried to help me up. It's a miracle that I didn't die and it's equally amazing that John Dover didn't die trying to save me. I did end up with a torn rotator cuff in my shoulder. Could have been a hell of a lot worse.

I wish I had never gone down to the train station. There are a lot of things I wish I had done differently. I still just don't understand why Jordyn lied and kept on lying even though she didn't do anything more than sneak out and try to pull a prank on a friend. She wasn't the one who sent Cora those fake messages and she wasn't the one who stabbed and beat her. But still she felt the need to accuse an innocent man, her teacher no less. I tried to get Jordyn to tell me why but she wouldn't or couldn't explain it beyond saying that she was scared and afraid they'd never let her come home again.

Tess tells me that we'll probably never fully understand our granddaughter. She's had a hard life. Her parents dumped her off on our doorstep. We've tried to be good parents to her, but it's not the same as having your real mom and dad there to sit down with you at dinner and to tuck you in every night.

Mr. Dover resigned from his teaching position and last I heard had moved out of state. Wherever he is I hope he's been able to make a fresh start.

After I fell on the train tracks and busted up my shoulder, I told Officer Grady about the book bag hidden in the chimney. He fished it out and it ended up there was zero physical evidence that linked Jordyn to any crime. By the grace of God, I

wasn't arrested for tampering with evidence. I guess no one saw
the point of throwing an old man in jail for trying to protect
his granddaughter.

Once a week we drive to Grayling and I drop Jordyn off at
her counselor's office and then take Tess to her physical therapy
appointment. The deal was Jordyn had to go to counseling or
be charged for making false statements to the police. The counseling seems to be helping. She's a lot quieter now, though, stays
pretty much to herself. Tess says that in a few months everyone will move on to the next scandal and Jordyn will be surrounded by friends again. But I don't know. Small towns have
long memories.

We packed up the car with our clothes, a few belongings and Boomer and left in the dark of night when the neighbors were asleep. Pretty much like how we arrived—fitting, I guess. I'm afraid, though, that no matter how far we run, Violet and Max won't be able to recover from our ten months in Pitch. I spent a long time talking with Dr. Gideon about the move. She warned us that running away from what happened wouldn't be good for Violet, for any of us, but she did think that it might be best for Violet, for all of us, to get a brand-new start. I was sure that if we stayed in Pitch Violet would forever be known as one of the Wither girls and Max would feel like he would always have to defend his sister.

Dr. Gideon also warned me about just up and leaving without having a real plan in place. She suggested that I research where we were going to move, look for a job, find housing and arrange for ongoing mental health support for Violet. She has a lot to deal with. Violet's best friend nearly died, and even though Violet was innocent, people still look at her like she's a criminal.

We needed to go to a place where no one ever heard of Joseph Wither and that terrible night in the train yard. Max wanted to go back to New Mexico and Violet wanted to move to Hawaii. I said no to both.

I finally decided on Rochester, Minnesota, because when I searched best midsize US cities to live in, it came up as number one. I haven't had the best track record in choosing where to raise my kids and I didn't want to decide where we were going based on a man.

I thought for sure the Petits would move away from Pitch. But it doesn't look like they will. My neighbor said that Thomas Petit had no intention of moving away from the place he called home for over forty years and that he couldn't bear the thought of selling the bar to someone who didn't know the heart and soul they'd poured into it, to someone who didn't know its history.

I just want to give my kids what's left of their childhoods. I want them to have fun, have some good memories, before they go off into the world on their own. Rochester has great schools, and a decent cost of living and the Mayo Clinic, one of the best hospitals in the world. Dr. Gideon even put in a good word for me when I said I was interested in getting a job there. I didn't care what kind of job it was—as aide, housekeeping, food service, hell, I'd have agreed to be a candy striper if it meant I had a steady income.

In the end, I was hired as an assistant in the dietetics department. I work with the registered dietitians and help process diet orders and menus to patients. Maybe not my dream job but it provides health insurance, which we're in desperate need of.

Violet still has nightmares about that night and sometimes wakes up screaming for me to get the blood off her. At night, in the dark, when I start thinking on these things I can almost feel his presence in the room and I have to remind myself he isn't real, that Joseph Wither doesn't exist.

In the end, no one was arrested for anything, although Jordyn was ordered to go to counseling for lying about her teacher being in the train yard. If you ask me, she got off easy. No one should be able to ruin someone's life like that.

And part of me wishes that Kendall Landry and her friend Emery had been charged with something for their catfish game. They lied and pretended to be someone else. They convinced a vulnerable little girl that the person on the other end of the computer loved and cared about her. Even though they may not have meant for anyone to get hurt, three little girls and their families will never be the same.

When Violet doesn't think I'm looking, I watch her. I watch as she draws in her sketchbook, while she reads, while she watches

TV on the couch with Boomer. I watch her when she is day-dreaming, staring up at the ceiling or into corners, and wonder if she's thinking of that night. Then I make myself stop. I don't want what happened in Pitch to define who she becomes. Dr. Gideon told me to be watchful but not to make myself sick with worry. I talked to Violet's counselor in her new school. She's going to meet with her once a week to help her make a smooth adjustment to seventh grade.

It's no surprise that Max is doing just fine in our new town, making plenty of friends and girlfriends, though I still catch him texting Nikki now and then. He watches Violet just as closely as I do. He worries and it makes me sad and proud all at the same time.

Violet is taking a while to settle in to our new life but she seems okay. She doesn't seem to have any close friends yet but she did join an after-school art club and they meet twice a week. I asked her if she ever misses Jordyn and Cora and she just shook her head and said not really. I check her phone and scan the bills to see if she calls or texts one of them, but she hasn't. I sneak into her room when she's at school and flip through her sketchbook, looking for drawings of Joseph Wither or tall grass or railroad tracks, but only find pictures of Boomer and attempts at anime. I'm relieved and hopeful and grateful. It's time for us to make new memories, good memories.

When we found Cora sitting in a pool of blood pulling out her stitches I was truly stunned. The nurses rushed in and whisked Cora away with Mara Landry right behind her. Cora was taken into surgery and the surgeons once more had the task of putting her back together again.

I remember standing in the middle of Cora's hospital room, my hands and knees covered with her blood and Jim Landry standing in front of me, his face red with rage. "This is your fault!" he spat. "You were supposed to help her! You were supposed to help my family!"

Kendall was sitting on Cora's hospital bed, crying anguished tears. I tried to step past Mr. Landry to go to Kendall, to comfort her, something her father should have been doing.

"No way," he said, blocking my way. "You stay the fuck away from her. You stay away from my family."

"She's upset," I told him the obvious. "You should go to her. She needs you."

"No!" He stepped toward me, forcing me to move backward until my back was against the wall. "You don't get to tell me what to do. Get out."

After Cora, I reviewed her case file over and over. I read and reread until the pages were dog-eared and smudged. I thought I would be able to pinpoint the mistakes I made, learn from them and hopefully never make them again.

And for a while I did just fine. I moved on. That's what we do as doctors. We assess and diagnose and treat and then move on to the next patient. The problem was, I didn't move on. I kept doubting myself. I'd make a diagnosis, then hesitate and change my mind. It got to be that I couldn't make a move without consulting with a colleague. I was losing sleep. I wasn't eating. And I wasn't good at my job anymore.

So I resigned. I quit because a little girl named Cora Landry and a fictional entity named Joseph Wither got into my head.

I don't tell people that, of course. I simply said I needed a professional change, a new challenge. So I moved three hundred miles away and began a second career as the head of the psychology department and a professor at a small liberal arts college east of the Mississippi.

Jim Landry's final words still echo in my head. The words he shouted after me as I left Cora's hospital room the last time I saw her. "You're going to pay for this."

And I have. In too many ways to count.

Sept. 14, 2018

Today is a good day. I get to use a pen to write in my journal and that is so much better than a crayon. It's hard to stab yourself with a crayon. But like I said, today is a good day, so I get to use a pen.

My doctor here, Dr. Kim, tells me it's a good idea to get my thoughts down on paper, that it will help me process everything that happened last April. I don't know about that, but I like to write, so I do.

Dr. Kim also likes to talk about what I wrote in my old journal, the one I dropped at the train station. He walks in with his file folders, the ones labeled Case #92-10945, and he'll say, "Good morning, Cora, how are you?" And I'll say, "Don't you mean *Good morning, Number Ninety-Two Dash One, Zero, Nine, Four, Five?*"

Dr. Kim laughs and says, "I like Cora." We do this before each of our sessions. Every. Single. Time.

I don't especially like talking about what I wrote in my journal. Imagine having to talk about every single secret thought you had. It sucks.

My arm is better and I didn't lose my eye. My face has healed but there are scars. When Kendall came to visit me last week, she told me not to worry about it, that the scars make me look interesting, that when I'm older I can tell people whatever I want about what caused them. So now whenever I meet a new kid in the psych ward I say that I was in a car accident or mauled by a grizzly bear or injured in a skydiving accident. But if I really want to mess with them, I tell them the truth.

Sometimes it's hard for me to remember exactly what happened that night. It was cold, but I barely felt it. It was the dark that scared me. But I was kind of excited, too. I thought Joseph was going to come and take me away from Pitch and we'd never come back.

I remember my arm hurt. Bad. Jordyn pushed me down after I grabbed her backpack. I was so tired of her bullying and teasing and tricks. She made me so mad saying that Joseph wasn't real. That it was all one big joke. We heard something then. Footsteps or maybe just the wind.

I hoped it was Joseph coming for me like he promised. I looked around but

I couldn't see him. Jordyn and Violet had run away and I saw the knife on the ground at my feet. Jordyn must have dropped it. For a second I wanted to find Jordyn and use the knife on her, I hated her so much.

Then I saw someone in the tall grass. I thought it was Joseph but they told me later I was wrong. They told me it was Gabe Shannon and that he was in on the prank. I can't believe I ever liked him. But at the time I believed he was Joseph and thought he was going to leave without me. I couldn't stand it. After all the messages and promises I thought Wither was going to leave me behind and never come back. And worst of all I thought he was going to take Jordyn instead.

I tried to follow him but he sprinted away from me and in that second I thought that nothing mattered anymore. I was going to be stuck here in Pitch forever. Our messages back and forth meant nothing. His letters meant nothing. He never loved me.

I don't really understand what happened next but it was like I was outside my body. Numb. Like I rose up above myself. That happens to me sometimes when things get too hard, when life doesn't make sense.

I took the knife and shoved it into my stomach. The pain was terrible and the blood pumped out but I wouldn't die. I was still there. I couldn't bear to stab myself again and I prayed for the train to come and run me over but it didn't. So instead I banged my face and head against the railroad tracks just wanting the world to go black. And I watched it all from above myself.

Dr. Kim tells me it's called depersonalization and I tell him that I call it being crazy.

The first time I was in the psych ward was after I tried to pull out all my stitches. It was in Grayling and I stayed there for about a month. One girl I met on the floor said that most kids get kicked out after a few days and I must be pretty crazy to have been there that long. The second time I ended up having to go all the way to a hospital in Des Moines because no other place had open beds.

My mom was so mad. She started yelling at the doctor and begging him to let me stay closer to home. He said it was out of his hands, that the patients had to go where there was room.

After Des Moines, they said I was well enough to go home. That lasted about a week. I don't remember much about it, but in the middle of the night my mom caught me in the dark, standing on my desk with my ear pressed to the air vent, talking to someone who wasn't there.

That was when I was sent to the Iowa Institute of Mental Health in Claiborne and that's where I'm at today. In a locked adolescent psych ward, in a rec room where sometimes I'm allowed to use a pen and, if I'm being really good, I might even get a scissors. And I'm trying to be good. You get more stuff that way.

At the time, I thought it would be better to die instead of being left behind. Sometimes I still feel that way. I remember hearing a dog bark and I remember seeing Skittles run by—and yes, I know that Skittles isn't real. Never was. But I still see her sometimes. And I hear things, too. I try to ignore them if I can and I don't tell anybody, not even Dr. Kim.

When I meet with Dr. Kim, we don't always talk about that night or Joseph Wither even, but between the medicine I'm taking and talking with him, sometimes I feel better. But usually I don't.

Last time my family came to visit, Kendall told me Mr. Dover quit being a teacher and moved away. She also told me that Jordyn got in big trouble by the police for lying to them and that she has to go to counseling and check in with a parole officer for kids and that Violet moved away. Good.

Kendall treats me like I'm a broken doll. I don't like it. Sometimes I wish she would just call me a pest like she used to. She feels so bad that she and Emery pretended to be Wither. But I feel bad that she tried to kill herself. Sometimes I wish she wouldn't even come to visit me at the hospital. We don't know how to act around each other anymore so most of the time we don't do anything or say anything. We just sit there quietly.

My mom and dad were the ones who told me they were suing Dr. Gideon. They thought she acted recklessly because she didn't alert someone soon enough when she learned that I had been talking with someone pretending to be Joseph Wither. My dad said Dr. Gideon committed malpractice because she failed to protect me from harm, which I think is hilarious. Maybe my parents should sue themselves.

They had to turn over all my medical records and a copy of my journal to a lawyer so they could be used in the court case against Dr. Gideon. I hope my parents lose. I liked Dr. Gideon. I think she really cared about me. But then, what do I know.

My mom says they're just trying to protect me. But if I thought my mom and dad were overprotective before I was wrong. Parents can be pretty clueless. And so can doctors and nurses. Computers are everywhere. Even in hospitals.

★ ★ ★ ★ ★

Acknowledgments

With each novel I write I am continually amazed at the generosity of others who share their time, talents and knowledge with me.

Special thanks go out to Chief Mark Dalsing, Eric Williams, Natalia Blaskovich, Carissa Gunderson, Teena Williams and Megan Wuest. Without their expertise this novel could not have been written.

Thank you to my agent, Marianne Merola. Her guidance and friendship mean the world to me. Thanks also to Henry Thayer and everyone at Brandt & Hochman Literary Agents, Inc., for their behind-the-scenes efforts.

Many thanks to my editor, Erika Imranyi, who with each novel provides thoughtful insights and spot-on suggestions. I so enjoy our conversations, collaboration and brainstorming sessions.

Thanks also to Emer Flounders, Natalie Hallak and the entire Harlequin, HarperCollins and Park Row team—I'm so fortunate to have you all in my corner.

Many thanks to Jane Augspurger and Grace Gudenkauf for reading early versions of the novel and offering priceless feedback.

My parents, Milton and Patricia Schmida, have always been my biggest supporters—all that is good and true I've learned from them. I thank them for providing a home that was filled with books, love, encouragement and the freedom to be imaginative. My brothers and sisters, Greg Schmida, Jane Augspurger, Milt Schmida, Molly Lugar and Patrick Schmida, are each a gift to me. I couldn't ask for better siblings.

As always, heartfelt thanks go to my husband, Scott, and to my children, Alex, Annie and Grace. I love you beyond words. I am blessed.

BEFORE SHE WAS FOUND

HEATHER GUDENKAUF

Reader's Guide

PARK
ROW
BOOKS

1. Cora, Violet and Jordyn are young girls with a turbulent friendship. Why do you think Cora keeps trying to remain friends with two people who don't seem to have her best interests in mind? What role do you think Cora plays in the friendship difficulties?

2. Childhood friendships can leave deep impressions, both good and bad. What childhood friendship impacted your life the most? Why?

3. Parents sometimes go to extreme lengths to protect their children. To what extent would you go to safeguard someone you love? Where would you draw the line?

4. Social media has become such an integral part of day-to-day life, even with children. What responsibility do social media like Facebook, Snapchat and others have in protecting youth? How about schools or government? And parents?

5. Several sorts of families are represented in the novel: Jordyn is being raised by her grandparents, Cora comes from a two-parent home and Violet is being raised by a single mother. How do you think the dynamics of each family played into the events of the novel?

6. Who would you describe as the antagonist or antagonists in *Before She Was Found*? Why?

7. How would *Before She Was Found* have been different if it had taken place in a different time or place?

8. What is the significance of the title? How does it relate to each of the main characters?

9. If you could ask the author one question, what would it be? Why?

What was the inspiration behind *Before She Was Found*?

Just like many of my novels, the idea for *Before She Was Found* was inspired by news headlines: a fictional online entity and real life collided with heartbreaking results. Not far from where I live, the account of two young girls who were obsessed with a character called Slender Man, who originated as an online meme, hit the news. Over the years, Slender Man, a tall, spidery figure with a blank face, has been the subject of short stories, videos, artwork and video games. The girls, believing Slender Man would hurt them and their families, lured a classmate into a wooded area and attacked her. The attack not only had a devastating impact on the victim and her family, but on the perpetrators, their families and the entire community.

The novel was also inspired by the many accounts of those who have misused social media by pretending to be someone else, bullying and encouraging others to hurt themselves. Through my writing I wanted to explore how social media, the lack of mental health services and family dynamics can impact actions and decisions that have life-altering costs to all involved.

Before She Was Found is written in several different voices and styles. What were some of the challenges you faced in writing this way, and how did you overcome them?

I love writing from multiple points of view and wrestling with the challenge of weaving different voices and writing styles together. It can be very difficult to balance the various perspectives throughout a novel and to know when a particular character needs to take center stage. As I wrote and got to know the characters, Cora's journals and online conversations with Joseph Wither emerged as the focal points of the novel.

Another challenge I faced was to make sure that I captured the voice of twelve-year-old Cora in her journals and other communications. As an adult, it can be easy to forget what it's like to be a preteen. To help with this, I thought back to my experiences as a classroom teacher and instructional coach. I also visited with younger family members for feedback so that as I wrote in Cora's voice, I could do it accurately and honestly.

The novel jumps back and forth in time, making it a challenge to keep the movements of the characters straight. To help, I created an extensive timeline that I taped to the wall so I could refer to it as I wrote, adding and moving events as the story evolved. I also created a handwritten map of Pitch, the fictional town where the story takes place, and had it right next to me as I worked so I could get the characters where they needed to be. Having these visuals was crucial for me as the story grew.

You are a school curriculum coordinator and also a mother. In your observations, how has social media changed the way young girls like Cora behave and interact with their peers?

The internet and social media have become so ingrained in our cultural fabric it sometimes feels like we've never been without them. Over the years, as an educator and as a mother I've seen how social media often replaces face-to-face interactions between young people and their peers. As a result, I think some are emboldened by immediacy and the impersonal nature of chatting via social media, and misunderstandings and hurt feelings are compounded. Then there's the permanency of what is posted on social media—what is posted has a life beyond what many kids (and adults!) understand.

On the other hand, I've also seen some positive things associated with some of these platforms. Students today are using social media for social action and for discovering different perspectives and ideas. What's crucial is that children learn how to navigate and use social media judiciously and appropriately. Nothing can ever replace person-to-person interactions.

As an avid reader, what are some of the books and authors that have inspired your own writing?

I think everything I've read over the years has influenced and inspired my writing, but a few standouts come to mind.

I read *Winesburg, Ohio* by Sherwood Anderson in high school and today it remains one of the most profound, emotional collections of short stories I've read to date. This haunting portrayal of small-town life taught me how much impact richly drawn characters have on a reader.

If I could choose a book to read again for the very first time it would be Betty Smith's *A Tree Grows in Brooklyn*. When you close a book and realize that you desperately miss the characters and can't stand not knowing what has become of them, you know it is a very special novel. Betty Smith had a way of writing and talking to the reader in such a way that I found myself saying, "Yes, that is exactly how it is!" There is such a truth to her stories, a turn of phrase that leaves you nodding your head.

Barbara Kingsolver's *The Poisonwood Bible* was one of the first novels I remember reading that was written in multiple points of view. I was amazed at how brilliantly Kingsolver was able to tell such a complex, heart-wrenching tale through the eyes of the Price women. Though I didn't know it at the time I read *The Poisonwood Bible*, it set the stage for my exploration into writing many of my novels in multiple perspectives.

Willa Cather's *My Ántonia* is my favorite novel of all time. The story is of an immigrant, Antonia Shimerda (my maiden name is Schmida) and her family's new life in a small frontier town. I love how Cather was able to perfectly depict time and place through her stunning descriptions of the heartland. I think this is why I spend so much effort in developing a sense of setting in my own novels. I read *My Ántonia* every single year and have been collecting multiple editions over the years to add to my collection.

All of your books have been set in Iowa. What is it about this region that you feel makes it good fodder for storytelling?

A picturesque college town surrounded by craggy bluffs and thick woods; a renovated bookstore settled near the banks of the rushing Druid River; a close-knit farming community; a large Midwestern city; a remote cabin on Five Mines River. These are just a few of the Iowa-inspired settings in my novels. Fictional accounts? True! Fictional locations? Not quite.

I've lived in Iowa since I was a young child, and in each of my books I have included meaningful real-life locations into my fictional settings. From my first novel, *The Weight of Silence*, where the forest is based on my favorite hiking spot, to my most recent novel, *Before She Was Found*, which borrows the feel of local small rural railroad towns, I never tire of writing about this beautiful, varied landscape.

It's not that Iowa and the Midwest make better settings than other regions, it's that Iowa is what I know, where I feel most comfortable, where I call home. Willa Cather, my favorite author, said it best: "Let your fiction grow out of the land beneath your feet." I love this quote so much that I have it hanging near my desk as I write.

Read on for an excerpt from Heather Gudenkauf's gripping thriller,
Not a Sound.

PROLOGUE

I find her sitting all by herself in the emergency waiting room, her lovely features distorted from the swelling and bruising. Only a few patients remain, unusual for a Friday night and a full moon. Sitting across from her, an elderly woman coughs wetly into a handkerchief while her husband, arms folded across his chest and head tilted back, snores gently. Another man with no discernable ailment stares blankly up at the television mounted on the wall. Canned laughter fills the room.

I'm surprised she's still here. We treated her hours ago. Her clothing was gathered, I examined her from head to toe, all the while explaining what I was doing step-by-step. She lay on her back while I swabbed, scraped and searched for evidence. I collected for bodily fluids and hairs that were not her own. I took pictures. Close-ups of abrasions and bruises. I stood close by while the police officer interviewed her and asked deeply personal private questions. I offered her emergency contraceptives and the phone number for a domestic abuse shelter. She didn't cry once during the entire process. But now the tears are falling freely, dampening the clean scrubs I gave her to change into.

"Stacey?" I sit down next to her. "Is someone coming to get you?" I ask. I offered to call someone on her behalf but she refused, saying that she could take care of it. I pray to God that she didn't call her husband, the man who did this to her. I hope that the police had already picked him up.

She shakes her head. "I have my car."

"I don't think you should be driving. Please let me call someone," I urge. "Or you can change your mind and we can admit you for the night. You'll be safe. You can get some rest."

"No, I'm okay," she says. But she is far from okay. I tried to clean her up as best I could but already her newly stitched lip is oozing blood, the bruises blooming purple across her skin.

"At least let me walk you to your car," I offer. I'm eager to get home to my husband and stepdaughter but they are long asleep. A few more minutes won't matter.

She agrees and stands, cradling her newly casted arm. We walk out into the humid August night. The full moon, wide faced and as pale as winter wheat, lights our way. Katydids call back and forth to one another and white-winged moths throw themselves at the illuminated sign that reads Queen of Peace Emergency.

"Where are you staying tonight? You're not going home, are you?"

"No," she says but doesn't elaborate more. "I had to park over on Birch," she says dully. Queen of Peace's lot has been under construction for the better part of a month so parking is a challenge. It makes me sad to think that not only did this poor woman, beaten and raped by her estranged husband, have to drive herself to the emergency room, there wasn't even a decent place for her to park. Now there are five open parking spaces. What a difference a few hours can make in the harried, unpredictable world of emergency room care.

We walk past sawhorse barriers and orange construction cones to a quiet, residential street lined with sweetly pungent linden trees. Off in the distance a car engine roars to life, a dog barks, a siren howls. Another patient for the ER.

"My car is just up here," Stacey says and points to a small, white four-door sedan hidden in the shadows cast by the heart-shaped leaves of the lindens. We cross the street and I wait as Stacey digs around in her purse for her keys. A mosquito buzzes past my ear and I wave it away.

I hear the scream of tires first. The high-pitched squeal of rubber on asphalt. Stacey and I turn toward the noise at the same time. Blinding high beams come barreling toward us. There is nowhere to go. If we step away from Stacey's car we will be directly in its path. I push Stacey against her car door and press as close to her as I can, trying to make ourselves as small as possible.

I'm unable to pull my eyes away from the bright light and I keep thinking that the careless driver will surely correct the steering wheel and narrowly miss us. But that doesn't happen. There is no screech of brakes, the car does not slow and the last sound I hear is the dull, sickening thud of metal on bone.

1

Two Years Later…

Nearly every day for the past year I have paddle boarded, kay-
aked, run or hiked around the sinuous circuit that is Five Mines
River, Stitch at my side. We begin our journey each day just a
dozen yards from my front door, board and oar hoisted above
my head, and move cautiously down the sloping, rocky bank to
the water's edge. I lower my stand-up paddleboard, the cheapest
one I could find, into the water, mindfully avoiding the jagged
rocks that could damage my board. I wade out into the shallows,
flinching at the bite of cold water against my skin, and steady it
so Stitch can climb on. I hoist myself up onto my knees behind
him and paddle out to the center of the river.

With long even strokes I pull the oar through the murky river.
The newly risen sun, intermittently peeking through heavy,
slow-moving gray clouds, reflects off droplets of water kicked up
like sparks. The late-October morning air is bracing and smells
of decaying leaves. I revel in the sights and feel of the river, but
I can't hear the slap of my oar against the water, can't hear the

cry of the seagulls overhead, can't hear Stitch's playful yips. I'm still trying to come to terms with this.

The temperature is forecast to dip just below freezing soon and when it does I will reluctantly stow my board in the storage shed, next to my kayak until spring. In front of me, like a nautical figurehead carved into the prow of a sailing vessel, sits Stitch. His bristled coat is the same color as the underside of a silver maple leaf in summer, giving him a distinguished air. He is three years old and fifty-five pounds of muscle and sinew but often gets distracted and forgets that he has a job to do.

Normally, when I go paddling, I travel an hour and a half north to where Five Mines abruptly opens into a gaping mouth at least a mile wide. There the riverside is suddenly lined with glass-sided hotels, fancy restaurants, church spires and a bread factory that fills the air with a scent that reminds me of my mother's kitchen. Joggers and young mothers with strollers move leisurely along the impressive brick-lined river walk, and the old train bridge that my brother and I played on as kids looms in the distance—out of place and damaged beyond repair. Kind of like me.

Once I catch sight of the train bridge or smell the yeasty scent of freshly baked bread I know it's time to turn around. I much prefer the narrow, isolated inlets and sloughs south of Mathias, the river town I grew up in.

This morning there's only time for a short trek. I have an interview with oncologist and hematologist Dr. Joseph Huntley, the director of the Five Mines Regional Cancer Center in Mathias, at ten. Five Mines provides comprehensive health care and resources to cancer patients in the tristate area. Dr. Huntley is also on staff at Queen of Peace Hospital with my soon-to-be ex-husband, David. He is the head of obstetrics and gynecology at Q & P and isn't thrilled that I might be working with his old friend. It was actually Dr. Huntley who called me to see if

I was interested. The center is going to update their paper files to electronic files and need someone to enter data.

Dr. Huntley, whom I met on a few occasions years ago through David, must have heard that I've been actively searching for work with little luck. David, despite his grumblings, hasn't sabotaged me. I'll be lucky if he can muster together any kind words about me. It's a long, complicated story filled with heartache and alcohol. Lots of alcohol. David could only take so much and one day I found myself all alone.

I come upon what is normally my favorite part of Five Mines, a constricted slice of river only about fifteen yards wide and at least twenty feet at its deepest. The western bank is a wall of craggy limestone topped by white pines and brawny chinquapin oaks whose branches extend out over the bluff in a rich bronze canopy of leaves. Today the river is unusually slow and sluggish as if it is thick with silt and mud. The air is too heavy, too still. On the other bank the lacy-leaf tendrils of black willows dangle in the water like limp fingers.

Stitch's ears twitch. Something off in the distance has caught his attention. My board rocks slowly at first, a gentle undulation that quickly becomes jarring. Cold water splashes across my ankles and I nearly tumble into the river. Instead I fall to my knees, striking them sharply against my board. Somehow I manage to avoid tumbling in myself but lose my paddle and my dog to the river. Stitch doesn't appear to mind the unexpected bath and is paddling his way to the shore. Upriver, some asshole in a motorboat must have revved his engine, causing the tumultuous wake.

I wait on hands and knees, my insides swaying with the river until the waves settle. My paddle bobs on the surface of the water just a few feet out of my reach. I cup one hand to use as an oar and guide my board until I can grab the paddle. Maybe it's my nervousness about my upcoming interview, but I'm anxious to turn around and go back home. Something feels off, skewed. Stitch is oblivious. This is the spot where we usually take a break, giving me a chance to stretch my legs and giving Stitch a few minutes to play. I check my watch. It's only seven thirty, plenty of time for Stitch to romp around in the water for a bit. Stitch with only his coarse, silver head visible makes a beeline for land. I resituate myself into a sitting position and lay the paddle across my lap. Above me, two turkey vultures circle in wide, wobbly loops. The clouds off in the distance are the color of bruised flesh.

Stitch emerges from the river and onto the muddy embankment and gives himself a vigorous shake, water dripping from his beard and moustache or what his trainer described as *facial furnishings*, common to Slovakian rough-haired pointers. He lopes off and begins to explore the shoreline by sniffing and snuffling around each tree trunk and fallen log. I close my eyes, tilt my face up toward the sky and the outside world completely disappears. I smell rain off in the distance. A rain that I know will wash away what's left of fall. It's Halloween and I hope that the storm will hold off until the trick-or-treaters have finished their begging.

Stitch has picked up a stick and, instead of settling down to chew on it like most dogs, he tosses it from his mouth into the air, watches it tumble into the water and then pounces. My stepdaughter, Nora, loves Stitch. I think if it weren't for Stitch, Nora wouldn't be quite as excited to spend time with me. Not that I can blame her. I really screwed up and I'm not the easiest person in the world to communicate with.

I'm debating whether or not to bring Stitch into the interview with me. Legally I have the right. I have all the paperwork and if Dr. Huntley can't be accommodating, I'm not sure I want to work for him. Plus, Stitch is such a sweet, loving dog, I'm sure the cancer patients that come into the center would find his presence comforting.

My stomach twists at the thought of having to try to sell myself as a qualified, highly capable office worker in just a few short hours. There was a time not that long ago when I was a highly regarded, sought-after nurse. Not anymore.

Stitch has wandered over to where the earth juts out causing a crooked bend in the river, a spot that, lacking a better word, I call the elbow. I catch sight of Stitch facing away from me, frozen in place, right paw raised, tail extended, eyes staring intently at something. Probably a squirrel or chipmunk. He creeps forward two steps and I know that once the animal takes off so will Stitch. While nine times out of ten he'll come back when I summon him, he's been known to run and I don't have time this morning to spend a half an hour searching for him.

I snap my fingers twice, our signal for Stitch to come. He ignores me. I row closer. "Stitch, *ke mne!*" I call. *Come.* His floppy ears twitch but still he remains fixated on whatever has caught his eye. Something has changed in his stance. His back is rounded until he's almost crouching, his tail is tucked between his legs and his ears are flat against his head. He's scared.

My first thought is he's happened upon a skunk. My second thought is one of amusement given that, for the moment, our roles have reversed—I'm trying to gain his attention rather than the other way around. I snap my fingers again, hoping to break the spell. The last thing I need is to walk into my new job smelling like roadkill. Stitch doesn't even glance my way.

I scoot off my board into knee-deep water, my neoprene shoes sinking into the mud. I wrestle my board far enough onto land so it won't drift away. Maybe Stitch has cornered a snake. Not too many poisonous snakes around here. Brown spotted massasauga and black banded timber rattlers are rare but not unheard of. I pick my way upward through snarls of dead weeds and step over rotting logs until I'm just a few yards behind Stitch. He is perched atop a rocky incline that sits about five feet above the water. Slowly, so as to not startle Stitch or whatever has him mesmerized, I inch my way forward, craning my neck to get a better look.

Laying a hand on Stitch's rough coat, damp from his swim, I feel him tremble beneath my fingers. I follow his gaze and find myself staring down to where a thick layer of fallen leaves carpets the surface of the water. A vibrant mosaic of yellow, red and brown. "There's nothing there," I tell him, running my hand over his ears and beneath his chin. His vocal chords vibrate in short, staccato bursts, alerting me to his whimpering.

I lean forward, my toes dangerously close to the muddy ridge. One misstep and I'll tumble in.

It takes a moment for my brain to register what I'm seeing and I think someone has discarded an old mannequin into the river. Then I realize this is no figure molded from fiberglass or plastic. This is no Halloween prank. I see her exposed breast, pale white against a tapestry of fall colors. With my heart slamming into my chest, I stumble backward. Though I try to break the fall with my hands, I hit the ground hard, my head striking the muddy earth, my teeth gnashing together, leaving me momentarily stunned. I blink up at the sky, trying to get my bearings, and in slow motion, a great blue heron with a wingspan the length of a grown man glides over me, casting a brief shadow. Slowly, I sit up, dazed, and my hands go to my scalp. When I pull my fingers away they are bloody.

Dizzily, I stagger to my feet. I cannot pass out here, I tell myself. No one will know where to find me. Blood pools in my mouth from where I've bitten my tongue and I spit, trying to get rid of the coppery taste. I wipe my hands on my pants and gingerly touch the back of my head again. There's a small bump but no open wound that I can feel. I look at my hands and see the source of the blood. The thin, delicate skin of my palms is shredded and embedded with small pebbles.

The forest feels like it is closing in all around me and I want to run, to get as far away from here as possible. But maybe I was mistaken. Maybe what I thought I saw was a trick of light, a play of shadows. I force myself back toward the ridge and try to summon the cool, clinical stance that I was known for when I was an emergency room nurse. I peer down, and staring up at me is the naked body of a woman floating just beneath the surface of the water. Though I can't see any discernable injuries on her, I'm sure there is no way she happened to end up here by accident. I take in a pair of blue lips parted in surprise, an upturned nose, blank eyes wide-open; tendrils of blond hair tangled tightly into a snarl of half-submerged brambles keeps her from drifting away.

Pinpricks of light dance in front of my eyes and for a moment I'm blinded with shock, fear, dread. Then I do something I have never done, not even once, at the sight of a dead body. I bend over and vomit. Great, violent heaves that leave my stomach hollow and my legs shaky. I wipe my mouth with the back of my hand. I know her. Knew her. The dead woman is Gwen Locke and at one time we were friends.